LOUDER THAN LOVE

JESSICA TOPPER

lunabloom books

"Three is a Magic Number" by Robert L. Dorough. © American Broadcasting Music, Inc. Used with permission.
"Catwings" © 1987 by Ursula K. Le Guin. Reprinted by permission of Orchard Books, an imprint of Scholastic Inc.
"maggie and milly and molly and may" by E.E. Cummings. © 1994 by Richard S. Kennedy Poems by E.E. Cummings.
"Measures", "Habit", "Funeral", "Syndrome Dreamer", "Censured" © 2013 by Stephany Sofia.

ISBNs: 978-1-953863-00-3 (trade paperback); 978-1-953863-01-0 (e-book)

For Bruce, because I once told him I would.

1

WEDNESDAY WARRIORS

"I'M TELLING YOU, you *need* to get rid of that bed."

"Why? It's a perfectly good bed."

I watched as Marissa repeatedly slapped two packets of sugar against her palm, like a cop beating the confession out of her suspect—me.

"Look, I totally respect your memories with Pete and all. But you should take into consideration the possibility of some bad mojo hanging around your marriage bed should you decide to bring someone else into it."

Her frosty manicured nails hovered over her coffee like it was a steaming cauldron. Any moment I expected an incantation to brew forth from her lips, meant to make me forget my broken heart. Or to at least get me laid for the first time since changing my area code from 212 to 914.

"It's been almost four years, Tree. And you want to move forward," Liz added. She detached the crumbly streusel, my favorite part of the coffee cake, from her slice and offered it in consolation.

I hastily sipped my latte, earning a scalded tongue to go

along with the aforementioned broken heart. "So what should I do with it? The bed?"

"You could donate it," Karen suggested. "St. Greg's is having a rummage sale after Easter." She gave me an encouraging smile, quickly looking to the others for backup.

Recently established in Lauder Lake with her shiny new family in their shiny new eco-friendly house, Karen was never quite sure how to blend in with my high school posse. Her knowledge of my situation was understandably less than that of my lifelong girlfriends. Not that I held it against her, of course. We met after Abbey and I had fled Manhattan, the wreck still rubbing me raw each waking morning and spurring me on to put some miles between us and the pain.

Home could not be where Pete had existed one day and not the next. So the place where I had existed before I met Pete became home once more.

"I suppose that's a good plan," I managed. The steam arm on the espresso machine behind me hissed and sighed.

Marissa gave me the sympathetic-best-friend-of-the-poor-widow nod as the other girls murmured their agreement; my very own Greek chorus clad in Lucky Brand jeans.

I turned and glanced out the window of Starbucks. It was odd to see almost the exact same view of the Main Street from my youth. Like walking through a dream, where familiar things are altered by the tiniest tweaks.

There was the hardware store, the post office, my dad's antique shop. The flavor of the day, dime-a-dozen coffee shop we were now sitting in had once been Colby's Five and Dime Store. Marissa and I used to spend our hard-earned allowances there on Lemonheads and Cow Tales when we were nine; it was where we had perfected our methods of shoplifting chocolate bars at age eleven.

"I'll bet Leanna can come help. Ed's got that truck." Marissa threaded her arm through the maze of cardboard cups and squeezed my hand.

"Where is she today?" Karen asked.

"Therapy," I explained. "Ed finally agreed to go with her."

Liz scraped her chair closer. "I'll help feather your new love nest." She gave my shoulder a bump. "You need a single chick's eye, not these yapping yentas trying to Martha Stewart you to death."

"Tree doesn't need a love nest, Liz. She needs a sanctuary," Marissa insisted. "Just a peaceful place for herself to enjoy and maybe . . . JUST maybe . . . a certain blond-haired, hazel-eyed ex-cornerback might come knocking." She let her great dark Sophia Loren bedroom eyes emphasize her point with a blink and a wink.

I laughed. "Give it a rest, Falzone!"

Marissa's brain had gone to mush from watching too many sappy *Lifetime* original movies and saw my bliss in the form of Grant Overhill, my first serious crush (for two long years) and my first steady boyfriend (for two short months) in the ninth grade. He also happened to be the man who took over my family's antique business when my dad retired five years ago. And he was single at the moment. It was all too much for Marissa to bear; she loved to torture me with the prospect, and I, in turn, loved to drive her nuts with my indifference. Not my type. Sloppy kisser. (Or at least he was at fifteen.) Sort of smelled like my dad, now that he worked in the shop. Like wood and old books. Yick.

"Oooh, I saw him in Wild Oats the other day, he's a hottie," Karen enthused. "He helped me get a box of quinoa off the shelf from the tippy-top."

"Trust me, Karen. He's what we called a poster boy in high school. Nice to look at, but once he opens his mouth . . . forget it," Liz said, allowing her tongue to half loll out of her mouth and her eyes to glaze over for emphasis. She had the most amazing eyes, ever-changing in their color depending on her mood, like those cheap rings we all loved to wear in junior high. Today they were a glinting, mischievous green.

"You weren't even in the same grade as us!" Marissa pointed out. "Plus you were too busy following Tree's brother, Kevin, around like a puppy dog to *notice* other guys."

Liz shrugged and smiled in dreamy defeat. She hadn't been the only one: Kev had had a lot of conquests in high school, probably due to the fact he was the only cute boy who dared take home economics three years in a row. My brother could bake the pants off Betty Crocker . . . and he sweet-talked them off most any girl at Lauder High.

"Anyway, one step at a time for this one." Marissa patted my head like I was one of her Jack Russell terriers. "First the bed . . . then the *accoutrement*." This made everyone giggle, since Marissa still possessed the thick accent she arrived with back in the third grade. Her family had moved upstate that year from Yonkers, which we all considered a very exotic, dangerous, and faraway place at the time.

"So when are you going to find some bling-bling for me, Mariss?" Liz wanted to know. "I've been single since . . ." She drained her cup and licked the foam off the brim. ". . . before coffee cost $4.85 a cup."

"Not my jurisdiction, dear. Move back to the 'burbs and then we can talk about it."

Liz raised her eyebrows under her fiery red bangs. She was 100 percent Irish, yet her hair color was 100 percent Goldwell Red. She was one of those creamy-skinned, black-haired Irish girls, but had begun hitting the dye bottle in college. It suited her devilish personality, a trait we'd all come to know and love over the years.

"It's been fun, ladies. But I have to be on the eleven forty-five back to town. The Naked Bagel cannot run itself." Liz's bakery was a little piece of heaven with a hole in it. Yum. One of approximately fifteen things I keenly missed about weekends living in Manhattan. Buying the Sunday *New York Times* on Saturday evening was another. Brunches with all-you-can-drink mimosas, lounging in Sheep Meadow reading the Style section while Pete lay with his head on my lap working on the crossword puzzle . . . Okay, I will stop there for now.

"Thanks for coming, I know it's a hike for you." I embraced Liz and got the ball rolling on the comprehensive, caffeinated hug exchange.

We had started our Wednesday coffee ritual last year, when Abbey and Marissa's youngest, Brina, began preschool. Lake-Shore Montessori encourages sending even the youngest children to school for a few hours every weekday, with the belief that they should experience the consistency of returning to the same environment. Lord knows Abbey needs some consistency in her days, other than my muttering to myself around the house and burning her breakfast waffles. And really, the "me" time had been great for all of us. Liz grumbled sometimes about schlepping, but we knew even she looked forward to shedding her tough city shell, if only for an hour of coffee and a short snooze on the Metro-North.

"So . . ." Marissa began as we got into my Mini Cooper parked out back. "Figure out what you're going to do for that children's library program yet?"

Our tiny town branch had an active Friends of the Library volunteer group. A far cry from the fast-paced research library I had managed in the city, but it had its moments. The group had fund-raised quite a bit of money with an auction last fall, and it had been allocated in many directions: collection development, new shelving, programming. I had come up with the bright idea of hosting a music program for children, which included busing in kids with autism from the local therapeutic day school in White Plains. My plan was to have a children's musician come perform and give the kids a chance to try out some instruments.

"Actually, yes. I believe I've had a Holy Grail moment." I slapped a CD into Marissa's hand and steered us out of the lot.

"Holy . . . Is this that dude, the Kitty guy? Who Abbey loves?" She suspended the cracked jewel case between her polished talons for inspection. It contained no liner notes or cover art. But the disc itself was stamped SONGS FOR NATALIE— ADRIAN GRAVES, along with a disclaimer notice: FOR PROMO- TIONAL USE ONLY—NOT FOR SALE.

"Pretty sure it's the same guy."

Abbey's all-time favorite PBS cartoon, *Maxwell MacGillikitty, Feline Private Eye,* was slightly insipid to anyone over age six, but had a wildly catchy theme song performed by the afore- mentioned Adrian Graves. Abbey was singing it from breakfast to bath time for months before it dawned on me to look into finding other works by the same musician. A surprisingly diffi- cult endeavor, despite my superpowered librarian research skills. It was as if the man didn't really exist. Or had a really crappy publicist. He just had no paper trail. Until now.

"Where the hell did you find him?"

"Well, I haven't found *him* yet. But that came from the Bruised Apple."

The Bruised Apple bookstore was one of my favorite places on earth. Most librarians would probably run screaming from the place, as the thousands of used books and CDs that filled the store were arranged by categories in handwritten notes and taped-on labels. But I adored it. It reminded me of being a kid in my dad's antique shop after school. I loved how the old bookshop floors creaked when you walked on them and how every available inch of wall space was covered with flyers from local artists and musicians.

Marissa snorted. "I don't know how you could find anything in that mess."

I had almost flipped past the disc in my haste, looking for something I so desperately wanted to exist but was not sure what shape or form the mirage would actually take. It turned out there was a whole case of them in the store's back room. "From the warehouse of that CD manufacturing plant near Nyack," the owner had informed me. "They bring us tons of music, mostly obscure stuff. Probably bands don't pay their bills, or never pick the product up. Just put one of these out though, to see if it would sell. Never heard of him."

Marissa slid the CD into the car stereo. "Ah, '*The Cat Came Back*,' good choice."

"Go to the next track."

"Oh my God, '*Señor Don Gato*'! Remember singing that song every year at summer camp? *Meow, meow, meow.*" She laughed.

"You've got to hear this, he sings it so adorably!" I increased the volume and sang along. "*There was not a sweeter kitty, meow, meow, meow, in the country or the city . . .*"

"If I didn't know you better, I'd say you have a crush on Señor Graves," Marissa teased. When I didn't respond in .02 seconds, she shrieked, "My God, you do!"

"Come on, I don't even know what he looks like—"

"Smitten!"

"—or anything about him."

"Smitten kitten."

"Very funny. Although I have to say, his voice is kinda sexy." It had a gravelly undertone, different from the bulk of syrupy-sweet kids' music out there. And there was an energy, like he really believed in the power and magic of music and wasn't just out to collect a paycheck.

"And I'd say there is something sexy about a guy who can entertain your kid for hours. I'm telling you," Marissa added, "even that furry red Muppet gets me—"

"DON'T go there."

She laughed. "He's really got a thing for cats, huh?"

"Seems to be the theme of the album." I didn't tell her I bought the whole case. I couldn't even tell myself why I did. "But now . . . to find the man behind the album." The box had a shipping label bound for Burning Barn Studios, LLC. It was the only tangible clue I had.

"I am confident you will find him. You are like a dog with a chew toy when it comes to that stuff. You won't let it go."

"At the rate I'm going, we'll probably end up with that clown Karen hired for Jasper's birthday party last October."

"The one that scared the crap out of the kids? God forbid!"

"He blows a mean balloon animal."

Marissa chuckled, reaching into her pocket. "Want one?" She proffered up a dark chocolate–covered graham cracker from a cellophane pack of two.

"Tell me you didn't swipe those from Starbucks!" I exclaimed, pulling into her driveway.

She shrugged unapologetically. "For old times' sake."

We dissolved into giggles and had our quick chocolate fix.

"Coming in?"

"Nah, I am going to attempt to unpack some . . . stuff."

"No rush, you've only been back for, what? *Three* years?" She blew a kiss through the window at me to soften her wisecrack.

Backing out, I pondered the fate of Don Gato and the cat that came back the very next day. And how much lighter you would take life if you knew you had nine of them.

2

PIGEON VS. STATUE

I DREAMED about Adrian Graves that night.

Which was weird and improbable, since I had never laid eyes on the man.

I blamed all that talk with Marissa. And the chocolate.

On Friday morning, I fanned my body out like a sleepy snow angel in my soon-to-be-donated bed and waited for Abbey to perform her ritual six a.m. tear-in-and-leap. Number-One Mom Rule: She had to fall asleep in her own bed, but she could come in during the wee hours to wake up with me. Although she often spun her little body around like a demented pinwheel during sleep, flopping arms and kicking legs, she was still a warm and delightful thing to curl up next to.

I flipped onto my belly and stretched. There was a time in the recent past when I could bury my nose into the sheets and still smell a vague lingering of my husband, his scent locked deep within the fibers of the mattress upholstery. Real or imagined, it was a mixture of his shaving cream, clean sweat, and that papaya shampoo he preferred, and was uniquely him. I inhaled deeply and realized I had slept alone in this bed for many more nights than together with Pete. Yet I still expected the smell and the memory of him to envelop me each time I lay down.

It was time. My friend Leanna and her husband, Ed, would arrive in a few short hours, and we would yank it out of the house and hurl it into their truck and be done with it. The thought was cathartic yet tragic at the same time. I felt like I was putting a faithful pet out of its misery. Crying my eyes out as it sat stoic and silent, accepting the end was near and waiting for it.

Rolling to my side, I placed one hand on the hollow of my hip, a place where Pete liked to rest his fingers. It wasn't supposed to be like this; it wasn't part of the plan.

Ah, but *Man plans and God laughs.*

Isn't that the most annoying thing people feel compelled to say when something bad happens? Now truthfully, does God, with all his divine wisdom, really have such time to waste? Does he get his kicks by squashing his thumb into each and every Day Runner and PDA out there, saying "Ha HA, take that!"?

I guess I'm not a very spiritual person. I don't think things always "happen for a reason," everything must be "God's way," or (and this is one of Karen's favorites) "He only gives you what you can handle." I simply believe, and I am sorry to sound crude about it, that shit happens. Period.

Sometimes you are the pigeon.

Sometimes you are the statue.

I heard the shuffle and drop of two feet in the next room and braced myself for the machine-gun pitter-patter of Abbey, my little whirling dervish of footy pajamas and sweat-soaked curls. The girl had yet to master telling time, but she had an uncanny knack for beating my alarm to the punch. The mattress bounced with all thirty pounds of her. Settling into that soft hollow between my armpit and breast, she quickly drifted back to sleep. Allowing me to drift back into my memories.

If you really are from the other school of thought, then I guess you could say Pete and I were doomed from the start.

WE MET the first day of our Intellectual Freedom class at Columbia. I fell for the cute journalism major sitting next to me amid a sea of information science students. And Pete fell asleep next to, as he later put it, the prettiest future librarian in the room. His head dropped on my shoulder that first day, and each day after. I had him pegged for a narcoleptic until my friends and I saw him working the door late one night at our local college music club.

I wouldn't call this door guy a bouncer. He wasn't like the thick-necked, tribal-tattooed, biceps-flexing guys from Brooklyn who paced around the West End Gate. But he was there every night to collect our five dollar cover charge and deposit a big *X* in black Sharpie on the back of our hands that wouldn't wash off for half a week. He always had a nice, albeit tight-lipped, smile for me and amused eyes, warm and brown. On one occasion, he'd had on a fedora that reminded me of a hat a 1950s newsman might wear perched jauntily on his head. All it needed was a press card tucked into the brim and he'd be all set.

"New hat?" I'd queried, watching as he Sharpied the thin skin between my wrist and knuckles. The guy grinned fully, exposing a crooked front top tooth and somewhat longer than normal canines.

"Nah. Bad haircut," he'd replied, pulling off the hat with a flourish to display a head shorn as close as a market lamb in spring. "Beware the barber of Astor Place."

"Whoa." I jokingly stepped back, then reconsidered. "Can I

rub it for good luck? I've got a final on Monday and I shouldn't even be out tonight." He had modestly obliged, lowering his head and allowing me to rub my palm over the soft stubble.

He had a laugh that you just wanted to bottle up for future use on a cloudy day. I liked the way his wolfy smile changed the whole look of his face, but had a feeling he perfected the closed-lipped version out of a self-conscious effort to avoid showing the world.

The rest, they say, is history. I got an A on my test, and Pete's hair eventually grew back. I finished my master's that year, one of the last students to graduate from Columbia's School of Library Service before they closed their doors. Pete had one more year of journalism school, so I moved into his tiny apartment on 110th and Broadway and we settled into domestic bliss. His first job out of school was copyediting for a major current affairs magazine, which he loved. Mine was the Public Library, which I hated. It was Pete who got me an interview at the magazine's research library. Within three years, I was heading up my own team of researchers as director there, and Pete was off making a name for himself at the *Observer*.

Jobs brought money, which bought a co-op on the Upper West Side and a glittery carat of promise. Silver Hammer, our favorite Beatles tribute band, was playing "In My Life" at the West End Gate as Pete met me at the door and placed a big black Sharpie *X* on my hand and a diamond on my finger amid cheers from friends and family. The same band played at our wedding a year later, and I can still remember twirling in my white Betsey Johnson dress and singing "When I'm Sixty-Four" with Pete. I think there is a picture of it somewhere, snapped that night by Pete's younger brother, Luke, a professional photographer moonlighting as best man.

News of Abbey arrived on New Year's Eve, 1998. She was definitely not something we had planned, but we toasted and kissed in Pete's office high over Times Square, squirreling away our little secret until the spring. She was due on both of our late grandmothers' shared birthday. We toyed with the idea of naming her after them, but figured Lily Millie Lewis was too much for one little girl to handle. Pete took one look at her dark hair swirled up into a slick Mohawk and her perfect matchstick fingers and was in love.

"Abbey," he announced, "after *Abbey Road*." And it was perfect. Exactly thirty years to the day the Beatles released their masterpiece, we introduced ours to the world.

We liked to think of ourselves as spontaneous practical minds, heads in the clouds with feet planted firmly on the ground most of the time. It was a delightful combination. Nothing was too impossible to dream up, yet we had several years solidly mapped out ahead of us. How about a family sabbatical? Why not France? On the day of the wreck, we were discussing our options abroad for the following year. We wanted Abbey to have the opportunity to *parlez Français* before she started nursery school, a well-researched one she had been placed on the waiting list for soon after the results of the first ultrasound. (Which is actually not that uncommon a practice in Manhattan.) The newspaper was willing to grant Pete his request, even after their generous allowance of six months of work-from-home paternity leave.

That had been another plan of ours, once the baby arrived: I would stay home for the first six months of her life, and then Pete would take over for the remainder of her first year. We wanted at least one of us to personally witness each and every milestone, rather than to be told "she took her first steps" or "she talked today" by a nanny as she punched the clock and rushed out the door.

Pete's paternity leave was forced to end three weeks early, when his senior editor needed him to cover a story down in Washington on some foreign diplomat from some country I had never heard of. He had tried to explain the significance to me the evening before, but it hadn't registered; too many two a.m. feedings had fogged my brain. France and the sabbatical couldn't come soon enough.

We commuted together that morning, the day of the wreck, for the first time since Abbey was born.

In my mind, it will forever be a wreck, not an accident. An accident is what happens when Abbey is too busy playing to make it to the potty on time. Or when a waiter carrying a tray of dishes crashes into a door swinging the opposite way. Accidents can be apologized for, smoothed over, explained away.

A wreck is different.

A wreck . . . does just that. It damages beyond repair.

I remember distinctly how it felt to be pushed against him on that packed A train during morning rush hour. I had my wrist curled on the pole for balance, and he had an arm curled around me to anchor both of us. It was jarring and disconcerting to be out in the fast-paced public together after months spent in that new parenthood cocoon. But I was able to block out everything, from the sardinelike suited travelers swaying silently in unison to the squeal and clack of the cars as we hurtled downtown, simply by pressing my face into my husband's neck and inhaling. Shaving cream and papaya shampoo.

To the casual observer, Pete could still pass for a college student, with his cocoa-brown locks forever in his eyes and his quick and warm lippy grin. He still reserved baring his goofy wolf teeth just for his two favorite girls. That day, he was wearing army green cargo shorts, a pair of All Stars, and a Yo La Tengo T-shirt that had clearly seen better days. The only things vaguely grown-up about him were the scruff on his chin and the wardrobe bag that carried his suit. The interview was scheduled for three o'clock, so he had plenty of time to head to his hotel and make the transformation from Manhattan hipster dad to Washington watchdog journalist.

Behind Pete's head and above the rows of orange and yellow seats of hard plastic ran a Poetry in Motion poster, the MTA's way of injecting culture into you whether you wanted it or not. I remember it was a poem by Stephen Crane, "*A Man Said to the Universe.*" The title sticks with me to this day, and I keep reminding myself to find and reread the poem, but never do.

We hopped off at Penn Station, and rather than kill time in the air-conditioned terminal, Pete walked me up to the steamy street level and bought me a coffee at our favorite street vendor. We had both forgone breakfast, choosing to spend maximum morning time with Abbey before turning her over to Ilana, our occasional babysitter turned regular nanny.

And so we spent our final moment together chatting while he chugged an Orangina and I blew across the top of my *We are happy to serve you* Greek key trim coffee cup. Nothing memorable or profound; had we been making a romance movie with a dramatic, tear-jerking good-bye scene, we never would have made it past the cutting room floor. No rainy, foggy airstrip runways in Casablanca, just a rushed good-bye at the doors of Penn Station as people careened around us from every direction.

"If you think of it, could you go to B&H on your lunch hour? I dropped some film off last week." His lips touched my forehead, my nose, and each of my temples as if performing an erotic sign of the cross. His own nose, so straight and Grecian, pressed against my earlobe. "The roll from Central Park."

"I'll try. What time does your train get in on Sunday? Maybe we can meet you."

"Not sure. I'll call you when I get to the hotel. Love you!" Our kiss was hasty as he allowed himself to get sucked into the flow of traffic heading down the stairs to catch the 7:05 Regional.

3

SUN KINK

I walked to my office, two blocks west of Penn. I loved getting to work before any of my staff. I could catch up on e-mail, work uninterrupted on a particularly tough query from an editor, or sometimes just sit with my cup of coffee and brainstorm. And occasionally, I would work out. The magazine had renovated the Tenth Avenue building that year, complete with a gym on the top floor and basketball courts on the roof. Having to close an issue weekly was stressful, and people tended to put in long hours and late nights. It was great having the gym to work off some energy, or to build some up.

In my case, it came in handy when working off the baby bulge. Not that I had a lot; I was one of those lucky ladies who all the other moms hate, fitting back into my pre-pregnancy jeans a few months after delivering. Still, I was having a hard time getting my abs in shape. Of course, my friends would only commiserate so much. "Kiss my big fat lily-white ass!" was Marissa's favorite retort if I complained about my weight or how my body looked. She had been heavier than me our entire friendship, but it was never really an issue; we joked, we complained, we complimented equally. But it was hard to press home to her that it's all in what you're used to. I was the heaviest I had ever been, so I felt it and saw it, even if no one else really did.

After an hour and a half of playing catch-up in my office, I beelined to the gym. My exercise of choice was running; outside of work, I would zoom Abbey through the park in her jogging stroller like it was our own personal rickshaw. At work, I used the treadmill. My favorite one was closest to the wall and to the TV, where I could catch up with the morning's news by reading the closed captioning as it flickered past. Sometimes I ran on my lunch hour, but that was really just an excuse to catch the trashy talk shows.

That morning, I set the timer for thirty minutes. I set the incline to 15 percent and the speed at four miles per hour. Al Roker was miming the weather on the screen, and I studied the day's highs as I began my ascent.

We had stepped into September, but the hot days scorched on. The subways smelled like piss and bologna baking in a thousand-degree kiln. People on the streets looked wilted and pissed off. Today would be no different, with highs in the mid to upper nineties. We were already at 91° F at 8:58 a.m., according to Mr. Roker.

As I advanced from a fast walk to a steady trot, I let my mind wander. Abbey's first birthday was approaching, and the in-laws were trekking in from Philadelphia. I had to figure out where to house them in our crowded two-bedroom apartment. They were threatening to stay with Pete's brother, Luke, instead, but he had yet to tell them the apartment he shared with a "roommate" was actually a studio he was sharing with his partner, Kimon. So Pete and I were taking one for the team. *23:58 to go, 40 calories burned.* Marissa and Rob had theater tickets next Saturday and had asked us to babysit. Maybe I would take the kids to the zoo. Did I pay the cable bill? It had been lying on the fireplace mantle for two weeks. Jennifer had better not be late to work today, that would make five times this month. Time to invest in a better jogging bra. Abbey had weaned herself a month ago, but good God, the girls hurt! Studying the TV rather than the treadmill display made time go much faster. Argh, *11 minutes to go,* my legs are killing me, let's run downhill. Incline at -1.5, *8 minutes to go, 190 calories burned.* Hmm, übercute guy Dan from the legal department just got on the treadmill two down from me. *1:51 minutes to go, 151 . . .* What are they saying? *7:05 a.m. train 151, 60 miles per hour,* Pete's train, *DC, 9:07 a.m., mile marker 42.5, train 151, DC, three dead, 94° F,* TURN UP THE TV, *230 onboard, 68 injured,* TURN IT UP, *7:05 . . . DC . . . 151 . . . 60 . . . 3 . . . 00:00 . . . 00:00 . . .* I can't turn it off . . . TURN IT OFF . . . TURN IT OFF.

I don't know if I was screaming out loud or just in my head.

I was helped off the treadmill by Dan from legal and Rich from marketing. They called up my assistant, Daisy. Somehow I was ushered home; somehow Liz was summoned from across town to come sit with me in silent vigil.

Somehow I knew it was Pete. I knew before the police came to tell me and before the coroner confirmed it.

My ears took in the information they gave me, and my brain filed that information into a cerebral cabinet that housed only my darkest thoughts and fears. What really happened to Pete sits there, written in an ancient guttural language I cannot decipher. The information that I am able to share out loud sounds more like a newspaper report: factual, objective.

Push a button. Hear me speak it.

An eastbound train struck a misalignment in the track at 9:07 a.m. on September 1 while traveling sixty miles per hour near milepost 42.5 between Newark, Delaware, and Aberdeen, Maryland. Four cars went down an embankment and over- turned against trees. At first report, three people were killed, five were in critical condition, and sixty-three others suffered from minor injuries. By the end of the day, the number of deaths had risen to seven. The misalignment, often referred to as a sun kink, was determined to be caused by improperly tamped ballast and excessive speed in the 94° F sunny weather.

Sun kink. I had existed for thirty years without ever coming across that term. Suddenly, it took over my daily life like some nightmarish mantra. One of the wrongful death attorneys once referred to it as a "thermal kink," causing me to actually laugh out loud in my shocked state. My mind conjured up a ridiculous image of people in their long johns, getting busy.

But *sun kink* . . . those words have taken on an almost mystical, pagan persona in my mind. A power possessed by a solar deity not to be messed with.

The funeral played out like a wedding in reverse. Instead of eagerly searching around town for weeks like I did before the wedding to find the perfect shoes in the exact cream hue to complement my gown, I listlessly hunted around in my closet on the morning of the service to find black pumps to go with my black dress, black mood, black soul. Abbey and I were picked up in a limo, although there was no champagne chilling like there had been when Pete and I jumped into ours on our way from ceremony to reception. Best man and matron of honor had caroused across town with us that night; on the day of the funeral, Luke and Marissa sat on either side of me, squeezing my hands. Both sets of parents rode silently across from us.

My groom was already at the altar awaiting our arrival in his best suit.

In a closed casket.

Pete's paper published a three-page, highly moving tribute to his life and short yet promising career. All the local city papers did a nice job, actually. Had Pete been there to read them, he would have rolled his eyes and mocked, "So *this* is all the news that's fit to print?" Seeing his face—from his grainy black-and-white mug shot press credentials picture to color

Corbis stills taken at a recent UN event—staring up from the pages for several days straight was like a cruel gift. My heart would flutter and sink, my hopes would spike and dive. My brain played tricks on me, allowing me to forget for nanoseconds at a time before flooding me with the knowledge and realization at the oddest times . . . while brushing my teeth, changing Abbey's diaper, buttering toast.

Gone. No more.

Friends and loved ones flocked and fed me that first week, as I struggled to remember there was a life before the after. Acquaintances and colleagues came out of the woodwork to pay their respects and offer what comfort they could. Pete's family and I would literally collapse at night, exhausted by the kindness of others that forced us to be social when we least wanted to.

And then, day by day and one by one, people began to get wrapped back up in their own lives again. I was relieved in a bittersweet way to have some of the pressure lifted, but the realization that life goes on was still a bitter pill to swallow. It was hard to believe the whole world wasn't sticking around to mourn in unison with me. Didn't they know? My whole world had come crashing down, after all. I would recoil in shock at the alien sound of random laughter on the street and stare curiously at the shopkeeper who requested I "have a nice day." Nice days were out of the question. How could they go on as if nothing had happened . . . How could I go on? How could I ever explain this all to Abbey?

As Piaget observed, the beginning of object permanence occurs when a child starts to actively look for an object that has been hidden or has slipped out of view. My wizened one-year-old took to peeking around corners with her wide brown eyes, plump palm opening and closing, as she would coo, "Da . . . dee? Bye-byeeee." A milestone heartbreakingly mastered.

Remaining in our apartment was unbearable, unthinkable.

I didn't know where Abbey and I would go, but during those numb days after the funeral, I robotically dismantled and packed up our life. As I carefully wrapped our wedding china in a week's worth of the *New York Times*, I noticed every monochromatic bride smiling up at me from her wedding announcement. Her marriage just beginning; mine abruptly over. I would place each wrapped piece into a box with the gentleness of a lover, all the while wanting to scream and fling it against the wall.

It was easy to torture myself with those "what if" questions: What if he had refused to cut short his leave? What if he had chosen to fly instead of take the train? What if Abbey had gotten sick that morning, forcing us both to remain in the cozy cocoon of our home? What if war had been newly declared on that country whose name I can never remember, keeping that diplomat far from Washington and unable to be interviewed? What if we had kissed good-bye longer and he had missed that train? Whatifwhatifwhatif. Then, on my blacker and most pathetic days: What if this was some kind of punishment for me? I had been checking out that cute guy on the treadmill, which kind of falls into the "covet thy neighbor" category, right? Was I an unfit wife? If there was a God doling out only what you can handle, did He think I couldn't handle a husband? Couldn't handle being a wife?

The magazine had no objections to my leaving. I was pretty much useless; the hard drive of my mind had shit the bed, and the only things I cared about were Abbey and leaving the city. My assistant, Daisy, sublet the apartment, and Abbey and I did the most logical thing I could think of at the time: We moved in with my parents. Which normally would be the most *illogical* thing, since they drive me slightly batty. Don't get me wrong, love and respect them and all that, but the twenty questions (Mom) and the "moral of the story" lectures (Dad) I ran from in my late teens had multiplied exponentially over the years. They were eerily silent for about two weeks after we moved in, and I almost wished for the zany dysfunction we had had when Kevin and I were kids. But they respected this fragile new unit that extended from their family tree, giving Abbey and me our space to grow as daughter and mother, but caring and supporting us as grandchild and child.

Abbey's first birthday was the first milestone to get through; everyone always says the first year of birthdays, anniversaries, and holidays is the worst after someone passes. Honestly, I was glad it was Abbey's day, because it broke through the melancholy and the mourning. How can anyone be sad at a first birthday party? The birthday girl put smiles on everybody's faces, especially when hers was ringed with chocolate buttercream frosting from her tiny three-tiered personal birthday cake Uncle Kevin had flown in from his restaurant in Portland.

My parents left for Florida a couple weeks later, keeping up their traditional migratory pattern as snowbirds who leave New York the minute it's time to turn on the heat and don't return until it's time to turn on the air-conditioning. My dad would be happy as a clam living in a sensory deprivation bubble, and my mom probably would, too, so long as she was allowed out twice a week to shop and get to the hairdresser.

"Don't forget to winterize the hose bibs" were my dad's parting words as we pulled suitcases out of the trunk at Stewart Airport. I had no idea what he was talking about, but assured him I would. "Keeps the pipes from freezing *and* conserves water." See, there was always a moral to his lectures.

"Tree, are you sure you're okay with us leaving? Keep the doors locked. I know it's a safe neighborhood, but I worry. Do you remember where our personal papers are? You know, in case—God forbid—anything should happen? Abbey, come here, give Grandma kissies, Grandma loves you, come visit us soon. Tree, I think she's hungry. Do you have a snack for her?

Do you want us to run inside and get something? Phil, go get a snack for your granddaughter."

"She's fine, Mom. I want you to go catch your plane. We'll be fine, we will lock doors and winterize hose thingamabobs." I hugged each of them awkwardly, Abbey in my arms and squirming. "What's this?" My dad was stuffing a manila envelope into my purse from behind, practically dislocating my shoulder.

"It's the deed to the house. We are transferring it to you, Treebird. We're tired of the dual households. We've decided to stay in Florida year-round."

"But—"

"It's all settled, honey. You and Abbey enjoy the house for as long as you need it. Our gift to you. If you decide you want to leave Lauder Lake, sell it and use the money for a new place, or for Abbey's college fund," Mom said.

"Gee, are we that hard to live with?" I joked lamely.

"Oh, Tree, the move was something your father and I have been considering for the last year or so . . . Your brother has no interest in the property, so it seemed like the logical thing. But tell us honestly if you are not ready for us to leave. We will postpone. Phil, we *can* postpone." She held up her hand authoritatively to prevent my dad and the porter from loading any more of their bags onto the cart.

"No, no, we will be fine. I just . . . I wasn't expecting it, but it sounds like a good idea." Truth be told, it was getting slightly claustrophobic in my childhood house; like being examined under a microscope for tiny cracks and signs of a breakdown. I had been juggling Mommy & Me with grief counseling sessions to cut down on our hours spent inside. Bounce 'n' Play in the morning, followed by bereavement group meetings in the damp basement of the senior center across town. Perhaps the two concepts could be merged: Bounce 'n' Grieve. I pictured the widows in their elastic waist lounge pants, defying gravity within the MoonWalk, bouncing their bereavement away. "Seriously, Mom. Go. We are okay."

Relieved, my mother hugged me. "We will call every day. And you'll be coming for Thanksgiving, we'll be up for the holidays . . ."

I went from city co-op dweller to wandering widow to hapless houseguest to suburban homeowner in the span of a month, which is enough to make the average head spin. My head, however, was floating somewhere between the clouds Pete and I used to occupy as we planned our blissful life and purgatory.

I drifted through the days with Abbey by my side, losing myself in innocent play with her only to be yanked back into reality each time I put her down to sleep. I lost interest in the playgroups and bereavement groups. The former was filled with moms chattering about their date nights and their kids' days out with Dad and the latter filled with women twice my age who had had the luxury of "for better or worse, in sickness and in health" for enough years to at least prepare themselves somewhat. Neither group applied to my situation. They did not make sense in my world.

My alone time was spent munching my way through bags of tortilla chips smothered in cheese, scarfing down store-bought cookies by the cellophane sleeveful, and devouring raw gritty cookie dough straight from its chilled tube—tasks that didn't require me to think and were best done when I didn't have to be a good example to my child. That fall, the local Girl Scout troop must've had a picture of me along with a map leading right to my house plastered on their wall. They just kept ringing the bell, and I just kept buying and eating more. There was no such thing as too many Thin Mints or Tagalongs when they were being delivered right to my door.

Halloween approached; Pete and I had been looking

forward to strutting Abbey around in an adorable chicken costume we had found at a shop in the West Village. Instead, I trussed her up and used her as an unknowing accessory in my quest for easy access to chocolate, eating all of her Halloween loot single-handedly (and single-mouthedly) in less than a week. Some people turned to drinking and let the alcohol wither them away under the same circumstances; I, on the other hand, liked the feeling of the heft and the weight I was gaining. My mind continued to hover above it all, but I liked that my body at least was still anchored to the place where Abbey was. I found it oddly comforting that my thighs now rubbed together when I walked, and I enjoyed the childlike swell to my belly. My body continued to exist and grow, even if my brain didn't.

Marissa would come over and, like any good friend would, eat cookies with me. She no longer told me to kiss her big fat lily-white ass, as I was toting around one of my very own. And then one day while carrying some of Abbey's baby toys to the basement, I spotted my dad's treadmill under a box filled with our Super 8 home movies and some questionable-looking bulky black garbage bags. My parents saved everything, which I guess came in handy when running an antique shop, like my dad had for forty years. I pushed the junk aside, gingerly running my finger over the dusty console. *Fuck you,* I mouthed to the evil high fructose sugar demon that laughed every evening as I stuffed myself to the point of nausea. What was I gaining, besides weight, by living like a robot, waiting for my blood sugar to crash so I could fall asleep at night? No more nachos, no more nonsense.

I remembered Pete's mother telling me the story of how he had flipped over the handlebars on his bike at nine years old, cracking a tooth, bloodying his nose, and embedding gravel into his forehead. She had feared it would prevent him from ever getting onto another bicycle again. But the next day, he was at it again. *He got right back on that horse,* she relayed. And I owed it to Pete to climb back on to my horse.

For Abbey. For myself.

Nighttime treadmill running became my drug of choice. The irony wasn't lost on me. Yet every time I climbed onto that treadmill and started my ascent, it was in spite of what had happened. My homage to Pete, I suppose.

After logging many lonely miles, I forced myself to seek out a more social situation. The local Y offered a daily spinning class, taught by a peppy lesbian with a hair color fetish named Donna who had the most killer playlists to accompany her regimen. The first class I took was not unlike the experience of childbirth: grueling and not sure what to expect, cursing as someone in a less torturous position yelled, "Come on, push!"

Making my mind up to attend that first class had been tough; returning for a second time was tougher. But my curiosity as to how short or purple her hair got or which songs we might hear each day coaxed me in. She would play everything from Johnny Cash to "The Imperial March." I began to attend regularly, making sure I was on the bike closest to the door in case I needed to bolt. Initially, every other song in her playlist could reduce me to tears; songs as inane as the Proclaimers' "I'm Gonna Be (500 Miles)" or as sappy as Queen's "You're My Best Friend." But soon, I broke through the wall, hitting that high runners often describe, and let the sweat replace the tears. I slept better, and I certainly looked and felt better. I could keep up with Abbey, whose legs had lost the baby Michelin Man look and were now long, toned, and coltish. I lost the tummy but gained a shapely butt and more boobs, much to Marissa's chagrin. She had lost her cookie-eating comrade, but had gained back her best friend.

4

BIG IN JAPAN

"Sure you don't want a drink or something?"

Leanna and I were standing on my enclosed front porch watching Ed secure the mattress and box spring with rope in the flatbed at the curb.

"Nah. You okay?"

"Yeah. It's a good thing. Change is good." I kicked the futon that served as a couch on the porch. "Can you help me bring this into my room?"

"You're kidding, right? You can't sleep on that!" Leanna folded her arms across her cashmere cardigan and fixed one of her signature stares on me. Barely five feet two, she commanded attention like a five-star general. "It's . . . porch furniture." Her tone sounded eerily like her mother's "*I'm the doctor's wife*" voice we mocked throughout high school. I wondered if she even realized she was doing it.

"It's a futon. I hear they're big in Japan."

"Duh. But you'll kill your back sleeping on that every night. Christ, what *is* my husband doing?"

"Sounds like he's going to leave without you." Ed was in the truck and honking impatiently. "This isn't permanent. Just until I buy a new bed."

"Fuck him. He can wait. I'm not going to come running because he's honking. Let's move this thing." She grabbed one end and tugged it. "Holy crow, this thing weighs more than your mattress and box spring put together!" We managed to drag it off of the wooden frame and down the hall.

"Good thing my bedroom is on the first floor."

"Good thing I love you like a sis," she replied. It was our motto, written in each other's yearbooks and at the bottom of notes we passed secretly in school. Leanna had been an exotic import from Chicago into my biology class freshman year. I could still see her as a sneering punker chick in her tiny combat boots, daring any teacher to catch us; jet-black eyeliner rimming her deep-set Asian eyes, her hair shellacked up into a spiky black mess with sugar water. She had fallen right in with Marissa and me, and with Liz rounding out the group, we became the Fab Four of Lauder High.

"My chariot awaits," she said sarcastically as we each dusted our hands on our jeans and walked toward the front door. The horn cacophony was approaching warp speed outside. "Like Eddie has anywhere important to go. The man has been unemployed for over two years. Sorry he's being such a prick."

"You don't have to apologize." Ed had never been too social with any of us, so his behavior didn't faze me. "How did the shrink visit go?"

"Fine . . . for me, anyway. Ed blew it off."

She shook her head in dismay, her smooth black hair fanning around her face. Gone were the days of sugar-watered Mohawks and most of her punk attitude. In fact, when she and Ed relocated back to Lauder Lake from the city after 9/11, she seemed about as foreign to me as she had upon first sight in biology class. At the time, I chalked it up to the fact she could have lost her husband, who had been in Tower 7 that day. But

as we renewed our friendship once again, I could see there was
much more at work breaking her spirit.

"Thanks for helping. And you know I'm always here if you
need an ear."

"Likewise, girl."

The door clicked closed behind her and, as if on cue, the
phone began to ring. I didn't peek at the caller ID; I suspected it
was Gwen. The director of the Lauder Lake Library had been
calling daily to inquire about the status of my program. I had
sketched out a rough proposal for her weeks ago, but still
needed to find the talent.

The ring seemed to take on her shrill and desperate
demeanor before finally clamming up. Well, the ringing phone
and she could wait a few more hours. I debated whether or not
to just break down and ask Karen for the name of her scary
balloon-twisting clown. I knew I could do better; I just needed
some inspiration.

The box of CDs sat patiently next to my old boom box on
the screened-in porch. I slid a fresh disc from the case of thirty
and contemplated it. I hadn't even played it for Abbey or
mentioned the program idea yet; I was hoping I'd track down
her elusive singer before getting her hopes up. Skipping past
the first few tracks, I slipped down to a seated position on the
floor where the futon had been, leaned back, and closed my
eyes. The same gravelly voice that wooed my daughter to watch
Maxwell MacGillikitty, Feline Private Eye every day began to sing
a song I remembered from my childhood about a garden and a
hoe. About weeds and stones and being made from dreams and
bones.

I could picture Abbey's face the minute she heard this. She
was going to love it. I clicked to the next track, "Transatlantic
Wake-up Call," which described a father's frustration trying to
reach his young daughter and the challenge of being in a
different time zone. Hmm, was there a deeper metaphor

running through there? The song had a somber sound to it, reminiscent of some of my favorite Beatles songs and nothing like any children's music I had heard before. My fingers smoothed over the bold print of the address label. Burning Barn Studios, LLC. The CD played on as I made my way back inside to my computer.

Amazingly, Hoover's Online had a listing, complete with e-mail address, for a studio of the same name in Hoboken, New Jersey. I quickly fired off an e-mail before rushing out the door to pick up Abbey.

"What's New Pussycat?" began to play from the copy in the car stereo as I pulled into the car line for dismissal. I hummed along with the funky bass line added to this old standard. Checking the rearview mirror, I noticed Marissa had pulled up right behind me. Between her minivan and the hulking Range Rover ahead, I felt pretty insignificant in my Mini. I caught her sticking her tongue out at me when I glanced up again. Then my cell phone rang.

"What, Mariss—you too lazy to step out of your car and talk to me?"

"Kiss my lily-white ass. You're up next." The Range Rover carrying the McGreavy twins pulled out, and I scooted up. I could see Miss Carly helping Abbey with the zipper of her coat behind the glass school door.

"I'll call you later . . . I may or may not have some exciting news. And you'll be happy to know, I am now bedless." Ending the call, I hopped out of the car. Abbey was carrying a large piece of manila paper that was boldly crayoned.

"Mom! I drew Maxwell MacGillikitty!"

"Hola, chica." I kissed her forehead in greeting and opened her door for her. "Cool drawing, very beautiful." Abbey had been on a creative kitty kick for about a week now. We had a watercolor Maxwell, an inkblot Maxwell, and a macaroni-and-glue Maxwell cluttering our dining room table already. I wrestled her car seat buckle closed as she held the picture high to kiss it multiple times. Oy vey.

"Katrina, I think it's great Abbey has a love of animals . . . but it's become an obsession with her lately. Did you lose a family pet recently, or has she been wanting a cat?" Miss Carly cocked her pretty blond head and smiled at Abbey through the window.

"No, we don't have a cat. Maxwell is just her favorite cartoon character. But hey, at least it's PBS, right? I don't let her watch all that much television, despite her preoccupation." I felt my cheeks redden. Was I embarrassed by Abbey's obsession or my own? I fervently hoped the studio would e-mail me back.

Date: Friday, April 9, 2004 12:02 p.m.
From: info@burningbarnmusic.com
Re: Adrian Graves contact information
To: bibliomama@gmail.com

Dear Ms. Lewis,
Thanks for your e-mail. I have not been in touch
with Adrian Graves for several years. The last
correspondence I received from him came from e-
mail—adriangraves63@yahoo.com. I'm sorry,
but I no longer have a valid phone number for
him. In response to your question, yes, he was
based out of New York when he recorded that
album ten years ago. Good luck.

Bill Bonovara

GRINNING, I quickly cut and pasted the address he had provided into a new e-mail and began to type.

Date: Friday, April 9, 2004 1:12 p.m.
From: bibliomama@gmail.com
Subject: Program Appearance Request
To: adriangraves63@yahoo.com

Dear Mr. Graves,
My name is Katrina Lewis and I am writing on
*   behalf of the Lauder Lake Public Library's*
*   Friends Group in Westchester County. We are*
*   interested in holding a music program for*
*   children at our library on Friday, April 23, and*
*   are hoping you might be available to perform.*
*   The program is geared toward ages four to eight*
*   and includes children from our community, as*
*   well as a number of autistic children from a*
*   nearby school. It would run about an hour in*
*   length. We can supply a PA and would reimburse*
*   you for your travel, as well as pay you a*
*   negotiable rate.*

Thank you for your time and attention, and I hope to
*   hear from you soon.*

Katrina Lewis
P.S. Maxwell MacGillikitty rules!

"Whatcha doing?" Abbey asked, her mouth spraying graham cracker crumbs.

"Oh honey, let's finish eating at the table. I'm sending a letter on the computer. Want to play a game? Go Fish?" I deleted and then rewrote my postscript, wondering if it sounded too corny. What the heck, may as well leave it.

"Can I watch TV?" Abbey asked hopefully.

"Abb . . . I think we need to take a break from TV. We could go take a walk to the lake. It's nice out."

"Oh! The lake! Thelakelakelakelake!"

Our street was one of eight forming a spoke-in-wheel pattern to the town's namesake, Lake Lauder. We could walk down the road past about nine houses to where the pavement became gravel, then dirt, and finally sand down to the mile-long lake. As kids, my brother and I would spend hours there, swimming out to the dock. You could see the bottom clearly ten feet in. We loved to stare in amazement at the fish, the stones, and our feet, looking pale and alien under the water. Burying our legs in the cool, quiet sand as evening approached, we'd swap stories about the Indians who most likely lived and died right by our house. One summer, we found five arrowheads between the beach and our own backyard.

Abbey and I pulled on Windbreakers and walked hand in hand toward Karen's house. I really hoped my e-mail to Adrian Graves would put Karen's scary balloon-twisting clown out of the running for the library program. We passed the Drimmers' house, where I spent many a teenage night babysitting their two boys. Then the old Rosen residence, now inhabited by Chuck and Kyle, life partners who commuted to the city with their matching Jack Spade messenger bags. Their toy poodle, Ruby Two Boots, was Abbey's second favorite thing on the block after the beach.

On past Hilda Franz's house, which seemed to have eyes looking out each and every leaded glass window. She was my mom's oldest friend and the self-appointed busybody of the street. She basically knew your business before you knew it was even yours. I didn't mind her so much now. Like my parents, she had become a snowbird. Her house now sat empty and gossip-free for half the year.

Liz's old house was next, a small Cape Cod still painted the same shade of puke-green we made fun of in grade school. Her parents divorced her sophomore year, and she moved with her mom and two younger brothers to the west side of the lake, where new condos had gone up. She could stand on her balcony and wave to us down on the beach. A red towel would let my brother know that her mom was out and that he could come over, back when they were dating. A white towel always signified defeat; if she was grounded or stuck doing chores, she would halfheartedly wave it around for a few seconds before hurrying back inside.

The last house on our road was a new build. A McMansion, as Marissa would say. The street's residents went ballistic over the proposal to build on the modest empty lot of grass closest to the beach, and many shouting matches at the town hall ensued. Joe Cippola, who had bought Liz's old house, was an attorney who stood to lose the most—his own view of the lake. He practically laid himself on the road as the backhoes came to break ground.

The house was Karen Mitchell's, and far from a McMansion. Her husband, Mitch, worked with a green architect to make the house environmentally friendly, and it showed—from the bamboo floors and the cement-based fiberboard siding to the rainwater collection system and photovoltaic panels on the roof. The 2,700 square foot house was completely independent of local power, water, and sewer connections, which my father marvels at each time he comes back for a visit. According to Karen, Mitch chose the exact location and layout, with most of the windows facing south toward the lake for maximum passive solar heating benefits.

They composted. They mulched. They recycled with a zeal that bordered on religious. Most of the neighbors had dropped their grudges toward the "new folk" once they saw how committed Karen and Mitch were to preserving the area and minimizing their carbon footprint.

Abbey and I met Karen soon after they moved in. We had been picnicking on the beach, enjoying the late summer weather. Abbey was approaching her third birthday. Her favorite thing to utter at least twenty times a day was a resounding and plaintive "Wazz*at*?" while pointing and demanding I explain everything from cigarette butts on the beach to moss on the rocks to bird calls from above to the egg salad on her sandwich. "Wazz*at*? Wazz*at*, Mama?" I had turned just in time to see her communing with a yellow jacket that was interested in the applesauce on her fingers. Her yowl of pain ripped right through me.

A woman came running up from the water with her hands cupped and outstretched. "The bees are terrible this summer! Here, use some mud. It will raise the stinger and draw out the venom." She fell to her knees in the sand in front of Abbey and began smearing a mixture of water and dirt from a grassy patch near the shore across the palm of my daughter's hand. Abbey was still sobbing and hysterical, but also curious as to the mess on her hand. "Wazz*at*?" she huffed through her tears, examining her hand as the mud began to dry.

"Garlic also works well if you have no mud handy," the woman explained, standing and brushing off her hands. "Hi, I'm Karen, by the way. And this"—she smoothed her hand over the spandex of her black bathing suit—"is Jasper." In all of the chaos, I hadn't noticed this woman was very pregnant. "Why don't we go to my house? It's close by, and you can wash her hand and have a cool drink." And so it was over mud and organic lemonade that we became acquainted with Karen, her husband, Mitch, and eventually little baby Jasper.

The second time Abbey got stung was an entirely different matter. I saw the bee flying near her face and her hand reaching to swat it. I rushed to her as she began to howl and noticed a rash quickly spreading up her arm. Wheezing replaced her crying, and as she struggled to vomit, I realized something was really wrong. Luckily, we were at a carnival on the grounds of the local fire station. Within seconds, we were surrounded by firefighters and EMTs. Anaphylaxis, explained the first paramedic on the scene. He gave her a dose of epinephrine and we were off to the nearest hospital. I now carry an EpiPen for her and have been trained in how to use it.

No worries about bees on this day; the air still had a frosty nip. Both our noses were runny and numb after a half hour of chasing birds and drawing our names in the sand. "Okay, Abb, time to go home. Time to start thinking about dinner." Abbey decided she'd hop on one foot from the picnic table down to the water's edge rather than think about dinner. "How about we race back?" I knew she'd never turn down the chance to win a challenge.

I half jogged, half walked to give her the advantage. As our house came into view, I remembered my e-mail and felt my stomach give an excited pancake flip. Perhaps there would already be a response waiting. I recalled a study I had read recently that reported 6 percent of Americans could be classified as "compulsive e-mail checkers." I hoped Adrian Graves would be among that elite group.

5

ADRIAN

Date: Friday, April 9, 2004 11:58 p.m.
From: adriangraves63@yahoo.com
Re: Program Appearance Request
To: bibliomama@gmail.com

Are you taking the piss?

~

Date: Saturday, April 10, 2004 9:42 a.m.
From: bibliomama@gmail.com
Re: Program Appearance Request
To: adriangraves63@yahoo.com

I've got a four-year-old girl here who lives and
breathes your Maxwell MacGillikitty theme
song. Your music is as serious to her as peanut
butter sandwiches with the crusts cut off—she is
passionately serious about what she likes.

You seem to have an interesting approach to
    children's music based on other songs I've heard,
    and I thought it would be a nice way to introduce
    children in the community to live music. The
    library can pay you a flat rate of $300.00, plus
    travel costs.

Sincerely not taking the piss,
Katrina Lewis

∾

Date: Saturday, April 10, 2004 1:06 p.m.
From: adriangraves63@yahoo.com
Re: Program Appearance Request
To: bibliomama@gmail.com

Dear Ms. Lewis,
Forgive me for my earlier response. I'm not used to
    being solicited to play; in fact, I have not played
    live for some time now. Are you sure the children
    wouldn't rather see those Australian blokes in the
    coloured shirts?

AG

∾

Date: Saturday, April 10, 2004 4:40 p.m.
From: bibliomama@gmail.com
Re: Program Appearance Request
To: adriangraves63@yahoo.com

Dear Mr. Graves,

*Not many public libraries have a budget that could
afford the Wiggles. That's the price we pay for
the charm of being a nonprofit! I can't speak for
every child, but I know my own couldn't care less
about those prefab kiddie bands. If you are not
available but can recommend a reasonable and
quality alternative, we would be grateful.
Disappointed, but grateful. Again, the date is
April 23, and we were hoping for a start time of
four p.m. I have attached directions from
Manhattan.*

Looking forward to hearing from you,
Katrina

Date: Sunday, April 11, 2004 2:15 a.m.
From: adriangraves63@yahoo.com
Re: Program Appearance Request
To: bibliomama@gmail.com

Katrina,
All right, count me in.
See you then.
Adrian

6

TIME MACHINE

THE WEEK before the music program, I became a one-woman street team. Grabbing a healthy stack of promo flyers from the library, along with a roll of tape and a stapler, I headed out to conquer Main Street.

The flyers were cute, featuring a guitar-wielding cat with shades and a cap perched between his ears. I hung several in the windowed entryway of the library, Starbucks, the Korean grocer, and at Stumble Inn, the local dive bar across the street from the YMCA. The owner of the bar laughed when I asked, but he assented to my request. I stapled it right between a flyer for a Van Halen tribute band and a want ad seeking musicians who played the didgeridoo. It takes all kinds, right?

I crossed over to the other side of Main, figuring I would hit the movie theater, the juice bar, and the antique store before heading back to meet Marissa and the kids at the park.

"Hey, Tree." Grant Overhill was coming out of the shop just as I was about to reach for the old brass doorknob I must've turned a thousand times during my childhood. I often had to remind myself the store was Grant's now, and not my dad's. The sign still read UNDERWOOD AND OVERHILL ANTIQUES, which my dad had thought was a clever play on our surnames once he and Grant became partners in the business.

It blew my mind to this day that my adolescent crush had actually become apprentice to my father. Here was a guy who had lived and breathed football, baseball, muscle cars, and girls, in that order, and seemingly overnight, he began walking around with his nose in the latest edition of *Kovels' Antiques and Collectibles Price Guide* and discussing with my father the merits of hobnail glass and Stangl Pottery. Marissa, ever the romantic optimist, likes to think he developed the interest out of a desire to woo me. But he began apprenticing a good two years after he had wooed, won, and walked all over me, so I didn't agree with her rose-colored notion at all. He was just the type of guy who never had motivation or a reason to leave Lauder Lake, with the exception of the unlikely event he would one day be called up and given a six-figure salary by the Jets or the Mets to play pro ball. When no scholarships or scouts appeared, he turned to his available options: community college and a part-time job.

My father, despite being less than happy with the state my ill-fated and short-lived courtship with Grant had left me in, was still a fair man. He must have seen some sort of potential in his charge. Sure enough, after getting his BA, Grant accepted a managerial job at the store, followed by part ownership, and then, when my dad retired, full reign.

"Hey . . . I was just coming in to see if you wouldn't mind hanging a flyer for the children's music program at the library. Jake might enjoy it, actually. It's next Friday."

He studied the flyer I handed to him. "Hmm . . . I'm working, but maybe his mom can take him." Grant never mentioned his baby-mama's name enough for me to remember it, but they shared custody of Jake.

"Cool, I hope so. It should be lots of fun for the kiddos."

Grant slipped inside to hang the flyer in the corner window, in front of a display of milk glass. I watched as he gingerly stepped around the display case, his head tilting toward the window. The late afternoon sun hit the top of his blond mop, showcasing all of his golden boy highlights. Poster Boy, Liz had called him. I had to admit, Grant was a rarity among most of the guys from our graduating class; he had managed to retain both his full head of hair and lithe athletic body he had proudly built up in high school. His chiseled biceps strained against the sleeves of his *10th Annual Lauder Lake Turkey Trot* T-shirt as he secured the poster prominently in the center of the window. He looked up at me for approval; I gave him a smile and a thumbs-up. He came back out and locked the door behind him.

"Closing time?"

"Yeah. I take Jake to karate class on Thursdays. It's a slow day anyway. Need a ride home?"

"Um. No. I'm good. Thanks. Heading back to the park. Abbey's there with Mariss."

"So what's up with Marissa and the other ladies of leisure these days?" Grant asked, jingling his keys.

"Hey! No woman with kids under age eighteen qualifies as a 'lady of leisure,'" I informed him.

Honestly, with the exception of Leanna and her freelance graphic design business, none of our Lauder Lake group was exactly bringing home the bacon. Marissa had worked in retail for years before halfheartedly going for her real estate license. A slump in the housing market coupled with her second pregnancy killed her desire to go further. Karen had spent several years and many dollars getting her MSW at NYU, but her current job duties consisted of running a renewable, sustainable, ethically responsible, and green household. It was an occupation that the rest of us didn't quite understand but admired her for nonetheless. And me, well . . . I was still studying the blueprint of the life I had built a decade earlier, trying to figure out where the design flaws and weaknesses were that had contributed to its major collapse. It was an endless and exhausting task that didn't allow for moonlighting. Insurance settlements, plus rent collected from the Manhattan sublet, allowed me to stay home with Abbey. Keeping her happy and feeling safe were my main objectives, even if it meant running our house like an underground bunker protected from any further disaster.

"Come on, my car's right here." He gestured to his red Saturn coup parked at the curb. "I can take you."

He opened the door for me, then quickly reached over to brush a *Sports Illustrated* magazine off the seat and to push a toolbox underneath it. I climbed in, marveling at the fact that the car still looked essentially the same as it had the last time I was in it. How old were we then? Nineteen? As Grant shut the door behind me, I felt as if I were being sealed into a time capsule. The sharp scent of Drakkar Noir assaulted my nose and my memory, along with the faint lingering odor of stale beer from a long-ago spillage.

"Wow, I can't believe this car is still going. I think the last time I was in it, we were cruising this very length of Main Street and cranking the latest Tesla cassette tape."

Grant laughed, throwing the car into gear and tearing out of his parking spot a little too fast. "She's treated me well, this old girl. Course, I added a CD changer and got rid of the tape deck. Lots of memories. Funny to think of all the action the backseat had . . . and now there's a booster seat back there."

"Yeah, well . . . that's what all that backseat action eventually leads to." I squirmed inwardly at the awkward mental image he had thrust upon me.

Grant had been the envy of us all, purchasing the zippy red Saturn SC Sport the first year they hit the market. It had those cool flip-up headlights and drove low to the ground. At the time, he was the epitome of sexy-cool to most of the underage female population. Then again, we were all wearing acid-wash jeans and scrunchies in our hair. It was depressing as well as disturbing, not so much that he was still driving it, but he was still treating it like a pussy machine after all these years.

"So . . . what belt is Jake up to in karate?" I asked, changing the subject.

"Green. The kid could pretty much kick my ass. He's getting big! Speaking of which . . ." We had pulled into the lot adjacent to the park. Abbey and Brina were taking turns on the small rock-climbing wall, with supervision from Marissa. "Look at those long legs on your little one. Was her dad tall? I never met him."

"You did, actually. He came to the ten-year reunion." I rested my hand on the door handle. "Pete was five-eleven."

Grant absently tapped his fingers on the steering wheel, clearly not interested in the physical attributes of any other member of the male tribe, living or dead. "Hey, Chad and Diane are coming into town in a few weeks. Why don't you come to dinner with us?"

The way he suddenly slid his arm across the seat back, along with his trademark flashing of a lazy smile, made me wonder if he still looked at me and saw a girl with second-skin Jordache jeans and teased hair. It was as if he swapped a John Hughes teen flick in his mind for what had really happened between us freshman year. And as if no time had actually passed between then and now.

"Thanks, but I don't think—"

"Come on. It would be like old times."

Clearly all the varnish and lead paint chips at the antique shop had gotten to him. Sure, I *knew* Chad, who had been on various sports teams with Grant. And his wife, Diane, had been a classmate of mine since elementary school. But we hadn't had any old times, good times, or fast times at Lauder High as a foursome. My girlfriend status with Grant had been such a short blip; it could barely be classified as a "time."

"I was actually just talking to Chad the other day, and your name came up." I raised an eyebrow at him in response, and he bumbled onward. "You know . . . about how you are, well, back in town and stuff. It's cool having you back." He leaned in closer. "You're so . . . down-to-earth, Tree. Not like a lot of the chicks around here."

"Yeah?" I pictured myself down-to-earth, all right; belly to the ground and squirming past Grant's land mines and foxholes. *You were right, Pat Benatar. Love is a battlefield.*

"So what do you say, Tree?"

I clenched the stapler in my hand, thinking of the many ways I could use it as a weapon if required. Like pinning his balls to the gear shaft if he inched any closer to me. "I'm really swamped right now, planning this program and all." My words came out in a rush. "Why don't you call me after it's over next week and I'll see how things look? You know, with Abbey and a sitter and stuff." I had the door open now. "Thanks for the ride, see ya."

"Hmm, so perhaps the bad bed juju has been lifted?" Marissa opened the fence gate for me as the Saturn spun a wave of gravel onto the grass in its departure. "I see he's still driving like it's 1999."

I laughed and folded the remaining flyers in half before Abbey's keen eyes could catch a glimpse of her favorite cat. Otherwise, I'd hear talk of nothing more for the remainder of the week.

"Can we do pizza, *please*?" Abbey and Brina began their twin nuclear assault to break us down.

"Aunt Miso said we had to wait to ask you." Abbey, ever since she began speaking, loved to refer to her favorite aunt-by-proxy, but wasn't able to pronounce her name quite right.

"Well, we've got no other plans . . ."

"We'd better stop home first," Marissa said. "Joey and Daddy would never forgive us if we went to Marino's without them." Taking that as a yes, the girls squealed and ran to Marissa's minivan. "Is that good with you?"

"Sure, I'm along for the ride."

"Speaking of rides . . ."

"He was leaving the shop as I was going there to hang a flyer and he offered me a lift. Hey, remember Chad and Diane?"

"Barely."

"They got married after graduation and moved to Texas. Anyway, he asked me to go out to dinner when they come to town."

"Hmm. Double date with superficial people you didn't care much for in high school. Not exactly an ideal first date." We loaded and locked the girls into their seats. "But then again, it's getting back on the horse."

"And you are beating a dead horse. Remember, I had a first date with Grant. And a second. And a third. It was a road to nowhere. If I get back on that road now, it'll be like admitting there is nothing better out there for me."

We watched out the window as a pack of boys from the high school track team galloped past along the shoulder of the road. Quasi-men, chins jutting and firm thighs pumping in adolescent adrenaline swagger.

Marissa gave me a long look as she waited for traffic to pass. "It's only regression if you tell yourself it is, Tree. A lot of time has passed. He could have a totally different set of values by now."

I glanced back at the girls, who were happily passing a stuffed animal back and forth between them, and remembered Grant's "backseat action" comment. "It's entirely possible he may have a different set of values, Mariss. But what if they are worse now than before?"

Marissa chose not to comment. Instead, she plucked one of

the flyers from my lap. "I still can't believe you found him . . . and he agreed to come to our dinky little library. You sweet-talk him?"

"Not exactly. We just e-mailed. But I think I did a pretty good job of convincing him it would be worth his while."

7

MAN OF THE HOUR

"ABBSTER, pick up the pace! We *gotta* go."

"I don't want to go to the liberry today, Mommy."

Normally, I would gently and patiently remind her that, while there were many fruits in the world, "liberry" was not one of them. But there was no time for a grammar lesson today. "Well, you don't have a choice. Mommy has to be there today, so come on." I did the hop-shuffle dance into my sandals as I began the search for my keys.

It was the day of the program, and of course we were beyond late. I pictured poor Adrian Graves (which wasn't easy to do—again, having never seen him) waiting at the train station for his ride to the library. He was supposed to call before his stop, but hadn't yet, so perhaps we would still have time to drop the CDs and instruments for the kids at the library before running to fetch him.

"But *Mom*." Abbey stretched the latter word out to three syllables. "*Maxwell MacGillikitty* is on! I wanna stay here!" I threw her sandals down beside her just as I spied my keys on top of the TV. I must've tossed them there when I turned it on to occupy Abbey while I dressed.

I hadn't anticipated the closet crisis until I pulled open the door that morning. What to wear? It was worse than I had feared. My B.C. (Before Child) working-girl wardrobe looked dated and sad. There was a ball gown, a barn jacket, and barely anything suitable in between. I had finally pulled on a dark denim pencil skirt and a cute wrap-blouse in plum I had picked up at Barneys on sale at the end of last summer. Sort of hmmm . . . sexy secretary, I now observed, tilting my head to inspect my reflection in the mirror and smoothing back my curls. As I raced to grab Abbey a clean dress from her room, I sent up thanks to the gods above that I had bothered to shave my legs that morning.

"Here. Put this on. *Now.* The TV is going off." Abbey shot me the juvenile version of a murderous look, eyes squinting and her head quivering. "It can go back into the closet, you know," I offered. She quickly hopped up and pulled the sundress over her head.

On September 10, 2001, I was still in a solitary state of mourning. By the next morning, the entire country had joined me. My world became that much more shocked and saddened. Like everyone else, I sat glued to the TV as it all came crashing down, over and over on a continuous film loop. I cried for all humanity, for Abbey's future, and, as ever, for Pete. I wondered what he would have thought had he lived to see what was happening in our former backyard: as a father, as a New Yorker, as a reporter, as an American, as a human being. On September 12, I unplugged the TV and pushed it into the closet, where it stayed for several months. I didn't need a twenty-four-hour network enabler to feed my sorrow. I canceled the cable and paid my respects by reading the Portraits of Grief via the *New York Times* website every morning until the last piece ran on New Year's Eve. Later that day, we bundled up and headed to Marissa's for a sleepover to ring in 2002. It was there, over monkey bread and morning cartoons, that my daughter's love for *Maxwell MacGillikitty, Feline Private Eye* was born.

Maxwell was a plucky little Maine coon cat who consistently found himself tiptoeing around one mystery or another in his tiny English fishing village of Mousehole. Luckily, with the aid of an unlikely sidekick in the form of a duck named Mr. Quackson, he was always able to wrap up the muddles within a thirty-minute, commercial-free time period. The show hadn't exactly exploded in popularity here in the States, but it had developed a small cult following. And my daughter seemed to be leading the campaign.

I found myself wheeling out our old telly soon after her first taste, like any indulgent mother would. After banging on the top for several minutes to beat some good reception out of it, I allowed her one show a day, which turned into one hour, followed by a full-blown addiction to PBS. She began to walk around the house giving props for whatever good things came into her life in the form of a public service announcement: "This donut was made possible by the generous support of viewers like you. Thank you."

Every episode ends with Maxwell humbly pulling down the brim of the tiny deerstalker's detective hat perpetually perched between his tuft-tipped ears and quipping the line, *"When you have eliminated the impossible, whatever remains, however improbable, must be the truth."* I was certain Sir Arthur Conan Doyle was rolling in his grave, but my daughter gobbled it up with a spoon, quoting his lines and relaying his adventures to any hapless child who stood within shouting distance at the playground, grocery store, or random parking lot.

Abbey was still grumbling from her booster seat as we cruised down Main in search of a parking space. The rear lot the library shared with Starbucks was full, forcing us to park down near Underwood and Overhill Antiques. Luckily, the Mini could wedge into spots the lion's share of Lauder Lake vehicles—SUVs and minivans—could not. I grabbed my box of program material with one hand and Abbey's shoulder with the other and maneuvered us across the street.

"What if I never find out what happens to Maxwell after he gets trapped in the Wild Bird Hospital while trying to rescue Mr. Quackson from the clutches of the evil Dr. Loveydovey?"

"Well, maybe you can ask Adrian Graves about it, since he makes part of the show."

"I thought *Maxwell MacGillikitty* was made possible by funding from the Corporation for Public Broadcasting," Abbey said, scooting under my arm as I propped open one of the library's double doors.

"Yes, sweetie . . . but someone still has to write the story and sing the song, right?" I hustled her into the large programming room located off the wing of the children's library. It was a great space, with tons of windows and lots of kid-size tables and chairs for crafts and summer reading club programs. Today, the library staff had pushed the tables to the back of the room and set up two curved rows with a dozen chairs each. There were already a few early birds eagerly awaiting the event, including Karen with Jasper and Marissa with Joey and Brina. I was relieved to have the friendly and familiar support. Abbey immediately fell in with her friends, which allowed me to hustle to the front of the room and set up the props I had brought. The dollar store had had small tambourines and egg shakers that fit into the program's supply budget, so I figured the kids could use them to join in with the music. I stashed the extra CDs I had purchased from the Bruised Apple in the corner, hoping if all went well, perhaps I could hand them out to the kids at the end of the program and Adrian Graves could autograph them.

"So are you nervous?" Marissa asked, trying out an egg shaker. "And where's our rock star? It's almost four now."

"Shit," I grumbled, low enough for the other parents and

kids not to hear. "I instructed him to call me just before he got to the station." I checked my cell and peered out the window down Main Street. "He'd better show. I'm not about to stand up here for an hour and pretend I can play music." There was a small PA system, consisting of a microphone on a stand and an amplifier, which I tested to make sure it was in good working condition.

"Need any help in here?" Gwen poked her head in. Instead of her usual cement-colored library director suit, she actually looked festive in a sack dress of a salmon hue.

"Nope, we are all good," I assured her.

"I can't wait to meet your singing sensation!" She smiled and greeted some more parents and kids, who settled themselves on the chairs and cross-legged on the carpet.

"Well . . . I wouldn't exactly call him a sensation. But I think he's fun and talented and the kids will like him," I replied, hoping he didn't show up with a swastika tattooed on his forehead. I didn't exactly explain to Gwen the limited knowledge I myself had of the man I had hired to perform.

"I'll keep an eye on the kids." Marissa nudged me. "Maybe you should go outside and call him."

I slipped into the main area of the lobby. It had the usual Friday afternoon pace of patrons returning and borrowing, studying and socializing. Amelda and Judy, two clerks who were probably working in the library before the birth of Dewey, were stationed at the circulation desk. I wandered over to the front door, debating whether to just run to the station or to stay put and pray for the best.

Leanna and her son, Dylan, were just coming in. Dylan, a quiet and broody nine-year-old, was out of the age bracket I was aiming for with the program, but I was thankful they came to show their support anyway.

"Hey, are we late?" Leanna gave Dylan a gentle shove. "In with you, no complaining. You've got your Game Boy, you can deal for an hour." He skulked toward the programming room. "What's up? You look freaked out."

We moved away from the front door and into the Fiction section as the van from the Rainbow School pulled up to the curb. "He's not here yet."

"Holy crow. What are you going to do?"

"I dunno. Maybe he missed his train or something. I'm so . . ." I stopped midsentence, noticing a man had breezed in moments ahead of the Rainbow kids. He had a softshell guitar case slung over his shoulder and was inquiring at the circulation desk.

"I bet he thinks one of those old biddies at the desk is you!" Leanna giggled. I took a moment to size him up. Not particularly tall, but of slim stature. His dark blondish hair, at least from my view, was somewhat raggedy, but perfectly respectable for a musician. He was wearing a black button down styled after an old-school tux shirt, with thin ruffles running down the front. His jeans were dark wash and looked expensive. I suddenly felt small-town and shoddy. I wished I had thought to pluck my eyebrows and give my chipped toenails a fresh coat of polish.

The clerks were gesturing and pointing toward the programming room. "Oh, but wait, here she comes now," Amelda announced as I hastily approached. He turned, displaying a face much more weathered than I had initially noticed from afar. Tiny wrinkles fanned from the outer corners of his eyes, and his hair had quite a bit of gray streaking through the blond, especially at his sideburns. For some reason, I had anticipated him being younger than me. I recovered quickly, sticking out my hand.

"I'm Katrina Lewis, thanks for coming."

"Lew?"

"No, *Lewis.*"

"No, I mean . . . do you 'ave a loo?" His watery blue eyes

widened to stress the urgency of the situation. "I'm afraid I'll burst if I don't go for a slash."

"Oh . . . yeah, down that hall." It took me a moment to register his accent and his slang, yet my embarrassment over the situation was fairly immediate. I stood rooted to the spot after he thrust his guitar into my hands and rushed off. Leanna was still standing there, a witness to the whole encounter. "He's . . . um . . ." I searched for the right words.

"Old? British? Drunk? Or D) all of the above?"

"He's older . . . but he's kinda cute," I admitted, surprising myself. "Come on, drunk? It's four in the afternoon at the public library! Please. Go get a seat. I'll be in there in a minute."

I waited at the end of the hall for my charge. After a moment, he came out of the bathroom, swaying slightly into the wall as he pulled a tin of mints out of his pocket. "Altoid?" he offered. The smell of Jack Daniel's and his peppery cologne, which was somehow subtle and intense all at once, were noticeably foreign to the hallowed halls of my local library. I got the feeling this was not the sort of creature who normally frequented places with drop ceilings and fluorescent lighting; perhaps not even the sort who functioned much before sundown.

"You *are* drunk."

"And you"—he popped two of the curiously strong mints into his mouth—"are beautiful."

"Jesus Christ."

"I'll sober up soon . . . and hopefully, you will still be beautiful." He grabbed back his guitar with a smile. "Are the throngs of screaming adoring masses here yet?"

"Yes, they've been waiting patiently for fifteen minutes. You were supposed to call before you got to the station."

"Well, I took a little kip on the train and overshot by one stop. So I grabbed a cab back. I'm here now, and I am ready. Let's have at it, shall we?" He raised his eyebrows, amused at the fact that I clearly was not. In fact, I was downright pissed off and wishing I had never contacted him. I hated the thought of Abbey or the others being disappointed. I led the way, secretly wishing he had taken a long "kip" and not woken up until Schenectady.

Just before we entered the program room, I remembered the CDs. "I hope it's okay, I brought some copies of your album to hand out to the kids after."

"Oh? And which album would that be?" he asked, again with that slightly amused, self-deprecating tone. It was as if he was making fun of himself and me all at the same time.

"*Songs for Natalie*—it was the only one I could find, and it wasn't easy."

The guy was taken aback; he paused and, for a moment, looked ready to bolt for the exit door. "Okay then" was all he replied, and proceeded in.

The room was happily buzzing with kids' chatter and moms' murmuring. Slowly, the noise died down and they all turned their attention to us. Adrian Graves nonchalantly began to tune what looked like a well-used twelve-string acoustic guitar, and I made a brief introduction before joining my friends in the back of the room. Abbey, her friends, and a few other curious kids were sitting cross-legged within spitting distance of the main attraction. There were six children who had been bussed over from the Rainbow School, and most were in chairs with their parents and teachers sitting next to them. Some were quite verbal, others not very responsive. It would be interesting to see how they reacted to the music.

Adrian cleared his throat. "Well, thanks for having me here at your library today, and thanks to Ms. Lew-*is* for arranging this." He flashed a smart-ass grin in my general direction. "I don't expect you have ever heard of me, but some of you prob-ably know this little guy called Maxwell . . . Maxwell MacGillikitty, Feline Private Eye." He sang the name exactly like the chorus, and his voice came through the mike, gravelly yet smooth and instantly familiar. He played a riff I recognized from the song, and Abbey's hand shot up.

"Yes . . . pigtails in the front?"

"Do you talk for Maxwell in the show? Your voice sounds like him."

"No . . . I just wrote the opening song."

"Do you know if Maxwell escapes from the Wild Bird Hospital today?" Abbey persisted. My child obviously inherited her maternal grandmother's interrogation skills.

"Honestly, I don't," Adrian admitted, thoughtfully strumming his guitar. He looked desperate to begin playing and stop talking. "But I bet he finds a way out; he always does." With a wink, he rolled right into the Maxwell theme song. "Feel free to get up . . . dance about," he murmured.

Marissa leaned close. "Sexy man, entertaining our children." I breathed a sigh of relief. Many of the kids were up and dancing in their spots . . . so far, so good. I found my eyes gravitating toward his fingers as he formed various bar chords with ease. He wore no wedding ring, only a thick silver band around his left pinky. I instantly chastised myself with the reminder that this was a cultural opportunity for the local children, not a vehicle for jump-starting my own sad social life.

"Awright, I was saving that for my encore," he joked as he wrapped up that first song, "but it made a good icebreaker." He took a sip from the bottle of water I had supplied for him. "Now . . . how about a request from the audience, a sing-along, perhaps?"

The kids suddenly all went shy, peeking out from behind their hands. Karen, sitting on the floor next to her toddler, got the ball rolling by raising her hand and suggesting Jasper's favorite song, "The Itsy-Bitsy Spider."

"Erm, yes but . . . that one's a bit naff, isn't it? How about a song about another spider? One named . . . Boris?" He began to pluck at the lower strings of his guitar, and pretty soon he had all the kids calling out the creepy crawly chorus of the Who's obscure song. Even Karen, shocked at first by his rebuff, was singing along. I couldn't believe he was really pulling it off. More kids and parents, lured by the sounds emanating from the programming room, came in and sat. Dylan had abandoned his Game Boy and was staring, fascinated, as Adrian did a few Pete Townshend–esque pinwheels on his guitar for effect.

In keeping with the animals theme, he launched into a song I remembered from my own childhood, "At the Zoo" by Simon and Garfunkel. Another interesting choice, especially considering the line about the zookeeper's fondness for rum. Leanna leaned over and whispered, "Yeah, the zookeeper's not the only one." I gave her a raised eyebrow and a smirk but said nothing.

The man of the hour was beginning to look less drunk and more relaxed as he sailed through one song after another. He handed out the egg shakers, and the kids formed a conga line for "Day-O (The Banana Boat Song)." He even had the kids from Rainbow moving and shaking eggs and singing. I loved how he began to change the words on the fly. "Stand on one foot and stick out your tongue . . ." The kids were happy to oblige. "Dance like a monkey, and talk on the phone . . ." Gwen was in the doorway with a wide smile of approval on her face.

For his final song of the hour, Adrian had the kids play a guessing game, asking them what number he was thinking of between one and twenty. "Right then, Dylan. Your prize is accompanying me on tambourine for my final song. I was thinking of the number three. And why three, you may ask? Well, because three . . . is a magic number."

I found myself having to step out of the room for a moment to compose myself. Pete and I, both children of the seventies, had grown up with fond memories of Saturday morning cartoons and *Schoolhouse Rock!* This was a song we had sung to Abbey from the time she was in utero. A song I hadn't actually thought of in years but, from the moment he began the first verse, sent the memories and visions flooding back. After several deep breaths, I was able to slip back in and catch him singing the final line. *"A man and a woman had a little baby, yes they did . . ."*

He was singing barely above a whisper, but his lips were communing with the microphone in a way that made it almost like an extension of his body. His eyes were turned down as he warbled: *"They had three in a family . . . and that's a magic . . . number."* I listened to him hold that last note as if he were trying to prolong some sort of magic himself, perhaps an enchantment he alone experienced while he was up there performing. Then I happened to notice all of the audience members over the age of twelve were, like me, holding their breath. And all of those under twelve were staring, completely enraptured, until someone started applauding, and then, simultaneously, the spell was broken for both the entertainer and the entertained.

The kids began swarming around Adrian. I watched him shaking hands, grinning, and slapping high fives. One mother walked up and hugged him, much to his amazement. "My son hasn't spoken or smiled in five months." Her voice choked with emotion. "Now he is singing. Thank you." She looked fondly at her son, a heavyset boy of about ten, who was still waving an egg shaker and singing, "Day-O! Da-a-a-y-o."

"That was truly awesome," I told Adrian when I was able to get within earshot. "Thank you."

"It was fun, my pleasure." Parents and kids began filing past us like a demented wedding receiving line, thanking both of us and shaking our hands.

"So you wouldn't mind signing some CDs for the kids, then?"

"Sure, sure." He hastily zipped his guitar case and joined the group of kids crowding around the table as I passed out copies of his music. Gwen brought him a Sharpie marker, and he went to work.

"Thank you thank you, Mommy, that was the best!" Abbey trilled, dancing around me and grabbing my hands. She was one of the last to finally fall into line and have her CD signed. "It's spelled *A-B-B-E-Y*, with an *E*, like the Beatles album," she informed Adrian. She had heard me recite this same line of explanation to people many a time.

"Ah yes, *Abbey Road*. I know the album—and the road—well." I stationed myself near the door to see people out but kept one ear listening to their exchange.

"My dad liked the Beatles, but then he passed out."

"She means passed on," Joey supplied. "Passed *on*, Abb, not passed out."

"Hey." Marissa placed her hand on my shoulder. "I've got to get Brina to her T-ball game. How about I take Abbey with us so you can finish up here? You can swing by later to get her."

"Are you sure you don't mind?" I glanced over at Abbey. She was quoting Maxwell lines to Adrian and doing her best cat impression.

"Have you ever been to Mousehole?" she was asking him.

"Yes, indeed I have. It's a real fishing village on the south coast of Cornwall, very lovely." I liked the way he considered each of her questions, no matter how far out of left field they seemed, and gave her legitimate answers.

"Do I mind? Come on!" my best friend scoffed. "I love your daughter. She nicknamed me after salty soy soup and I *still* love her! Go on. Take him to dinner or something."

"Or something," Leanna chided, much more wickedly than Marissa had intended it. Leanna had an uncanny way of pulling naughty thoughts out of your head you didn't know were there. I always thought she had missed her calling as the next Dr. Ruth. Or a dominatrix. He was entering earshot range, so I gave them both the stink-eye.

"Adrian, this is Marissa and Leanna. Oh, and Karen." She had just come over with a wiped out–looking Jasper in her arms to say good-bye.

"Nice to meet you . . . that was fabulous!" Marissa enthused. "Truly the best thing I have ever witnessed at this library. Not that I come here a lot. Only when Tree drags me here. But seriously, so great." I rolled my eyes at her, and she took the hint. "Okay, off to the T-ball fields. Abbey, you're coming with us, honey." Abbey came running over to give me a kiss.

"Good-bye, Adrian Graves," she said solemnly.

"Cheers, Abbey-with-an-*E* Lewis." They shook hands.

"Bye, Tree. I'll talk to you soon. Nice to meet you, Adrian." Leanna waved. She and Karen walked out together with their kids, leaving me and Adrian and a bunch of chairs pushed all willy-nilly.

"I'll give you a ride back down to the train," I offered as I busied myself straightening the room back to its original order. Without fail, every time I found myself within five feet of a man in close quarters, my mind would race to the point of virtual incoherence. Like with Grant in his car last week, and now with Adrian. After living exclusively with a four-year-old for so long, my small talk was limited and my flirting mechanism had rusted up beyond belief.

He began to help me push the tables back to their original spots, apparently not too keen on much conversation either. "You don't have to do that," I assured him, but he didn't pay me much mind. "Listen, you were really great with the kids today. Sorry I doubted you."

"I'm sorry I gave you a reason to. In all honesty, I was nervous as hell playing and needed a couple of drinks to steady my nerves. I haven't played in front of anyone in a long time." He rubbed his temple. "A *really* long time."

Gwen breezed in, gushing with compliments and waving a check cut from the programming budget for Adrian. I watched as he slipped it into his back pocket without so much as a glance at it and nodded his thanks. Then I hustled him out before Gwen could begin her usual tirade about how my talents could really be of use around the branch full-time. I quoted the train timetable as an excuse, and we escaped onto Main Street as the late afternoon sun began to dip behind the buildings.

8

FIGHT OR FLIGHT

THERE IS something inherently cool about a guy walking down the street with a guitar case in one hand and a cigarette in the other. Especially on our sleepy little Main Street. He had lit up immediately upon leaving the library, which didn't surprise me since his singing voice had that nicotine-laced tone.

I was secretly glad my car was not parked right out back, as it was pretty thrilling to walk with him. There was a feeling of innocent camaraderie as we fell into an equal pace. As we passed the antique shop, I caught sight of Grant standing inside, broom in hand, watching us. Jake had not been present at the program, and I wondered if Grant had even bothered to mention it to his son's mom.

"Here we are." I touched Adrian's arm to indicate where my car was, enjoying the contrast between his soft cotton shirt under my fingers and his solid biceps.

"Smashing color," Adrian complimented as he stashed his guitar behind the seats and climbed into my Mini Cooper. When it had come time to buy the little bulldog of a car, I had gone with the electric blue/white top combination, figuring I would never lose it in the mall parking lot.

"Thanks . . . Marissa's husband, Rob, calls it my Smurf." I laughed.

"My first car was a 1975 Mini 850 in British racing green. Loved that little gem." We both reached for the automatic window buttons that resided in the middle of the dash and our fingers collided. The electric zing of physical contact reverberated through my hand and made a beeline right for my pleasure points. As Leanna would say . . . *holy crow*. If pheromones actually existed, mine were out of Rip Van Winkle mode and ready to make up for lost time. It took all of my faculties to remember how to put the car in drive.

"I like the feel of your town, how it isn't too posh," he commented as I waited at the light to hang a U-turn. "So many small towns in the States seem homogenized by the influx of yuppies and Starbucks opening on every corner."

"We've managed to keep a lot of the charm. Although it has definitely changed since I was a kid. I love that it's far enough from the city to not have the trash and overcrowding, but close enough to have many of its perks: a diverse ethnic population, cultural outlets . . ." I cringed, fearing I sounded too much like a tour guide. "Oh . . . and the best Thai food in the tri-state area."

"Oh, nothing beats this little Thai place I know on 48th," Adrian insisted. I knew exactly which place he was referring to, as it had been my favorite in Manhattan as well. "How about we grab dinner," he suggested when I respectfully disagreed with his opinion, "so I can judge for myself? The trains are plentiful, despite what you told your boss."

"Ugh, bite your tongue . . . that woman is *not* the boss of me! I volunteer at the library, so technically, I don't really work there. I lied about you having to catch your train because she has the tendency to talk and talk and not shut up." Realizing I must've sounded like the pot calling the kettle black, I cut myself off by simply nodding and throwing the car into park in front of Saigon Spice.

The restaurant was cozy and inviting, with dark walls and a plethora of bamboo accents. Adrian escorted me to a corner table and went so far as to pull the chair out for me. His display of chivalry was certainly making up for the crude potty talk he had begun our acquaintance with. In fact, the dim and sophisticated atmosphere, coupled with his soft-spoken demeanor, made him seem like a different person altogether.

I ordered a glass of Pinot Grigio, relishing the opportunity to be out at a restaurant that did not have crayons and butcher paper on the table. Adrian pulled a pair of reading glasses seemingly out of nowhere and began to study the extensive menu. He decided on the panang curry chicken and a Singha beer. I debated but ended up with my usual favorite, pad Thai.

Our drinks were delivered and we were left on our own, no menus to hide behind. "So, um . . . what part of England are you from?"

He took a swig of his beer. The thick silver ring encircling his pinky gleamed in the late afternoon sunlight. It had some lettering etched on it that I couldn't decipher from across the table. "Hampshire . . . about two hours from Londontown, southeast. Until seventeen . . . then I moved to London with my two best mates."

"And how long have you called New York home?"

He had to think for a moment. "I was in and out of the States a bit for work," he began slowly. "Mostly in the eighties. I moved here permanently in 1994, so . . . crikey, it's been ten years!" He swished the remainder of his beer around in the bottle. "Imagine that," he added, more to himself than to me.

"So how did the whole Maxwell MacGillikitty song thing happen for you? Have you done any other jingles for TV?"

A nervous bark of a laugh flew out of his mouth, followed by a more subdued but still amused titter. "No, no . . . not my scene at all. My cousin . . . he works for the BBC and was involved in the development of the show. I think it was around

1998, we were down the pub, boozing it up on one of my visits home. He was telling me all about this brilliant kids' show and this cat, so for a laugh, I started throwing out silly song lyrics. Before I knew it, I had an offer from the producers to submit a song, so I figured, what the heck, I'd have a go."

He leaned forward then, elbows on the table and arms crossed. "So Katrina—"

"My friends call me Tree."

He smiled. "I think I'll call you Kat."

I let out a laugh. "My grandma used to call me that. Okay. I'm fine with that."

"Have you always lived here, Kat?"

"Born and raised here in Lauder Lake . . . moved to Manhattan at eighteen for school . . ." Neat and tidy short version or long and painful torturous version? I decided to go with the former. ". . . and moved back here with Abbey in 2000."

I hadn't really noticed his goatee until he began to rub it musingly. It was slightly darker than the hair on his head and started with a little soul patch under his bottom lip. I had never been a fan of much facial hair, but I decided I liked his.

"So . . . Abbey's dad. He . . . he's gone, then?"

"Just before her first birthday, yes. I . . . It's hard to talk about it. We're doing okay," I managed.

Instead of the usual head-tilt/auto-reply of "I'msosorryfory-ourloss" people tended to offer before moving on to a safer topic, Adrian actually gripped both of my hands across the table, riveted his eyes on me, and murmured, "Bloody hell, Kat. How old was he?"

I let my hands be held as I answered, gazing at them intently. If I stared and didn't blink or look away, I could possibly stave off the tears.

He shook his head, sighing. "Twenty-nine is no age. How do you go on?"

"There are times when my grip on reality gets slippery," I admitted. I still couldn't look up at him for fear I would lose control. *New topic,* my brain screamed. I concentrated on his fingers gripping mine. "Can I see your ring?" I asked, grazing my right pinky against the ring on his left.

"This? I've had it for yonks." He slowly extricated his hands to pull off the ring and plunk it into my palm. "Picked it up in my travels somewhere."

I turned the band around to read it. *We know what we are* circled the outside. On the inside was inscribed *but know not what we may be.* I recognized the quote from *Hamlet.* "It's a nice thought . . . taken delightfully out of context," I pointed out, sliding it back across the table to him.

"Oh?"

"Sure, considering Ophelia was a raving lunatic at that point."

"I'm impressed." He held the ring to his eye and looked through it as if it were a spyglass before slipping it back on. "No one I know has ever placed it."

"Don't be." I laughed. "I was the understudy for Ophelia in our high school play. Never actually had to go through with it."

Adrian ordered a second beer. "Always a bridesmaid, never a bride, eh?" he joked.

"Always a playground instructor, never a killer," I quipped back, raising my wine glass.

"Now wait . . . I know that one—Morrison?" He pointed his fork at me. "I can't believe you quoted Shakespeare and the Doors' frontman in the same breath."

"Yeah, I'm kind of a walking *Bartlett's Familiar Quotations.* Probably why I became a librarian in the first place."

"I must confess . . . when you wrote me and told me you were a librarian, I thought you would be much older." I laughed, not daring to tell him I'd imagined he'd be much younger. "You know, that dowdy Marian the Librarian stereotype. You definitely shattered my expectations."

I blushed. "It's all right; it's not the first time I've heard that." Two matching hipster hairstyles bobbed past the window, and my neighbors Chuck and Kyle entered, waiting in the frosted glass vestibule to be seated. The restaurant had been steadily filling up while Adrian and I were busy chatting, but I had hardly noticed anything beyond our intimate table. "It took me a while to make my peace with it. I'd practically hide under bar stools in college when guys asked me about my major. You know, those types of questions that always come up on that first date."

"Brits normally don't use 'So what do you do?' as a breaking-the-ice kind of thing," Adrian explained, draining half his beer in a smooth fluid swallow. "We're too worried about sounding impolite. And it's not terribly imperative in the grand scheme of things."

"That's actually refreshing to hear." I dabbed my lips with my napkin and made a mental note not to ask what else he did besides sing about cats. "One thing I loved about my job was being able to find out about anything. I loved the challenge. Being able to prove the existence of something, that was cake. But having to prove something *didn't* exist, well . . . that was infinitely harder."

Adrian pondered that notion for several moments. I enjoyed watching his eyes, amused and intelligent, flicker across my face as he intently absorbed what I had to say. "I get that," he mused, rolling up his sleeves as our entrees were brought out. Four black paw prints were tattooed on his arm in an uneven pattern, as if a cat had walked through paint and then tiptoed up his forearm. He saw me sneaking glances at them. "I've got a thing for cats, as you may have guessed. Osirus, a cat I had back home, inspired these."

I proudly displayed my own feline-inspired ink, tilting out

my right ankle for him to inspect. "My one and only. Inspired by an illustration from a children's book, *Catwings*. By Ursula K. Le Guin. I got it with my first library paycheck, in fact." I remembered my chipped toenail polish then and hastily pulled my foot back under the table. "It's now one of Abbey's favorite books. 'Mrs. Jane Tabby could not explain why all four of her children had wings. "I suppose their father was a fly-by-night,"'" I recited, laughing. "It's sweet and quirky."

"Your Abbey seems sweet and quirky. How old is she again?"

"Four and a half. She's a character! I marvel at her every day." I couldn't resist listing some of her unique qualities with pride. How she could draw for hours, with her favorite subject being rainbows and her medium of choice being the scented marker. How she had a love for seventies soul tunes and Christmas songs in June. "How about you, any children? Is Natalie your daughter?" I noticed a muscle twitch in his jaw and hoped I hadn't tread into dangerous waters.

He contemplated an ear of baby corn that sat quivering on the tines of his fork. "That she is. I wanted to call her Chelsea after my favorite football club, but my ex wasn't having it a bit." He gave a short laugh. "So Natalie it was. My only child . . . twenty this year, believe it or not."

"That's nice you dedicated an album to her."

"Well . . . I wasn't around much when she was young . . . always working. Away a lot. I wasn't too keen on writing letters, so I used to write her these songs. You know, just funny, queer little songs to make her laugh, and I would send tapes to her." He sighed, fiddling with his ring. "The album was an homage, I suppose . . . but a little too late. We really have never had a close relationship. I was a bit taken aback, I guess, when you told me you had copies of it. Wherever did you find them?" I explained the secondhand store and he nodded. "I recorded the songs on the fly in a friend's home studio. The resulting CD was never for sale or anything . . . I think I had to order a minimum of a hundred for the manufacturer to press it. This was before most people had the ability to burn CDs from home, of course. Spot of luck they—and I myself—fell into your hands." He smiled a weary smile, the wrinkles around his eyes creasing like Asian paper hand fans. I wanted to reach out and trace the delicate lines with my fingertips, to flutter down his cheeks and across his lips. The urge hit me quick and sharp, dragging me back to my reality: longing and desire such strange bedfellows with sadness and loss. My hands remained in my lap.

"How's the food?" I remembered to ask. He held up his hands over his spotless plate to admit defeat, and we both laughed. "I told you so! Would you like to try some of mine?"

"No, thank you, I am practically too podged to walk as it is! Everything was ace. Good call." He discreetly signaled for the check. "Don't you dare," he cautioned as I reached for my wallet. "Please just humor this poor geezer, will you? I'm in your debt for getting me out of the city . . . hell, out of my flat! Left to my own devices, well . . . drunkenness would have been the order of the day, I reckon." His tone was joking, but his eyes reinforced at least a modicum of truth in that statement.

"I'm glad I spared you from that." I smiled. "Well, thank you. For agreeing to play this afternoon, and for dinner."

The front vestibule was now three rows deep with eager diners waiting for empty tables. A hand rested tentatively yet somewhat protectively on the small of my back as we threaded through the crowd. I was glad Adrian was behind me so he couldn't bear witness to the silly grin that insisted upon gracing my face.

Back in the car, we watched as the sea of briefcased commuters poured from the station toward Main Street. "If we hurry, you can make the 6:35." I was suddenly very aware of the intimate quarters once again and had trouble finding the ignition with my key.

"I'd rather kiss you and take the 6:55."

His lips had barely pushed out the words before mine sprang into action. The moment was beautifully surreal, as I had been imagining it vividly during the last twenty minutes at dinner. Catching his top lip between mine, I felt it broaden into a grin. It seemed my eager and bold assent shocked him at first, but he recovered quickly, threading his fingers through my hair and pulling me closer. As his tongue gingerly hit mine and his thumbs traced slow concentric circles behind my ear lobes, I felt a jolt firing up my synapses and waking body parts I had forgotten about.

"Easy, tiger," I murmured breathlessly, resting my forehead against his. He was breathing hard as well, and his body leaning on mine across the car's center console felt warm. I touched his cheek and moved to kiss him again when I noticed his lips were swelling. His breathing had turned to a wheezing, and I could see the panic rising in his eyes. It was the same look Abbey had given me after that second bee sting. *Help me, do something!*

My hands hastily went into autopilot mode, navigating blindly through my purse to find Abbey's EpiPen. "I'm sorry, but I have to do this!" I gulped, flipping off the activation cap and plunging the auto-injector into his thigh. "One, two, three, four . . ."

"Owww! What in bloody hell?" he managed to get out, sweating and shaking and, to my horror, slumping back onto the seat.

". . . nine, ten . . . I think you're having an allergic reaction," I exclaimed, but he had already lost consciousness. "Shit!" I tossed the EpiPen aside and massaged the injection site as I had been taught. Then I swung the car across the double yellow line in the middle of Main Street and gunned it. The closest hospital was in Peekskill and only six miles away, but with the onset of rush hour traffic, I knew it would take some maneuvering of back roads to get him there in good time. Luckily, I had spent much of my youth on the back roads.

I kept checking his pulse with my right hand as I drove with the left, sneaking looks when I could to make sure he was still breathing. His wrist was clammy beneath my shaking fingers. Abbey's EpiPen dose was only half of what an adult should have, so when we stopped at the next light, I fumbled in the glove box for another pen. It had been in there awhile, and I wasn't sure if temperature could lessen its effect, but I figured it couldn't hurt to give him a second dose. It would buy us another five minutes until I could get him into the ER. I counted to ten again as I rubbed his leg, thinking that this was definitely not the kind of intimacy I had had in mind twenty minutes earlier.

A nurse and an EMT were outside of the Hudson Valley Hospital, having a smoke the requisite distance from the ER doors, and I enlisted their help to get him inside. "I think it's anaphylaxis. He's had epinephrine." I clutched the two empty injectors as proof. They grabbed a wheelchair sitting vacant between two sets of automatic sliding doors and away he went to triage. I had a moment to gather my wits, move my car to a legal parking space, and wander in. The reality of the situation was beginning to descend upon me.

"Mrs. Graves?" A hefty nurse thrust a clipboard at me. Her name tag read DAWN JACKSON, RN. Adrian was nowhere to be seen, so I could only assume he was being tended to. Before I could correct her or decide how to answer, she dumped Adrian's wallet and cell phone into my hands as well. "Fill out the top portion and the section on insurance information and sign and date both sides," she explained impatiently as another triage nurse, with an accent that sounded like South Bronx by way of Puerto Rico, began firing questions at me.

"Do you know if he has any history of heart disease?"

"No, I don't know. He's not my husband. I just met him today."

"High blood pressure, diabetes, thyroid disease?" she rattled off.

"I'm sorry. I don't know." *I can tell you he likes Chelsea football and cats,* I thought. *But that's about all.* I felt uncomfortable going through his wallet, but the nurses and that clipboard with its blank pages were staring me in the face. "All I know is he had shortness of breath, wheezing, and swelling around his mouth. I administered .15 mg of epi right away, and then another .15 mg about five minutes ago."

"You a doctor?" Nurse Jackson demanded.

No, but I play one on TV. "I'm a mother whose child has an anaphylactic reaction to bees. I had the pens in my purse and car." I began to sift through the documents in his wallet so I could at least fill out the identification portion of the forms. I found his license and was surprised to see his first name listed as Douglas, not Adrian. He had a Central Park West address, very ritzy. Also interesting was a birth date of 1963; he was just seven years older than me.

"I wouldn't suppose you'd know if he had any allergies?" I shook my head. "Has he eaten anything in the last hour?"

"Chicken . . . curry chicken. Beer."

"ICE?" Nurse Rivas, according to her name tag, asked. "Does he have ICE listed on his phone?" I must've looked clueless. "In Case of Emergency." She had clearly given up any hope of my solving the case. "Check his phone under *I* for *ICE*; some people list a next of kin there."

He had nothing like that listed, so I scrolled through and looked for the obvious family members: Mom and Dad, Home, et cetera. No dice. I did find Natalie listed, with a 917 Manhattan cell number, but it was out of service. Not that I had really looked forward to talking to the estranged daughter anyway. Most of his contacts had odd names or were made up entirely of initials—AJ, Biff, KK, Mutt, Zakk. Many were 818 numbers, which I recognized as California, or overseas numbers with confusing dialing codes.

Nurse Jackson was still hounding me. "Did he have any shellfish?"

"No. Just chicken. I had shrimp in my dish, but he didn't . . ." It suddenly hit me that our kiss must have triggered the reaction. "Oh! We, um . . . came into contact after I ate the shrimp." Both nurses raised their eyebrows at me. "We kissed, and ah . . . that's when . . . oh dear."

Nurse Rivas murmured, "Hmm, yeah. You go, girl," clicking her teeth with her tongue. Nurse Jackson allowed herself a smug smirk, not looking up as she scribbled something on a chart.

"I know, I know, I know nothing about him," I admitted, as if I were confiding in Marissa or Leanna instead of two nosy and judgmental nursing nazis. "It's crazy." What *was* I thinking? It had been pretty reckless of me, way out of character.

Embarrassed, I turned my attention back to his phone. Under *D*, I found a number for a Dr. Rosenblatt. I called, hoping it was his primary who could shed some light on his medical history for the form. The snarky secretary who answered informed me she couldn't reveal any information to anyone who was not family. "Can you at least tell me what kind of medical practice this is?" I asked, desperate for any clues.

"*This* is one of Manhattan's *preeminent* psychiatric institutes," she huffed, as if I should have my own head examined for not knowing this information.

With a click of the phone, I turned back to the nurses and admitted defeat.

"It's all right, honey, he's conscious now," Nurse Jackson informed me, hanging up a phone herself. "He's on antihistamines and oral steroids . . . and he's asking for you."

Hospitals intimidate me; similar to entering a church or

synagogue, I always walk slowly and quietly through them feeling awestruck and out of place. I had never broken a bone in my life or needed surgery. Besides being born, delivering Abbey, and then her bee sting adventure, my hospital exposure had been very limited. The real kicker was the smell: always that same lingering odor of institutional gravy from the cafeteria mixed with antiseptic and old skin.

I allowed myself to be led behind a curtain to Adrian's bedside, half expecting to see him hooked to machines and tubes. To my surprise, he was sitting up in the bed with nothing but a pulse oximeter clipped to his finger and one of those oxygen nose prong things dangling around his neck, no longer in use. He was still fully clothed, which I took as a good sign. Surely they would have put him in one of those dreaded hospital gowns if they needed to keep him longer or required further examination. I wasn't sure if my sigh of relief was due to his apparently successful resuscitation or the fact that I didn't have to see him wearing one of those flimsy gaping garments. Seeing him puff up and pass out was enough excitement for one evening.

"Hey," he greeted me weakly. Followed by, "Where's my guitar?"

"Locked safe in my car."

"My friend Randy gave me that, I can't lose that."

He let his head fall back against the raised half of the hospital bed. The way his voice drifted off at the end of the sentence made me realize how thoroughly drained he was. "They told me you saved my life. I seriously thought you were trying to kill me."

"Nah, I don't try that until at least the third date," I joked lamely. I still lingered with my back against the curtain, not exactly certain what my role should be at this awkward point.

The attending physician breezed in, carrying a handful of familiar white-and-yellow boxes. "Ah, this is the knight in shining armor, then?" he queried. "Your friend here is highly allergic to shellfish. If you hadn't given him that first dose of epi and gotten him here so fast, I think we'd be having a much different conversation right now."

"Cripes. Good to know my neurotransmitters cooperated— Lord knows I have mistreated them over the years," Adrian commented, carefully scratching the back of his hand. I noticed it was all taped up and realized they must have started an IV line there.

"He's all right then? Does he have to stay?" I had Abbey on my mind. Although I knew she was in the capable hands of Marissa, I was beginning to feel anxious about being away from her for so long, and under such strange circumstances. The clock over Adrian's bed read 7:28. Usually we were in pj's and reading stories in the big beanbag chair by now.

"Given his medical history and age and the limited oral exposure"—the doctor was studying the chart and thankfully wasn't privy to our embarrassed expressions—"and taking into consideration the swift administration of meds, I don't think he needs to be admitted. However, I'd like to keep him here for a few more hours to make sure he doesn't have any secondary reactions." He turned to Adrian with the EpiPen boxes and began to instruct him on proper usage, should the need arise in the future. I excused myself and went out into the cell phone area to call Marissa.

"Hey, how's it going?"

"Well, I kissed him—"

"Woo!" Marissa whooped. "Rob, you owe me five bucks!" she yelled away from the mouthpiece. I heard a distant and amused grunt from her husband in reply.

"—and I almost killed him."

"*What?* Get the hell outta here."

"We are at the hospital." I explained the whole mess, from

the amazing dinner to the futile search for personal information to the additional three hours of observation.

"I can keep Abbey here overnight, Tree. Right now they're
watching a movie and she hasn't mentioned home once." I
wasn't surprised, as Marissa's kids and Abbey were frequent
overnight guests at each other's respective houses. Our closets
and car trunks were stocked with surplus Aerobeds and booster
seats just for that purpose.

"Are you sure? I feel like I should stay and make sure he gets
home all right."

"As long as you feel comfortable. Do you want me to send
Rob down to keep you company?"

"No, no. I'm fine. How was T-ball?"

"Cute. They weren't keeping score. You know . . . the whole
'everyone's a winner' thing. But Joey's first softball game is at
ten tomorrow, and that's the real deal."

"Cool. I'll come get Abbey long before that so you can all
get ready."

"I want a full report, you know," Marissa informed me.

"Yeah, yeah. I know. My future juju mojo depends on it."

"Was it at least a good kiss?"

I smiled into the phone. "Ask me tomorrow when my pulse
rate returns to normal."

9

CELESTIAL CHARM

"Absolutely not. I won't have you driving into Manhattan at all bloody hours of the night to get me home." We were standing in the hospital parking lot, arguing. Adrian wasn't given his walking papers until close to eleven p.m., and the last train back to New York had departed ten minutes prior. "I'll take a taxicab."

"A cab'll cost you over a hundred dollars, that's ridiculous. And you can't just hail one up here. First you've got to call a car service. Then you have to tell them where you are and where you want to go. And then you have to wait and hope they show. I can drive you and be back home before twelve thirty. It's not a big deal."

"And what if you were to break down at the side of the road? No. If I can't get a taxi to the city, then drop me at a hotel. Preferably one close to the train." He sucked the last bit of nicotine from the cigarette clamped between his fingertips and then flicked it toward the streetlight. It bounced across an empty parking spot, sending orange sparks cascading. "Or I will walk to one." He exhaled over his right shoulder as he glanced into the car to make sure his precious guitar was still present and accounted for.

I was exasperated and exhausted. "Look. It's late. We are both tired. And you've been through a lot. I trust you. You can stay the night at my place, no funny business, and I will drive you as much or as little as you want me to tomorrow morning."

He fixed his gaze on me, expelling one final tendril of smoke from his nostrils like some great pissed-off leviathan. His eyebrows crumpled in, and I caught the hint of a sheepish smile. "Are you sure? That's awfully kind."

"I got you into this mess in the first place, didn't I?"

"You're underestimating the power of free will, Kat." I enjoyed the way my newly acquired nickname rolled off his tongue, as if he had perfected it over years of enjoyable conversation. I, on the other hand, was having a hard time thinking of him as Adrian, now that I had learned his given name was Douglas. Douglas Graves . . . Doug Graves . . . *Dug Graves?* I wondered if that had been his parents' idea of a joke, or perhaps it hadn't occurred to them at the time. I wrestled with the decision of whether or not to ask him about it. I was curious to know more about him. Yet I had put the poor guy through enough for one night without the additional insult of learning I had dredged through his personal belongings.

He climbed into the Mini and was promptly asleep before I got to Route 6, leaving me no choice but to wonder.

The house loomed dark and still as I coasted silently into the drive. The motion-detector lights my father had installed last summer suddenly blinked wide-eyed and alert, greeting us as we neared the front door. I was reminded of my mother. From the time I was old enough to have an after-dark curfew, she would wait up for me. It used to drive me nuts, but now as a mom myself, I understood her logic. Attempting sleep was futile when your child was out at, as Adrian would probably say, "all bloody hours."

I glanced over at the slumbering stranger in my passenger seat and wondered what my parents would think of the present situation. No doubt it would warrant a lecture about "stranger danger" and include the latest sex-crime statistics. Lauder Lake hadn't had a murder since 1973, but seeing as I had imported this unknown personality in from the boroughs, all bets were off.

Adrian was snoring slightly, his lips pursed as if to blow out birthday candles. There was something angelic and forlorn about him that kept me from thinking he was plotting any dastardly deeds. "Hey." I nudged him gently. "Adrian. We're here."

"Wow. Those antihistamines are kicking my arse." He rubbed the bridge of his nose and outward across his eyes, yawned, and proceeded to follow me in.

"Careful, there are a lot of boxes." Many of Pete's and my marital belongings, too important for deep storage yet not important enough for daily access, lived in a few dozen cardboard banker's boxes stashed in various corners of the house.

"Did you recently move?"

"No . . . just taking our time settling." Abbey and I had learned to live around them or, in some cases, repurpose stacks of them as end tables and staging areas for various Barbie play scenes. Seeing the boxes through the eyes of an unfamiliar bystander gave me a queer feeling.

"Whatever became of Abbey?" he thought to ask, gingerly setting his guitar case near the piano as I flicked on lights.

"I called Marissa from the hospital. She's keeping Abbey overnight."

Adrian was studying the pictures that spanned across the top of the piano, mostly Abbey in various stages of child-chub. There was one picture of Marissa, Leanna, and me taken at someone's basement rec room Halloween party during high school. We were dressed as three blind mice, complete with ears, tails, whiskers, dark shades, and canes. "These are the ladies I met today," he commented. "You've been friends a long time."

"Yeah, since forever. I never imagined we would all end up back here."

"Once I hit London, I vowed never to go back home," Adrian murmured. "Onward and upward." He was now standing in front of a trio of frames by the stairs. "Do you miss the city?"

The words caught in my throat. "More than I know how to say."

It pained me to look at what I called the Carousel Prints. Yet not a day went by that I didn't.

I never did make it to B&H that day, as Pete had asked me to. As many times as I relived our final conversation because he never could, the task of picking up those photos never dawned on me. His last request unfulfilled. An entire year passed before Pete's brother showed up at my doorstep with them. As a professional photographer, Luke was a regular customer at the photo center, and a thoughtful employee took the time to make sure the neglected prints had ended up in the right hands.

Luke had taken the negatives and made enlargements in black-and-white, giving them a timeless look. The trio of prints portrayed a sequence of events occurring mere minutes apart, but they spoke volumes on a lifetime of emotions: fear, trust, and joy.

The first photo was all Abbey. Pete's disembodied hands, his fingers looking huge as they spanned her rib cage, placed her on the wooden saddle molded to the body of the carousel horse. Her tiny head was bowed so she was all cheeks, lashes fanning across them and little mouth drawn up like a young rosebud. *What is this new creature?* Hands instinctively reaching for the pole jutting from the horse's mane.

The next photo is Abbey's face in protest, and Pete's

bending close in consolation. Her eyes are flashing, betrayed by the daddy person and looking toward the lens for the mommy person's help. Pete's lips are pursed in a half smile, frozen in mid-coo. His lashes, in profile, mirror hers. Dumb cow eyes, he used to call his big brown ones, with their impossible lashes.

The third photo is absolute rapture. The realization of her eleven-month-old world spinning, with its methodical ups and downs and Daddy safe next to her, has brought a gleeful, gummy smile to her face. Cheeks wide, eyes shining, and the hint of two bottom front teeth at her gumline about to break through. Pete is absolved, vindicated, rewarded. Grinning point-blank at me as I manage to capture, unknowingly, our little unit's final experience of jumping into the great unknown together. The photos speak volumes, yet they say nothing. The moment, like the ride, was too short.

A cacophony of bells fractured my reverie. Along with 80 percent of their furniture, my parents happened to have left behind a half dozen of their noisiest antique clocks. Abbey and I no longer noticed them, but to the unsuspecting visitor, midnight arrives in quite a jarring fashion. Adrian marveled, surrounded by grandfather, wall, and mantel clocks with their chime rods and tubes pealing in their splendor. They weren't quite in synch, so midnight arrived at 11:58 and continued until about 12:03. "Sorry, I should have warned you . . ."

"No, no, they're brilliant! I hear the Winchester chimes: '*O Art Divine, exalted blessing! Each celestial charm expressing!*' Makes me feel like a kid again." He cocked his head. "And there's the Westminster, and the Whittington chime. It's like time-traveling back to London and being in two places at once." I loved the way his smile came so quickly and naturally that it almost surprised even him.

"My dad owned an antique shop," I explained. "I sort of inherited the house when they moved, along with a lot of the inventory." While most of the heavy antique furniture was out of both my price range and my scope of style, I still enjoyed the history each piece had. Not only its history from whatever period it happened to have been created in, but also the history it played in my own life. It was somewhat comforting to serve Abbey dinner at the Horner solid quartered oak dining table, round with its full-winged griffin carved base. My family had celebrated countless Thanksgivings at that table; it was where I had wished over numerous birthday cakes, and where Pete and I had first announced our engagement.

"It's . . ." He scanned the room, stalling for the right words. "Quaint. Homey." His eyes rested on me, and it seemed like he wanted to add another adjective, but instead fell silent.

I hastily flipped on the attic light at the bottom of the stairs. "Um . . . the spare bedroom is upstairs. You can smoke up there if you want, just make sure you open the window. Towels . . . extra toothbrushes . . . all that stuff is in the linen closet in the bathroom up there." Liz had recently stayed with us over Easter weekend, so I knew the bedding was freshly laundered and the dust couldn't have settled too much since. It was no Four Seasons, but it would have to do.

Standing back, I allowed Adrian to proceed up the stairs. He paused three steps up, hand lingering on the railing, and turned. "Thank you. I know this is . . . weird and unexpected. Thanks for being a good sport." He disappeared up the rest of the stairs.

My nightly bedtime rituals were performed, albeit with slightly racing heart and shaking hands. I tried hard not to be aware of every little creak and moan from the floorboards above me. Brushing my teeth, I reflected on when the last time was that I had been on my own in the house overnight with another adult. Certainly well before Abbey was born. It felt strange yet natural, all at the same time.

Footsteps approached the top of the stairs. "Erm . . . Kat?"

"Yes?" I called. He didn't answer me right away. "Everything okay?" I hiked halfway up the steep staircase before he came into sight at the top. His black shirt was unbuttoned, and I caught a glimpse of a plain white T underneath. His hand was cupping an unlit cigarette.

"Just curious. Was this . . . your room growing up?" he asked, appearing slightly flustered.

"God, no! It was my brother Kevin's." I hopped up the last few steps. "I know it looks like a shrine, but don't worry, he isn't dead. He's just in Oregon." I laughed, casting a sweeping glance around the room and trying to imagine seeing it for the first time. Posters of metal bands lined the walls and slanted ceiling like a claustrophobic cocoon. His bed was directly underneath the largest poster, which appeared to pulsate with flames, Marshall stacks, and men pounding on their guitars. Light from the stage spotlights in the picture bounced off the crotches of their tight spandex pants, creating an almost three-dimensional effect. "Abbey calls it the boogeymen room and won't come up here."

"Cripes. I don't blame her."

My eyes lingered on the forgotten high school track trophies in one corner and the milk crate full of dusty vinyl albums in another. "My parents never made him clear out his stuff, and now he's halfway across the country. I should take matters into my own hands. But he'd probably kill me if I so much as breathed on the tape holding these posters up."

Adrian heaved the small dormer window frame a few inches, lit up, and gazed at the silk Iron Maiden tapestry tacked up above it, serving as a curtain. "Older than you, or younger?"

"Two years younger. Kev lived and breathed Iron Maiden, KISS, Judas Priest . . . all those bands in high school." I sat on the bed and stared up at the huge Corroded Corpse poster. "He never forgave my parents for not letting him see these guys, though . . . his favorite band. We weren't allowed to go to concerts until we were sixteen, and the band split up that year, so he never got to see them play live."

"Hmm, that's a shame."

"Sixteen years later and he still bitches about it."

"My brother is the same age. Well, half brother. We aren't very close. But he loved Corroded Corpse, too. Gutted when they broke up."

Adrian tapped his ashes carefully into a small tin ashtray left behind from Kevin's Marlboro-smoking days. Big Blue, his favorite bong, was still parked behind the old couch on the opposite wall, as if waiting for its faithful master to return and spark it up once more. Kev's room had been a virtual no-mom's-land during his teen years. I remember her insisting on a once-annual fumigation, but beyond that, she never stepped foot in there to see what he was up to. Whenever my parents came to visit now, I usually camped out up here and let them have my room; technically, their former master bedroom. No sense in popping their blissful bubble of domestic denial after all these years. Abbey was in my old childhood room. Thankfully, the Pepto-pink walls and Tiger Beat posters had been replaced with a fresh coat of lilac paint.

"So what about you?" Adrian asked, his steel blue eyes twinkling. "Were you a metal chick growing up?"

"Nah." I absently pulled a curl from my ponytail and twirled it. "I was more of a hippie chick. I liked the classic stuff, Doors, Hendrix, Beatles . . . peace and love and all that."

"Peace and love, eh?" He had finished smoking and ambled toward where I was perched on the bed.

"Yeah . . ." I watched as he took my hand in his. "Hey, no funny business," I lamely joked, my heart hammering.

He slowly knelt down in front of me, still clutching my hand. "No, I consider this very serious business. What are you thinking right now?"

"I'm thinking I want to kiss you again, but I'm scared to.

Maybe I could kiss you on a safe spot, like your elbow." My giggle was a defense mechanism that sounded ridiculous and foreign to my ears. "What are you thinking?"

"I'm thinking anywhere you kiss me could become an instant erogenous zone, Kat," he breathed, leaning over and kissing the hollow of my neck. His lips on me felt amazing . . . but everything else felt wrong. We both reeked of hospital. Dozens of heavy metal dudes were leering down at us from every crack and crevice of the room. And like the carousel ride captured in those pictures hanging one story below, my own joy and fear were oscillating at a dizzying pace. As much as I was enjoying Adrian's company, I felt the intense need to be alone, to absorb and reflect upon the strange events of the evening.

"Adrian . . ." I rested my hands on his shoulders, and he nodded. He knew. I was grateful I didn't have to say more. Standing, I pulled him up with me. "You need your rest."

I judged him to be about three inches taller than me, as his lips were at perfect forehead-kissing range. I chose to stand on my tiptoes and kiss his brow instead. "Good night."

"Sleep well, Kat."

In the darkness of my room, I pulled on my usual sleepwear ensemble: a pair of Pete's plaid boxers and one of his old T-shirts. People would probably find it bizarre that I chose to keep his underwear, of all things. But when the time came, I couldn't bear to put such an intimate and everyday item in the trash. Settling onto the low futon, I ran my hand comfortingly around the waistband of the boxers, feeling the elastic stretch under my fingers. *This is so strange.* I don't know if I was talking silently to myself, or to Pete. *Is it okay? It feels okay.* Above me, I heard the springs of the bed sigh as they compressed under the pressure of their occupant's body. I wondered what Adrian was wearing upstairs. Boxers or briefs?

Jeez, stop. Go to sleep.

10

SCRIPT FOR A JESTER'S TEAR

Two rare occurrences were instantly apparent to me upon waking. Another adult was breathing under the same roof. Although Abbey was great company, I liked the notion of that. And the air was devoid of the scent of coffee. I had gotten in the habit of setting the coffeemaker on the timer each night to create the illusion of someone making coffee for me. (A bit pathetic, yes. But it got me out of bed each morning.)

I crept into the kitchen to begin brewing, dialing Marissa from the home phone at the same time. It was 9:24 according to the clock on my Krups, so I was surprised she hadn't called me first.

"Um . . . he's still here." I quickly and quietly explained how he had missed the last train and defended my decision to house him overnight, with Marissa clucking, gasping, and good-naturedly chiding me all the while.

"Did you—"

I didn't let her finish. "Of course not." The evening had been surreal and awkward enough. Pleasantly surreal and awkward, if such a thing was possible. No need to add cheap and cliché to that as well. "Major medical trauma, remember?"

"Guys don't care about that. They could be on their deathbeds and still have boners."

"Seriously, Mariss . . . that was some scary shit. I am never going to eat shellfish again."

"Not if you want him to stick around," she joked. "Look, should I keep Abbey with me then? Till after you drive him home?"

"No, no, you've helped more than enough, I will think of a way to explain it to her."

I had enough time to take a few swigs of coffee, brush my teeth, and concoct an explanation Abbey might understand. Marissa let herself in with her key, along with Abbey and a sack full of groceries. For Marissa, food is love. She must've gone shopping for me in her pantry, which was perpetually stocked to the ceiling.

"Breakfast stuff. So you can be the hostess with the mostest, darling. Where is he? Think he sleeps in the buff?" Marissa whispered that last sentence as Abbey catapulted herself into my arms. Above my child's head, I used one hand to point a finger up and the other to draw a finger across my neck in warning to Marissa, who laughed and hightailed it back out to her minivan full of waiting kids. "Call me later!"

"Hi, my love. Did you have a good time?" I tried to keep my voice even-keeled and on the quiet side, hoping she would follow suit. But like most four-year-olds, Abbey hadn't quite mastered the practice of vocal volume control.

"We watched *The Lion King*! Aunt Miso made POPCORN! We had a pillow fight and Joey lost a TOOTH! What's a tooth furry?"

"You mean tooth fairy? Well, um . . ." I hesitated. As with Santa Claus and the Easter Bunny, I was somewhat reluctant to pass on another sugarcoated traditional rumor to add to her pile of eventual childhood letdowns. How was she supposed to accept the idea of a father who could never return, yet believe

in the existence of a fat guy, a giant bunny, and a winged creature who spanned the globe year after year with the trivial tasks
of stuffing stockings, hiding eggs, and hoarding teeth?

She was already on to the next big question. "Mommy, is
that a GUITAR?" She rushed over to the case Adrian had set by
the front door last night. Before she could do any damage, I
scooped her up and half tickled, half carried her to the couch.

"Listen, Abb. You know how you get sick if a bee stings
you?" She nodded solemnly. "Well, it turns out Adrian Graves
gets sick when he eats certain things, like shrimp. But he didn't
know shrimp would make him sick until yesterday. And
remember how we were visiting Grandma and Grandpa Lewis
in Philadelphia last year, and you got the flu?"

"When I threw upped in the bed." Abbey nodded, pulling
her eyebrows and her mouth down to express her horror of the
memory. It was a face so uncannily like one Pete used to pull,
especially during the grim task of dispatching the honking
huge cockroaches that would find their way into the tub of our
apartment near Columbia. I was amazed at how she could pick
up a trait or habit of someone she had barely had time to
witness. Nature really had a stacked deck over nurture in some
cases.

"Yep, that's right. We were supposed to leave that day, but
ended up staying longer because it was a long trip home and
you were too sick to travel. Well, that's sort of what happened to
Adrian yesterday . . . without the throwing up. He got so sick, I
had to take him to the doctor, and now he is resting here."

"Is he going to get better?" Abbey wanted to know.

"I'm sure he's feeling much better after a good night's rest.
But why don't we draw him a get-well card, just in case?"

Abbey got right to work, pulling buckets of markers from
the bottom drawer of the china cabinet. I unpacked Marissa's
bag of surprises in the kitchen: pancake mix, OJ, bagels and
cream cheese, blueberries, eggs. Then I joined Abbey at her

insistence. She was already putting the finishing touches on her picture of Adrian and his guitar, his feet pointing out sideways and floating an inch above the grass she was expertly inking at the bottom of the page. I helped myself to a piece of paper and quickly got lost in doodling rows and rows of flowers. It was a frequent activity I found quite therapeutic; it allowed me to space out while still participating. I was so engrossed that before I knew it, I heard the clocks chiming eleven and the soft tread of Adrian's stocking feet on the attic stairs.

"Oh hey. How'd you sleep?" I was painfully aware I was still wearing Pete's boxers, and now I had green marker smeared up my arm. Abbey stole my thunder, though, with pink ink on her chin and a purple streak high on her left cheekbone, like eye black on a football player.

"Adrian Graves! Come see my room!" My child was certainly no shrinking violet.

"Slept very well, thanks." He smiled. "Hello again, Abbey."

"Come on, come on!" Abbey insisted, hopping up. "I want to show you things."

It didn't seem all that appropriate for my child to invite an adult stranger into her bedroom, but I didn't know how to discourage her without making Adrian uncomfortable. "Just a quick look, Abb. Then let's get our guest a cup of coffee." I trailed them down the hall. "Or tea, if he prefers."

"Coffee sounds fantastic." He ran his hand over his hair, which had taken on a mad scientist look sometime in the wee hours.

Abbey's room was its usual chaotic clutter of toys suspended in midplay, art projects paused pending her next creative thought. Plush bears, cats, and bunnies were strewn about, facedown on the floor as if there had been a mass murder. Plastic jeweled necklaces dripped from her dresser drawers, and her favorite purple dress-up tutu had been repurposed as a lampshade, apparently.

"Who's this guy?" Adrian gave a yank on the gray rubbery bat hanging from the pull-chain of her ceiling fan. Abbey had won him last weekend at Karen's church carnival. When the parish wasn't busy praying, they were fund-raising. Last month it was the rummage sale, then the spring carnival, and come summer, nubile church teens in their bikinis would be holding signs on Main Street enticing car owners of all denominations to come on through the lot for a car wash. Karen often volunteered, although she drew the line during frozen cookie dough sales, as the partially hydrogenated oils and artificial vanillin were against her code of ethics.

"Matt. Matt the Bat," Abbey christened him on the spot, laughing. "Can we write a song about him, Adrian?"

"Certainly. He's elastic. And fantastic!" I admired his ability to wax poetic on something as ordinary as a crappy made-in-China toy.

Abbey hopped through the stuffed animal massacre on her way over to her art wall. "Look at all my Maxwells." We had hung up her latest efforts earlier that week, including an endearing kitty created with tiny fingerprints of gray and black paint and a large piece made up of cotton balls on a blue background. "Maxwell in winter," she announced, contemplating it.

Adrian stepped over a large inflatable Shamu to inspect the wall. Abbey had begged endlessly for the useless thing during our last visit to SeaWorld, yet it had sat untouched on her floor ever since I had lugged it the thousand miles or so home. "Wow, those are something else!" he enthused, running a finger gingerly over the macaroni-and-glue Maxwell. "How long did it take you to make these, Abbey?"

She pointed to each one as she recited the days of the week. "They do art every day at school," I explained. "Hey, speaking of Maxwell, I have a geographic problem with him."

Adrian raised his brow, chuckling. "Oh really?"

"Yeah. How did he end up in Mousehole if he is a breed native to the state of Maine?" I wanted to know. Abbey crossed her arms and waited expectantly for the answer as well. "That's *New* England, not original England."

"Well, legend has it," Adrian began, affecting a heavily accented Cockney not unlike the narrator of the show, "our fearless feline stowed away on a ship leaving the Port of Maine as a young kitten, bound for the Motherland." He continued in a dramatic fashion, eyes wide and lips pursed. "His presence went undetected until one day, a trail of cheese and crumbs led one passenger to discover our hero, cold, flea-ridden, and homesick inside a shipping container. This chap, a certain Mr. Bradstreet, who you may have heard of, was a detective from the infamous Scotland Yard. He took pity on poor Max, feeding him and grooming him, and once they docked, he brought him to the headquarters of the Metropolitan Police to live. There, Maxwell quickly learned the art of expert sleuthing. One day, Max was out accompanying Bradstreet on a case deep in the East End, and inadvertently rescued a duck that had been sold into slave labor at Spitalfields City Farm. The duck, Mr. Quackson, was actually heir to a huge estate in Cornwall, but he had run away from home in search of a more exciting life than his posh comfortable existence. He and Maxwell forged a strong friendship and became partners in fighting crime. They left London in the capable hands of Bradstreet and Scotland Yard, choosing to settle in Mousehole, where they spend their time protecting the mice, fish, and birds who reside there from less desirable felines and, of course, from the clutches of the diabolical Dr. Loveydovey!"

Abbey applauded, and Adrian bowed in response.

"Okayyyyy. That was five minutes of my life I will never get back," I teased as Abbey led the way back to the living room.

"Who would've guessed you were a Maxwell MacGillikitty geek?"

"Actually, the only episode I ever saw was that pilot episode. But don't tell Abbey that!"

Abbey had pulled out her LEGOs from under the piano bench, and Adrian joined her on the living room rug while I fetched coffee. I made an extra effort to find two matching cups and saucers. Besides my parents and my girlfriends, we so rarely had company. It was nice to make a bit of a production out of it. I set out my mom's vintage Heisey sugar bowl and creamer, eavesdropping as they discussed who lived in the castle they were building.

"Well, there is a princess," Abbey drawled, loving the attention, "and a queen. The queen is the princess's mommy. Sometimes I pretend I am a princess, and my mommy is a queen."

"Okay, so we've got the princess and the queen mum. You and your mum. And I can be"—he made a comical yet snarling face—"the ogre who lives under the bridge!"

"No, silly, you can be the prince."

"I think I'd make a better jester than a prince," Adrian admitted.

"What's that?"

"A funny guy who plays music and makes up songs about the king and queen."

"Oh!" Abbey nodded enthusiastically. "You can definitely be the jester."

"Thank you, my dear."

"Coffee's up," I called. "Abbey, are you hungry? There're bagels."

"I had one at Aunt Miso's."

"And . . . ?" This was a daily exchange of ours, in pursuit of reinforcing her manners.

"Oh yeah . . . no, thank you." She smiled sweetly and turned to Adrian, who was picking himself up off the Persian rug. "Can you play a song . . . pleeeeease?"

"Abbey. Let the man have his coffee."

"It's okay, Kat," he assured me, padding over to his guitar case and flipping it open. Winking at me, he slung the strap over his shoulder and began to finger-pick what I recognized as the shortest song in the Beatles' repertoire. He harnessed his raw and raspy voice into a smooth and breathy one as the words tumbled out along with the notes.

"I know that! 'Her Majesty'! It's from *Abbey Road!*" Abbey crowed, but didn't look up from her growing fortress of LEGO. I didn't dare look up, either; my face had instantly heated as he sang about love and a belly full of wine.

Adrian sauntered over, pleased with himself, and took a long swallow of black coffee before resuming his jesterly duties. He took a seat across from me, plucking out a slower, bluesy riff. Live guitar was certainly a new sound in the walls of my house, but not unwelcome at all. He fixed his gaze solidly on me and began to sing in that husky, pack-a-day voice I found myself gravitating toward. I knew the song from the first verse; I had mentioned its artist last night as one of my favorites. The significance wasn't lost on me.

He chose to break his stare and concentrate on his fingers hitting the chords as he sang throatily about a weeping queen somewhere.

"And somewhere a king . . . has no wife," I quietly finished, stirring my coffee and raising my eyes to finally meet his again. People talk in clichés about sparks flying, but damned if we didn't have our own little pyrotechnic show happening right in my dining room.

"Adrian! We didn't finish the castle!" Abbey called.

"How about you continue with the walls and then I will come and finish the turrets?"

She skulked through the open entryway that separated the

living and dining rooms. "Actually, they are crenellations," she informed him before stalking back out.

While Adrian was clearly amused that such a big word could come out of such a small kid, I was not enamored with her tone. "Is someone already in need of a nap?" I countered sternly.

Abbey scuttled woefully back in. "But . . . naps are for babies!"

"Naps? No, naps are very rock-and-roll, Abbey." Adrian winked at me. "Why, John Lennon was known to stay in bed for an entire week!"

His smile sent Abbey giggling all the way to the living room and sent me blushing into my coffee mug. Sudden fantasies of stealing him away for our own weeklong stay in bed came to mind. Napping next to him, waking up to those eyes . . . Something about him got my mind racing. No longer in that foggy, incoherent way, but rather in luxurious possibilities that were long overdue.

"Thanks for humoring her." I hesitated, but when he looked up expectantly, I continued. "And spending some time with her."

"Are you kidding? She's great. I forgot how easy it is to talk to kids. Natalie, well . . . It's a pity she had to grow up so fast. Mostly my fault. I haven't seen her in three years."

"That must be hard on you."

"Yes. And no. I'm afraid we mostly fight like Kilkenny cats when we're together. It feels like it has always been that way. Like her mother raised her to be at odds with me." He fell silent, and I didn't know quite what to say.

"Mommy, my stomach is crumbling." Kudos to Abbey for coming in and lightening the mood.

"You mean rumbling? How about some pancakes?"

"Only if they are blueberry. Do you like blueberry?" Abbey asked Adrian.

"Yes indeed, I am a fan of the blueberry."

"Then blueberry it is," I announced, and I whipped up, thanks to Marissa, an admirable breakfast before driving Adrian to the train station and ending what had to be the weirdest twenty-four hours of my life.

11

LOST IN TRANSLATION

THERE ARE a couple of things I've come to expect every Saturday in Lauder Lake. David Mahoney mowing his lawn before seven a.m., for example. Inevitably, whenever I would just love to sleep in, that idiot is out there before the dew dries. The farmer's market near the train station is another. Well, since we're up by seven a.m., we might as well hit the market! Love, love, *love* their roasted garlic kalamata olive bread. But the best thing about Saturdays, hands down, is sauce day at the Falzones'. Which means a big pasta dinner that evening.

Rob and Marissa are great cooks. And not the measuring cup, recipe book–type cooks. They are the kind who taste a dish and can decide it needs a dash of oregano or a splash of vermouth. And when they get their sauce cooking, it's a family affair. No matter Brina is only four; she's peeling garlic. Joey is all of six, but he is working the blender. The sauce begins to simmer at around ten a.m., and it bubbles on a low flame through dance lessons, baseball games, work picnics, cold and flu season, birthday parties; getting an occasional stir by whoever happens to whiz through the kitchen at any given time. The invitation to their friends and family is open-ended:

Come and eat if you're hungry, come and chew the fat if you are not. Some Saturdays, there are upwards of twenty people sopping up the gravy.

Tonight there were only five of us; Joey had been invited to mini-golf and pizza with a friend from school. Brina and Abbey relished the rare opportunity for girl power and ran outside after dinner to the backyard clubhouse with plans of outfitting it into a "Girls Only" paradise. Teddy bears in dresses, tiny porcelain tea cups, and about two dozen strings of colorful plastic beads left over from Marissa's last Mardi Gras party went out with them. Lickety and Split, the family's two Jack Russells, happily followed the girls back and forth.

Marissa and I lingered at the table, dipping the last of the farmer's market bread I had brought into the sauce left over on our plates and washing it down with chocolate milk. It sounds disgusting, I know, but the unique blend of cocoa-sweetened cold dairy and zesty sauce-covered meatballs somehow works. Marissa and I had been doing it since we were kids during Sunday dinner at her mom's house, so we would accept no substitute. Rob was doing the dishes, occasionally lending his two cents to our conversation.

"So any word from Shrimpy McLobster?"

"Very funny. No, but whatever, it doesn't matter." I picked the olives out of the bread on my plate and popped them into my mouth. Seven days of silence from my answering machine was a bit disheartening, but it certainly wasn't a world record.

"He said he would call, though, right?"

"I believe the words were 'ring you up.' Yeah. But he didn't say when."

"Well, no law says you have to sit around and wait." Marissa brushed crumbs off the tablecloth into her hand. "You have his digits. *You* contacted *him* to begin with, remember?" I gave a noncommittal shrug. "Well, if he doesn't call you, he's an idiot. Or should I say, if he doesn't *ring you up*, he's a *wanker*." She sipped her chocolate milk as daintily as if she were the Queen of England at afternoon tea, and continued in her piss-poor attempt at a British accent, "You are one smashing lass . . ."

"Smashing!" echoed Rob from the kitchen.

"Oh, stop, you two. I don't need a pep rally." I got up and began to collect the last of the dirty dishes. Marissa, sensing she was losing me, resorted back to her tough Yonkers tongue as she followed me into the kitchen.

"Seriously, Tree, I don't think you realize you are quite a hot commodity. You're witty and intelligent, financially stable, fiercely independent, you've got a ton of interests, hair like Julia Roberts wishes she still had, a great figure—"

"Rockin' bod, Tree," Rob agreed, squeezing his sudsy sponge for emphasis.

"Really. You are the only person I know who could gain twenty pounds, then whittle it all off your middle and redistribute it into your butt and your boobs. Kiss my lily-white ass! This guy should be begging at your doorstep for a chance to take you out."

"Pleading!" Rob chimed in. I watched as he arranged and rearranged dirty dishes in the dishwasher as quickly as a tosser in a street corner shell game, the wheels in his math-geek head spinning as he aimed for maximum load capacity.

"Well, he's not, and neither is anyone else, so perhaps that should tell you something." I scooted alongside Rob to ditch my glass of chocolate milk in the sink and reached for the Pinot Grigio on the counter. I prided myself on my iron stomach, which never rebelled over beverage combinations like milk and wine. It was definitely time for wine, if they were going to continue to rah-rah me to death.

"Like . . . ?" Marissa prompted, handing me a wine glass.

I watched out the window as the girls ran in and out of the clubhouse, bringing more things in to feather their nest like busy little birds. "Like maybe I'm damaged goods? Or I've got some extra baggage?"

"If he thinks that, then he really is crazy," Marissa said, her anger flaring. "And he doesn't need a fancy-pants city shrink to tell him that."

"Easy, killer. I'm not ready to string him up just yet. Or write him off."

I watched as Marissa handed her husband the last saucy pot, kissed his cheek, and smiled. There were couples that went through the motions on autopilot, and then there was Marissa and Rob. I don't know if it was the Italian thing or what, but he was like the meatball to her chocolate milk; they complemented each other perfectly.

Marissa poured herself some wine and leaned against the counter. She swished the contents of her glass and studied it. "He couldn't keep his eyes off you, you know."

"Really?"

"Yeah, the whole time he was playing, he kept sneaking little glances, making sure you were still in the room. He needs to shit or get off the pot. I wonder if there's a British translation for that."

12

PATIENCE AND FORTITUDE

"IS DADDY IN THE STARS?" Abbey came trotting into the bathroom just as my wet foot touched the bathmat. "What do you mean, honey?" I pulled the shower curtain closed and squeezed some of the moisture out of my hair. "When I slept at Brina and Joey's, we watched *The Lion King*, and they said in the movie that all the great kings are in the stars."

"Well . . . that is a nice way to think of him, I suppose. Like he's watching over you." We weren't religious; there had been no talk of heaven in our household. There were times when I fervently wished I had been brought up believing in some doctrine of afterlife, if only to pass that unquestioned comfort on to her.

She sat down on the closed toilet lid and sighed. "I wish I could hear his voice."

"He sounded a lot like Unkie Luke," I offered. Our wedding video was collecting dust somewhere, but I had never mentioned it to Abbey. I wasn't ready to see it myself just yet. Someday . . .

Abbey fondled all of my jars of creams, sniffing their

contents. She opened and closed every pressed powder and eye shadow compact like a pearl diver searching for that one lucky oyster. Then she sampled my dental floss. "Mmm, minty. Can I watch PBS? There's a *Maxwell MacGillikitty* marathon on all day today."

"Abbey." It was barely eight o'clock and I was already exasperated. Knowing the whole day stretched out in front of us without a plan made me panic. Sundays often crept up on me and smeared me in the face with the reminder that, for most people, Sundays meant cherished family time after a long week of work. For Abbey and me, Sunday was just another day in a long string of days with each other for company. And as much as we enjoyed each other, along with lots of activities in and out of the house, there were times when we needed a break, an escape. I knew *Maxwell* was a bit of an escape for her, but couldn't in good conscience let her sit in front of the TV on such a beautiful day. Not to mention, every time I heard the opening notes to the *Maxwell MacGillikitty* theme, I thought of Adrian and his noncommittal 'Can I ring you up sometime?' It made me want to wring his neck. Well, not quite. But it stung and saddened me that he hadn't, despite what I had said to Marissa the evening before. "One episode," I said firmly. "Then we are going to the zoo."

For many kids born and raised in Manhattan, Central Park becomes their backyard paradise, their playground. Despite the fact I dragged Abbey out to the suburbs before age one, I didn't want her to miss out on the opportunity to learn every inch of that wonderland. It was her legacy. Pete and I had happily squandered many a summer day in Sheep Meadow, Frisbeeing with friends, reading the *New York Times* under the stately oak trees, eating Naked Bagels from Liz's shop, and dreaming away the hours. We never did skate on Wollman Rink, although we had always meant to. But we took many walks past it during the crunchy cold winters, bundled and leaning into each other as our conversations frosted over in front of our faces.

From the time Abbey was born, we would bring her there. As she people-watched from the BabyBjörn carrier on my chest, you could tell she was absorbing it all. We would take turns pushing her stroller through fallen leaves and whipping around pigeons, and when she would finally surrender to a nap, hand in hand we blissfully glided along the paths we knew so well. Chatting quietly about what we would show her there when she was two, five, ten. The statues of Alice in Wonderland and Mother Goose. The zoo. Cleopatra's Needle. Bethesda Fountain. Strawberry Fields. The carousel.

Abbey's favorite place in the city was now the park, thanks to our regular visits. And her favorite thing to see in the park was the zoo. Although the Bronx Zoo was a borough closer, we preferred the more intimate surrounds of the Central Park Zoo. We could walk the whole thing and still have energy for other things, like playing at Heckscher Playground, climbing Cat Rock, and pretending we lived in the Dairy.

Traffic was nonexistent that morning, and the parking gods were on our side. To our shock, the gates at the brick-and-wrought-iron zoo entrance were still closed. "Gee, Abb, we're early," I explained, pulling out my cell phone to glance at the time. "They'll be open soon. Why don't we sit on a bench and have a snack?"

The path that led to the zoo was deserted, save for some Asian tourists posing cutely for their companions' cameras. East Drive had the occasional cyclist zooming past, but all was relatively calm in the park at this hour. I breathed deeply and gazed at the canopy of emerald green over my head. I felt like a stalker, knowing we were so close to Adrian's place. It was a silly thought. He wasn't aware that I knew where he lived. And Abbey and I were only two of the thousands of people who came to enjoy the park every day. No crime in that.

"I can't wait to see the sea lions!" Abbey crowed. She bounced her tiny butt, clad in denim shortalls, up and down on the bench.

I handed her a bag of peanut butter crackers and began searching through my pocketbook for a juice box. "Do you remember their names?"

"Of course! There's Scooter . . . April is the cutest one . . . Clarisse . . . Adrian!"

"What?" I had just turned, juice box in hand, to see Abbey take off like a shot, running toward East Drive. I took off after her, yelling her name as bikes whizzed by at a dizzying pace.

How she recognized him, I'll never know. First off, he was wearing one of those ridiculous aerodynamic bike helmets that made him look like an alien life-form. Add mirrored shades to that, and those obscenely tight spandex bike shorts. Plus he was off his bike, kneeling and pumping air into his tire with a small handheld pump. He was totally wired for sound and shut off from the world, iPod clipped to his arm. Precisely as I was about to snatch her by the scruff of her neck, he glanced up, smiled big, and I recognized him. It was one of those moments that made Manhattan truly feel like a small place, just a hunk of bedrock twelve miles long and two miles wide.

He stood to his full height. Luckily, the Chelsea football jersey he was wearing covered most of his spandex-clad nether regions. He pulled the earbuds off, and I could hear tinny guitars and drums screeching a million miles an hour. "Hello, ladies."

"See, Mom, I *told* you it was him." In actuality, she had just yelled his name and gone running without looking both ways, but I figured there would be time to scold her later. "We're going to the zoo. Like in your song, but we didn't take a crosstown bus. We drove. Wanna come?" Abbey offered.

"Thank you, Abbey, but . . ." He turned his head theatrically from side to side, pretending to make sure no one was eavesdropping, and said in a stage whisper, "If I go back there, I'm afraid they won't let me back out." Then he crossed his eyes and scratched under his arm like a gorilla, much to Abbey's delight.

He turned to me. "They should really lock me in the loony bin for not calling you. I've no excuse, other than being a fool."

"So redeem yourself," I challenged, trying hard not to study the rambling topography of his spandex. Arms. Arms are safe. His biceps strained against the tight blue and yellow cuffs of his football shirt. I forgot how cute he was. I liked the way his hair curled out from under his helmet and down around his collarbone.

"We have to go, good-bye, Adrian Graves! Mommy! Come on!" The gates were opening and Abbey was making a beeline back toward the zoo.

"I will . . . tonight!" he called after me. "Watch out for those reactionary zebras, Abbey!"

WE ARRIVED home to the longest message in the history of our answering machine. Adrian left his cell number, his home phone number, his e-mail address, and his IM screen name. "Since you are a librarian and love information, now you have every possible way to contact me. So whatever works best." I fulfilled my starving daughter's request for ravioli with a perpetual grin and grabbed my laptop. The only person I regularly instant messaged was Kev; it wasn't a medium I particularly loved, but with a cranky, hungry, wiped-out child in the room was less stressful than a phone call. I signed on and there he was.

K: Boo.
A: Ah, redemption!
K: Just a keystroke away.

A: So when can I see you again? Pick a place, anywhere. I will meet you there.

K: Are you sure? I think I am hazardous to your health.

A: On the contrary. What are you doing tonight?

K: It's a school night, not a good idea. How about Friday night?

A: Okay, now you ARE really trying to kill me, woman.

K: Can you find Patience?

A: No, I'm worse than a kid, I'm into immediate gratification.

K: Well, find Patience and meet me there on Wednesday at 10:30.

A: Meet where?

K: I just told you, silly.

A: Patience . . . is that some new rave club?

K: Ha. No.

A: You're making me work for this, aren't you?

K: Yep.

A: Well . . . can I ask you the rating on this date?

K: Isn't that a tad premature? I don't know, I'm hoping 8.5 out of 10, maybe? LOL

A: No, I meant, will it have a G rating, PG rating, etc.?

K: Oh, you mean will Abbey be there? No, she has to be at school by 9. So the date can contain some mildly crude language, adult references . . . partial nudity, if you are lucky.

A: LOL Who needs redemption now?

K: <looking for little blushing emoticon to send you>

A: So 10:30 . . . AM?

K: Is that too early for you?

A: Yes. But I will be there.

"Favor to ask."

The crunch of Marissa's potato chip crackled through the phone line. "Shoot."

"Can you grab Abbey at school one day this week, in case I'm late?"

"Late because of . . . ?"

"A playdate with the kiddy musician." I grinned at the notion.

"Oh my God!"

"Well, can you?"

"Of course. But tell me, tell me! What took him so long to contact you?"

"Don't know. I guess he was working up his nerve?"

"So do you think he's rich?" Marissa had been intrigued since learning of his Central Park West address. "He could pass for the wealthy eccentric type, don't you think? Rich and crazy. Better than poor and crazy."

"I wish I never told you that stuff."

"Just kidding, Tree. So . . . give him a chance, I guess."

"I am," I replied. "I'm meeting him in the city on Wednesday." I had been reluctant to tell her that part of the story, as it meant our yearlong Wednesday coffee-klatch streak was broken.

"Where?"

"At the NYPL."

"Oh, that is sexy." Marissa snorted in my ear. "A date at the library."

"No, I just told him . . . well, I kind of implied I would meet him in front of the library." I shared my off-the-cuff riddle of finding Patience and what it meant.

"Girl." She sounded alarmed. "You should call him and tell him. Not everyone is literary. If he doesn't show, you won't know if he intentionally blew you off or if he didn't get the reference."

"I have faith in him that he will find it; he seemed up for the challenge. Where is your sense of adventure?"

"He'd better show—I'll break his little guitar-strumming fingers if he doesn't!" she threatened. I could picture her flexing her elbow and baring her fist, rings glittering like a knuckle-duster, to send her point home.

"Mariss, who isn't giving him a chance now? Let's give him some credit."

"I just want you to be happy."

"No, you want me to be safe," I pointed out.

"What does that mean?"

"You'd rather see me give someone like Grant a chance, let the jerk prove to me that deep down he has a heart of gold, and then we can neatly merge our little broken families and I can live happily ever after and be the comfy wife of the local antiques dealer, like my mama before me. Honestly, the known terrifies me more than the unknown at this point."

Marissa sighed on her end of the line, and I held my breath on mine. Finally, she responded. "Well, chica. Wednesday is Cinco de Mayo. If our coffee morning is off, I propose a margarita evening so we can hear all about it."

13

BIG APPLE

I DROVE in on the tail end of rush hour. Seeing the large green-and-white highway signs for New York City always produced a herd of butterflies in my gut. Some people lived their whole lives only seeing such signs in movies; I felt lucky experiencing them for real. Excited to be on the road to a place of legend.

It was strange going to the city without Abbey. More than once I found myself about to talk to her, peeking in the rearview mirror only to glimpse her empty car seat. She had given me her blessing to travel into town today, along with a new Maxwell drawing for Adrian. And she wasn't the only one dedicating art to him—we had killed a few hours at the library the day before, and Gwen had given me an envelope of thank-you cards and drawings by the kids from the Rainbow School to pass on. Three other branches in the county were interested in booking him for programs, she had informed me. I took the business card she gave me for the director of outreach programming with mixed feelings. I was happy my idea had been such a success, but wasn't sure I wanted to share Adrian with the rest of the world yet.

Tuesday had ticked by slowly. I made good use of the time

by making sure all the required maintenance was out of the way: mani-pedi, waxing hair that had no business growing in certain places, testing out the best sandals to wear, filling the gas tank for the drive into Manhattan. Trains were simply no longer an option for me. I harbored no illusions that tragedy automatically inoculates anyone, and I wasn't taking any chances.

Looping off the Saw Mill Parkway, my butterflies turned into jumping beans. The roofs of houses, row after row, appeared to have been cut from the fabric of the landscape with pinking shears. Soon the houses gave way to buildings. I scooted down the West Side Highway and navigated over to one of my favorite parking lots near 42nd and Eighth. Even with wandering through Duane Reade drugstore for ten minutes, I was still early for our rendezvous. And nervous as hell.

As I approached Fifth Avenue, I heard Marissa's voice in my head. What if he didn't figure out my lame joke? I quickly attempted a few rounds of alternate nostril breathing like we did each week in yoga class. With my right thumb, I closed my right nostril and inhaled deeply through my left. Then with my right ring finger, I closed my left nostril and exhaled through the right side. Within seconds I felt like I was in the basement of Karen's church, on my mat in my bare feet and yoga pants, instead of the middle of Manhattan in a floral Anthropologie dress and impractical but dead-sexy wedge sandals. Luckily, I *was* in the middle of Manhattan, where such freaky behavior is barely noticed.

Calmer and feeling better balanced, despite my tottering shoes, I plunged onward toward the ever-majestic Central Research Building of the New York Public Library. Although the library had employed me early on in my career, I had been stuck in one of the borough branches, which was like being the poor Appalachian cousin. In fact, I had only been in the

research library a handful of times for meetings and to covet
pretty items in their gift shop. I wondered if Adrian had ever
been inside, or even paid notice to the impressive tower of
stairs and the regal cats, known as Patience and Fortitude,
flanking them.

I spotted him instantly, despite the crowds already clus-
tered about. He was sitting right in the center of the steps,
elbows up on the stair behind him and basking where the
eastern sun struck the pavement. He had his sunglasses
pushed up on top of his head, displaying those great sideburns
and a silver hoop earring I hadn't noticed the first time. He
struck me as boyish, much younger-looking than I remembered. When he saw me, he jumped to his feet and bounded
down the steps enthusiastically, like a child. Hopping down the
last one and landing right in front of me, he marveled, "I found
him. How perfect! They are both magnificent! Which one is
Patience?"

"I'd like to think that this one is." We jogged up several
steps toward the southern lion, pausing so a tourist didn't catch
us in his photo, and then over to the lion's marble haunches. I
reached up and ran my hand along the tip of his tail in greeting. "Did it take you long to figure out my riddle?"

"Well, once you told me Patience was not a bar, I started
thinking about city landmarks and decided I would make you
proud by venturing into my local library to school myself." He
grinned. "The librarian there was most helpful."

"Librarians aim to please." I blushed. I had to get used to
that smile, the accent, those startling blue eyes all over again.
"Oh hey, these are for you. From some of the kids who attended
the program. The top one's from Abbey." I pulled the envelope
from my purse and I studied his face as he read them.

"These are brilliant. Thank you. I've got something, too, for
Abbey, actually." He pulled a jewel case out of the pocket of his
cargo shorts and replaced it with the envelope of artwork. "I

made her a mix CD. Just some fun songs I thought she would enjoy. We jesters aim to please as well."

"That's so sweet. She will love it." My eyes caught a glimpse of the playlist. "'*Lust for Life.*' Really?"

"My own version. Changed a few bits and bobs," he was quick to supply. "Left out the striptease and lotion."

He surveyed my reaction with a wary yet somewhat impish expression, as if he was testing me. "Punk for preschoolers. Iggy Pop would approve."

Relief and dimples broke out at the sound of my laughter. "Shall we walk a bit?" We hiked back down the stairs and strolled up Fifth Avenue. He patted the right side pocket of his Western-style shirt, unfastening the pearly snap on it. "Will it bother you terribly if I smoke?" I shook my head. He lit up, inhaling deeply. It occurred to me he might be just as nervous as I had been while alternate nostril breathing on the corner ten minutes ago.

"So, Gwen, the library director . . . she said a few other branches would love to have you perform." I added quickly, "If you're interested, of course. I told her I would tell you."

He laughed. "Perhaps you should be my booking agent."

"Depends. What's my cut?" I quipped, causing him to laugh again.

"Tell her I am flattered. And I will consider it." I snuck a glance at him, but he was shyly looking at the pavement in front of him. I was able to make out yet another tattoo, thanks to his shirt being short-sleeved; this one a Celtic cross on his right bicep, whose black ink had gone slightly greenish with age. Still, the detail in it was mesmerizing. Cat paws and crosses . . . I began to wonder what other interesting stories his body art told. We fell into a rhythm, bumping arms as we paused at what felt like a red light on every corner.

"Have you had breakfast yet?" I asked.

"No. You?"

"In my world, it's almost time for lunch." I grabbed his hand and steered him east on 51st Street. "Come, I am going to treat you to the best bagel in all the five boroughs."

"The Naked Bagel, eh?" Adrian pondered as he held the door open for me. The inside wasn't half as erotic as the name made it out to be. It was mostly a take-out place, with a long narrow area for seating. The counter line snaked around toward the restrooms, but the seated area at eleven a.m. was sparsely populated. Liz waved from behind the cash register, motioning for us to take a seat. I had warned her in advance that we might stop by.

"Well . . . 'naked' meaning the bagels taste so good, they can be eaten plain," I explained. "But there are so many amazing things to put on them, why would you?" We both studied the huge chalkboard that lined the wall behind the counter. Each sandwich combination was written out in Liz's neat handwriting using colorful chalk. She had had great fun creating monikers for her sandwiches, often naming them after friends, family, and regular customers. I pointed this out to Adrian, explaining that Liz and I had grown up together.

"See the Tree Hugger bagel? That's mine—avocado, carrot, provolone, and sprouts on whole grain," I said with pride. "I always say I'm going to try something different, but I never do. Creature of habit."

Adrian squinted at the sign. "Heavy Metal Hangover? What is that?"

Liz, materializing instantly at our table in her signature *Happiness Is a Warm Bagel* T-shirt, piped up, "PBBP—peanut butter and bacon on pumpernickel." She had all the combos memorized by acronym and often joked she could recite them with the speed and skill of an idiot savant.

"Ugh, my brother Kevin's surefire hangover cure when we were teens. Liz adopted it," I supplied.

"Gotta love a guy who knows bacon cures all," Liz commented.

"Liz, Adrian. Adrian, Liz."

"A pleasure to meet you."

"Likewise." I could tell she was impressed with the firmness of his handshake. One of her biggest pet peeves was having a guy give her a limp fish to shake. "Tree told me what an awesome job you did at the library. I'm bummed I missed it." She turned to me. "Let me guess . . . Tree Hugger? How about you, Adrian?"

He studied the board again, tapping his finger to his lips, definitely overwhelmed. "You put my local bap shop to shame. That's what we would call a sandwich like this in England . . . though more on a roll than a bagel, really."

"You can build your own combination, too, if there isn't enough variety in my choices," Liz teased. She glanced down and gave me her wiggly eyebrow of approval. Today, under the warm glow of the pendant lighting, her eyes reminded me of gooey amber. I smiled back, biting my lip and waiting to hear Adrian's decision.

"Bacon-brie-cranberry," Liz parroted back his choice, not bothering to write it down. "BBC, that's funny. Be right back . . . help yourselves to coffee." She practically skipped away, back to the bustling counter to personally prepare our order.

Adrian smiled. "You've got some cool friends, Kat."

"Well, I think you've met all of them. Exciting life I lead, eh?" I joked. "Shall we?" I pointed to the coffee bar. It had mismatched mugs hanging from a mug tree, along with three carafes of different kinds of coffee. It was like hanging out in a friend's kitchen, where you could help yourself to a refill at any time.

"Allow me." Adrian stood. "How do you take yours?"

"One sugar, two splashes of skim."

"One Tree Hugger for you . . . and one BBC bap for you." Liz presented the sandwiches with a flourish. "On the house, and don't fight me on that!" she snapped with a mock–tough guy tone, and raced back to the lunch crowd trenches.

I shook my head, laughing. "Nut job. But I love her." Adrian practically swooned over his first bite. "See? Maybe people *should* get naked and do a dance on the tables."

"They are *that* good," he praised.

We settled into a second cup of coffee. "Can I ask you something?" He raised his brows, which I took as his assent. "I wasn't snooping, honest. But the nurses gave me your wallet and wanted me to fill out all those forms, so I looked at your license. Your name is Doug?"

Adrian regarded me over the rim of his cup, and then slowly lowered it from his lips. "My father's name is Doug," he explained. "I never wanted to be called a junior, or 'Dougie,' or any variation. So while my Christian name is Douglas Adrian, I choose to go by the latter. You can imagine the delight the lads had in taking the piss out of me in school with a name like Doug Graves," he continued, smirking. "Go ahead, you can laugh."

I shook my head and declined in polite protest, but couldn't help myself when he admitted he had married a girl named Robyn. "Ah yes, Robyn Graves. It's true, I'm afraid." He laughed along with me. "Half the reason she probably divorced me, in the end." He wiped his eye and gave another chuckle. "Anyway. I've gone by Adrian for so long now, I've pretty much forgotten Doug. If someone were calling that name down the street, I probably wouldn't even turn my head, you know?"

"Everyone's always called me Tree, despite my average height. Except my dad calls me Treebird. And his mom, my grandma, always called me Kat. Like you do. I love it when you call me that." He fussed with his mug, eyes averted, and I wished that hadn't come out sounding quite so eager.

"Your eyes remind me of a cat's. Calm . . . calculating. Not crafty, but more . . . cautious. Like you observe first, before acting." I had never had anyone comment on my eyes before, other than the fact they were green. "Wise and full of mystery," he added, lowering his voice as he looked up from under his brows at me. I felt like I had drunk ten cups of coffee, rather than a mere two. "Shall we walk some more? Get some fresh air?"

We waved to Liz, and Adrian left a hefty tip. In unspoken agreement, we began to walk north and then west. Grand Army Plaza loomed ahead of us. We strolled in silence past the stench of the horses, with their garish colored flowers and ever-hopeful coachmen.

It was a comfortable silence, although my mind was skittering through questions I had no answers to. *Have we run out of things to talk about? How long should this date last? Should we have come up with a plan? Is he going to kiss me again? What's he thinking?*

And then out came a question quite spontaneously, before I realized I was saying it. "Ever thought of jumping in the fountain?" I covered my mouth to stifle my own shocked laugh.

"Come again?"

"The Pulitzer Fountain." I gestured toward the cascading landmark in front of the Plaza Hotel. "Pull an F. Scott and Zelda Fitzgerald. You know, something totally off-the-cuff, out of character?"

His grin led me to believe he didn't think me totally insane. "I've spent half my life out of character," he admitted, "trying to be someone I was not. I've jumped *off* things, the proverbial cliff and whatnot. But rarely have I jumped *into* things." We crossed over to get a better look, admiring the water spouting from the mouths of carved heads above into the basin below. "Care to take a dip, my little creature of habit?" he egged me on. But I had already turned my gaze up to the green-trimmed windows of the legendary hotel to our right.

"You know, all these years living here and I have *never* been inside."

"Seriously?"

"Never. I've walked by it a thousand times."

"Your mum never took you for tea at the Plaza?"

"No. She totally deprived me," I said in mock sadness. "I don't even know if they serve tea there anymore, do you? Hasn't it changed hands a bunch of times?"

Adrian nodded. "I've heard talk about it turning into condos. That would be a shame if it were true. I took Natalie here for tea during her first trip to New York. She was three."

"Let's go in."

"Really?" He let me take his hand, but he balked at the red carpet leading up to the stained glass and gilt entryway.

"Just to have a look," I coaxed.

"Oh, all right." We climbed the wide stairs along with a half dozen tourists and a random rich old broad, allowing ourselves to be swept into the opulence. I felt exactly the same way after finally stepping into Radio City Music Hall after years of merely hurrying by: in total awe. I took in the mosaic floor, the Italian marble of the concierge desk, and the chandeliers dripping their light, all with the wonder of a child.

Adrian, meanwhile, seemed to exude a strangely calm and familiar sort of comfort as he escorted me through. "That's the Palm Court," he said as we passed by the large potted palms and marble pillars. "And here is the Oak Bar."

Like its name plainly described, the place was floor-to-ceiling wood panels and murky murals. The place was empty, other than a few men in suits seated at the bar, their martinis sweating expensively. The bartender looked up from the glass he was polishing and nodded to Adrian.

"Drink?" Adrian pulled out a heavy brown leather chair for me at a table near the windows. Central Park was still in full swing outside, but in the Oak Bar, time was standing still at a more gentile period. I half expected to see vintage cigar smoke still lingering around the sconces and Cary Grant to come gliding in.

"But we just had breakfast," I halfheartedly protested. He sidled over to the bar and came back moments later with a screwdriver in one hand and a mimosa in the other.

"Breakfast drinks," he explained. "Full of vitamin C."

I laughed. "Do you always drink before noon?"

He stabbed at his drink with his stirrer. "It's better than shooting smack, right?" He winked at me, but then fixed his attention on his stirrer once again. "Did you know at one point, women weren't allowed in here? Certainly no unescorted women." He watched as I sipped my fizzing beverage.

"Do you come here often?" I had to snicker because it sounded like a bad pickup line. He did, too. "You seem quite at home," I observed.

"It was one of the last public places to smoke in Manhattan," he offered as a way of explanation. Then he leaned across the table toward me. "You look really, really amazing, do you know that?" I blushed and he continued. "Completely beautiful. Every man in here is staring at you."

"Probably because I am female and I don't belong here," I whispered.

"You belong just as much as that Pomona statue belongs in the fountain out there," he argued. "You are like a goddess." I didn't know if it was the champagne bubbles or his words making my head giddy. "Thank you for meeting me today."

"I was losing hope that you would ever call me," I admitted.

Adrian sighed, knuckling his goatee. "I've been in the habit of denying myself for a while now. Retribution for my Bacchian days." I raised an eyebrow at him to see if he would continue, but he only turned his gaze toward the gilded, coffered ceiling. I followed suit.

"What do you think people are doing up there?" I asked.

"Sleeping, fighting, shagging, dying . . . same as they are at the fleabag motel down the road." His ice received another stab with the stirrer. "Doesn't mean their lives are any better, just because they can afford to stay here." His words caught and burned in his throat, like the vodka did. He cleared it. "What do you think they're doing?"

I allowed myself a moment's pause. "I'd like to think maybe somewhere up there, someone is putting the finishing touches on their manuscript, maybe the next great American novel . . . or taking their time making love for the first time in a golden bed."

He dragged his stirrer along my wrist. "Your optimism is quite a turn-on," he observed as I shivered in delight. Leaning over, he kissed the icy trail of alcohol.

"Mr. Singer-for-the-Children is not a glass-half-full kind of guy?"

"Hey, I sing about things for kids that are just as serious, as real as the heartbreaks adults feel. Whether it's about your dog running away or your lover running off, it's the same emotional center. It's the same . . . *yearning*," he pointed out, quite passionately.

Suddenly, I had grown weary of being out in public on a date. It shouldn't have bothered me, since we were practically alone in the bar, being discreetly ignored, but I wanted to be with just Adrian. Just with him, no one else around.

"I want to be alone with you . . . to get away from all these businessmen ogling you," he whispered, and the look on his face mirrored mine; our brainwaves didn't need us to speak the rest. "I'll be right back."

I concentrated on draining my drink both for something to do and for courage. The bartender was preparing a bloody Mary and smiled at me as he garnished it with a plump pink shrimp. It made me think of Adrian, unresponsive in my car. My heart tripped in my chest, and I glanced at my watch.

Twelve thirty. We had spent two solid hours in each other's company. I still felt I had no clue who he was at all, but was so incredibly drawn to him. I wanted him back at my side; I wanted to know what our next adventure would be.

More minutes ticked by before he rushed in and grabbed my hand.

"Where are we going?"

"To jump in the fountain."

WE SCURRIED out past the lobby. The emptiness of the corridors seemed surreal, like Times Square emptied out in preparation for a movie scene. I wondered if he had paid off the bellhop, the elevator operator, the concierge. No one was in sight as we hopped into the wood-paneled elevator, and with a satisfying sweep of the doors, we were finally alone.

"Adrian Graves, what have you done?" I giggled, pulling him toward me as we traveled upwards.

"I done rented us a room, darlin'." He grinned, kissing me long and fierce. A strange thought suddenly occurred to me: Pete had been twenty-nine at our last kiss . . . I had skipped a whole decade and was now kissing a man in his forties. It was different, yet I refused to get sucked into fruitless comparisons. Adrian had worked his way down my neck and, as the elevator climbed, he dropped to his knees and put his mouth on the skirt of my dress. I felt his hot breath on me; it was wildly sexy. I frantically pulled him back up, literally popping the snaps on his shirt in the process, and we necked like a couple of teenagers until the door slid open with a sophisticated ding.

We half stumbled, half dragged each other down the corridor to our door, Adrian doing a stellar job of still being able to work the key as I kissed his neck and ran my hands over his firm backside. He lifted me up with one forearm under my bottom and the other arm supporting my neck, fingers tangled in my hair as he kissed me and slowly brought me into the room. I helped the best I could, kicking off my shoes, wrapping my legs around him, and leaning my heaving chest to his. His hand moved under me, grazing my panties, and he murmured, "Oh my, you are ready, aren't you?"

"It's been so long." I sighed, letting him lay me down on what was, indeed, a golden bed. Stripes of teal and gold ran up the duvet, folded down midway to display a crisp plump white featherbed and a dozen decadent pillows waiting for us to crush.

"I have condoms," I blurted. "In my purse." Adrian's face, just centimeters from mine, looked amused. "I got into town early. Killed time in Duane Reade. You know . . . gotta be a Girl Scout. Always prepared."

"I thought Girl Scouts brought cookies," he teased, lightly biting my left earlobe as I turned my head to locate my shoulder bag. Marissa always likened it to a clown car, impossibly tiny and yet stocked with an unlikely quantity of goods: juice boxes, baby wipes, animal crackers, book, umbrella. And now birth control.

"Ha ha," I intoned, pouting in order to kiss the tip of his nose. "Not to spoil the moment, but perhaps we should discuss . . ."

He entwined his fingers through mine, pulling them up to his chest. "I've been tested regularly. Not recently, but I haven't been with anyone in the last year. I've learned to be a good boy. Clean bill of health." He kissed my knuckles and smiled. "Now then, luv . . . I'm happy you arrived prepared, but I'm in no hurry . . . I plan on enjoying you at a leisurely pace."

The way he said that, all the while running his fingers still entwined through mine down the side of my face and over my lips, made me want to strip him down and have him right then and there. Instead, I breathed deeply, allowing myself to relish the feeling of his solid body straddling mine. We were still fully clothed, exploring with our eyes, our hands, our mouths. Drinking in and marveling at each other's presence.

Adrian began to peel off my panties, never taking his eyes, or his lips, off my face. "I have to taste you" was all he whispered, and in a flash, I felt hands gently push my dress over my thighs, the softness of his hair as he ducked down, and then one amazing, rough stroke of his soul patch before he zeroed in on the spot deeply with his tongue. He lingered, he teased, and steadily began to increase the speed of his pleasuring. Gasping, I tried to go for longevity, but it was hopeless. My toes with their pretty paint job were curling against his shoulders, and the climax hit me sharply before rolling slowly up me in waves that left not only my lips but my fingertips buzzing and numb as well.

I could barely breathe as he kissed his way down one leg and up the other, taking a moment to unbutton the front of my dress and lightly tongue from my stomach up over my cleavage, bra still intact, and back to my neck as I rasped, "That. Was. Amazing." Reaching down, I frantically unbuttoned his shorts and helped free him, all while kissing, nibbling, licking his ringed earlobe, his chin, his neck. His approval was apparent and rock-hard against me as I slowly began to make my way down.

"No, no, I won't last a second, come 'ere," he mumbled, and pulled me on top of him. My brain was starting to come back to earth as I leaned to kiss him, feeling him suck a breath of air as the heat of my skin burned through the thin cotton T he wore under his unsnapped shirt. I went to remove both, but again, he stopped me. "I have . . ." He reached up to touch my face, and I kissed each of his fingers. "Burns . . . some scars . . . I don't want to scare you . . ."

"Do they hurt?" I whispered, lightly running my fingers

down his biceps. I traced the inked outline of his Celtic cross with my nail.

"Nah. They're just ugly. I want to keep this moment beautiful." He smiled up at me, those eyes a gentle yet tormented rocking sea of blue, dark with desire. Without another word, I slowly pivoted my hips and began to gyrate against him in small circles, not taking my eyes off of his. He groaned, arching his back and aching to meet me. "Quick," he breathed, "do me the honor . . ." He reached, grabbed, and tossed my purse onto the bed in one deft move. "Before I soil your dress, luv."

Our ragged sighs echoed one another as our bodies finally locked. The pinnacle he had brought me to earlier allowed each thrust to induce multiple aftershocks deep within me, and I could tell he felt and enjoyed each one. "Oh, Kat," he moaned, biting and twisting his bottom lip as he reached to pull me closer, deeper. Our breath and movements flowed evenly, measured, in unison. He brought his torso up to meet mine as he heaved, hands grasping at my bra straps, my curls, anything tangible to keep him from floating into the ether. I witnessed his face speak a thousand words as his lips just uttered one: my name again. He was all at once demonic, blissful, tortured, humble, and at peace.

"Why are you crying?" I whispered as we both collapsed into the ballooning channels of the featherbed.

"Only because you are," he whispered back, wiping my cheek with his thumb and kissing the moisture left behind. I hadn't even realized I was. "You all right?"

I nodded, letting myself be gathered into his arms for a moment. We were both spent and silent. My back was against him, and his wrists were clasped under my breasts. I studied them, marveling at their sinewy detail, their delicate veins. His hands leisurely rubbed my ribs as if strumming his guitar. "I should get rid of the rain gear."

He was up swiftly, walking bare-assed to the bathroom and

whistling a dead accurate intro to the Violent Femmes' "Blister in the Sun." He grabbed his underwear in a smooth move along the way. I wrapped my arms around the area that his had just vacated, a smile breaking through on my lips. Now where the heck had my panties gone? I popped up and peeked around, finally locating them under his cargo shorts on the floor. I pulled them on, entertaining the notion that I could retain a modicum of mystery after he had been all over me. Then I paused to take stock of the room for the first time. Decent size for Manhattan, tastefully decorated. A bit too stuffy *beaux-arts* style for me. I had been in a few luxury hotels, none as famous as the Plaza, but ones that certainly had rooms that compared. The big showstoppers here were the windows, each as large as a pool table and faced out over the northeast view of Central Park. Not too shabby at all.

Adrian returned, now wearing his black boxer-briefs and fishing in his shirt pocket again for his cigarettes. "Will you look at that!" He leaned over the bed so I could inspect the pack. All had broken during our frolicking, save one.

"I'm sorry," I managed, reddening.

"Don't be." He kissed my shoulder. "I've been meaning to cut down." I wanted to pull him back into bed, but respected his need for nicotine. Besides, I didn't have the energy.

"How's the view?" I asked, sinking into the crisp sheets and plush down. He struggled with the window and positioned himself so he could lean and flick ashes between the bars of the Juliet balcony.

"Meh. About sixty blocks of trees, lakes. You know. Not bad," he wisecracked, looking back at me over his shoulder. "But pale compared to the view I see right now."

"Oh please." I laughed, stretching out on the bed into an advanced tree pose, my palms meeting over my head in a V and my right foot pressed high into my upper left thigh. It was a delicious stretch, made more glorious by Adrian's eyes. I knew he was watching me, even with my own eyes shut. All my connective tissue felt relaxed, having been warmed and loosened by his touch. The pillow had captured his cologne and caressed me with its scent. I tried hard to pull out the notes, like those professional noses who get paid for smelling. Definitely the essence of black pepper. Bergamot? Maybe basil as well. It was masculine and mysterious and so completely him. I allowed it to envelop me.

Sex with Adrian had swept clean the corners of my brain I had long ago abandoned, dusty and cluttered with despair. I couldn't help myself. I was falling. Falling for him, and falling asleep like I had been drugged.

The next thing I remembered was focusing in on Adrian, who was sound asleep next to me. We were facing each other with only our hands touching, our fingers locked and elbows bent at an angle as if we were getting ready to arm wrestle horizontally. I studied his lips, relaxed in slumber. My own lips felt swollen and bruised, overdosed on kissing. I gently ran my hand along his hip, noting how his boxer-briefs clung to the muscle of his thigh and how the hair on his legs looked golden in the afternoon sun. He was deep in sleep and didn't stir. The T-shirt he still wore was slightly askew, and I could indeed see a scar that traveled around his midsection, deep purple like the sun setting over the beach back at the lake. Home.

I started. Abbey. The bedside clock read 2:18, and I double-checked my watch. Wednesday was Abbey's long day at school. Dismissal was at four, and Marissa had assured me she would collect Abbey if I didn't make it back in time. Still, I wanted to be there for her. I was a good hour drive from home, so long as I beat rush hour traffic. But I still had to get to my car. "Adrian . . . hey," I whispered, but he seemed as drugged as I had felt earlier. A note seemed stupid, and shaking him awake seemed cruel. I crept out of bed to make quick use of the bathroom, hoping he would wake up in the meantime. The shower had two rain showerheads, which made me long to stay, but instead I buttoned my dress, smoothed my hair, and surveyed myself in the beautifully adorned mirror above the pedestal sink. I approached Adrian a final time. "I have to go," I whispered, kissing his prone lips. "I have to get home to Abbey." It felt like he kissed me back, but he still appeared sound asleep. "I'll call you later, okay?"

Getting in the elevator was a whole new experience this time. I kept my eyes on the doors as everyone else around me did the same. The elevator made me think of the picture book Abbey loved to hear about Eloise, a little girl who lived at the Plaza. I was so anxious to get home to my little girl. Hotel staff was abundant now, stepping lively, and the lobby was abuzz as I glided out on shaky legs. I probably looked like countless other guests that day, breezing out to do some retail therapy.

My phone sprang to life as I was gunning the Mini Cooper through the Bronx. I grabbed it before it could vibrate down into the crack of the passenger seat.

"I had the most glorious dream that you were here with me in this golden bed . . . but then I woke up and you were gone, and it nearly broke my heart." I smiled into the phone upon hearing his voice. "Was I what the kids refer to as a booty call?"

"Oh my God." I sputtered a laugh. "Hardly!"

"Come back. We'll order room service and make crumbs in the bed."

"A third breakfast of the day sounds tempting . . . but I have to get back. Abbey, school . . ." I drifted off. "Thank you, though . . . for a most delightful afternoon."

"It was a pleasure."

"That it was," I agreed, feeling my stomach do an hourglass flip with the memory of what we had been doing a short while ago.

"When can I see you again?"

"I'll check my calendar. My people will call your people."

He laughed, and now I could absolutely picture his smile. Before meeting him again today, it had been hard to conjure it up in my mind, but now I knew the image was there to stay. "One condition next time," he warned. "You bring Abbey along."

"Really?"

"Yeah, definitely. We need a chaperone."

14

KISS AND TELL

HAD I conjured up the afternoon's events? The burn between my thighs and the tingling of my lips told me no. It was surreal and strange to be back in the neighborhood A&P, watching customers squeeze melons and listening to children beg their moms for sugary cereal. Abbey drove the little plastic car attached to the front of our cart, swinging the wheel to the left as I maneuvered what was roughly the size of an El Camino down the narrow aisles, contemplating boxed items, canned goods. Dreamily savoring the press of Adrian's mouth and the smell of his skin, I tossed in chips, fresh salsa, and limes, paid, and found myself in my kitchen without even remembering the drive home.

Following dinner, the Falzone minivan swung into the driveway. "Trade you these two for your one," Rob offered, thumbing back toward Marissa and Leanna. "We're going for ice cream."

He didn't have to ask Abbey twice; she was already jumping into the chair with the built-in booster seat. Brina and Joey waved from the back.

"Come on, we've probably got forty minutes before they

come back, all sugared up," Marissa announced as soon as the van reversed out of the drive. "Spill the dirt, Tree."

"Great second date?" Leanna prompted.

"Yep."

"No attempted killing involved?" Marissa wanted to know.

"Nope." I led the way to the kitchen.

"He was where you wanted him to be?"

"Exactly."

"Oh, you're killing us, Tree!" Leanna groaned, crunching a tortilla chip in frustration.

"Drinks first." I uncorked a new bottle of Patrón Silver. "Talk during."

Marissa pulled perfect avocados, a Spanish onion, and a lime from a bag and got to work at the kitchen countertop. She had a knack for spotting avocados in their exact stage of ripeness; it was truly a gift.

They carried the food into the living room, and the drinks and I joined them. I could see they were practically keeling over in suspense.

"So . . ." Marissa prompted as I handed her a glass, and then one to Leanna.

I casually crossed my legs and took a sip. Then I began. "Incredible. We had an amazing time."

"And the sex?" If Marissa had been waging bets tonight, I would have won in knowing sex was going to be the first bullet point on her agenda.

"What sex?"

"Come on! You slept with him, didn't you?" She kicked my bare foot dangling near hers. "You got rid of the monkey paw," she noted, referring to my freshly exfoliated heel, "your nails have red polish on them for the first time since Brina's christening—"

"I bet you got a Brazilian, too," Leanna challenged.

"No, just a bikini wax."

Both women practically spilled their drinks all over the couch in gloating celebration. I told them briefly of how we ended up at the Plaza.

"Ahh, hotel sex . . . that's the best," Marissa said.

"The hell with that, *daylight* sex," Leanna added. "I haven't had that in years!"

"Jeez, a night at the Plaza would probably be Rob's whole weekly paycheck." Marissa sounded wistful as she dredged a chip through the bowl of salsa in front of her.

"And you were only there a couple of hours. Nicely played." Leanna toasted me with her margarita glass.

Marissa waved her hand. "Wait a sec, doesn't he live just a few blocks from there? Why would he spend several hundred bucks on an afternoon delight there and not take you back to his place?"

"I don't know. The topic never came up. We were working off the spontaneity, you know?"

Leanna licked a bit of salt from her glass. "You don't think he has a wife hidden away or some torsos in his freezer, do you?"

"Uh . . . I do *now*, Leanna! Thanks a lot." I laughed, but I felt a tiny nagging seed of doubt burrow its way into the back of my brain. Was he hiding something? We had talked a lot, but I still knew so little. I was enjoying getting to know him slowly, although our romp this afternoon had certainly accelerated some familiarities.

"So how was it getting back on the horse after almost four years? Was he a stud?" Marissa pried.

"He was . . . very sweet," I admitted. "Romantic, but not in a thickly laid, thinly veiled way. Sincere. He didn't get weird after or anything . . . even when I fell asleep. It was nice waking up next to him, I have to say."

"Ah, romance. The first thing I wake up to every morning is

Eddie ripping a fart," Leanna drawled. We howled with laughter.

"Rob and I are still pretty passionate, but I don't know if I would call it romantic after fourteen years. Maybe we know each other too well. But it's still pretty hot."

Leanna scooped a huge chunk of guac, cupping her other hand protectively underneath it. "So when are you going to see him again?"

"I was thinking Abbey and I would take him to Bear Mountain, maybe this weekend . . . if he's free." I hopped up and came back with a freshly made pitcher to refill our drinks.

"What does he think of the fact that you have a kid? Is he cool with it? Did you tell him the deal?" Despite Marissa's recent tirade about the bad bed vibes, she and my other closest friends treaded carefully on the details of "the deal," as Marissa sometimes called it, although "ordeal" was probably a more apt term.

The truth was, they had dealt with Pete's death in the trenches right beside me. They had witnessed the shock and horror and the aftermath, and had fought hard not to let it redefine their relationships with me. There had been a short time of walking on eggshells for each of them, naturally. But they knew I didn't want pity or comforting ad nauseam, and I knew they weren't going to forget or dismiss it simply by not speaking of it, so we had reached a quiet middle ground; a peaceful purgatory, I guess you could say. My baggage remained, like those forlorn items traveling round and round the conveyor belt at the airport, but we chose to ignore it, to not claim it and own it and drag it around with us. They had picked me up and healed me more so than any counseling session or grief book ever could, and I loved them fiercely for that.

"He's been made aware." Why *was* I finding it so difficult to tell Adrian what had happened? Everything else with him came so easily. Should I hand him the newspaper articles to read and tell him to get back to me should he have any questions?

I mulled it over as I chewed on a tequila-laced ice cube. It had been a long time since I had had to lay the whole thing out. Living here, I didn't have to. Small towns are perfect for preserving, or petrifying, one's personal history. My family's beeswax buzzed down the power lines and grape vines of the town along with everyone else's. Bride becomes mom becomes widow, all recorded in the annals of Lauder Lake even before I reestablished myself as a resident. But the whole story . . . not exactly first-date small talk. Nor was it second-date pillow talk. My body temp increased by ten degrees at the last thought, and it wasn't the alcohol's fault. Memories of our hot afternoon romp lingered like a dream, and I quite liked the mystery and fantasy we had each brought to the bed. What had he called me . . . a goddess? Sheesh. The less he knew at this point, the less likely I would become his charity case. Or scare him away. Keep the moment beautiful, as he had said about keeping his scars covered. The same could be said for mine, lying below the surface. My first-class, Louis Vuitton–size excess baggage could stay in cold storage for a bit longer.

"As for Abbey . . . he actually said he thought she should be with us on the next visit." The Patrón was softening the edges and making my tongue lazy. "Bad sign?"

"No way. They had chemistry, too. I saw it in the library. And not just because she adores that freakin' cat he sings about," Leanna pointed out. "He seemed very comfortable around her."

I was secretly glad I wasn't the only one who had picked up on that. Seeing him interacting with her the morning following the library program had further reinforced the notion that he seemed to genuinely enjoy her company as well as mine. Yet his relationship with his own daughter sounded so tumultuous. I was curious to learn more about that. "He's got a grown daughter, actually, from a previous marriage." I tested the words out loud, getting used to them. I had dated several breeds of the male species in my day, but never the type labeled "Divorced Dad." It sounded so . . . mature.

"There are my three lovely senoritas." Rob had let himself in. I heard Abbey on the porch, cranking up her new Adrian mix CD for Brina and Joey. "Did you get your drink on, my lady?" He leaned down to give Marissa's lips a short kiss.

She sucked the dregs of her sweet drink and grinned. "Hell yeah. Glad you are the DD."

"Yeah, thanks for picking me up, too," Leanna said. She turned to me. "The Volvo is in the shop, and I wasn't about to drive that truck."

"Of course not." I humored her. "That truck" was Ed's 1958 Chevy Apache Street Rod, as well as the bane of Leanna's existence. He had blown his entire severance pay on the truck after 9/11 and his separation from the insurance company that had employed him. And he had spent most of his time since then restoring it to its original cherry-red brilliance. Lauder Lake was small enough a town to relish such oddball behavior; besides Manny Mietta, the octogenarian who drove a Cadillac predating my birth by one year, no one here antiqued when it came to cars. Although Grant's fifteen-year-old pussy wagon may have run a close third.

"If this is his midlife crisis, couldn't he have at least gone and bought a Maserati? Something cool?" she continued. Marissa and I both rolled our eyes sympathetically; Rob just shrugged, unwritten guy code for not coming down on another member of the tribe. Secretly, I sort of liked the truck. It was actually the one thing that made Ed vaguely unique. Ed Brown was . . . well, beige, for lack of a better descriptor. Nice enough guy, cute and smart enough, but for our Leanna . . . *not* enough. A powerhouse like that deserved a man who could match her.

Soon after Leanna's vows of "for better and for worse" had

been exchanged, Marissa, Liz, and I had a powwow in our identical teal dupioni silk dresses, Cosmos in hand. We vowed to always build our friend up, no matter what in life brought her down. And extended the pact to mutually include all of our futures as well.

"Thanks for coming, you guys. Sorry I broke the usual Wednesday plans." We lingered by the door, watching as Rob chased the kids around the lawn and through the minivan via both open side doors as if it were a jungle gym.

"No biggie. This was a nice change. And come on. It was worth it, right?" Marissa teased.

"It was a nice change," I admitted with a grin.

15

LAKE VIEWS

THE RAIN SEEPED into my dreams early Saturday morning, drumming on the dirty skylight over Pete's bed in his studio on 110th and Broadway. We lay with our legs intertwined, facing each other. He was wearing his favorite T-shirt from the eighties, a red shirt so washed, it was now a dull orange. It sported a huge MTV logo on the back. "There are all different kinds of love," he was telling me, pushing my hair back behind my ears.

I woke up to the sounds of Abbey crying in bed next to me and rain falling on the leaves of the Japanese maple outside my bedroom window. "What if he doesn't come?"

"Oh sweetie, I doubt a little rain will stop him." I drowsily kissed her and rolled back over, wanting to get back to the dream. What had Pete been telling me? What had felt so life-like a moment ago seemed vague now. I let my eyes close, willing the dream reel to loop back and continue. Next to me, I could hear the scraping of Abbey's long lashes as she blinked against the pillowcase.

"But what about Bear Mountain?" she whimpered.

"It won't wash away in the rain," I assured her. "If we can't show him Bear Mountain today, we'll do it another day." It was

7:46 on a sopping wet Saturday, with no hope of sleeping more now. Adrian's train wasn't due until 11:25. Following Abbey as she padded to the kitchen, I began to revamp the day's plans in my head. Picnicking at the mountain was out. I had planned on grabbing bread from the farmer's market after we collected Adrian from the station. Assorted European cheeses had been carefully selected from the import store. Instead of whipping up the pasta primavera salad I had in mind, I began to prep the vegetables for soup. It was definitely a damp-to-your-bones soup kind of day. I added the tiny tubes of pasta for a heartier result. Then I dragged out the bread machine and involved Abbey in making a fresh loaf of our own from my favorite Amy's Bread cookbook. We definitely had the time this morning, and I needed to burn off some nervous energy. My dream was still hovering close. Funny I had dreamed of Pete in that old apartment. Usually my dreams of him took place outdoors, in the wide open where I couldn't contain him. He felt close to me now, as he had been so close in the dream. Yet here Abbey and I were, so far away from that place. Her little hands were on top of mine, measuring and adding ingredients. The rain spilled from the gutters and beaded into tears that rolled down the kitchen windows.

"Our house feels cozy today," Abbey observed.

"It sure does."

Finally, after breakfasting and showering and putting the kitchen back together following our impromptu cooking session, it was time to go meet the train. The rhythmic thumping of the wipers was like a metronome that paced the beating of my heart. Breathing deeply, I swung down the long drive into the lot of the commuter station, letting my eyes survey the scene. The 11:25 had just pulled out, and a meager handful of passengers were sifting down the steps from the station. Umbrellas began to blossom up, obstructing my view. I pulled up as close as I could and popped the door locks open.

Seeing him was a delightful gift, an assurance I hadn't conjured him up in my lonely mind. He was indeed there, hunched and hurrying to the dry sanctuary of my car and inside before I could relish the vision any further.

"So much for Bear Mountain!" I greeted him as he dripped a rainy kiss onto my cheek. He was wearing a black leather jacket that took the brunt of the weather. It had the cut and thickness of a motorcycle jacket, but without all the goofy zippers and buckles. Very clean and classic, perfectly broken in.

"No problem, I'm easy, whatever you gals want to do. Hiya, Abbey." He smiled into the backseat.

"Hello, Adrian Graves," she said earnestly. I could hear the mixture of shyness and delight in her tone. "Guess what we've been listening to!"

"Um. *Led Zeppelin IV*?"

Abbey laughed, even though there was no possible way she understood his humor. "Silly Adrian. Your CD!" As an afterthought, she quickly added, "Thank you!"

"You're welcome." We spent the short trip back to the house singing along to the CD, including a raucous rendition of "Octopus's Garden" with Adrian belting out the chorus in his best Liverpudlian baritone.

"We have a surprise for you. It involves yeast," Abbey said mysteriously as we entered the house.

"It smells amazing in here!" Adrian, shrugging off his jacket, allowed Abbey to proudly lead him into the kitchen to marvel at our freshly baked bread. "Nice thing to do with your daughter," he commented to me. She had scampered off to the piano, pretending to provide us with a reprise of "Octopus's Garden" in G position.

"It's pretty easy. We used the machine today, but sometimes we do it by hand. You just have to devote the time to the rising up and the punching down." I handed him plates from the cupboard for the table. "My mom used to bake a lot with me . . . so it's become a household tradition."

"Lots of rising up and punching down in my household, too," he admitted. "My dad was a man of few words." He mimed the jabs of a prizefighter to finish the sentence. "As for my daughter . . . I *did* take her for her first tattoo." Adrian chuckled at his confession. "That's about as close as we got to any sort of tradition. She and her mum, well . . . they shop together. Bonding on Bond Street." He ducked in and kissed me. "Has it really only been three days?"

Soft and low, his voice liquefied a part of me.

"Crazy, right?" We held each other, listening to the rain compete against Abbey's piano playing. "It's cozy in here, isn't it?" *Great, Katrina. You've been reduced to stealing one-liners from your preschooler.*

"Very. Let's never leave," he murmured into my hair. Although he had abandoned his jacket in the other room, I swore the heady and smoky smell of the leather still lingered there on his skin, mixing with that peppery scent I was quickly becoming addicted to.

"Well, if this rain ever stops . . . I am sure Abbey would love to show you the lake."

"So there really is a lake in Lauder Lake, then?"

Abbey grabbed both of our hands and practically dragged us down the street after lunch. "Wait till you see my lake!" We paused at the wet sand to peel off socks and shoes, then rolled up our jeans and walked around the bank of pine trees until the lake came into view. The beach was deserted, not surprisingly. Abbey ran ahead, yelling insults at the gulls and galloping to the edge of the water.

"This is lovely. I had no idea it was so close to your house." Adrian bent to pick up a smooth stone and effortlessly skipped it toward the dock. "You've got a nicely kept secret out here."

"More like a forgotten secret. Lauder Lake used to be a

resort community, before all the wealthy New Yorkers moved on to more luxurious digs in the Catskills." We sat on an area of sand that had been dried by the emergent sun and watched Abbey scavenge for interesting bits of shell and pebbles along the shore.

"Their loss." Adrian dug his toes into the wet sand.

"When I was little, I assumed everyone had a lake at their disposal within walking distance," I admitted. "I spent every day of every summer here. Except when I was twelve and I tried sleepaway camp, which I hated."

"I think I would come down here every day, too, if I lived here. Even in winter. Growing up in a port town, you learn to appreciate the grounding, calming effect of water." He had been squinting out across the lake before turning his gaze on me.

"*For whatever we lose (like a you or a me), it's always ourselves we find in the sea.*"

"I like that."

"It's not mine. Cummings." He tossed his hair back. "I'm glad you have this sanctuary here for you and for Abbey."

I looked down at our sandy toes. "All those years I lived in the city . . . this place was never far from my mind." We gazed past the sand, dimpled from our steps, to the gentle push-pull of the small ripples and the lush thicket of green that bordered it far across the surface. "Like a reminder it would always be here for me when I needed it." It had certainly been a comforting constant after my heartbreak and homecoming four years ago.

Adrian nodded, tracing around my hand splayed behind me for support. Here and there his finger would touch one of mine as he outlined it in the sand, sending that delicious zing of electricity I remembered feeling in my car that day we met.

"New York feels that way to me," he said quietly. "From the first time I visited, I felt like I knew it well. Like I had conquered it in one huge bite. And then I went back home to London and felt like I was wearing a cheap, ill-fitted suit. New York was like a love affair that I didn't allow myself to commit to fully, like I didn't deserve it. I thought of it a lot, though, especially when things got tough back home. My career . . . hadn't turned out like I'd imagined, and things with the wife had turned bloody ugly, and I felt like all my friends there . . . well, they were different, too. Maybe it was me who changed. Anyway. I knew I would end up there eventually."

He hoisted himself up abruptly and half jogged, half ambled to the water's edge. Abbey ran across the sand to meet him, holding out her hand to show him something she had scavenged. I sighed, feeling as if our talk had unwittingly brought a melancholy down upon us. Determined to change that, I hopped up, leaving behind my handprint Adrian had traced in the sand, and ran toward them. "You're it!" I tagged Abbey, who squealed and took up the chase. Round and round she barreled in pursuit before giving up on me and catching Adrian on the arm as he did an exaggerated slow-motion jog away from her.

"Tagyerit!" she bellowed as Adrian turned to chase her. She zigzagged back up the beach, screeching with anticipation of being caught.

"Gotcha back!" Adrian lightly reached out and stretched one of her curls as she tried to fake him out with a feint to the left and then to the right.

"Aw, Mommy hasn't been it yet!" Abbey complained, quick to pout like many a four-year-old is wont to do when the game doesn't go exactly as planned.

"Let's both get her, all right?"

Delighted once again, Abbey tag-teamed with Adrian and they chased me until I was out of breath with laughter and fatigue. I shrugged out of my red zippered hoodie and brandished it like a brave bullfighter. They brought me down to the sand in a fit of giggles, then collapsed next to me, breathing hard and grinning.

"Oh Abbey, look at you. Where'd all that mud come from? Come on, dirty monkey, let's get you home and cleaned up." We hiked back to the road. Adrian hoisted Abbey up in a piggyback ride so we didn't have to put her muddy feet into her clean shoes. From her perch, she happily sang over his shoulder as we walked.

"Dirty clouds."

Adrian tilted his head in the direction she was pointing. "You're right, Abbey. Do you think that means more rain?" I loved the way he took the time to respond to her observations.

"Yep."

I hosed off her feet by the side of the house while Adrian had a cigarette and admired my mom's hydrangeas in the front garden.

"Can I watch my show?" Abbey whispered. She was a creature of habit even with company around.

"Abbey . . ."

"You're going to do boring stuff. Like talk." I had to stifle a laugh.

"I will think about it, okay?" I turned to Adrian. "I'm going to help her get changed. If you want a drink or anything . . ." I gestured vaguely toward the breakfront sideboard.

"That's Mommy's happy drink." Abbey pointed to the squat, bubbled glass bottle of tequila with its big nobby cork that had been left out after Wednesday's powwow with Leanna and Marissa.

"Abbey!" My embarrassment was plain, but Adrian just looked amused. I ushered her into her room, and she pulled on the clean pants I handed her. Out the window, the three p.m. sky looked like a seven p.m. spring evening, darkening as a distant thunder rumbled.

"Please can I watch *Maxwell* now?" Her face contained a

mixture of remorse and innocence. I could tell she didn't know exactly how to read mine.

"One show. As your quiet time. In my room."

"Yes!" she hissed in victory.

Adrian had the fireplace ablaze with one popping log and some driftwood and was inspecting the liquor over in the dining room. I normally didn't imbibe while home alone with Abbey. In fact, most of the collection was the leftovers of bottles friends had brought over at one time or another. He disrobed a half-full bottle of Canadian whiskey from its purple felt bag; Liz liked to drink it with ginger ale and had left bottles of both after her most recent visit. I watched as he mixed a big one the exact same way.

He looked up. "Can I interest you?"

"Mmm. Ginger please, no Crown. I'll get some ice."

We settled on the couch across from the fire. "To happy," Adrian echoed Abbey's adjective. We clinked glasses.

"To happy."

Adrian stretched his legs, crossing ankle over ankle, and put an arm around my shoulders. "And where might Abbey be?" he asked into my hair.

"She usually has an hour of quiet time in the afternoons. Sometimes it leads to a nap, but these days, mostly not." I strained my ears and finally picked up a few notes of the *Maxwell* theme song. "Do you hear that?" He concentrated, squinting and biting his bottom lip until the hairs underneath stuck straight out. Finally, he shook his head in defeat. "It's your song: *solving crimes without claws, he always lands on four paws . . .* " I prompted.

"Ah. Max." In the half-light of the fireplace, it was hard to tell if he was blushing. "My ears aren't what they used to be."

I leaned and kissed him right under his lobe in consolation. He returned the favor by peppering my cheek lightly before finding my lips and lingering there.

I silently cursed my mother's choice of couch; it was a red velvet Victorian affair, hand-carved in mahogany. Its deep tufts and weak springs made it comfortable for sitting, but if leaning back, the crest across the top was murder on your neck. It had been acquired during my college days, and while I had always thought it looked nice in front of the fireplace, I had never tried to get cozy on it with another human being. Abbey and I usually chose the overstuffed chair to cuddle on or the big beanbag chair in her room. Pete and I had had more modern tastes, opting for a low long IKEA sofa in highly impractical ivory to grace the hardwood floors of our co-op. In storage with so many other relics from that time, it wouldn't fit in here any more than Adrian and I fit on this tiny uptight thing. I grabbed him and we rolled with a plunk and a laugh onto the Persian rug.

I was having a hard time discerning whether the heat I felt was coming off the fire or off of our skin as it came into contact with lips, with fingers. We lay across the rug, facing each other. All around us the clocks kept track of the minutes as we stared and explored. I delicately placed my palms on his chest, enjoying the rise and fall of his rib cage under my touch. He ran a finger gently down my cheek, across my semi-parted lips, and down my chin past my neck and leaned in to kiss me.

"This is nice," he breathed, and I nodded, too woozy to speak. "I'm not normally . . ." He searched for words as I ran my hands from his chest to his shoulders and down his arms. "I usually find it tough to be . . . tender," he admitted. "But the moment I touch you . . ." He pushed my hair back behind my ear and I had an instant flashback to the morning's dream, the rain and Peter and his cryptic talk of love . . .

"I'd better check on Abbey." I hopped up, nearly upsetting our drinks next to us on the hardwood. With shaking legs, I quickly made my escape. God only knows what Adrian was thinking of me, whether I was a loon or a cock-tease or what. I tried to shake off the lingering dream of the past and bring my head back, sharp and focused, to the here and now. Abbey was curled up on my pillow, rump in the air. Her head was turned toward the television in the corner, but when I moved around the futon to get a better look, I could see her eyes were closed. I sat down beside her and pushed her hair off of her face. She sighed but didn't wake.

Adrian was still on the floor, but sitting upright, nursing his drink as he stared into the dying embers of the fire. His profile looked a bit worn in the glow. "Everything all right?" he asked, not turning as I approached.

"She's sound asleep, would you believe? All that running at the beach." I lowered myself beside him.

"And you?" He turned now, and those pale blue eyes, absorbing the reflection of the fire and rebounding back a shimmering purple, were just inches from my face. "I'm sorry if I—"

"No . . . it was all me. I had a momentary lapse of . . . I don't know what. I'm . . . trying hard to remember how this all goes."

"How what goes?" Adrian asked, setting his drink aside.

"The tender stuff. Being romantic. Getting turned on. It's just been . . . it's been a long time since . . ."

"I know. It's been another lifetime," he agreed. "Don't try to retrace steps. We'll find new ones. We did pretty well the other day, yeah?" He raised his brows at me.

"True." I smiled.

"I wrote something. A poem." He spun his silver Shakespeare pinky ring with his thumb in what appeared to be a mixture of nervousness and nonchalance. "The other day in the hotel. After you left."

"Oh?"

"I had assumed it was about me, but now . . . I think I wrote it with you in mind."

"Wow." The only guy I had ever inspired poetry from was

Shawn Fisher. He had worn a bandanna headband exactly like Axl Rose and could whistle the intro to Guns N' Roses' "Patience" spot-on. And he had presented me with an embarrassingly bad poem sophomore year of college. I had a hunch Adrian didn't rhyme words like *moon* and *June* when he wrote.

"Does that freak you out?"

"No. I'm flattered. I guess." I took his hand to halt his ring-spinning, as it was making me antsy. He wove his large fingers through mine and curled them down.

"Things, feelings . . . morph for me sometimes. Into songs. Poetry."

"Cool." I squeezed his fingers. "Care to share?"

"Nope." He laughed. Leaning close, he murmured softly, "It's a work in progress. Sorry."

Each kiss with Adrian was a different experience. That first kiss in the car had been hesitant yet determined; a tentative exploration of a brave new world. Then, in the elevator, urgent and exciting, madly searching. Up in the hotel room, luxurious, transporting. And now, with what felt like relief after our strange conversation, his lips tasted hungry and new, our connection deeper and our movements almost mirrorlike in their synchronization. I fluidly felt like I knew what he needed and when; it was a delicious play as he responded fully in mind and body.

As my hands slid down and reached for the button of his jeans, he audibly gulped. "Yeah?" he breathed, as if to ask if I was sure. I kissed him in response, letting my fingers roam gently. I felt his body relax under my touch, but soon heard his weak protest as my body moved south on top of his. "None of that, lass." He took advantage of the fact that I was supporting myself solely on one elbow and deftly flipped me over.

"Adrian . . . no fair!"

"There are no rules. All's fair in love and lust," he teased me, working to unsnap my jeans.

"But . . . I'm told I am really good at it," I coaxed, trying to find my dignity, joking yet confused.

"I am sure if it were an Olympic sport, you'd medal in it, luv." He kissed my temple and ran his fingers around my loosened waistband.

"I want to make you feel as good as you make me feel." I gasped and lost the ability to form a sentence as his fingers began to lightly play.

"You do. You make me feel amazing." He sighed a ragged sigh as he slipped into my perfect spot. "You've got some sweet voodoo, I'll tell you what." I was helpless under his nimble caress and gave in. He stifled my moan with an openmouthed kiss as I bucked up against his hand. "Mmm, that's beautiful . . ."

"You're beautiful. I want you." I clawed at his shirt, threading my legs through his and grinding up against him.

"What about our drowsy chaperone?"

I grabbed his hand. "Come with me."

Our house had been built in the early 1930s and still had every original brass doorplate. Kev and I had lost most of the skeleton keys while playing with them in our youth, and my mom had hidden the remaining ones once Abbey came along for fear she would lock herself in somewhere. The only truly secure room in the house was the bathroom, with its hook and eye latch. It was too high for Abbey to reach just yet. "We're going to have to be quick," I whispered as we snuck past my bedroom doorway. Abbey hadn't budged from her spot.

"I don't think that's going to be a problem, luv," he murmured, practically climbing me like a ladder the moment the door was safely locked. The sconce to the right of my head rattled as we slammed together against the wall, kissing and pulling at each other. "You as prepared as last time?"

"Top shelf, medicine cabinet."

He hopped over our puddle of discarded denim as I

contemplated our surroundings. The tile floor looked pretty cold, and the curved edge of the clawfoot tub looked precarious and unforgiving. I needn't have worried; Adrian simply hoisted me up and had me right against the wall, next to the bar with Abbey's ducky towel hanging from it. He hooked an arm under my leg as I pressed my heel into the small of his back. It's amazing what kind of stamina sex can provide; I knew we would both be bruised and aching tomorrow, but lost in the moment, we defied the laws of physics and managed to knock some of the plaster off the wall in the process.

"God, Kat. Oh Christ. Fuck," he growled, catching my eyes with his own wide and wild ones as we both came together. He continued to hold me against him, his heart knocking against mine. "Bloody incredible."

"And imagine how good it would be if we ever fully disrobed." I was still in the sweatshirt I had thrown on to walk to the lake, and he had only lost his jeans and boxers.

"I'd love nothing better," he assured me. "We've just got to learn some self-control around each other." He winked as he lowered me with shaking limbs. "Next time, I promise . . . fully naked, proper bed . . . I will feed you grapes and read you poetry."

"And I will schedule a babysitter," I said, already zipping my jeans. "I'd better go make sure she isn't having any nightmares of earthquakes or the walls falling down." I picked a fleck of drywall out of his hair and giggled.

"Cripes, that was a bit rough, I reckon." He looked pleased and not a bit guilty. "Marlboros are safely out in the living room, thank Christ."

I tiptoed into my bedroom. Abbey had rolled onto her back, arms splayed out in an "I don't know" shrug. Sometimes I was amazed at how tiny she was. When in full motion and chatter, she appeared larger than life. Now, I marveled at her small nose, tiny lips, her whole face in utter relaxation and calm.

Lashes fanned out on crab-apple cheeks. One little foot was dangling off the futon, its sock slightly askew. Out in the living room, the piano was softly being played.

"Is that a new picture?" Adrian cocked his head to the left, never lifting his fingers from the keys as I joined him at the bench. A framed picture of Pete and me, standing with Kofi Annan, was perched upside down on top of the piano.

I righted it. "No, old one. Abbey likes to make off with pictures. She must've had it in her room for a while and brought it back." I watched his hands as they spanned a scale of notes. "I didn't know you played."

"'*Malagueña*.' I didn't know you know the UN secretary-general."

"Um, I don't. Pete had interviewed him at a United Nations Association awards dinner, and he posed for a picture with us." I remembered the night well; there hadn't been too many occasions where his work actually led to a glamorous free meal out on the town. More often, I was bringing in sandwiches to his cubicle as he churned out words and burned midnight oil to meet a deadline.

"That's him, then? His name was Pete?" His song dwindled into a soft diminuendo as his fingers and his gaze lingered on the keys.

"That was his name. Yes." And those were his hands. His veins. His hair and skin. I looked at his eyes, forever unblinking, and tried not to think of what was left of him now.

"Okay." His thumb tapped absently at middle C. "I took lessons as a kid. Three years. My mum insisted. I hated it at the time."

It took my brain a minute to switch topics. "Me too. Five years. I don't think I'll force Abbey. But if she wants to . . ."

As if on cue, Abbey came stumbling into the living room like a drunken sailor, her breath slightly soured and curls matted from slumber. "Hungry."

"And?"

"Food."

"I only answer to complete sentences," I informed her. Adrian hid a smile behind his glass of whiskey.

"Let's take Adrian to Basilica!" she said, clearly proud of her brainstorm. Honestly, I hadn't contemplated how long the date would last, but realized we were headed into the dinner hour. "Please, Mommy?"

"Are you up for dinner out?"

Adrian smiled. "As long as we don't wind up in the ER, sure."

LAUDER LAKE HAD two Italian restaurants: Ralph's, your basic red sauce joint, and Basilica, which relied more upon garlic and olive oil to win over its fan base. My parents had had a weekly standing reservation there since forever. And Abbey and I ate there at least once a month. Their pastas were homemade, and the cannoli literally melted in your mouth. Plus the waitstaff always gave kids a hunk of raw dough to keep them occupied so the adults could enjoy their wine in peace.

The hostess instinctively grabbed two menus when she saw me coming with Abbey in tow. When it became obvious that Adrian, holding the door and bringing up the rear, was in our party, she recovered quickly and deftly grabbed a third menu. With a broad smile, she sat us at a cozy corner table in the back and fetched a double order of raw dough for Abbey.

"Tree Underwood? Is that you?" We had barely glanced at the menu before an unfamiliar couple came bearing down on our table. It took me a moment, but I eventually placed them, right as I remembered Grant's invitation to dinner three weeks back.

"Diane . . . Chad . . . hi!" I awkwardly half stood as Chad

came swooping in with a kiss on my cheek, infusing me with the stench of his heavily applied cologne. He looked the same as I remembered him in high school, thick-necked and stocky, although his crew cut was graying gracefully. Diane was very pretty in high school, and clearly she must've decided it had been her best look. Her hair still smacked of eighties bi-levels and her eyes were still ringed heavily in kohl black eyeliner. Attempting to hang on to that youthful look actually made her look older than most of the female classmates who I still had the pleasure or displeasure of seeing around town.

"We were wonderin' if we were gonna see y'all, and here ya'll are! And here's your little one! Let me get a look at you, darlin'!" Diane had apparently picked up a Southern accent instantly upon relocating to Texas, even though she had lived in New York her entire life. Abbey looked at her skeptically, but politely said hello.

"Grant had mentioned you were coming into town . . . nice to see you." Chad's cheap cologne marched up my nose; it was as if I had dipped my face in it. "This is Abbey . . . and Adrian . . . Adrian, Chad and Diane Snow. We went to school together." Adrian barely had a chance to open his mouth to say hello before Diane jumped on his accent.

"Oooh, I love your voice! Are you Australian?"

Adrian chuckled. On just our third date, I could see by the gleam in his eye he was holding his tongue from adding a quick-witted retort. "No, I'm British," he allowed himself.

"Oh, I've never been good with accents," she drawled with a wave of her hand, and I couldn't resist giving Adrian a light kick under the table.

"We're meeting Grant. Better grab a table while we can. You're looking great, Tree. Really good to see you."

"Enjoy your stay." I let my smile linger until Chad had ushered Diane safely out of earshot. "Yiiiikes. Homecoming king and queen, back in town. Haven't seen them, or that hairdo, since prom. Wild."

Abbey flattened the dough with her palm. "Mommy, can I go see the fish?"

"Let's wait till we order, Abb." Our server, Christa, appeared with the wine Adrian must've requested while Chad was smearing his stinky stubble against my cheek. She was the younger sister of a classmate, and we had spent several torturous figure skating lessons together as preteens.

"I'll take her, Tree."

"Thanks, Christa."

She smiled, expertly uncorked the bottle, and poured a sampling for Adrian. After he nodded his approval, she filled our glasses, took our orders, and then took Abbey by the hand to visit the big tropical fish tank near the kitchen.

"I like how everyone knows you," he confided, leaning in with a smile. His warm fingers brushed a stray curl off of my cheek that had escaped from my barrette.

"Please. I miss the anonymity of New York City sometimes." I threaded my foot between his under the table, and we held each other's gaze for longer than most people would find comfortable. Adrian finally broke it and settled back with a grin as the back waiter swooped in with bread. We left our feet entwined in intimate privacy below.

"Pardon," Adrian murmured, "my mobile." He had his phone to his ear before I could place the familiar-sounding ringtone. "Wotcha, mate? Actually, yes . . . I'm out to dinner . . . *yes*, with a living, breathing lady friend." He smiled at me. "Two, as a matter of fact."

Our table, positioned a few steps up from the rest of the dining floor, had a central vantage point. As I kept my eye on Abbey, I couldn't help notice when Grant came breezing in, his head careening around like a bobblehead doll. *Just keep walk-*

ing, I silently willed. *Go find your friends and refrain from trying to turn this town into your own personal Peyton Place.*

"Sorry, luv. My mate Sam. He can gab, given the opportunity. Normally he's the jammy git, out with more ladies than he can handle."

"Oh? Are you having a hard time handling us?" I teased, yet peripherally I was focused on Grant. His head jerked in surprise as his eyes landed on our table.

"You," Adrian began, a delicious tone to his voice as he curled his fingers around mine, "are a pleasure to handle. And spending time with Abbey is a delight."

I watched Grant's confusion and shock quickly morph into arrogance as he swaggered over. Giving Adrian's hand an advance apologetic squeeze, I internally braced myself.

"Hey, Tree. Sorry I didn't *call* you like you *asked* me to." Grant made a point of completely ignoring Adrian. His patented lazy grin flashed a little too big.

I remained unfazed; allowing so much as an eye roll would appear as juvenile as his behavior. "No problem, Grant. Diane and Chad are over there . . . we got to say hi."

He turned on his heel at the mention of his friends and joined them without another word. Abbey got an unrequested hair tousle from him on her way back to the table as she passed him.

"Dare I ask . . . who's the rude bloke?"

"He was Mommy's boyfriend," Abbey supplied simply, climbing back into her chair and reaching for her apple juice.

"Whoa . . . ho ho. Let me clarify. We dated in high school for a couple of months. End of story," I assured them both. "Love can be blind . . . but puppy love is deaf, dumb, *and* blind."

"Ah, a high school sweetheart . . . At least you stayed in school long enough to have one." Adrian paused. He took a gulp of wine. "I dropped out when I was all of fifteen, stubborn as I was stupid. Met my wife in the 'real world,' if you want to call it that."

Abbey practically did a spit-take with her apple juice. "*You* had a *wife*?"

"Hard to believe, yes," Adrian replied.

She looked worried. "Is she in the stars now?" Whether a typical four-year-old contemplated the living versus the dead on such a regular basis, I wasn't sure. My child may have been a bit more inclined to, given her limited body of experience. "Mom says it's a nice place to imagine people."

"No, she's in Belgravia." Adrian's tone implied the ritzy section of London was in his mind akin to the fourth circle of Dante's Hell. "With her new husband. Leopold. The banker," he finished flatly. I was secretly glad Abbey was asking the questions, because I didn't dare.

As tactfully as he could in front of young ears, he told us his wife had decided she'd be happier married to a "dreary sod with a bloody dull job he witters endlessly about" rather than to the father of her child. Abbey quickly lost interest in our conversation, despite her attempt to hang on to and decipher some of the more colorful adjectives in Adrian's vocabulary. She began to manufacture a dozen tiny doughnuts across the table, rolling the spongy dough into a snake under her hands and pinching the ends together.

"Once upon a time, he was the family's accountant. He lured her with promises of domestic security and the material bliss she craved, all the while funneling *my* funds into various accounts to ensure it. All tidily tucked under 'ancillary relief' when the decree absolute came down. What he lacks in personality he now makes up for in pounds sterling, which in Robyn's world counts for substance." I was at a loss for what to say, but gave a grim little smile of empathy. "Put it this way," he said, reaching for the sealed bottle of San Pellegrino left on the table for those so inclined. He spun the pale green bottle until the label was facing me. "She liked to think she was *this*, whereas I"—he took a sip from his glass filled with tap water and tilted it toward me in a toast—"consider myself more like *this*."

"So she was overpriced and pretentious and you were the real deal."

His laughter fluttered down on me like a ticker tape parade. "Spot on, Kat!" He refilled both of our wine glasses, killing the bottle.

"How old was Natalie when you split?"

Across the room, Grant was guffawing embarrassingly loud over something, or nothing.

"Two. God, she was just a babe. We shared guardianship until she was eight, and then . . . well. We need another bottle of wine before I get into that."

"Skeppi, no neatball." Christa had arrived with many plates, reciting Abbey's order exactly as she had requested it. Adrian had played it safe with the chicken Marsala, and I, too, had steered clear of seafood, opting for the pesto tortellini. "Can I get you three anything else?"

"Another bottle of wine?" Adrian turned to me.

"Sure, what the heck."

"And let's send one to the loud git at the booth down there on the left, all right?" he suggested with a gleam in his eye.

"Adrian! Don't you dare."

"Come now, let's toast the prom king and queen . . . and the class clown." I couldn't help but laugh at his keen observation. "And another apple juice for the young lady," he added with a wink.

"You're crazy," I said, bumping his knees under the table. We watched as the bottle was presented with little verbal explanation but quite a bit of gesturing. Heads turned in our direction, and we reciprocated by raising our glasses in a silent and amused mock toast. Abbey saluted them with her kiddie cup of juice. Diane was all teeth and probably would have shouted, "Thanks, y'all!" had she not been so busy sucking down a healthy first glass. Chad gave us a dorky thumbs-up, then looked to Grant for reassurance. Grant looked like he had just swallowed a bug.

I helped Abbey cut up her spaghetti. "What's that saying about revenge? It's a dish best served cold?"

"Or a wine best served chilled?" Adrian chortled.

"Eh. I have no beef with him. Life's too short. But he does have a way of making this town feel claustrophobic."

Wine and endorphins had us giggling and bumping into each other on the way out to the parking lot. "You all right to drive?" he asked, but then answered his own question. "Cripes, we're not going anywhere with that tire."

"Oh . . . sugar," I said as Abbey swung on my hand over to the car. "A flat?"

"I thought all Minis were equipped with run-flats?" Adrian bent to inspect it.

"I opted for regular tires," I replied, cursing the salesman for not coming on stronger with the pros of having the fancier tires.

"Honestly, I don't think a run-flat could have survived this. Christ, someone did a bloody hack job on it. Screwdriver, maybe?" He straightened up. "Tell me you have a spare in the boot?"

"Spare in the boot," I affirmed, popping it.

"What's a spare? Do cars wear boots? What makes a tire flat? Can people die from flat tires?" Abbey had a million questions and kept a running commentary while Adrian removed the tool kit and spare and began to jack up my Smurf.

"I'll have this fixed in a jiffy. Why don't you wait inside?" Abbey and I headed back toward the restaurant. In the vestibule, I sat in a black padded chair while Abbey sat on my lap, wistfully staring at the bubble gum machine. I could hear

Grant laughing his brain out of his head. What an idiot. I felt bad for all the diners still in the restaurant.

Adrian was back to fetch us in what could still be considered a jiffy. I hiked a sleepy Abbey up on my hip and took his hand. He had smears of grease across his knuckles and a satisfied smile on his face. "My dad was a mechanic. Never taught me to kick a football, but he taught me how to change a tire. I worked at his garage to save up for my first guitar."

"Lucky for me."

I began the slow drive to the train station, heeding Adrian's warning about driving under fifty on the spare and savoring the last moments of what had been a fairly perfect day. *The Magical Mystery Tour* on the stereo comfortably replaced conversation. Abbey and I primarily listened to the Beatles and Broadway show tunes while in the car. Safe stuff. Nothing that would cause me to veer off the road in a teary mess.

"Abbey, who's your favorite Beatle?" Adrian asked, twisting around in his seat to face her.

"Ringo." She shrugged. "Rhymes with *bingo*," she added logically.

He turned back to me. "Pretty heavy album. Has she asked who the walrus is yet?"

"No, but she does have a lot of questions about how one can sit on a cornflake."

"Bright girl."

"Hey, Abb," I called back to her. "I'm just stepping out of the car with Adrian for a minute. I'll leave the music on." Abbey nodded, her eyes glassy. It was rare for her to see the inside of the car at nine p.m.; usually she was tucked snug in her bed before the streetlights came on.

"Good night, Abbey-like-the-road." I watched them smile at each other. Adrian reached his hand back as if to shake hers, although the distance and car seat buckles made it impossible.

He pumped her foot instead, eliciting laughter that could be heard even after we had closed the doors.

Adrian and I leaned against the car, delaying the inevitable good-bye. Adrian began to speculate whether the sabotage of the tire had been random or deliberate.

"I'm the only person in town driving a blue Mini with an *I love my library and I vote* bumper sticker on it. I doubt it was a case of mistaken identity."

"And to think I bought him wine, the prat," Adrian fumed as I shared my suspicions. Grant had arrived late for dinner with his visiting friends. His car, I now recalled, had been parked diagonally in front of mine. I thought of the random tools he had shoved under the seat, and the look on his face when I had blown off his cocky dinner invitation a few weeks ago...

"Was he your lover, Kat?" I felt Adrian's lips graze my earlobe.

"He was the . . . the first. Once." Thoughts of the old boathouse by the lake, long torn down, surfaced. I could still smell the damp wood, the mildew from the life jackets hanging on the walls. I remembered looking up to the rafters, watching two balloons left over from a neighbor child's party bob gently above as I left my childhood behind. "I wanted to get it over with." I rested my head on Adrian's shoulder, and he gave my forehead a gentle kiss, right where my widow's peak began.

"I wish it could've been me. Although I was already a dirty old man by then . . . What were you, sixteen?"

"Fifteen. Come on, you aren't that much older than me . . . seven years?"

"I was a different animal at twenty-two." He wrapped his arms around me. "Come meet me in town. Would Wednesday work again?" I nodded. "My turn to pick the place." The distant whistle of his train could now be heard on its approach into the station. He opened Abbey's door once more to say good-bye. Then he turned to me.

"I have a place riddle. Nothing is real there." He rocked back on his heels, pleased with himself.

"That's not much of a clue."

"Abbey will be able to tell you." His sole perplexing hint got the wheels in my head turning.

"You'll feed me grapes and read me poetry?" I whispered as we hugged long and tight.

"Darlin', I'll grow the grapes for you . . . and write the poetry."

I sighed. That was poetry to my ears right there. I watched as he took the stairs to the station two at a time, but couldn't bear to stay as his train pulled out. Abbey perked up slightly as I hopped back into the car. "Is he coming back soon?"

"I think so." The compact front cabin of the Mini felt cavernous. Something vague was creeping through my brain and my body. An emptiness, turning more tangible by the minute as we crept home along darkened roads on our uneven tires. It was an ache. I ached for him. Was this all too quick, too soon? I glanced at Abbey in the rearview mirror, wondering if she detected the loss. She was gazing out the window as the blackened foliage whizzed by. I tried to shove the feeling into the junk drawer section of my brain, a place to harbor it safely until it could be dealt with at a later time. And I concentrated instead on the riddle that would lead me back to him in three days.

Nothing real.

Made up.

Imagined . . .

As we pulled onto our street, Abbey began, as if on cue, to softly sing along with "Strawberry Fields Forever."

16

CEREBRAL CITATIONS

I ADORE LISTS.

It must be the librarian in me.

Alphabetical, chronological, with numbers or bullet points. I like the tracking and the order of things and delight in ticking items off any sort of checklist. The morning after my ten-hour date with Adrian, I found myself creating a brain bibliography as I gave Abbey a bath, based on what I knew of Adrian's story so far. Like a dutiful librarian, I mentally cited my sources. Most were primary, directly from things he said or did.

- Born in 1963 *(from driver's license)*
- From Hampshire *(note: look at a map)*
- Dad was a mechanic
- Mom ??? *(made him take piano lessons)*
- Likes soccer *(Chelsea football)*
- He's got at least one sibling (half sibling) Kev's age
- Dropped out of school at fifteen
- Moved to London at seventeen
- Has a daughter who is twenty, divorced when she was two, so ... marriage ended around 1986?

- Married AND divorced by age twenty-three *(no subsequent marriages?)*
- Lost wife and money to Leopold the banker *(and seems slightly bitter, understandably)*
- Moved to NYC in 1994
- Lives on Central Park West *(according to driver's license)*
- Wrote a kids' cartoon theme song in 1998 *(for a laugh, apparently)*
- Good with kids *(although not with his own)*
- Hasn't been in a relationship in the past year *(or at least, hasn't gotten laid)*
- Rides a bicycle and smokes cigarettes

I wasn't very satisfied with my mental pathfinder. There were ten years between his divorce and relocation to the States that I knew nothing about. And he never did say why he lost custody of Natalie. He can't just smoke and bike around Manhattan all day. Way too many holes. *But,* I reasoned silently as I soaped Abbey up, *we've only had two dates . . . three if you count the dinner with the side of epinephrine.*

How much did he know about me after three dates? That I have a kid obsessed with a cartoon cat, a dead husband who I can't bring myself to talk about, and an ex-boyfriend who might possibly be a tire-slasher but is most definitely a wanker? That I am game for afternoon delights in five-star hotels and am putty in his capable hands?

I sighed and slicked back Abbey's hair, flattening her mass of ringlets. She was an amazing mix of Pete and myself. My dominant widow's peak was apparent at her hairline, and my curls bobbed to the middle of her back. Pete's big brown eyes had been perfectly replicated, brows, lashes, and all. It was too soon to tell whether she would inherit my nose, which was on the longer, thinner side, the tip turned down. Or whether her baby teeth would give way to Pete's wolfish adult ones. Her smile did remind me of his. When I looked at her, I understood why couples must go for baby number two, if only to see what the next stunning custom blend would be.

"Abbey," I ventured, "what do you think of having Adrian Graves visit again?"

Her little eyebrows flew up. "Today?" She grabbed her rubber seal squirt toy from the watery depths and inspected it.

"No, today is Mother's Day. But soon?"

Abbey seemed to like that idea. "Is he your best friend?"

"No . . . he's a new friend. You know Aunt Miso is my best friend."

"I thought Daddy was your best friend, too."

"It's hard to explain . . ." I started. We were running late, and the weekend had been too full of new emotions to dive into such a philosophical discussion with a four-year-old. "We always have room in our lives for more friends, right?"

"Except for Jake Overhill. He called me stinky at school and said he isn't my friend." She applied a death grip to the poor little seal until he spit every last drop of water he held.

"Well, we know you're not stinky," I said, kissing her damp head. "Jake must have been having a bad day."

"Mommy, someone is knocking." We stopped soaping and splashing. Sure enough, I heard a light but persistent thump. Who the heck could that be? "I'll be right back. Don't stop singing, okay?" As long as I could hear her voice, I'd know she wasn't drowning.

I cinched my robe tighter and glanced at the grandfather clock in the hall. Eight forty-five. Through the front window, I glimpsed the white Underwood and Overhill delivery truck parked outside. Oh good Lord. Grant had entered the screened-in porch and was deliberately knocking slowly and steadily on the heavy wooden front door. Grumbling, I yanked it open.

"Hey. Happy Mother's Day." He brandished a blooming

hydrangea branch, presumably from my mom's bushes outside. "I sold the French hunting chairs, finally!" he exclaimed, rolling his eyes upward and letting out an exaggerated whistle of relief. All prickish behavior from last night seemingly had dissolved with the rain. "You know, the oak and rattan?"

"Mazel tov."

"Yesterday . . . for two grand, cha-ching!" He peered past my shoulder into the house. "I only had one on the sales floor. Your dad says the other three are in your basement. Need to deliver them today, so . . . here I am." He spread his arms as if offering himself up to me.

"You could've called first," I said flatly. "And when did you speak to my dad?"

"Sorry." The word dropped from his mouth as unapologetically as the hydrangea petals dropped to the floor in his wake. "Why, is your date still here? Sleeping?" His tone was lecherous; obviously he was implying Adrian. "Called your dad this morning. Talked to your mom, too." He grinned. "Nice chat."

I chose to ignore the latter comment. Any "chat" he had with my mom would no doubt end up meaning an inquisition later for me. "Do you really think anyone could sleep while Abbey is singing at the top of her lungs?" She was currently belting out "The Cat Came Back." "I left her in the tub. So if you'll excuse me . . ." I jerked my thumb over my shoulder toward the basement door to indicate my consent.

"Is it Adrian again?" Abbey wanted to know.

"No, it's Jake's daddy, sweetie. He needed to pick up some of Grandpa's chairs." We could hear him clomping downstairs with the grace of an elephant.

"How does *he* know Grandpa?" she demanded suspiciously.

I handed her the ducky towel. "He worked with Grandpa." I plucked her and her little seal of disapproval out of the tub. "Go get dressed. We're late for Aunt Miso's."

Back in the living room, Grant was struggling with a pair of bubble wrap–encased chairs.

"Found two. Where's the third?"

"I don't know," I said, impatient to be rid of him. "Try upstairs."

He went up and soon returned carrying the third chair. "I see your brother's still flying his heavy metal freak flag up there," he grunted under the weight on his way down, almost missing the last step. "So . . . tell me about Cuppa Tea."

"Excuse me?"

"You know, your *mate*. Your *bloke*." He dropped the chair with a plop, rattling the china cabinet. "He seemed a little . . . oh, I don't know. Smooth Slim Shady. Who spends that much on wine? And how much do you know about this guy?"

"I know he can fix a flat tire," I tested.

Grant picked up the chair again with fabricated nonchalance. "It's just, well . . . Tree, your dad is like a father to me. And so I feel like you are my sister, you know? I don't want to see you get taken advantage of."

"Yeah. Okay. You're one to talk." We stared each other down for a tense moment. "You know what? It's Mother's Day. Don't harass me," I finished, slamming the door on him.

17

QUEEN FOR A DAY

I HAD GOTTEN up for a four a.m. feeding on my first Mother's Day. Foggy-brained and swollen-breasted, I had needed a moment to process why on earth two envelopes were propped up against the inside rails of Abbey's crib. Pete had placed a card from her and a card from himself there, presumably before he went to bed. I remembered smiling in the half-lit dawn as I brought Abbey to my chest.

I faithfully received cards from my parents and my in-laws every year since, and I reciprocated by sending my own to them. And Abbey never failed to bring home some construction-paper-and-tissue-paper creation from school in honor of the day. Today, we would fill the day with brunch at Marissa's and the slew of people she had invited over. I was grateful for not being left at home with my memories.

"*Haha-no-hi*—that's Mother's Day in Japanese. I Googled it!" Marissa said proudly, pushing a glass of sake and cucumber into my hand. "Rob is a sushi-making fiend in the kitchen."

Abbey and I followed her inside. The Falzones lived in a cute converted cottage two streets away from us and just one house away from the beach. It was a lot like my place, only two more bedrooms had been added on with an addition to the back. Marissa's mom had found the fixer-upper for a steal eight years ago. Luckily, Rob had the patience and Marissa had the eye for decorating. It was homey and warm without being too cutesy-country. A poor gal's MacKenzie-Childs, Marissa liked to say.

The TV blared from the den, no doubt the men watching some sort of NBA pregame nonsense. Abbey ran to join the other kids up in the attic playroom, and I popped into the kitchen to pay my respects to Marissa's mom, who refused to relax on her day and was insisting upon being Rob's sous-chef.

"Hey, Ma," I said affectionately. "You're all dressed up." Dora Filletti was decked out in a pantsuit of muted gray with fancy buttons. A pair of her signature stilettos graced her tiny feet.

"Yeah, got an open house from two to four," she explained, flicking a piece of rice off her apron with manicured nails that rivaled her daughter's. "No rest for the wicked."

"That's why you are *the number-one realtor in the tri-state area*," Rob boomed, quoting the commercial from his mother-in-law's realty company that aired on the public access channel. "The gals are out on the deck demolishing the first round of California rolls," he said, kissing my cheek hello as he squeezed his bamboo rolling mat.

I took my sake and joined Karen and Leanna out on the deck.

"No Liz?" I asked, knocking glasses with each of them.

"Nope. Took her mom to a Broadway show."

Marissa joined us a few moments later, kicking up her feet on an empty chair. She toasted me with her own big glass of sake. "Where are the boys?" I asked.

"The Nets are on tonight," Marissa explained. "My dad no doubt has some money riding on the game. I think he's holding Ed and Mitch hostage in the den with ESPN. Jasper too!"

"Oh please, the only way I could convince Ed to come today

was the promise of sports." Leanna brushed wasabi like war paint across her piece of sushi. "So Tree . . . how was round two?" The girls exchanged knowing smiles, and with some nudging, they got me talking about the glorious day with Adrian.

"Wow, bathroom sex." Marissa high-fived me.

"Wow, *standing up* sex . . . I swear, if you regress to kitchen table sex, I'm taking over your life!" Leanna warned me. Karen sat shaking her head and smiling, eyes wide with wonder. "More juicy details, please."

I obliged. "But what do you think is up with the oral?" I finished.

Marissa shook her head. "I've never heard of a guy cock-blocking himself! Maybe it's a power thing?"

"Maybe he's too respectful of you?" Karen suggested.

"Maybe he just doesn't like it. For some people it's a turn-off. Honestly," Leanna confessed, "the thought of *servicing* Eddie after a long day of me doing everything and him doing nothing . . . I'm just not attracted to him like that anymore."

"See now, I think it's the toilet bowl theory," Marissa announced. "Once you move in with a guy and are reduced to cleaning his pubes off the toilet bowl, the romance and mystery are gone."

I burst out laughing. "So do we never clean the toilet?"

"No, you get a cleaning woman. Or you make him clean his *own* bowl," Marissa advised.

"Somehow I don't think hiring a maid is gonna bring the spark back for me," Leanna said. "Even if it was a sexy French maid!"

Karen spoke up. "You just get so tired when you have kids, you know? Mitch is always too busy, too stressed. Luckily I have Jasper to hug and kiss and snuggle. Obviously it's not sexual, but makes up for some of the lack of physical contact."

I nodded, knowing exactly what she meant.

Marissa was strangely quiet. More sushi was consumed, eventually the men came out of their sports coma to eat, and the kids stopped playing long enough to gobble up the sushi-inspired pizza rolls Rob had invented. After everyone else left, Joey, Brina, and Abbey commandeered the television. Marissa and I kicked back with the rest of the sake.

"You're so quiet. Is everything okay?" I asked her.

"Yeah . . . actually, that's just it. Everything's great. I don't have any of these complaints the other girls have. It's almost creepy," Marissa said. "I worry about them." I understood. Leanna increasingly never had a good thing to say about her marriage—or her life, for that matter. "But you . . . you're doing okay?" Adrian's voice emanated from the den; the kids must've tuned into *Maxwell MacGillikitty.* "The sexy man is still entertaining you and your child?"

"And then some." I smiled at the thought of him. "He is great. I forgot what it's like to have a man around the house. He changed a tire for me, and he got dirty. I miss having a guy around to kill the spiders, you know?"

Marissa laughed, munching a sake-soaked cucumber slice. Tires and spiders aside, I was enjoying Adrian's company; his wit and his way with Abbey melted me. And obviously we had chemistry. I wasn't quite ready to take Marissa's toilet bowl theory seriously, but I did wonder where the newness and novelty of this relationship was going to lead us. We had already taken several leaps in a short period of time. I thought back to the Plaza and the fountain and the order of things. Should one jump in feetfirst? Headfirst? Or heart-first?

MEASURES
*

I want to tell you about my scars but
it's unthinkable
I will not face
that particular pain
I will not pick that wound
there are fissures
where there were none
before
I want to smash it all
down from the shelf
and grind it into a
flammable dust
won't you curve
yourself around me
I surrender.

(A.G.)

18

ILLUMINATION

I WAS ETERNALLY grateful to Karen for talking me into yoga class. It was during my post-depressed, slightly manic phase where I was constantly in an adrenaline-pumping survival-of-the-fittest mode. I was running on the treadmill at home, spinning like mad at the Y, playing with Abbey during all of her waking hours, and leaving no time for inner peace. Karen, on the other hand, was doing baby yoga with newly born Jasper and was way blissed out. When I asked her what her secret was, she brought me to the basement of her church on a Tuesday morning. There, men and women of all ages and from all walks of life were stretching in their bare feet on thin mats. We were asked to sit and silently set our intention for the session and for the rest of the day. I begged myself for calmness, for focus, and felt a wave of well-being and self-love wash over me. I needed this.

Now, while working through the sunflower-moonflower series of movements, it struck me. The time had come to reclaim the top half of my house. Kevin's bedroom should become a proper guest room, a playroom, or some sort of retreat separate from the rest of the house. Or at least a place to store all the boxes currently inhabiting the first floor. I would have two hours to begin dismantling it before I had to fetch Abbey from school. I figured I could at least get the posters down and the bong out of there.

Back at the house, I surveyed the room and started my ambitious task. Still dressed in my yoga clothes for maximum flexibility, I stood on Kev's bed and steadied myself. Reaching both hands up, I began to gingerly peel the highest corners of the largest poster from the slanted ceiling. A spider carcass circa 1985 sifted down and practically landed in my left eye, but that was not what sent me cartwheeling off the bed with a shriek.

Oh my freaking God.

I had caught a close-up glimpse of Corroded Corpse's lead guitarist.

Adrian.

The hair was longer, straighter, dyed jet-black with two inches of bleach on the tips. But it was definitely Adrian. His lips were twisted up and to the left with concentration, his eyes half shut in ecstasy as he wailed on his guitar: a mirror image of his expression on the bed at the Plaza as I had climbed on top of him.

I racked my brain, trying to remember back to all the silly stage names these metal guys gave themselves . . . Ozzy, Lemmy, Nikki, Blackie. Thunderstick, King Diamond, Riff Rotten . . . and this guy was . . .

Digger.

The poster clung for dear life to the slanted ceiling it had considered home for the last twenty years. I hopped back up and smacked the corner back in place. Then I sat on the bed for a good long time. Finally I brought myself to grab a stack of Kevin's albums. Sitting cross-legged on the floor, I began to pour through them. *Metastasis,* Corroded Corpse's third album, shook in my hands. I remembered the album well. Back in the mideighties, it had been as commonplace in my family's household as the Sunday comics and Lucky Charms on the breakfast table. A huge Blakean sun graced the front, black yet shining, with its rays seeping out toward the edges. Writhing souls seemed both captured and captivated by its dark light. A large white ring had worn away some of the cover art, probably from the number of times the album had been slipped in and out of the sleeve.

I turned it over and there he was again staring out at me, this time with a snarl on his face and more eye makeup than a crying Tammy Faye Bakker. His posing made me laugh, even though I was shocked and hurt. *"Digger" Graves, Lead Guitar* read the caption. The other heavily made-up scowling cast of characters with him were Riff Rotten, rhythm guitar and vocals, Adam Archangel, drums, and Samson Steel, bass guitar. The song listings dripped in red down the back: "Blood Oath," "Slaying of the Firstborn," "Funeral," "Queen of the Guillotine," "Siren's Song," "Godforsaken," "Spoils of War."

There was another picture on the inner sleeve in black-and-white—he stood naked to the waist and wielded his guitar as if he were using it to do a behind-the-neck shoulder press. A gruesome, rotting zombie tattoo ran up one side of his chest, perhaps the real reason for his reluctance to disrobe in front of me. There was the Celtic cross tattoo, but no cat paws . . . and no burns yet that I could ascertain.

I didn't know what to think about any of it. I was still reeling. I carried the album downstairs, picked up the phone, and then put it back down. Calling him seemed ridiculous. I needed to get a handle on my emotions. Did I have a right to even feel betrayed? He hadn't lied. He just failed to share many truths with me. And I hadn't exactly been wearing mine on my sleeve, either.

I decided to call my brother instead. I wasn't exactly sure what I wanted to tell him, or to have him tell me. He was an expert on all things Corroded Corpse, even though the band had called it quits half his lifetime ago.

No answer, but perhaps that was a good thing after all. I left a vague message before heading out the door to get Abbey. "Hey, Kev, I'm thinking of turning your old room into a guest room. Do you want me to ship your records and stuff to you? Call me."

I drove to school in a fog, the last few weeks swirling over my head in a storm cloud full of questions. So many of the puzzle pieces were falling into place: his initial reluctance to perform for the children, his vagueness about his job and why he had traveled so much when Natalie was young. The weird names and numbers in his cell phone. His reaction when I mentioned finding his CDs for the children attending the library program, not to mention the one he had upon entering Kevin's room . . . it all made sense now. Had he been relieved or astounded to realize I had honestly not known who he was? How long had he been in hiding, using his middle name and staying out of the public eye?

For every question I had, one word screamed in my head in response: *RESEARCH*. It took all my willpower not to just jump onto the computer once Abbey and I returned home. If there wasn't an official Corroded Corpse Web site, there were sure to be loads of fan pages, music sites, album reviews, and years of full-text news articles to enable me to piece together the life he hadn't made me privy to. The librarian in me burned red-faced in shame and yearned to methodically gnaw through every source out there to make up for lost time, but my heart told me to let it be . . . let it be. My heart couldn't take the pain of learning yet another person who had touched my life and Abbey's life didn't really exist.

Kevin returned my call that night, but I was too exhausted

to answer it. "Hey, sis. Miss you. But if you so much as mess with any of my Corroded Corpse stuff, I'll kill you."

SLEEP HAD SHARPENED my memory and strengthened my resolve. I would only meet him at Strawberry Fields today to say good-bye. Throughout the night, my dreams had scoured my subconscious for those random factoids one learns about various celebrities simply by the sheer luck of living simultaneously on God's green earth with them. I had come of age during the debut of MTV News and the rise of *People* magazine. Even if I hadn't been interested in the trials and tribulations of Digger Graves, some of it had been absorbed by the osmosis of our overconcentration as teenagers on pop culture, as well as from the concentration the media devoted to burning it subliminally into our brains.

Heroin. Rehab. Assault. Jail.

I may not have recalled all of the details surrounding those actions or events, but upon waking, I remembered those words could accurately describe Digger Graves just as much as the standard cliché "*sex, drugs, and rock 'n' roll*" could. How darkly droll it must have been for him, romancing the naive widow. Millionaire rock star junkie being invited to a library, to my house for soup! I slapped clothes upon myself, cursing every good thought I had had about our blossoming relationship. Cursing myself for exposing Abbey and opening her up to disappointment. Cursing him and his sadomasochistic attempt to play along.

I couldn't bring myself to face Marissa that morning during drop-off. She had called the night before to see if our Wednesday coffee date was back on regular schedule, and I had given her the noncommittal go-ahead to gather with or without me. Even if I only cruised in to tell him off and got back in time to join them, I didn't think I could handle the chatter and gossip today. I made sure I was the first one in and out of the lot. I gave Abbey extra kisses and hugs and tried not to let my face betray my emotions when she instructed me to tell Adrian she missed him.

I already missed him, too.

19

IMAGINE

CENTRAL PARK OPENED its lush green arms and instantly comforted me. I took my time walking down familiar paths and past favorite landmarks on my way west. As I passed the kids playing in Heckscher Playground, oblivious to the abundance of concrete, I missed Abbey desperately. There was a bevy of those brown squirrels she loved to chase flitting about; as I walked I pondered why we didn't have any brown squirrels around Lauder Lake. Hipster squirrels that eschewed the suburbs, no doubt. People were scaling Umpire Rock like it was some urban Everest, with the nonchalance only New Yorkers and tourists could have on a hunk of bedrock a half billion years old.

Before I realized it, I was upon Tavern on the Green and its wonderful menagerie of topiaries. I fervently wished to hide myself within that leafy fantasyland, but continued trudging up the bridal path instead. It was deserted, but there was evidence of freshly dug horseshoes in the dirt. I rejoined the paved path leading to Strawberry Fields well before the Riftstone Arch, which was desolate and creepy even on a sunny morning. And then I began to brace myself.

Willing myself to stay calm and cool was a futile task. I could no longer enjoy the peaceful beauty of the trees on my path. There was the faded Lennon Imagine mosaic, so much smaller in real life, and the endless parade of people paying photographic homage. And there he was, sitting along the curved triangle of benches that bordered it. His elbows rested on his denim-clad knees, and he was leaning forward into a small book.

I stopped short, almost causing a pileup of French backpackers behind me who had been close at my heels, eager to see the New York City landmark. I needed a moment to collect myself, to survey the situation. To capture his image before all hell broke loose.

Black faded Norton Motorcycles shirt, tattered jeans, brown leather boots that looked like they had journeyed across a hundred dusty desert miles on a Harley. At his feet were two Starbucks cups of coffee, which almost broke my heart. Our fourth date and the man not only brings coffee, but I knew it was exactly how I liked it, too: one sugar, two splashes of skim. Adrian was the type of guy who noticed the details. *A shame he didn't bother to clue me in on some of his own important details,* I thought bitterly. "*Nothing is real*" indeed.

He kept gazing periodically to his right, figuring I'd enter the Fields like most people did, through the 72nd Street entrance. He glanced at his watch more than once, and I observed his shoulders rise in what could only be a gusty sigh. *Does he think I failed in solving his riddle? Too thick—or thin-skinned—for the challenge?*

I remembered his remark in the Naked Bagel. If someone were to call his given name, he had said, he would barely think to turn his head. I felt all the rage return. Who *was* this guy really? He was a lie, a stranger.

Before my brain had a chance to chicken out, I let the word

fly. I knew the moment it exited my lips and entered his ears, there was no going back.

"*Digger!*"

What was meant to sound strong and absolute came out as a quivering bark. But sure enough, he jerked up his head in a pitiful Pavlovian response and met my gaze across the mosaic. I had vowed to stomp off the moment I received confirmation, but somehow I just couldn't. The look in his eyes could only be described as haunted. *Go, go go.* My feet finally obeyed my brain and twisted me back the way I had come.

"Kat! Katrina!" I had only taken a few steps before I heard the collective gasp of tourists and pigeon-feeding bag ladies alike. Glancing over my shoulder, I saw Adrian hurtling across the middle of the mosaic, which had to be some sort of sacrilege. He deftly hopped over the lit votive candles and the bouquets of limp roses carefully strewn across the shrine, making sure he didn't tread upon John Lennon's resounding and timeless single word on his way to me.

I dodged bumps in the pavement and people and dogs in my effort to leave gracefully as he pursued. "So that's it, you're just going to walk away because you think I'm a washed-up scumbag who doesn't deserve a chance to prove himself?"

"No!" I yelled, causing the people and dogs in our path to leap and scatter. "I'm walking away because you didn't trust me enough to tell me the truth." I stood rooted to the spot, my body white-hot and twitching as adrenaline flooded it. Many times I had witnessed shouting matches in the streets of New York, but I never imagined I would find myself in the middle of one. It was mortifying but strangely liberating.

"Trust?" he sputtered. "All my life I *trusted* people to do right by me, and I was burned at every turn! Made a commodity by those who I thought cared about me—my friends, my wife, my own daughter . . ." His voice dwindled as he drew a ragged breath and stared me down.

I held my ground. "Well, I'm thinking of *my own* daughter! She trusted you! I let her get close to you, and you hid the glaring fact that—"

"The fact is, Kat, I'm never going to fit into the neat and logical order you're used to!"

Logic? He was really going to play the logic card with me? Life had already pulled the mother of all tricks, pulling the rug out from under me and leaving me to ponder the ultimate disappearing act. Could he blame me for wanting life to play nice for a while?

"I'm not asking you to *fit* into anything. I . . . I . . ." I had no idea how to express what I wanted, what I needed. My heart wanted to ask plenty, but my head was afraid to.

"That isn't me anymore," he explained calmly, approaching me slowly as if I were a Central Park hipster brown squirrel that would scurry off with any sudden movement.

"What—did you go to prison and find Jesus?"

"*No*, I went to hell and back and found myself." Three giant steps and he was nose to nose with me. "I sprouted wings and I carried myself far away and started a new life!" He shook his book at me. One glance at the cover and my heart soared.

It was Ursula K. Le Guin's *Catwings*, the book I had mentioned on the day we met. "But until you and Abbey came along, I wasn't really living it. I know that now," he finished softly, resting his forehead on mine.

"I was going to tell you; I just needed the right time. I brought you here"—his arms swept backward toward Strawberry Fields and upward vaguely toward the high-rises that lined Central Park West—"because I had decided I was ready. It's not so easy to say, *'By the way, while you were walking down the aisle at high school graduation, I was snorting lines off some groupie's arse.'* I told you, I was a different animal back then." I heard the weariness in his voice and saw the years lining his frown, but his eyes were what led me right down to where he was laying his soul bare. I had thought for certain his eyes would be different, seeing him in a new light today. I had feared they would be cold and unyielding steel. But they were as deep and as pliable as ever, and they began to well as I finally embraced him.

Only a few smells in life instantly bring me back to a happy place. Most of them are tangled up in childhood memories, of feeling safe and loved. The fruit and spice of pipe tobacco always brings me back to my grandpa, raking leaves on crisp autumn days. A just-extinguished match brings blowing birthday candles to mind, along with their gritty, sugary secret wishes. Shaving cream and papaya shampoo will always break my heart yet keep Pete close. And now Adrian, with his mixture of coffee and leather, combined with that peppery richness and the smell of cigarettes in his hair . . . for sure his scent will hit my memory triggers every time. His T-shirt sleeve darkened with the press of my tears against it. "You've got to understand . . . I haven't let anyone . . . not since . . . and . . ." My exhale of words weren't getting anywhere fast, so instead I stopped, inhaling what I could of him.

"Listen . . . come . . . just come home with me," he murmured, his fingers weaving through my hair. "Listen to what I have to say. Or you can watch some rock bio flick on MTV and make your own judgment, I won't stop you." I shook my head to his latter suggestion and allowed him to lead me back through the wisteria arbor, its vines exploding with purple and violet blossoms, past the street vendors still commercializing Lennon with their T-shirts and monochromatic prints.

"How did you . . . not that it matters, but . . . did someone—"

"Kevin's room," I managed to get out. I snuck a look at him and thought I detected a mixture of relief and embarrassment slide across his face.

"Ah yes. The shrine. Imagine a place where all your biggest

triumphs and blunders were on public display. And then imagine trying to fall asleep there."

The ridiculous irony of it all made me want to laugh, but one more sideways glance at Adrian quelled the urge. The grim set of his mouth made me wonder what other demons he may have had to contend with that night in my attic.

As we walked onto Central Park West, he began to carve out a rough time line of events to bring us to the here and now, vague pinpoints that were safe to be overheard in public. But I could tell by the tone of his voice and the way he linked his arm through mine, steering me as we walked, he was eager to get me somewhere private to speak candidly.

"We were huge, beyond our wildest dreams. Everything we recorded flew off the shelves, every promoter wanted us; the guarantees thrown at us were staggering. Kids rioted in the streets in Europe and South America when we came to town, and Stateside, every red carpet was laid out for us, in any direction of excess we chose. Stretch limos, girls, five-star hotels. When we were young and starting out, we swore if we ever made a name for ourselves, we would never sully it with overdoses or bad publicity stunts or fights about birds or money. It would always be about the music, plain and simple. But all that other stuff comes out of the woodwork and finds you. We had it all: addiction, involuntary manslaughter, infidelity, embezzlement." Each word came off his tongue like a curse, and each breath in like an invocation.

"Everything went to hell around '88, I got kicked out of the band, and then the whole bloody operation dissolved. I spiraled into a depression that lasted a good four years. Losing custody of Natalie was a real wake-up call. I realized I had been an addict as long as I had been a rock star, which was downright terrifying, if not pathetic. That's when I picked myself up by my bootstraps, kicked my habits and, when the situation presented itself, moved here." He bumped my hip with his to move me onto the grass and deftly stepped around shards of a smashed bottle directly in our path. "But the real story can't begin at the end, as much as I would like it to. To truly explain things, I need to tell you about Rick. Simone. And Wren. Names I don't often like to think about."

He stopped in front of a brown and redbrick prewar building with a navy blue awning. The doorman was quick to greet Adrian by name, formally but warmly. The buttons of his double-breasted coat matched the ample brass on the door. We breezed in and were met by the elevator attendant, who was also full of salutations and pleasant remarks as he whisked us up to the fifteenth floor.

"I like how everyone knows you," I said, echoing his words to me from Saturday evening as a tease, but they hung pregnant with their meaning in the hallway as Adrian chuckled and unlocked his door. How well did they know him here? He was a name on the buzzer and certainly a healthy tip in their pockets come Christmastime. Who was he to his neighbors? A daily reader of the *Wall Street Journal*, as evident from his subscription lying on the doormat. But what lay in wait beyond the threshold? That album cover from Kev's room with its ominous song titles, its graphics of fake blood mixed with stage makeup flashed through my mind. We all use various props as we move through the scenes in our lives. I was eager to see beyond the dress rehearsal of Adrian's act.

"It's no San Remo, but it's home," he said modestly, ushering me into a cavernous space of hardwood with huge fixed pane windows that framed the treetops of the park.

"You're kidding me—your living room is bigger than my whole Manhattan co-op was." I spied a set of wrought-iron stairs spiraling up in a far corner. "Is that what I think it is?"

"Um, it's called a staircase, and it has these things called steps that connect this floor to the one above it."

"Smarty-pants. I've just never known anyone who had an

upstairs in Manhattan!" I looked around in delight like a child as he watched me, hesitantly gauging my reactions. Three shiny electric guitars leaned on stands in one corner like ultra-modern objets d'art. "I think you'll need to put a velvet rope around those if Abbey ever visits."

"Like a museum? Bollocks. She can have free run of the place." He tentatively placed his hands on my shoulders from behind. "How about some coffee? I abandoned ours in the park."

I was reluctant to leave the light-drenched room with its boxy gray couches and lush ebony drapes, but I assented. He led me down a hallway, our feet falling softly on a beautiful Persian runner. I wondered if he had decorated the place himself or if he had had help. Noticing a powder room to my left, I excused myself and ducked in. Marissa would be happy to hear my report of no pubes on the toilet seat. With water from the tap, I erased the tearstains from my cheeks. No pubes in sight and L'Occitane verbena hand soap—he's got to either have a maid or a wife.

I found my way to the kitchen, first passing through a dining room large enough to seat twenty and impressive double pocket doors. It was a modern affair of stainless, slate, and teak. My brother would keel over to cook in a room like this. The pictures from the Rainbow kids were displayed prominently on the door of his refrigerator, along with Abbey's get-well drawing. Adrian was grinding coffee beans in a European-looking machine, flipping switches to start the brewing process. He pulled open the fridge, and over his shoulder I spied a shrunken lemon and several ancient-looking takeout containers. "No skim for your coffee," he said apologetically. "Will two percent do?"

"Sure."

He held the door wide in a sweeping gesture. "Ah, and here

we have a prime example of early take-away from the Mesozoic Era."

I laughed. "See? And you said this wasn't a museum!" I picked up one of the paperboard oyster pails delicately by the handle. "And you will note here the detail in early paper construction, indicative of the development of fast food during the Western Han Dynasty," I said as enthusiastically as a museum curator.

"Okay, I'll admit it. I don't do much cooking in here. Manhattan makes it too easy. I had the local deli send up a pack of cigarettes one winter because I couldn't be arsed to walk down and get them myself!"

"My fridge isn't much better," I assured him. "Marissa always tells me food is love. I keep wondering when I am going to be arrested for neglect." A sauerkraut jar of indeterminate age rattled on the door shelf. "Is that left over from the Nazi occupation?"

"Nah, that was from the Luna Rose occupation. My relationship with that fräulein expired long before the jar did."

"Luna Rose . . . sounds like an exotic dancer."

"Lingerie model, actually," Adrian said matter-of-factly, pulling mugs from the cupboard. An apparition of a long-legged, small-pored beauty with a gleaming updo and a push-up bra, all smoky eyes and no cellulite, perched on the kitchen island in a vision before me, pouting shiny swollen lips and tapping a stiletto heel.

"Okay, I'm going to shut up now," I mumbled, feeling the heat flame to my face.

He put a hand on each of my cheeks to cool the burn. "All the beauty in the world can't help an ugly relationship," he said softly. Pulling his fingers down along the edge of my jawbone and lingering on my chin, he tilted it ever so slightly. "This . . . now this is pure beauty."

His lips found mine in that slow and strong way, and I was

lost to the world. The coffee machine began to gurgle and spit rudely and, to my utter surprise, speak in tongues.

"*Ó Senhor Graves! Dê-me licença.*"

Adrian pulled back abruptly, and I saw we were not alone. A girl of about twenty, with a curtain of long dark hair, stood rooted to the spot. She wore sweat pants rolled up to the knees and flip-flops around her pretty pedicured toes. A cross of gold peeked in and out of her tank top as she labored to catch her shocked breath.

"*Desculpe, Ana . . .*" Adrian stuttered as he searched for the right words, and I was amazed to hear them slip from his tongue with relative ease. It sounded similar to Spanish . . . Portuguese, perhaps? "*Esta é a minha amiga, Katrina.* Katrina, meet Ana . . . I completely forgot she was coming today."

She smiled brightly. "*Olá!*"

"*Olá*, Ana." I echoed the only word I was pretty sure I knew and gave a friendly little wave.

"One minute, luv?" Adrian asked me, and beckoned to Ana to follow him. They chattered back and forth amicably out of sight, and then I heard the latch of the door. He whizzed back into the kitchen, grinning apologetically. "So sorry. Housekeeper." He pointed to a bucket of cleaning supplies stashed near the sink that neither of us had noticed.

"I figured she wasn't the German lingerie model." I thought of my deliberation between wife and maid and was relieved to have confirmation it was the latter. "I didn't know you were bilingual, Mr. Graves." I sidled back up to him. "Very sexy."

"That's *Senhor Graves* to you . . . hmmm, yes. I've spent a bit of time in Portugal. Wonderful people." He kissed my earlobe. "Come, I have something to show you."

"We're not going to run into any butlers buttling, are we? Or gardeners gardening?"

"Nope. Jeeves and José have the day off."

We left the kitchen the way he and Ana had and found

ourselves back in the foyer. Adrian proceeded straight ahead to
another set of double pocket doors off the living room. He slid
them open to reveal a library, its four walls lined with floor-to-
ceiling bookshelves in rich mahogany. "I knew you'd like this. I
don't own nearly enough books to do it justice." I gazed around
in wide-eyed wonder, instantly in love with it. There were
brown leather couches beckoning invitingly and small brass
table lamps like the ones found in the Main Reading Room of
the New York Public Library.

"Curses, I forgot the coffee. Be right back."

I made a beeline for the shelf nearest me. Rows of colorful
spines with their thick fonts called out their siren's songs. I ran
my index finger along *The Rolling Stone Illustrated History of
Rock & Roll,* volume two of *The Complete Beatles,* and several
other coffee table–worthy music books until I came to *Godforsaken: The Truth and Turbulent Times of Corroded Corpse* by
Alexander Floyd. Hmm. *A librarian's job is to thoroughly and
objectively evaluate and validate printed matter,* I reasoned,
peeling it off the shelf and cracking the stiff binding.

Under the rigid social structure of pre-Thatcher-era Britain,
Douglas Adrian Graves and Richard David Rottenberg had
only a snowball's chance in hell of ever crossing paths. The
younger of two rough-and-tumble sons of divorced working-
class parents, Digger (as he was christened early on by his
friends "for my early fascination with the sandpit, not due to
the wordplay on my surname") spent his youth in state comprehensive schools and hanging out near the Portsmouth docks.
Riff, by contrast, grew up sheltered in Hampstead, the only
child of wealthy educated Jews. Art historians by profession,
they would take their young son with them regularly to Stock-
holm, Paris, and New York. Private tutors had provided him
with the bulk of his early education. But at thirteen, both lads
found themselves enrolled in a newly established independent

day school located in a stately home known as Ditcham Park. And so the snowball avalanched.

After divorcing the elder Douglas, Polly Graves remarried up; her new husband taught math at the elite public school, akin to a private prep school in the United States. She thought the secluded environs and smaller class size would be good for her teenage sons, who were slipping through the cracks of society under the not-so-watchful eye of their hard-drinking, hard-working motor mechanic father.

Dual sabbaticals for the Professors Rottenberg at NYU's prestigious Institute of Fine Arts landed Riff under the care of his favorite aunt in Petersfield. His parents, keen on providing him with a proper British education, were impressed with nearby Bedales School, but his aunt Barbara, or "Bootsy," as she was affectionately known, convinced them Ditcham Park would be a better fit. The two boys became thick as thieves there within the first week, with Riff turning Digger on to fantasy role-playing games like Dungeons & Dragons, and Digger in turn introducing Riff to a whole new religion: heavy metal. Second only to his wife, Simone, metal music became Riff's lifelong love.

Rick. Simone. And Wren. Names I don't often like to think about. I remembered Adrian's words, my fingers flying to the index and locating Wren in the order. Chapter five. As I flipped through the pages, I caught a glimpse of a wedding picture. *Rick and Simone, 1982.* The groom's haystack of dark hair needed a postal code of its own, and Simone radiated happiness from everywhere, especially her cavernous blue eyes.

Three more pages and . . . Wren. I found myself staring down at a suited slim man with an easy grin and hair too short to be trusted. The mirrored shades, fashionable at the time, didn't improve my opinion of him. Judging from the tone of the paragraph, I had a hunch Alexander Floyd wasn't his biggest fan, either.

Wren Blackmoor had worked his way up the chain. He had paid his dues as a dogsbody, doing grunt work at various major labels and playing assistant to prominent A&R reps of the day at EMI and Columbia. He vaguely alluded to projects he had been involved in with famed producers Mutt Lange and Martin Birch, and would name-drop and pull quotes from management greats like Peter Grant, Don Arden, and Malcolm McLaren with such ease that one was easily convinced he had had intimate dealings with such heavy hitters.

At the time the band met him, over pints and pool at an Earls Court pub, Wren claimed he had sorted the key steps in the formula for commercial success and was ready to strike out on his own and develop a band and a brand, a household name that would keep back catalog profits churning for decades to come. All he needed was a young and talented band with the beginnings of a loyal following and a strong work ethic that wasn't afraid to go for broke.

"Oh, no you don't." Adrian was back. He handed me my coffee and snatched back the book. "Now don't pout. I promise I will give you a no-holds-barred exclusive peek into the sordid lives of the tortured souls who made up Corroded Corpse."

My eyes followed him over the top of my mug as he tossed the book aside and made his way to a bookcase in the far corner. "Check this out."

The bookcase revealed a hidden doorway. I hesitated for a moment, thinking about Leanna's torsos-in-the-freezer comment. Peeking in, I saw numerous gold albums, leaning in their frames against the walls of the small room in piles, none hung up. I thought back to the children's drawings prominently displayed on his fridge. Ironically, his own accomplishments were hidden out of sight. "Welcome to my lair."

One corner of the room was dedicated to a workbench for fixing his guitars. There were guitar strings of various gauges coiled tight like tiny silver and gold snakes. On the wall above the bench was a pegboard completely filled with keys—hotel keys. The old-fashioned kind, complete with heavy plastic ring tags sporting various hotel names. What didn't fit on the pegboard was spilling out of the drawers of a tall black-and-gray metal case. There had to be at least two hundred of them. The case was on casters, with CORRODED CORPSE stenciled in white on all sides. I assumed it was some sort of road case that used to travel with him.

"I see you're admiring my collection. From the good old days, before key cards spoiled all the fun."

"Why did you take them?" I picked up one and inspected it. The thick silver was engraved with the words DO NOT DUPLI-CATE; the turquoise diamond-shaped tag was emblazoned with the word PHOENIX in gilded lettering and the number 22.

"Dunno. Just something to collect, I guess. We played over one hundred cities a year. After a while, I felt like I was leaving a little piece of me behind every day I was on the road. I needed to take something in its place to remember who I was." He touched the key in my hand. "Our debut in San Francisco, during our first US headlining tour. Dodgy neighborhood, but a gem of a motel. All-night jam sessions by the pool with topless ladies in attendance, and no one seemed to mind." He began to finger several others, as if the anecdotes lay in their raised lettering and colorful geometric designs. "We were staying here when we learned our album went platinum. I was here, in Belgium, on Natalie's first birthday. And this is where I was"—he shook a key ring embossed with Japanese Kanji —"when Robyn left me. She rang me up at four in the morning

Tokyo time and informed me she had moved out." His voice
trailed off, lost in thought.

My eyes rested on a key from the Plaza. His eyes must have
followed mine. "Ah yes. You commented on how at ease I had
seemed there. We stayed at the Plaza every time we played New
York. My favorite hotel."

"So I wasn't the first one you brought there." Sordid visions
of groupies, trashed hotel rooms, and nights of excess swam in
my head.

"Actually . . . yes, you were." He began to explain that
despite all of the nubile and willing temptations presented to
him on the road, he had managed to keep most of his wedding
vows to Robyn intact until she dumped him. "Sadly, Robyn had
never fully trusted me on the road. And I had met her at a gig;
imagine that. The moment she got her claws dug in me, she
was suspect of any girl in the audience. I suppose I made
matters worse when I told her I didn't want her or Natalie on
the road with me." He explained the reason behind his decision, painting a picture of walking into his dressing room one
night in Los Angeles to find a beautiful young girl servicing two
of his bandmates simultaneously. "She had invited me in on the
fun, but I politely declined, opting for a pre-gig line of quality
blow with some friends." He had assumed she was some
random groupie until, after the concert, he was introduced to
one of his all-time idols, a well-respected musician "whose
name I don't dare reveal," and the man's fifteen-year-old daughter, said beautiful girl whose lips had been wrapped around the
organs and other sundry parts of Adam and Rick backstage. "I
knew right then I didn't want Natalie exposed to that kind of
life, so I put my foot down. Not so *I* could do whatever I wanted
on the road, as Robyn later accused, but rather to shield them.
That was the beginning of the end, as she didn't like playing
second fiddle to anyone or anything, especially not to the road."

"So being on tour really is like all those rockumentaries

describe. How big of a rock star were you? Like, panties-thrown-at-you-onstage big?" I ventured.

"Panties-thrown-with-phone-numbers-written-in-them big," he admitted. "But I never snorted ants or bit the heads off bats or any of that crazy business."

"Yet you kept company with those who did?" I was incredulous.

"Do you still want to be with me?" he asked, a hopeful yet heartbreaking look on his face. I dropped the keys and took his hands in response. "It used to be women wanted to sleep with me after they learned who I was. Kind of ironic . . . now that you know, I'm worried you *won't* want to be with me."

"I just want to get to know the real you, whoever you are. I want the tap water."

He pulled me close, an impish smile on his face. "Might want to turn those taps on pronto, let 'em run for a bit full pelt. Shake the rust loose."

"Oh, yeah?" I murmured, my lips grazing the ringed lobe of his ear. "I think I know exactly how to turn them on . . ."

ADRIAN'S BEDROOM was a tranquil masculine retreat of brown, gray, and crisp white. I was delighted to find his bed was a futon, although it was actually on a frame and ten times more comfortable than mine. Large square wall panels behind the headboard in a rich dark grain matched the wood on the floor and gave the room an insulated-from-the-world effect. Thick velvet drapes lent themselves to the mood as well. Adrian lit a large candle the color of the darkest chocolate, and the room instantly simmered with the same peppery smell that infused his skin. Fifteen stories below, the hushed and steady thrum of traffic could barely be heard, with just the occasional chirp of a truck horn or police siren breaking through.

He slowly began to undress me. "Nice plaster. Sexy," he whispered, kissing my knee. I had cut myself earlier while shaving in the shower and had hastily slapped on the closest bandage I could find. I saw now it was one of Abbey's Hello Kitty Band-Aids.

I pulled his T-shirt over his head. "I wasn't exactly thinking of how good I looked this morning. More preoccupied with how I was going to bring myself to say good-bye to you . . ." He was kneeling on the bed before me, all those tattoos I had only begun to glimpse in pictures now fully exposed.

A thin, simple dagger ran down the middle of his chest, starting at his clavicle and ending with the point at his navel. "That's a *misericorde*—used by knights to deliver the final 'mercy' blow to the mortally wounded." His chest trembled as I kissed my way, openmouthed, down the blade. "Something I would have needed had you actually brought yourself to say good-bye . . ." The sharp tip was bordered by delicate red writing that looked vaguely Nordic.

"What's this say?"

"Don't you read Old Icelandic?"

"And you do? Come on . . . Portuguese is one thing . . ."

"If I tell you, I'll have to kill you," he deadpanned.

I cocked an eyebrow, and he relented with a smile. "It reads *að blanda blóði saman*—'to mix blood together.'" He took my finger between two of his and traced around the text.

"Rick and I were big fantasy geeks in school, you know . . . Dungeons and Dragons and all that. His father was an art dealer, seventeenth century Swedish art mostly, and so we learned a lot of the Norse mythology from looking at all the paintings. There was a tale of these two blokes who were blood brothers, and we thought that was brilliant so we did the same, with an old flick knife I had, see, right here?" He extended his arm at the elbow to display a faded *X* in the hollow. "We were too young to have tattoos back then, but once we started getting

inked, Rick brought up the blood oath thing. We chose identical daggers, and he pulled the quote from one of his dad's old
books. Kept its meaning a secret, even from the rest of the band.
Stupid now, I suppose."

"Not if it meant something to you at the time."

"Yeah, it did. I wrote a song about it. 'Blood Oath.' Based on
Orvar-Odd's saga."

"Over-what?"

"Orvar-Odd. You've never heard of him? Or the love story of
Hjalmar and Ingeborg?" I shook my head. He pulled the sheets
down and me up to the pillows. We twined our bare limbs
under the crisp linen, and Adrian wove his version of the
Norwegian warrior Orvar-Odd and Swedish warrior Hjalmar as
he gently stroked my hair. "Orvar-Odd was hell-bent on testing
his fighting skills against Hjalmar's, so he sailed to Sweden with
five ships and met Hjalmar, who had fifteen ships. Hjalmar
wouldn't accept such an uneven balance of strength and sent
away ten of his own ships so the forces would be even. Which
was so like Rick and me. His family was well-off and had so
much, and I didn't have much of anything, but we were always
equal, you know? We'd take the piss out of each other, but we
were best mates. Anyway, the two warriors fought for days with
a lot of blood-letting, drama, poetry, blah blah blah. But it was a
draw. When they finally realized they were equals, they became
blood brothers. Hjalmar confided in Orvar-Odd about this
beautiful princess who he was in love with, named Ingeborg.
Orvar wanted to help them elope, but Hjalmar dragged his
heels until these twelve crazy berserkers came along and one of
them wanted to marry her. Typical man, yeah? The king let his
daughter choose, so of course she chose her true love, Hjalmar,
and the berserkers went . . . well, berserk. A big duel ensued,
with lots of gore and yuck, and at the end, all the bad guys were
dead, but sadly so was Hjalmar. So Orvar-Odd took his blood
brother's body back to Ingeborg, who of course dropped dead

at the news. All he had to do was give her Hjalmar's ring"—
Adrian slipped off his Shakespeare ring and placed it on the
index finger of my right hand resting on his chest—"and she
knew. And that was it."

"Wow. That's some story. I can see how it could inspire
some good songwriting. Death and romance." I fell silent as I
contemplated how the subject matter was something I was
sadly versed in. The metal was surprisingly hot against my skin.
My finger felt heavy as I used it to trace a thorny tattooed vine
snaking around the blade on Adrian's chest and trailing to a
rose that wound around his rib cage. It blossomed at the
approximate spot of his heart, and *Natalie* was etched into the
tight center of the petals in a spiral pattern. "It's beautiful," I
whispered, taking it all in. He had a smattering of realistic-
looking bullet holes across his breastbone, narrowly missing
the rose. They appeared three-dimensional. Beauty, darkness,
danger, pain. "You are beautiful . . ."

"Yeah, right." He gestured to the demon on his other breast.
"You can tell Abbey I'm the original boogeyman." The half-
bone, half-flesh corpse had pins sticking out of his head,
voodoo doll–style. The skull was dusted greenish blue as if it
had been pulled from a swamp somewhere, and the flesh was
yellow, oozing red. Its teeth were of varying lengths and in
different states of decay. "So can you see why it's not easy to
woo the ladies toting around that one?" His tone was sardonic,
his expression sheepish.

"Does he have a name?"

"Corpse Guy? Nah. He appeared on our first album, but
then we did away with him and started using this." He pointed
to the Corroded Corpse logo above his appendix, which
consisted of two *C*s hooked to each other and linked vertically.
Their color, shading, and texture suggested they were made of
bone or claw, pitted and ridged, with a bit of gristle for
emphasis hanging from where they were seemingly ripped

from whatever body they belonged to. "I regret him some-what . . . especially when fans would come up to me and proudly display their own Corpse Guy tattoo in honor of their love for the band. It's just such a personal, permanent statement."

"Well, some of those fans probably lived and breathed your music."

"True . . . even after I stopped." He rolled over, stretching and pushing his hair off the back of his neck so that I could inspect more of his body artwork.

On his back was a large, lone tattoo, and judging by the color and crispness, it was relatively younger compared to those on his chest. An intricate compass rose inked in black, robin's egg blue, and scarlet spanned across his shoulder blades. "Blake's Four Zoas," I breathed, tracing the slanted script. Each prominent point identified one of the directions in Blake's cosmology, rather than the traditional four cardinal directions.

"I was going through a major William Blake phase last year." He shivered as my lips touched down on his cervical spine and I paraphrased from memory.

"Eternity had *Urthona*, the Imagination, in the north. *Urizen*, or Reason, was its opposite in the south." I ran my index finger gently down to the small of his back. "*Tharmas*—the senses—lies west, and *Luvah*, Passion, in the east, right?"

"Correct. Blake felt the Zoas resided within each human being, but when the Zoas fell from Eternity into Experience, they each split into two, a male and female counterpart, and they were no longer in harmony."

"So what does that say about us, male and female?" I wanted to know.

"Good question, luv." He rolled over and smiled at me. "All I know is you and I are currently"—he kissed my left breast—"together in the eastern quadrant." His warm and calloused hands played lightly across my shoulders, fingertips exploring my flesh. I reveled in it, enjoying the way he looked at my body, as if quenching his thirst after many desert miles. "And in a proper bed," he reminded me, his eyes celestial in the dim candlelight.

20

PURGE

"So where are those grapes and that poetry you promised me?" I chided, barely a breath left in me. We loosely held each other, waiting for our hearts to resume their normal rhythm.

He delicately placed hands on both sides of my jawbone and kissed me, as deep and soul-searching in his afterplay as he was in his foreplay. "Consider that the *amuse-bouche, mon amour*," he breathed.

I ran my fingers past his dewy temples into his hair and gently pulled him close again. "Who am I kidding? I can get by on this sustenance just fine," I whispered.

"But since you brought poetry up . . . this is what I've been pondering over lately." He reached across me and pulled a red leather-bound book from the nightstand, along with a pair of reading glasses. I settled into the crook of his arm as he arranged the glasses on his nose with his free hand and pushed his thumb in between the pages bookmarked with an old MetroCard.

What is the price of Experience? Do men buy it for a song?

Or wisdom for a dance in the street? No, it is bought
    with the price
Of all that a man hath, his house, his wife, his
    children.
Wisdom is sold in the desolate market where none
    come to buy,
And in the wither'd field where the farmer plows for
    bread in vain.

Adrian stopped reading. He removed the glasses with a sigh and turned to face me. He lowered his head in a way that was slightly boyish, a chunk of hair falling over one eye. I gently kissed his forehead. "Don't be sad."

"Ach, Kat. I've been alone with my memories so long. The thought of bringing them to the surface verbally is . . . overwhelming."

I understood completely; it was as if he had plucked those two sentences from my brain, where they had been stewing for years now.

"I know. It's one thing to ruminate, but another to enunciate." My voice trembled. Where that tightly knit gem of wisdom had come from was beyond me.

Adrian gazed at me for a long moment, his eyes smooth as worn sea glass against his weathered face. "Cripes, I hope you don't think me a selfish prat. Here I've been pissing and moaning about the life I've lived, when—"

I put my finger to his lips, shaking my head.

"God, no. I'm grateful, actually. In time . . . thank you for being patient."

"No one has ever used that word to describe me. From you, I'm learning patience . . . and fortitude." He took a deep breath. "That being said . . ."

We spent the next two hours holding each other, Adrian's fingers kneading his history across my skin. My vertebrae became pinpoints on the time line he lingered upon, as I kissed my questions along his shoulders and neck.

"We were nobodies going nowhere fast. Until Wren found us. When we signed with him, he immediately put us on the road. I remember the tour exactly: London, Kingsbury, Burton-on-Trent, Warrington, Blackpool, Liverpool, Birkenhead, Retford, London, Swindon, Bristol, and back to London for Christmas." His ticked off each city across my body as if it were a map of the UK, his thumb traveling from London at my pubic bone, up to my navel, circling my entire right breast and across to my left before coming back to my pelvic area, then over to linger on my right hip, and returning back to London with a smile.

"Fun trip?" I asked wickedly.

"The best." There was a devilish gleam in his eye. "The camaraderie was brilliant. Wren showed us he wasn't afraid to get his hands dirty. He was our security at the back door as well as the number-crunching maniac who refused to back down when some of those promoters tried to pull fast ones. Like the fifth member of the band by the time we arrived home. Little did we know, he would end up on the other side as soon as the stakes were high enough."

Each player in turn—from the musicians themselves to the girlfriends, wives, manager, and crew—had a unique role in constructing the beast that was to become one of the most successful new wave of British heavy metal bands. "We were monstrous, unstoppable. But the fame . . . fame was like the mob. It was relentless, tireless. Attacking our personal lives. Drugs, money, excess—those were the pitchforks and torches the mob pursued us with. The monster had to burn and die."

My eyes traveled to his abdomen.

"Ironically, that happened when professionals were in charge of our pyro. I got too close to the spot on stage where a six-foot flame was programmed to ignite. I realized my error just before it went off and moved away, but not before suffering second-degree burns. My guitar actually shielded most of the blast, and the leather pants helped as well."

The white sheet was a sharp contrast next to the sunburst of his scar. I tentatively touched the raised purple ridge close to his navel. "It doesn't scare me," I said quietly.

He fingered it lightly as well, and then ran his hand over mine. "I probably would have healed better had we not been in the middle of a world tour."

"No worker's comp for you?" I joked, lifting both of our hands together and gently kissing his.

"Nope, no rest for the wicked. Skin grafts, compression garments, and a whole lot of morphine got me through that first month. Which is a chapter far from where we are now." We slipped deeper under the sheet, Adrian winding and unwinding my curls as he progressed and digressed.

Wren vowed if they stuck with him, their albums would soon be on turntables in the bedrooms of every teenager on earth. "How do you say no to that?" He leaned over to blow out the candle, which had burned down to a thick dark pool. "You don't. You say 'yes please' and 'thank you, sir' and you sign your name on the dotted line. You make a deal with the devil."

My eyes followed his gaze, and we both stared at the candle, its orange-hot pinprick pulsating brighter as it gasped for air before finally succumbing.

"I think that's enough purging for one day." Adrian leaned back against me and closed his eyes, inhaling deeply. "Like a purification . . . watch the smoke." A black ribbon sifted its way up to the ceiling from the extinguished wick.

I laid my cheek on the top of his head, my hands resting on his rib cage. "Hey, you never explained these." If I spanned my hand wide enough, I could cover each tattooed bullet hole with a finger, as if I had the ability to staunch the old wounds.

"Bloody hell, I've been prattling for hours now and I haven't even reached these parts of my tale. They tell the story better than I can." He took my finger between his thumb and pointer, guiding me across them. "This one here is for Wren; for what he eventually did to the band. The next one is when Robyn left. This one, well—I inflicted myself, losing custody of Natalie. This"—he lingered on the bloodiest one—"was Adam. He killed our roadie, Cass."

I gasped, my fingers instinctively jumping from his chest to my mouth.

"The minute Rick mentioned Adam and a car, I knew the news couldn't be good. Most days on tour he was over the drink-drive limit simply upon waking. Cass was just trying to get home to Essex for Chrimbo," he commented softly.

"How horrible."

"How did Wren put it? Oh—'At least it wasn't one of the band.' Like Cass was somehow less of a loss because he wasn't lining this guy's pockets! I was devastated. I had practically grown up with Cass . . . salt of the earth, he was." He breathed deeply. "That's when I really began to look at Wren in a different light. Suddenly, everything he said could be taken more than one way. I didn't like his colleagues, starting with the prat he hired to handle our money. I distrusted him, but felt powerless. I was nursing the loss of Cass, the breakup of my marriage, and the disillusionment I felt toward my mentor and didn't know where to turn."

"What about Rick?"

He pointed to the largest and final bullet hole. "This. Was Rick."

I didn't know what to say. His recollections had caught me up in their spellbinding details, and yet I felt as if I had been woken prematurely from a dream, or a nightmare. The best and the worst had yet to come, I surmised. He had painted such a vivid picture of his humble beginnings, but there were still years to go to get to the man I saw before me now.

"Want to hear a secret?"

I leaned closer, but he shook his head. "No, really *hear* a secret?" I nodded. "Wait here."

He yanked on his jeans and disappeared down the hall. I began to wonder how many rooms he had upstairs and how they were filled. More guitars and memories . . . I slipped on his Norton T-shirt and sat up to wait. Adrian returned, guitar in hand. It was his signature Ibanez, recognizable from so many of those posters in my attic. An amp I hadn't noticed doubling as a nightstand began to buzz warmly as he united guitar and power cord. He began to shred a complicated melody, fingers nimbly attacking the frets, and I could instantly see this was what he really loved, he was so alive.

His gaze was concentrated on his playing while mine was zeroed in on his face. The pure rapture was apparent, although there were glimmers of what could only be described as an exorcism. He was simultaneously reaching for something yet trying to rid himself of it at the same time as he ran through a smooth and fast legato. It was as heavy as any Corroded Corpse material I had heard in the past, yet fresh and timeless. I had a feeling it was the first time he had actually played it for ears other than his own.

His eyes were on me now, and he was grinning as his fingers changed their direction and their mind, working up a heavy groove that tingled down my spine.

"You should do something with this." It was the only thing I could think to say as he stood in front of me, his torso slick and heaving with the labor. My own heart was thumping its muted applause.

He unharnessed himself and joined me on the bed once again. "The only person I can see myself playing this with is Rick, and we aren't exactly on speaking terms anymore." He ran a hand up my bare leg. "It's going on sixteen years. I have no idea where he is." His phone began to ping next to our heads; I had asked him to set the alarm so I could get back home before school dismissed. "Ah, the bell tolls," he murmured apologetically as I groaned.

"Already?"

"No. I set it a half hour early. I like long good-byes," he breathed, crossing his legs over mine.

21

REALITY BITES

As I NAVIGATED the Mini up through the borough toward home, I couldn't shake the essence of my lover's mesmerizing story-telling. The overcast afternoon reinforced the mood, painting the concrete landscape even grayer than usual. I felt like I had been dropped into eighties London; my native city had never looked so foreign.

But with each underpass and highway ramp, modern-day reality began to creep in. I checked my messages while in standstill traffic on the bridge. Two texts from Marissa, two hours apart: *WE MISS U* and *LEAVING S'BUCKS, C U @ BALLET?* I had forgotten we had signed the girls up at the dance studio across town. I had no doubt Brina would take to the lessons without a fuss, but wondered if Abbey would make it through this first class without pirouetting to her own tune, right out the door. She often followed a sound track that resided in her head and had a hard time with step-by-step instructions.

My thoughts drifted back to Adrian as the road opened ahead of me, and my stomach grumbled a reminder that we had not consumed a single thing, other than each other. The coffee had grown cold, food hadn't been a thought, and Adrian didn't touch a cigarette in those three-plus hours he had been in my company. I couldn't remember the last time I had been able to shut out the world so exclusively with another individual.

But I could remember the first time.

If I had to pick a defining moment in my courtship with Pete, the moment in time when I knew he was "the one," I would have to rewind back to that first year. I can't remember all the details of our date; I recall the coal oven pizza we shared at Arturo's and escaping into the air-conditioning of the Angelika for a few hours. I remember sharing a lot of laughter, a lot of stories. Typical early date stuff. The excitement and anxiety of asking him in for the first time. Having him examine my CD collection, comment on my book collection, kiss me in front of the wall of grungy appliances that passed for a kitchen in that dimly lit, ground-floor sublet. Pulling him across the threshold into my closet of a bedroom. I rarely closed its door because it was far too claustrophobic. But that night, Pete and I shut ourselves in and closed off the world.

We lay talking and touching into the small hours, when a presence right outside froze us both. Someone was just inches from the bars covering the window, and therefore only inches from us. We could hear him muttering and breathing, rummaging through the bins of garbage pushed up against the brick wall.

I had been a city girl going on five years, but it had been a first for me. Pete could tell I was freaked out. "Shhh, he's just looking for cans and bottles," I remember him whispering, holding me tight. "He'll go away in a minute."

People use that descriptor, "the one." As in, "How did you know he was the one?" I had never been the kind of girl to read the happily-ever-after stories or practice bridal walks with a pillowcase on my head. Love at first sight had always sounded impractical, and soul mates didn't seem possible. But I remember being in Pete's arms that night, the thrill and the fear of it all, and I just knew.

I thought again of the rainy morning dream, of being in Pete's arms again. Having him remind me "there are all different kinds of love" and speak through my subconscious the unspeakable.

ALTHOUGH ADRIAN HADN'T COME out and asked me directly, I had promised him two things that afternoon: I wouldn't reveal his identity to my friends—or God forbid, my brother—just yet, and I would let him finish telling me about his past without the aid of Alexander Floyd or what he called "unofficial, unauthorized, wildly inaccurate accounts published purely for monetary or shock value." It was hard to stay composed, but I managed some level of normalcy as Marissa and I settled onto a bench outside to wait out the girls' first dance class.

"I can't believe the ballet teacher is going to go through all five positions on the first day." I accepted the smoothie she handed me and peeked over my shoulder into the dance school's window.

"Speaking of *positions* . . . what's it really like, sleeping with the kiddy musician? I'm trying to imagine him talking dirty, and all I'm coming up with is 'do me, my little sugared gumdrop of love!'"

"Don't be such a goofball, Mariss." I bit my straw. "I'm done giving you gory details. The sex is great. I would go as far as to say mind-blowing."

"Yet he still won't let you—"

"I'm not so worried about that."

"Hey, hon!" A distinct Baltimore accent curled around us from across the plaza parking lot. The mother of Grant's son was lugging karate gear toward us. "Was that you I saw the other day, driving on your donut?"

"What's her name again?" Marissa asked under her breath, lips pasted into a ventriloquist dummy's smile.

"Not a friggin' clue." I smiled right along with her, shaking my head.

"That's what my daddy calls it, driving on your spare. Your donut!"

"*Oh, Marone.*" Marissa had low tolerance for anyone south of the Verrazano-Narrows Bridge, and the woman's fronting back vowels and bouncy boobs probably didn't help matters any.

"You could have Jake's dad take a look at it, he's real good at fixing flats." She beamed at her son who, even dressed in his karate whites, couldn't have looked less angelic. He was towheaded and snarky like his father, yet had his mother's wide dark eyes, reminiscent of a fruit bat. "For real, that's how we met. Jacked up my car in the driving snow and fixed *my* flat tire better than any cob job I could do!"

We knew the town gossip: Grant had hooked up with this girl as she passed through town, increasing the population of Lauder Lake by two. But hearing the origins from the source was particularly interesting, considering the recent attack on my Mini.

"Thanks . . . it's all good," I assured her, and locked my lips to my straw so I wouldn't have to converse with her further.

"Bye now, hon!" They continued on their way to the neighboring karate center.

"Jacked her up, then knocked her up with the devil's spawn," Marissa murmured, her eyes mascara-ringed saucers. "Talk about a cob job!"

"Rosemary!" I remembered triumphantly.

"Huh?"

"Her name. Like the horror movie, *Rosemary's Baby*. You know, devil's spawn?" I sputtered a brief laugh. "But seriously." The similarity of the dire tire situation was a little too coincidental. Adrian and I had speculated as to whom, but now pieces were falling together as to why. Originally I had suspected malice on my ex-boyfriend's part. I now wondered if Grant, upon seeing my car in Basilica's lot that night, had assumed I was dining out with just Abbey as usual and thought he'd try the old knight-in-shining-armor bit with me. Especially with his friends in town to make him look good. Thinking back to the way he had strutted into the restaurant, and how utterly stunned he was at the sight of Adrian . . . it made sense. "Lauder Lake has its very own serial tire slasher."

"Serial town idiot, more like it."

I laughed, twirling Adrian's ring. My new finger trinket didn't go unnoticed by my best friend.

"You know I'm happy for you, Tree. I was only teasing before. Although I am bummed we lost our coffee day." Marissa attempted to fold her napkin into a hat, or a swan, and pouted.

"I've missed two Wednesdays . . . don't write me off that quickly! I'll be back."

"Good, because someone needs to be the buffer between Debbie Downer and Perky Patty, and you know Liz and I aren't always so good with the tact."

"Leanna's really losing it, huh?"

"I think I would, too, if my kid gave me such grief and my husband had his head up his ass. And Karen . . . you know I really like her, Tree, but sometimes . . ." She trailed off, looking at her watch. It was time to head inside and collect the girls.

"I know." I held the door for her. "Karen's in la-la land sometimes. She doesn't realize her advice kinda makes things worse."

"Bingo."

"Bingo? Rhymes with *Ringo*!" Abbey slid toward us in her leotard, with Brina skidding right behind her. "We're hungry, can we get pizza?"

22

HITS AND MRS.

AFTER PUTTING Abbey to bed that evening, my laptop greeted me like an old friend. I wouldn't break my promise to Adrian, but my desire to at least "see" what was out there led me to run his name and the band's through a search engine or two.

There were 1,976,000 hits for *Corroded Corpse*. Not too shabby for a band that hadn't existed for twenty years. And 1,050,000 on *Digger Graves* alone! I ignored the urge to read the fan blogs, the speculation, or the news articles about him. Instead, I searched for images and 17,300 hits popped up. How does one get used to having that many pictures floating around for the entire world to peruse? I tapped his ring to my lips as my eyes swam over page after page. Most of the images were posed band pictures, press photos, album cover shots. What fascinated me were the rare candid ones. None looked to be more recent than fifteen years ago. Digger concentrating in the studio, Digger gaping wide-mouthed onstage. A black-and-white shot of Digger with a baby, presumably Natalie, being held poolside in his tattooed arms. His face was barely recognizable, much rounder with youth and bloated with the admitted excess consumption of ale.

There was a thumbnail picture of him with a tall skinny blonde. Against my better judgment, I clicked on it to get the bigger picture and saw the caption. *Corroded Corpse's Digger Graves with wife, Robyn, BRIT Awards, Grosvenor House Hotel.* Still married in cyberspace, frozen in time. My heart felt like it had been regurgitated and stuck in my throat. He looked stuffy yet handsome in a tux; she looked a bit too bare and underfed in a strapless number. As Marissa would say, like a skeleton with a mop on her head. Blech. The computer is not my friend.

If only we could clear the cache of our minds as quickly and easily as the computer's. In a click and a blink, I wiped clear the history, deleted temp files, and got rid of all cookies. The FBI might find evidence of my peek at Adrian's past life, should they have reason to seize my computer, but no one else would be the wiser.

Wandering into the kitchen, I retrieved the album once more. After contemplating putting it on the ancient turntable, I once again fell back on technology. Within five minutes, I had purchased the album from iTunes and downloaded the entire thing onto my iPod. Amazing. I carried Digger and the gang downstairs to the treadmill. Music has always had the ability to transport and spur me on while running; but with the first telltale lick of Adrian's soloing, this music ripped right through me.

What I remembered as being a cacophonous sound track to sibling strife during my teen years had been replaced by a complex, almost orgasmic tapestry. Although Rick sang the leads with all the vigor and vibrato one would expect from an eighties metal singer, I could hear Adrian's deeper and rougher rasp, strong and understated, behind the choruses. The crunch of his power chords injected themselves into my very marrow. The music poured over me. I was in deep.

23

CHEMISTRY AND CHAOS

Adrian and I fell into a wonderful pattern, spending as many days together as the week would allow us. He would roll sleepily off the train to spend hours with me. Together we would collect Abbey after school and take her on adventures, some as close as Bear Mountain or the lake, others as far as Chinatown or Coney Island. Adrian started teaching Abbey scales on the piano, and they continued working on their ode to Matt the Bat. Not only was Matt "elastic and fantastic," but he would now "go spastic if you called him plastic." Some evenings, Adrian would call just to talk to Abbey and discuss a new lyric. Abbey reveled in the calls, grinning into the receiver. "Sure, Adrian, bats can wear party hats."

I learned to love rather than dread the anticipation of waiting at the train station, watching as all of the harried businessmen jumped onto their Manhattan-bound trains. Smiling because I knew my man was on the reverse commute up to me in ripped jeans and a T-shirt with no plan for the day but to be utterly happy spending it together.

Some days, I would slip into the city for the luxury of lying in his arms for hours. He continued to slowly unfurl his past, but mostly we marveled at our present, a gift to each other in the here and now.

"All that time spent together and he still doesn't keep a toothbrush at your house?" Marissa wanted to know. "I can't believe he doesn't want to spend the night."

"It's not a matter of not wanting to," I explained. Despite the number of hours Adrian and I logged lounging in each other's beds, we always made sure to vacate before bedtime. We had Abbey to think about, after all. Her comfort level was paramount and a good excuse for us to pace ourselves in terms of "too much, too soon."

Abbey delighted in every Adrian encounter as if he were a new episode of *Maxwell MacGillikitty*. In fact, she had found in him a willing viewing companion. One afternoon I found both of them—Abbey sprawled on the floor, Adrian sitting low and grasshopper-legged on the edge of my futon—riveted to the TV. "This show isn't half-bad, Kat. Amazing how he manages to solve *every* muddle, the cheeky little bugger."

One day, he emerged from the station with a slip of paper in his hand. "Can you take me to this address?" It turned out to be the CD manufacturing plant up in Nyack where the rest of *Songs for Natalie* were stored. "They aren't doing any good sitting there." He stacked the remaining boxes in the Smurf. "I'll think of a use for them."

Sometimes, he would bring bags brimming with food from Myers of Keswick or Dean & DeLuca. With his reading glasses perched on his nose and my mom's pin-striped apron slung around his tattooed torso, he looked positively adorable. Like the badass metal version of the Frugal Gourmet. He'd spend hours slowly cooking, refusing help, and carefully consulting cookbooks. The end results were traditional English meals that even Abbey took to, like roast chicken with bread sauce and sage and onion stuffing, shepherd's pie, and what Adrian called "proper fish and chips," with mushy peas, baked beans, and

gherkins. If Abbey appeared leery or unwilling to try something, the simple assurance that "Maxwell MacGillikitty eats
this stuff all the time" would quickly change her mind. She
especially loved the foods with funny names, such as bubble
and squeak. Like a sponge, she was soaking up many of Adrian's English expressions, throwing "crikey!" and "huzzah!" into
conversations whenever possible.

Often, Adrian would wander up to Kev's room and silently
study the shrine. He approached it with a mixture of curiosity
and caution, not unlike a deep-sea diver inspecting a ship-
wreck. I gave him his space, but some days he would invite me
along. One artifact after another would turn over in his hands,
and he would look at them in wonder, as if he were thinking, *I
was once a part of this?* And, after carefully setting them back
down in their dust-marked place, *And I survived.*

He emerged from the attic after one of his excavations
carrying an album in each hand. "Erm, Kat, how much homeowner's insurance do you have, luv?"

I had been catching up on e-mail and twisted away from my
laptop to face him. "Why? Are they really worth that much?"

"He's got an Italian twelve-inch promo of *Blood Oath*. And
this is *Spoils of War* on green vinyl. I think only twenty-five were
pressed. Not that I really pay too much attention to
collectibles."

Since I was on the computer already, I ran the items
through eBay. "Holy crap."

He leaned over my shoulder. "Ridiculous what some people
find value in, no?"

One morning, he arrived lugging a heavy odd-shaped box
off the train.

"Flowers for me? You shouldn't have!"

"This," he said, "is better than flowers. Came all the way
from the UK." It was a car bike mount. "Most I found wouldn't
fit your model year. But this one"—he went to work with the

spanner from my trunk right there in the station lot—"holds two bikes."

"Perfect for you and Abbey. Bear Mountain awaits."

"There's a bike down in your basement, you know. A Rock-hopper, and it's a bloody good one."

"Oh, Kev's old bike. He saved up all of his paper route money to buy it, and then had a growth spurt."

"Perfect size for you. It just needs some air in the tires," he said.

"I don't know . . ."

"When was the last time you rode?"

"Does spinning class count?"

"Tosh! You might as well do karaoke and air guitar. Come on. You've got to get out and feel the wind in your hair. I'd love to take you to one of my favorite parks. Fort Tryon."

"I've never been there."

"You call yourself a New Yorker! For shame, Kat!"

I laughed. "I never ventured above 125th Street when I lived in Manhattan."

"Well, you should." He smiled.

The next day he showed up with his own bike and a dozen roses. He was very hard to resist.

MORE OFTEN THAN NOT, music accompanied Adrian on his trips upstate. CDs were brought by the handful to play in the car, in the house, at the beach. He mixed playlists for Abbey, ranging from the Stray Cats to Etta James to Peter Gabriel, the Ramones to Jethro Tull to 10,000 Maniacs. He delighted her by including some of his own renditions, throwing in her name and funny rhymes on the fly about loving LEGOs and blueberries. If I was a walking *Bartlett's Familiar Quotations*, Adrian was *Baker's Biographical Dictionary of Musicians* personified. He knew scads of fascinating information on every genre of music.

There was an ever-changing sound track to our lives those weeks; the only time we didn't listen to music was when we made love—frequently, intensely, and with every nerve alive focused on each other. Silence punctuated only by our sighs, truncated one word at a time, until we found our voices once more. Gentle pillow talk often ensued.

It was fairly easy for Adrian to talk about rock and roll and his role in its history; *Metastasis* had quickly gone gold in America and platinum in the UK, resulting in ample material that he could pull from. However, discussing the two remaining parts of the trifecta—sex and drugs—often left him searching for the right words in order to properly press home his experiences.

We were at the lake. It was a mild Monday morning, and we had wandered down from the house with a blanket and breakfast. Adrian had stopped by the Naked Bagel en route to Grand Central and had brought some of Liz's finest with him. Breakfast was soon abandoned for other delicious pursuits, taking advantage of the secluded haven of soft sand where the old boathouse had once stood. Large thick pines had encroached upon the empty space, allowing us to be sealed off from all sides save a small slice of the beachfront. Once again, I attempted to slowly and seductively make my way down a certain path of pleasuring, and once again, he managed to detour me.

Adrian's tongue still tasted of Irish butter, the decadent and smooth Kerrygold that Liz always used in the shop, as he kissed me into bliss. We fell into talking afterward, as the breeze swept across our hot skin and we allowed our pulse rates to calm. Unprompted and as eloquently as the situation would allow, he began to describe the heartbreaking spectacle of the endless parade of nameless women, on their knees in a lewd receiving line, all eager to suck down the seed of stardom.

"No doubt you've wondered why I won't let you . . . I just . . . I want to have something different with you." He watched my fingers as they trailed the length of his thigh, and shuddered happily. "I *do* have something different with you. Maybe, in time . . . I can learn to enjoy it again. It isn't a sexy thing to me."

Adrian's opinion of groupies was certainly not the norm among his bandmates. "Sam fell in love with every girl he touched, poor sod. It earned him nothing but headaches, lawsuits, and many cases of the clap. Adam, he was the star-fucker of the group. Sure, he would let any anonymous bird backstage get him off, but when it came to a shag partner for any lengthy period of time, she'd have to have at least equal, if not more, star power. Page Three girls in Britain, *Baywatch* girls in the States, swimsuit models in Spain."

"What about Rick?" I knew at this point, Rick and Simone had had not only two-year-old Paul, but twins on the way as well.

"Rick . . . oh, Rick relished the depraved excess of it all. Multitudes of girls with their tongues in his every orifice simul-taneously was his way of unwinding after a show. In his mind, he had figured out how to, as he so eloquently put it, 'separate sex from love.' A knob jerk was just a job perk. What he had with Simone was *love*. Yet he hadn't the decency to fill Simone in on his epiphany." This disgusted Adrian then, and still upset him to talk about it now. "Simone and I had an amazing rela-tionship. I had never bonded with a woman on such a platonic level. If he was my blood brother and she his soul mate, well, that made her my soul sister. I loved her . . . and that scared the hell out of Rick. Mind you, it was never on a sexual level. But rather, a level Rick either couldn't bring himself to or wasn't able to go to. It drove a real wedge between us."

The wedge resulted in their inability to collaborate on

music, for the first time in their decade-long friendship. Drugs
were also beginning to cause a rift between the two bandlead-
ers, Adrian explained. While Rick would partake in the occasional joint, he wasn't interested in any other chemical
enhancer. The others, Adrian included, were delving into bags
of black beauties by the handful to keep up with the rigors of
the road. He had been well on his way to becoming a speed
freak until his accident in 1985, when he was introduced to an
intravenous opioid for burn pain management in the hospital
—morphine. His brain and his body did a 360-degree turn.
"The euphoria was full-body and like nothing I had ever experienced before. I craved it long after my burns had healed." He
rolled into the comfort of my arms, pulling with him a section
of sandy blanket over his back to cocoon us. Pressing his
scarred torso against me, he sighed.

My fingers fell onto the hypodermic needle etched between
two ribs, protruding from Corpse Guy's head. A nuclear neon
green substance filled the chamber, with a few cartoonlike
droplets spurting nearby. "What ... I can't imagine ... what was
it like?"

A silence ensued, one so long I almost thought he hadn't
heard the question.

"It's . . . complex to explain." He cleared his throat. "A
powerful dance."

Back on the road, there was no pure morphine to be had,
and no one he trusted enough to inject him with anything
else. "I quickly discovered convenient substitutes: oxycodone,
hydrocodone. Great little helpers . . . for a time." Snorting
heroin became the next viable option, as he quickly developed a tolerance to the oral painkillers. That was easy on the
East Coast, where the drug was in powder form. "But once we
hit California, Portland, Seattle . . . it was like tar. Brown
lumps you had to cook down and soak up with a cotton ball.
Junkie science," Adrian explained. Shooting was a massive,

immediate rush. Any pain—mental, physical—was chased away. "It brought on something I hadn't experienced in ages: comfort."

"Comfort?" A mixture of hurt and sadness stirred in me. I kissed along his forearm. I wanted to be his drug, his only indulgence.

"Getting ready for the high," he explained, his finger absently circling in the hollow above my collarbone, "was as warming as the high. You've your spoon and your lighter. You have your bundle, your razor blades for cutting it. Your needle is bleached out and it's clean." The details rolled off his tongue, but he paused between each, as though relishing the memories one by one. "The ritual itself is relaxing; the high is imminent." His lips brushed my temple, dry and hot. "Getting ready was the opening act."

Wren, desperate to keep his puppets happy and under his thumb, ensnared each of them deeper according to their individual weaknesses. For Rick, it was the constant assurance that he was the glue holding the band together, as well as the star power. For Sam, Wren made sure there was ample snatch to be had, and for Adam, a constant party. Adam's drinking had become the stuff of legend, and the antics that ensued kept the publicity wagon running. And for Adrian...

"Wren provided me with a 'personal assistant.' Basically, someone to teach me how to shoot up and not die." Heroin was now not just the drug of choice, it was the drug of necessity. "I needed it to rapidly cross that brain-blood barrier in order to function and perform, so injecting it was the only way."

"I don't understand. Why would Wren encourage . . . no, sabotage the band?"

Adrian pulled on his jeans and sat up to light a cigarette. "The best way to conquer is to divide," he answered quietly. "What little soul was left in us, he began to steal one by one."

He took a deep drag, and we both watched his exhale of

smoke. It danced and dissipated toward the water, as if it were
the very essence of the souls he spoke of.

Lyrics from "Habit"—a song he had written for the *Hell
Hath No Fury* album—rolled into my memory:

home
creates an addiction
opens a vein
to boredom
the infinite evil
get it
before
it gets
you
let me explode
let me corrode . . .

"I swore it would only be a tour thing." He slowly shook his
head. "Off the road, I attempted—fruitlessly—to fall into the
swing of home life, the roles expected of me as husband . . . as
father. I forgot what it was like to live off the road. I was at a loss
without the load-ins, the sound checks, the bus callbacks. I had
a purpose when I was taking the stage, playing the encores. At
home, I felt useless . . . bored. Robyn and Natalie had all these
routines; the schedules they conformed to were foreign to me.
Man, how I envied and resented them! I was miserable."

"How did Robyn react to . . . your usage?"

"The Jekyll and Hyde act got old fast. She was a road widow
seven months out of the year, so when I came home, she
expected action and glamour and all the perks. Instead, I was
turning into a depressed and cranky mess who only left the
house to score. I won't lie, my habits soured the marriage and
most likely led her to seek companionship outside of it."

As the band embarked on its most ambitious tour to date,
163 shows in seventeen countries that would last an entire year,
he found himself single and seeking. "Seeking companionship,

as I no longer had a wife or a best friend anymore. Rick was increasingly cut off from the rest of us, spending more and more time with Wren and becoming obsessed with the organizational and commercial aspects rather than the creative process it took to get there. As for female companionship . . . I craved drugs far more than I craved sex. When I did, I chose to turn to the paid professionals, escorts with an elite clientele who flawlessly fabricated whatever I wanted." He insisted the names *Digger* and *Corroded Corpse* or the label of rock star never enter those bedrooms. "Anonymity was an escape for me. While girls were screaming 'I love you!' and 'I want you, Digger!' from the crowds, I was paying hand over fist for girls who had no interest in knowing me. Pathetic, no?"

"No. It's understandable, given the situation."

"You're not disgusted by that?"

"Adrian. No." I paused. "A little . . . intimidated, maybe." I thought back to our discussion on the Plaza's golden bed. He had been tested . . . and I trusted him. Still. It was quite a history to look past.

"Please don't be."

"Pleasured by women from all corners of the world . . ." I pointed out.

"Give me my East Coast mama any day." His lips pressed the words against the curve of my throat, making me smile. "Anyway, those moments of need were few and far between, as I was seeking a much more important and rapid release. Music had always been my primary escape, but with the label demands, Rick's single-minded perfection, and Wren's slave-driving, it began causing me anxiety to the point where I could barely function. I was trying to chase away the self-hatred and self-doubt my past had left me to wrestle with. My parents and my peers never believing in me, my wife telling me she had never really loved me, my child never really knowing me . . . tales as old as dirt."

"What did your bandmates think?"

"Oh, they dealt with it like anything else; accepted it as a character flaw and moved on. So long as tickets were moving, the band was a success. Adam was the drunk, Sam was pussy-whipped, Rick was the control freak . . . I was the junkie. Together, we created Corroded Corpse." I must have looked skeptical, or horrified. "What I am trying to say is . . . we continued to function as a dysfunctional unit. We were still the same guys. We were making gold records and money hand over fist . . . and we didn't care. Wren wouldn't let us slow down enough to care."

Although we left the conversation behind at the beach, the proverbial dragon chased us into the afternoon. I had so many more questions as we pulled up to Abbey's school. But when surrounded by the cheery walls, the chattery din of dismissal, and the telltale smell of tempera paint, it hardly seemed proper. I watched as Abbey balanced her little feet on top of Adrian's, he hooked his arms under hers, and they Frankenstein-walked out to the car. It was hard to reconcile the man before me with the monstrous description he had earlier conveyed.

24

SIREN'S SONG

WE DECIDED to revisit the beach after dinner. "Bring your guitar, Adrian. Please!" Abbey pleaded. He may not have kept a toothbrush at our house, but there were guitars in almost every corner now.

"Any requests?" Adrian hopped on the lopsided bench by the pines with his Guild, the acoustic he had used at the library that first day. It was one of his favorites, I'd learned, given to him by the late guitar great Randy Rhoads.

"'Siren's Song'!" I called. Abbey fist-pumped the air in agreement. We loved being his audience of two.

Adrian grimaced good-naturedly. Although I had just discovered and claimed the song as my favorite, he had written it eighteen years ago and had essentially written it off. "Okay. But like you've never heard before," he said.

It was a mellow yet heavy selection from the Corpse body of work, but played on a twelve-string acoustic it became as pretty and haunting as any classical piece. An evening breeze shivered off the water and through our hair as Adrian's fingers vibrated off the frets. The ragged hem of his jeans caught under the sole of his black All Stars as he tapped sneaker to bench.

He harnessed his sexy, raspy voice and playfully smiled as he sang the slowest, most soulful version the song had ever known. It was a tale of being sucked sweetly down to the ocean floor, resplendent with ripped limbs, eyes gouged from the head and swollen tongues yanked out. Amazing how a lyric, gruesome on paper, could transform gorgeously given the right treatment.

The Cippola boys arrived and began busily digging to China near the water's edge. They quickly enlisted Abbey's help.

"So who was she?" I teased, once we were alone.

"The Siren?" With the guitar pick between his teeth, he grinned. "She was New York. My love affair. Remember I told you the first time you brought me down here?" He slowly removed the pick and began playing again, creating a new lyric in reference to earlier memories of us.

> *"Raising red down at the lake's shallow shore,*
> *she spurs me on and lures me to her*
> *like a matador . . ."*

He stopped playing abruptly, muting the strings with a closed fist around the neck. "Maybe New York was merely the vehicle to lead me to you."

My fingers loosened his grip; he let me take the guitar from his hand. Abbey ran by, a streak of pink plaid and denim. singing, *"Maxwell MacGillikitty . . . feline private eye!"* as Ryan Cippola chased her with seaweed on a stick.

Maybe *she* was the vehicle. Without Abbey's love of that fantastical cat, could any of this exist?

Without Abbey.

Without Pete's love, there would be no Abbey.

Without Pete.

I plucked down all twelve strings. How could a hollow body

release such clarity? I wished my thoughts were as in tune. But they were conflicted, murky like the water at shore's edge.

Do things really happen for a reason? Had my previous theories been blown out of the water?

The sun bathed the condos on the west side of the beach in scarlet as it set. I remembered Liz up on her balcony, waving those red and white flags years ago. Adrian's last lyrics echoed; I saw myself raising red during his first beach visit. Luring him, and he had come charging.

Was I ready to wave the white flag, to surrender fully to him?

25

GHOSTS OF COLUMBUS AVENUE

"Abb, can you unpeel yourself from the glass, please?" We had been inside Adrian's apartment for the better part of an hour, and Abbey had stayed hinged to the eastern quadrant for most of it, playing I Spy and huffing little clouds of condensation onto Adrian's spotless living room window. Adrian sat amused, watching her from his long gray couch, but I was appalled by her manners.

"But Mommy, I can see the Lennon bushes!"

"Yes, Strawberry Fields."

"And I see a giant girl poodle!"

"How can you tell it's a girl?" Adrian asked her, pulling me down next to him.

"She's making me nervous," I told him.

"She's fine."

"Because she's got pink bows on her ears." She pressed her fingertips above her head. "Mommy, look, I'm flying!"

Enough. I pried her body away from the smudged pane and suggested lunch.

"There's great sushi on Columbus," Adrian suggested.

Abbey made a face. "Hot dog," she countered.

"She's not a big fan of sushi. Um, how about Mexican?"

"Hot DOG!" It had been a somewhat challenging day. Abbey hadn't been in the best mood upon pick-up at school, but I had hoped a nap on the way into the city would rectify that. The minute we hit the highway, however, she became too excited to sleep. It was Fleet Week *and* her first visit to Adrian's —Manhattan didn't get much better than that.

"There's a Gray's Papaya on Broadway." Adrian was being a good sport. I was sure the last thing he wanted was a cheap dog on a dirty street corner. "We could grab her a dog and a smoothie, then sushi takeaway and eat in the park."

"Smoothie!" Abbey roared.

"IF there's good behavior. Starting now."

"Brilliant. Shall we?"

We made our way out of the building, Abbey wowing the doorman with a low bow and impeccable manners. Hands on her hips and her little butt jutted out, she craned her neck to scope all nineteen stories. "Adrian," she hollered, "do you *own* this whole building?"

"No, Abbey," he called back. "Just twenty-six hundred square feet of the Manhattan sky."

She smiled and trotted along beside us, the prospect of that smoothie looming just two avenues away.

We wound through a temporary wooden maze erected to provide safe pedestrian flow while some sort of major construction was going on above our heads. Despite the stark stencils warning POST NO BILLS, someone had brazenly plastered the entire length of the walkway with posters advertising the album by the newest flavor-of-the-month pop diva. "Ach. She's on Wren's client roster," Adrian muttered.

"Really?" It hadn't occurred to me that Wren was still out there, passing himself off as a legitimate businessman. I couldn't decide which was more alarming, that he was apparently succeeding or that Adrian was still keeping track.

"Oh yeah. He's not loyal to any genre when it comes to the almighty buck." I loved how he automatically reached for Abbey's hand as we raced to cross against the light.

Abbey was beginning to drag her heels. I noticed her staring longingly at children of various ages being whipped past us in pimped-out, shock-absorbing jogging strollers and titanium Maclarens. A method of transportation my daughter firmly eschewed in the suburbs and dismissed as babyish suddenly looked appealing as the city blocks stretched out endlessly in front of her.

"So had Corroded Corpse been a country band . . ." I giggled at the notion.

"Wren was a chameleon who changed his spots so long as there was green involved. His favorite buzzwords were 'universal accessibility'—he was the mastermind behind what was to become Corpse's biggest success, and our downfall: 'Simone.' The song."

"The dreaded eighties power ballad?"

Adrian gave me a wry smile. "Not only had Wren the audacity to suggest it, but the bollocks to pit his once-harmonious songwriting duo against each other to see who could come up with the better song. At the time, we didn't realize it, of course."

"You so lucky, my man. Surrounded by your two angels. Spare fifty cent, my lucky man?"

Abbey had slowed down to covet a dirty stroller saddled with the paper bags and bottle collection of a homeless man, who was looking imploringly at Adrian. In one deft move, Adrian gave his head a negative jerk in one direction like most New Yorkers were conditioned to and swung Abbey up onto his shoulders. She rode like a conquering hero down Broadway right into Gray's Papaya and ordered her hot dog and drink from high above.

"Make it the two dog special," Adrian said, reaching for his wallet even with his arms hooked around Abbey's legs to aid her balance.

"Changed your mind about the sushi?"

Adrian leaned so I could extricate Abbey. "No . . . be right back." Handing Abbey one of the crispy dogs, he jogged across the street and offered the other to Dirty Stroller Man. I watched the man hold up his free hand in praise.

"Back up you go, lass," he said to Abbey. "Mind the ketchup!"

Abbey munched on her dog from her perch and saluted every Navy sailor who passed in his crisp crackerjack whites.

"Cripes, Kat. Is everything okay?" We had rounded Columbus to pick up our takeout and I literally felt my color drain.

"Mommy looks scared," Abbey observed from on high. "And she's sweaty."

"Mom's all right," I assured them. "We used to . . ." I vaguely gestured up Columbus toward the eighties blocks. "We lived. Up there. 88th and Columbus."

"Me and you and Daddy?" Abbey asked, incredulous. I nodded.

Adrian caressed my arm with one hand, his other rubbing Abbey's ankle. Now he looked as if he was seeing a ghost; perhaps mine as I crossed his path in that other life. I caught my reflection in a dark shop window, and various ghosts looked back at me: newly wed and carrying home flowers, Pete's paper under my arm, and a pound of his favorite coffee from the Sensuous Bean to celebrate his first major byline. Eight months pregnant and staring wistfully into Betsey Johnson's storefront, fondly thinking of the days when that wardrobe fit. Waiting out a downpour under an awning with the stroller as Pete ran to meet us with an umbrella and a smile.

"Come on, guys. Sushi's getting cold," I joked softly.

We picked up our order and walked silently west, entering

the leafy wilderness of Central Park. Abbey connected her smoothie straw to her lips and cloud-watched nearby as Adrian and I broke apart wooden chopsticks and dug in. I had regained my composure and my appetite.

"I had no idea you'd lived so close," Adrian began. A warm wind kicked up from somewhere south, sliding through the trees and buildings before rushing up to ruffle leaves and rake our hair across each other's faces. A wayward balloon on a stick bounced past Abbey, and she gave chase around the meadow, laughing.

"Another lifetime ago."

"This will sound selfish." He clicked his chopsticks. "But I wish I'd known you then."

"You wouldn't have known me." Adrian looked stricken. "Meaning, I would have been just another face in the crowd." His world had been so much bigger than mine. "And I was different then." With Pete.

"And I was already inner tubing down the River Styx while you were still splashing in the paddling pool."

"You make me sound so . . . goody-two-shoes. I wasn't sheltered." I rolled closer to him. "I was *orderly*."

My life had followed the grid of good grades, decent colleges, and impressive résumés, which landed me professional nine-to-five employment with solid benefits. I had lined up and shelved those accomplishments as deftly as books on a library shelf and stood back with the calm and cool satisfaction of a job well done. Next came Pete and love . . . then Abbey. I watched her streak past after the balloon, shrieking with uncontrolled delight. And then nature's cruel curveball: the unnavigated fork stabbed in the middle of the road. The sun kink. Whatever you wanted to call it.

Despite all my organizing and arranging, I had never noticed the logical order to it all. The Dewey Decimal System placed Marriage and Family at 306.8. And Death and Dying at

306.9. How very tidy. Grief and love, hand in hand. Yet beside me sat Adrian, and what I felt for him defied classification.

"You look troubled, luv." Adrian's brow wrinkled in sympathy.

"I'm trying to figure out where you fit into the order." Was there a place for reclusive rock stars? For a heavy metal hero with a heart of gold? "You," I kissed each temple, then nose tip and chin. "You are glorious chaos."

26

TRUTH OR DARE

IT WAS MEMORIAL DAY WEEKEND, and Marissa and Rob were having a party. The invitation read *Bring your ass, your sass, and your ability to raise a glass* and had arrived addressed to me, Abbey, and "Shrimpy McLobster."

"He's coming, right?" Marissa demanded in the days leading up to it.

"So long as you don't call him that to his face. Best behavior, right?"

She gave me an exaggerated *Who, me?* bat of her lashes. "We just want to get to know him, Tree. And make sure he's treating you right. No inquisitions, I promise. Bring Abbey's suit; Rob's got the pool open. Oh, and there's a sitter coming, too, for the kids. It's gonna be a blast."

Marissa may have promised best behavior, but Adrian was another story. I could tell he was in a rare mood the minute I spotted him in the station lot. He was smoking with an agitated ferocity and barely smiled as Abbey waved through her open window.

"You don't seem in the party mood," I observed cautiously.

He dropped a fat white envelope in my lap. "Looks like I'm being forced into it."

It was addressed to him in enviable script. "I'm shocked it's not addressed to 'The Wallet.' I know that's what they call me," he muttered, yanking the stiff announcement from inside. "'*Mr. and Mrs. Leopold Smith joyfully request the honour of your presence . . .*' bugger, bugger, blah, blah." He proceeded to read the entire thing as I slowly navigated us through holiday traffic. "I can't believe my daughter's marrying that bolshy Scouser. And at twenty! So much for learning from your parents' mistakes."

"A bushy who, now?"

Adrian laughed. "Bolshy Scouser. Scouse is the accent from Liverpool. So one is called a Scouser if they hail from Liverpool. And *bolshy* meaning . . . obstreperous."

"Ah, much better."

"He gets on my tits . . ." Adrian glanced sheepishly into the rearview mirror at Abbey. "Look at that, my endless prattle put her to sleep."

I rolled into the driveway and we quietly got out, leaving the windows down, to allow her the much-needed nap. Marissa's parties always guaranteed a late night. I ran in to grab us a cold drink and then joined Adrian on the porch steps.

Across the street, Colin Drimmer rinsed suds off his Subaru with the garden hose. I waved. He gave a grin and lifted a big sponge up in greeting. The cocky guitar strut of AC/DC's "You Shook Me All Night Long" could be heard from his radio.

"Bloke a friend of yours?" Adrian moved to the step above me and gave my shoulders a gentle massaging. I closed my eyes, enjoying the touch and the breeze.

"Colin? I used to babysit him, if you can believe that. He just finished law school and moved home." Adrian's fingers tapped up my spine with the beat of the song as I shifted my own American thighs off the scorch of the hot step and leaned back.

"For fuck's sake . . ." His hands froze on my scapulae. "Do you hear that?"

Colin was hunched down, polishing the headlights with his back to us. The next song drifting over from his car stereo speakers sounded innocent enough. In fact, it was one of those songs turned generic due to oversaturation on the airwaves. I myself had heard it rotated countless times . . . but not since meeting Adrian. It clicked. Rick was singing, "*Sanitize my insanity . . . cleanse me, make me whole again, Simone . . .*"

"Well . . . that's a kick in the arse."

"Rick's love song for Simone?"

"Not exactly." I waited while he lit a cigarette. "Wren confided in me one day, expressing 'concern.' Rick was falling short in his attempt to write a metal ballad. He tactfully suggested I try my hand at a few lines to help Rick out of his writer's block, wording his request in such a way that I truly felt I was helping. He showed me what Rick had, and honestly, it was weak. Rhyming *Simone* with *phone* and *home*. It was embarrassing. Sappy has no place in metal. If love was going to appear in *our* music"—he tapped his chest like it was currently going on inside him—"it had to be doomed, damned, or deadly. So perhaps my lyrics were a bit tongue-in-cheek; a stab at Rick by saying he would never really know how good he had it until he lost it."

"Is that how he took it?"

"No, worse. He thought I fancied her! Wren called a meeting and presented both sets of lyrics to the entire band. Rick took one look and punched me square in the jaw. I wasn't a doomed soul pining over my ultimate love any more than I was standing on a bloody field on Samso in 'Blood Oath.' It was called *perspective*. Something Rick clearly lacked."

"So why didn't you guys just scrap the whole idea?"

"Well . . . truth be told, mine was a bloody good song. The rest of the band loved it. The label was timing the release carefully to be in the running for the Christmas number-one single in the UK that year. Rick begrudgingly admitted it was a solid song. But when it came time to credit publishing, he wanted lyrics credited to him, music to me."

"He didn't want Simone to know."

Adrian nodded wearily. "What could I do? I let him have it. He was my best friend."

"So you wrote a number-one song?"

"Number two, actually." Adrian clicked his tongue modestly. "Good thing it didn't make the Christmas number one; my mum would've had a heart attack. Oh yes, she had burst out of the woodwork that year. No matter it was the lowest point in *my* life emotionally. She was there riding the coattails, hounding me for tickets and bragging to her friends. 'Ickle Dougie Graves, playin' at the Hammy-O!'" He cackled. "We were scheduled to play London right before Christmas, then over to the States for three nights at Radio City to kick off the North American leg. Suddenly I was getting calls from her about 'my number-one fan.' Rodney, my half brother."

"The brother Kevin's age."

"Yes. He was fifteen and she was taking him to London." I could tell it was difficult for him to continue telling me the tale. How he had sent a car to bring his family to the show, set them up with the best tickets, with backstage passes. "And then like a selfish bastard, I pulled a runner right after the concert. Jumped into a waiting van and left without a word. Holed myself up in my flat and proceeded to shoot Christmas right up my arm."

"Oh, honey . . ." He let me pull him into a hug.

"The seats were so close, I could see them out there in the crowd." His voice cracked. "The lights usually prevent you from seeing beyond the first few rows. But there they were. Rodney looked so *happy*. I didn't acknowledge them, couldn't even glance in their direction the rest of the night. Where was *my* happiness at fifteen?"

Without another word, Adrian went into the house.

I sighed. Colin was gathering his rags and sponges, oblivious. The song ended, and the disc jockey began yammering, pulling Abbey into the waking world.

"Mom . . . so thirsty . . ."

I unhooked her sweaty torso from the seat and she gratefully downed the remains of my water, relishing the cup between her little hands. Slowly, we made our way inside as if we were first-time houseguests.

"Where's Adrian?" Abbey squinted, her eyes adjusting to the late afternoon interior light. She followed up with her own reply. "He's up in the boogeymen room." Her fuzzy pigtails quivered in defeat; Adrian was one of the few adults she would follow to the ends of the earth, but when it came to the second floor of our house, all bets were off.

"It's okay, sweetie. He'll come down soon."

"Maybe if I turn on PBS and *Maxwell's* on . . . ?" Selfish motivation or a four-year-old's simple optimism; either way, I felt a surge of tender sympathy.

"That's a great idea, Abbey. You go check and we'll be down in a few minutes." I paused on the third step until I heard the demented cackles of Dr. Loveydovey.

Adrian was stretched out on Kevin's old bed, hands folded corpse-style over his sternum. Had he been shirtless, he'd have resembled a knight girding his sword to his stony chest in a dusty tomb.

"You okay?"

"Just needed to be alone with myself." He turned his eyes ceiling-ward and chuckled.

The bedsprings protested as I helped myself to a corner, but Adrian did not. "Can't stand that ruddy song," he murmured, tracing undecipherable shapes along my back. "Don't know why people always wanted to hear it played live. Funny, Simone herself rarely got to hear it; by that point in the evening she had usually left the venue and was putting the children to bed at the hotel. She didn't bring nannies on the road, with Rick's track record and all. Meanwhile, every bloke in the audience wanted to be with her, every girl wanted to *be* her. She became a celebrity by association."

I leaned my cheek on my shoulder, looking back at him. "Do you think she knew you were the one . . . the one who wrote it?"

"I think . . . there wasn't much that Simone *didn't* know." He cleared his throat. "So yeah. I reckon."

"When did you last see her?"

He clasped his hands behind his head, regarding the posters above him once again. I let my fingers fall on the tip of the *misericorde*, peeking out from below his shirt. "Winter, late '87. We were playing the final show of that three-night stand at Radio City. The partying went on into the small hours. We were staying at the Plaza . . . but I was wired. I needed a fix get me to sleep. I found myself walking to Eighth Avenue to see a guy I knew who was always good for some quality H. I snorted some at his apartment to mellow me out for the walk back, pocketing the rest to shoot up at the hotel.

"Anyway, I'm on Broadway passing this all-night diner, you know that place right near the Ed Sullivan Theater? No trendy coffee shops in those days. And there's Simone, inside by herself. And I thought, *Bloody hell.* I really just wanted to be alone, get stoned, but there's my best mate's girl, and she's got the raccoon mascara, the ashtray overflowing with half-smoked cigarettes. So I go in and sit across from her. I can see what she was wearing, to this day. These rust-colored platform suede boots up to here"—he smacked at his thigh—"skinny black pants and this studded halter. In New York City she could've been a high-class hooker, but she was just Rick's wife, beautiful mother of his three kids. Of course, he was balling girls on the tour every chance he got; it was a disaster the moment Simone came on the road. That tour she left the children with her parents to reacquaint herself with the stranger she was married to. Meanwhile, she found herself facing a different monster in each of us: Rick's philandering, my drug-dabbling, et cetera. My therapist always said the three of us had addictive personalities: mine involved the drugs, Rick's was the fame . . . and Simone was addicted to him. So we're sitting and she's smoking and I order a coffee and we don't say a thing, not a word. My coffee comes and I drink and she smokes. It's quiet and the place is ours. There was a napkin on the table and I was never without a pen so I start to write and she's watching me the whole time but I don't think she's seeing me. Dawn was breaking through the window behind her and it was a picture I couldn't *not* paint with words. I didn't feel right, showing her. Like I had taken advantage of her sorrow when I should've been comforting her. So I added it to my pocket and I took her hands. 'I'm leaving this time,' she said, 'for good.' We just sat there, holding on for I don't know how long, felt like hours, till the vampire paparazzi were tipped off and began closing in; snapping away with their cameras and firing questions at us about our affair, how long had it been, did Riff know, and I'm throwing chairs at them and breaking plates over their heads . . . would have driven stakes through their hearts if I could, the bloodsuckers. The diner calls the cops, and Simone . . . bless her. She grabs me and pulls me close and I feel her fingers in my trouser pocket and then she's pushing me away from her as they grab me and haul me off to jail. She took the heroin, and the words I penned on the napkin, and I never saw her again."

"Oh my . . ."

"Yeah. She saved my neck. Bad enough to be arrested for assault, but a drug charge would have gotten me deported, banned . . . So I'm behind bars and everyone is waking to the news. Rick and Wren come to bail me out and I lay into them, saying things need to change, this can't go on, you're killing Simone and Wren's killing us . . . making us tour 230 days a year, we've got no bloody life. Meanwhile I am shaking with DTs and sweating and still bleeding from those broken plates and the police scuffle; probably looked like a raving lunatic. But if Rick could have slowed down for one minute, he would have come to the same conclusions himself."

"No such luck?"

Adrian smirked. "Tour bus left for Boston without me that day. They pulled some twonk to replace me so they wouldn't void the contracts. The tour tanked; not saying things would have been different had I been there. We just couldn't weather the perfect storm of personalities, mismanagement, and the downfall of the genre. Corroded Corpse ended up like that mascot on the first album cover—a smoking bloody corpse digging its own grave. We thought we owned the world back then. Well, the world showed us just how fickle it could be; it buried us and moved on. Barely cold in the ground before the likes of Alice in Chains, Corrosion of Conformity, Tool, My Dying Bride, all started signing label deals. Brilliant acts, all will tell you they were heavily influenced by Corroded Corpse, but the music world had already written us off."

"I can see why you're bitter."

"Corroded Corpse was like an ancient spider; we spun a huge, ugly egg sack before crawling into a corner to die. All these other bands emerged like tiny spider babies, floating off on their tangent web strands, creating new genres—grunge, alt-metal, sludge, indie, nu-metal, emo. Some climbing higher than we had ever gone. So, bitter . . . yeah. A bit. But proud, too. We started a revolution of sorts. Only we imploded before we could build our defenses. Too many traitors in our midst. And the hardcore fans thought we had sold out with the ballad."

"What became of Rick? And Wren?"

"I saw them here and there. Our lawyers met. We dissolved everything. But there wasn't much. Wren's dirty dealings and 'back commissions' we owed him were just the tip of the iceberg. Yes, he made a lot happen for us. But he made a lot more happen for himself. For years he was making deals behind our backs that weren't exactly in keeping with his contract, but there was just enough of a loophole for him to squeak through. And we hadn't solicited enough legal advisement to catch it. Luckily, the song publishing and our back catalog remained ours, or I'd be living in a paper bag right now. The bastard had copyrighted our name *himself*, not on behalf of us as we had originally assumed. So even if we ever wanted to reconcile, he'd be able to sue us if we tried to use the name."

"You're kidding. Why would he do such a thing?"

"Well, remember his whole 'success formula' he sold us over that game of pool?"

"Developing a band and a brand?"

"Yeah. I think he had imagined churning out a metal Menudo of sorts; replacing each of us after we burned out with an equally young and angry, hungry musician. Almost two decades later and I still wouldn't put it past him."

"And Simone . . . do you think she left?"

"Whether she did or didn't . . . I'd like to think she's happier now, somewhere out there."

"Did Sam stay in touch with them? And where's Adam?"

"Sam was always my mate, not Rick's. He's enjoying life as a session musician in LA. I doubt they've maintained a friendship. I'd be highly surprised. Adam? London. Kind of a nutter, became born-again after Cass. Harmless enough, I suppose. Met a girl in the flock and settled down. I think he's wiped most of Corpse's sins from his mind . . . and the blood from his hands." He sighed. "We were gods . . . but no one has the right to be that almighty. To think nothing and nobody could stop us. That was our fatal flaw."

With his eyes still skyward, he put a finger to his lips, tapping them yet pointing at something simultaneously. My eyes fell upon a poster ripped from the pages of a rock magazine, hanging in the corner. A decades-younger Adrian, chiseled arms clamped around his childhood chum. A heavily silver-ringed finger of Rick's pushed against his friend's nose, flattening it for comic effect. Both man-boys mugged pouts and grimaces for the lens.

"I'll do my best to find him . . . if you want me to."

Adrian assumed the same exaggerated pout he had pulled for the camera years ago. "My supersleuth," he said softly, beeping my nose flat with his finger. "Thank you."

"Information scientist," I corrected, with a kiss to his finger. "Your supersleuth is downstairs with Maxwell MacGillikitty. You'll catch the last five minutes if you hurry."

"Come on then." He pulled at my hands with a smile. "I'm not leaving you up here alone with the boogeymen!"

ADRIAN'S MOOD had lightened considerably by the time we arrived at Marissa's. We could smell the festivities as we pulled up; steaks over apple wood chips and Kahlua-brushed salmon, one of Rob's specialties. My entire posse was gathered on the lawn like the Welcome Wagon. Or perhaps they were circling the wagons in preparation for attack. I hoped not; Adrian had been through enough that day.

"Hey!" Rob greeted us with his customary broad smile. He wore an apron that read GRILL SERGEANT over his Hawaiian shirt. "Nice to finally meet you, man." Adrian accepted Rob's non-spatula hand and they half shook, half slapped in a manly guy way.

"It's about freakin' time!"

"Sorry, Mariss. Naptime ran long."

Adrian kissed her on both cheeks. "Nice to see you again, Marissa." From anyone else, she would've considered the action as pretentious as air-kissing, but I could tell from Adrian, she didn't mind one bit.

"Naptime? Yours or Abbey's?" Leanna laughed devilishly. She had what looked and smelled like a strong Jack and Coke in her hand. Ed was nowhere to be seen, which didn't surprise me. He rarely accompanied her to social functions, and she barely seemed to care.

"Hello, Miss Abbeycadabra," Liz greeted Abbey, giving her a high five. "Brought you something." She pulled a kid-sized cap from her bag and plopped it on Abbey's head.

"Awesome!" It had a glittery skull with a sequined pink bow on top; happy girly skulls were a favorite. "Thanks, Aunt Lizzie!" Abbey left me to protect it as she galloped toward the splashing and laughter coming from the aboveground pool in the backyard, leaving a trail of clothes in her wake as she stripped down to her suit. Sarah, the Falzones' babysitter, was waist-high in the water and throwing diving sticks for Joey, Brina, and Dylan to fetch.

"Hellooo!" Karen ambled up, huge salad bowl in her hands. Mitch, with a swim diaper–clad Jasper wiggling in his arms, managed to shake hands with Adrian as I made the last of the introductions.

"Come on, ladies. I'm gonna put you to work." Marissa tilted her head toward the house.

"I'll keep Rob company out here," Adrian said, accepting the beer Rob offered with thanks.

"Eeek, Tree, he is so adorable," Marissa said as soon as we were in the kitchen door and out of earshot. "Cuter than I remember!" She began to pull fruit from all corners of the kitchen. "Le, grab that big bowl over there for fruit salad. Seriously, girl, he's a keeper."

"Thanks." I winced as Leanna whacked a pineapple in half.

She had all of the fury and none of the humor that John Belushi conveyed in his TV role as a Samurai chef.

"Someone needs to get on building that cloning machine," Liz murmured.

"I could close my eyes," Karen said with a sigh, "and listen to that accent forever."

Leanna hacked into the poor kiwis next. "My next husband is going to be sweet like that." She ticked off a few other qualities, as if she were talking about the next car model she was going to buy.

"Leanna!"

"I wish Ed would develop a prostitute fetish or gamble our life savings away . . . something to give me a clear sign," she joked sardonically, pausing her fruit genocide to take a long haul of her drink.

"Bite your tongue!" I wanted nothing more than happiness for her, but wished she would take charge like the Leanna of old. "And hand over that knife. You're making me nervous."

"THINK we can get the kids to clean up?" Marissa leaned back with a glass of wine. We were lounging around in a post-glut state watching the little ones chase Lickety, Split, and the Frisbee the dogs had gleefully absconded with. Every now and again, a child would whiz by the table for a bite of a ketchup-smeared hot dog or a sip of lemonade before taking off again.

"You sit, chicky. We'll do it." Liz, even buzzing on several beers, could swiftly and expertly bus a table. Adrian and I gathered the mountain of empties and took them around the side of the house to the recycling bin.

"How am I doing?" Adrian kissed me behind the lilac tree.

"You haven't run screaming from the premises, so I'd say you're doing great."

"Go on. Your friends are nice."

I hooked my thumbs through the loops on his cargo shorts and pulled him close.

"Get a hotel room, you two." Liz had popped around the corner. "Smoke time?" She grinned sheepishly.

"Are you enabling her, Adrian?" I scolded. Liz was the type of ex-smoker who fell off the wagon at the prospect of having a drink in her hand and a butt in the other. Yet she hated the smell of cigarettes, so she would wash her hands with OCD frequency and chew wads of gum guiltily afterward. Why she tortured herself was beyond me.

"Apparently. Looks like I've created a monster." Adrian kissed me on the cheek as he fished out a fresh pack of Marlboros from a pocket. Liz grinned, guilty as charged.

I brought the last of the dishes inside. Marissa was stashing the leftovers in the fridge between gulps of wine. "Sarah started a movie for the kids upstairs. You guys are going to stay awhile, right? I sent Robbie down to the beach to get a bonfire going." She saw me sneak a glance at the clock. "You're not thinking of taking him back to the train tonight, are you? Abbey can sleep here, you know that."

"I know. Thanks. We'll see."

"Come on, you'll have to get over the flatulence and morning breath thing eventually, just bite the bullet!"

"Funny, Mariss. I just don't know if Abbey is ready." I thought about Abbey's early morning tear-in-and-leap and whether I wanted to subject Adrian to that yet. "Or if he is, for that matter."

"For Christ's sake, we could make it one big pajama party so everyone sleeps over and no one feels weird. He's great, Tree. Really. I love how he took your hand at the table after dinner. And how cute was that when he started playing soccer with the kids?" We took a new bottle of wine out onto the deck. "Think we seem like dumb boring Americans to him?"

"Oh, come on. He was psyched to come and meet everyone. I'm always talking about you guys."

"Check that out." She nodded toward the far corner of the yard, where Adrian, Liz, and Mitch were all puffing away, laughing and talking.

"Mr. Health Nut, sneaking a smoke while his wife is inside changing diapers?"

"Yeah, let's go bust his balls."

We strolled across the lawn. Liz was folding a piece of gum into her mouth and giggling.

"H&H blows."

"You're on, Big Red," Mitch said, crushing the cigarette under his Tevas. "We'll have a bagel challenge."

Liz gave a sloppy laugh. "He keeps calling me Big Red," she told us. "Isn't that funny? You know, because I'm chewing Big Red. And I have red hair." Liz was rather tall and somewhat big-boned, but not overweight. She enjoyed her bagels and beer, and would never have a yoga and tofu-toned body like Karen.

I could tell Marissa took offense. She has no problem calling herself big, or calling her friends out when it comes to looks, but heaven help the outsider who comments on them. "Is that *not* hilarious, Tree?"

"Hmm. Indeed. Since when do you smoke, Mitch?"

"*And* he's gonna eat some carbs," Liz said in mock horror. "Adrian's my witness, right?"

"What will we learn next? That you were piloting the *Exxon Valdez*?"

Mitch smirked. "I'm not the choirboy you think I am, Mariss."

His wife was waving from the deck, no Jasper to be seen. Karen was pretty in a sharp way. Her face, rounded in pregnancy when I met her, had resumed a more angular shape after giving birth. Her cheekbones glowed under the dim light of the colored lanterns hanging overhead.

"Better give him some sugar, Big Red. Karen's gonna smell him from a yard away. Come on, I need your help inside." Mitch took the gum Liz offered and then let his eyes linger a bit too long on her backside as she followed Marissa back to the house.

"Adrian's been telling me about your bike rides, Tree. We should all go sometime." He put his arm around Karen as she walked up. "Adrian and Tree have been biking with Abbey at Bear Mountain. Wouldn't that be great to do, too, honey?"

"Oh, absolutely. We just got the Chariot Trailer for Jasper."

"What's the farthest distance you've ever biked?" Mitch asked Adrian.

"I did the Five Boro Bike Tour last year with a mate of mine. That was forty miles. It was a bit of a cock-up with thirty thousand other cyclists, but it was fun."

"Wow, forty miles. And you *smoke*?" Mitch was incredulous.

"Cut down from three packs a day when I started riding," Adrian admitted. "I'm at about a half pack a day . . . less when I'm with Kat and Abbey." His fingers played with the strap of my dress and he smiled. "Abbey tells me I smell like her Uncle Kev."

"What!"

He laughed at my mortified look. "I'm glad she told me. It's been a long time since I've had anyone around to smell me."

"Bonfire time!" Marissa bellowed from the deck. She and Liz led the procession through the side yard and down to the lake. Leanna trailed behind, carrying her bottle of Jack by the neck like a cocky rock star. Karen and Mitch went inside to check on Jasper's mood with the sitter before following.

"You know," I started, reaching for Adrian's hand as we navigated the sandy path, "Kev actually started smoking because of Digger." Adrian and I often referred to his stage name in the third person as if, indeed, it was a third person in the room; like a mythical, larger-than-life character. It was Adrian's turn to look mortified. "I didn't mean that as an accusation," I hastily added. "Just a weird . . . I don't know. Ironic coincidence?"

"Well, if I ever meet him, I will apologize." We walked in silence toward the tiny beacon of light that was Rob's bonfire. He had set up a spot far from any of the pines or houses.

"So who is this bloke called Todd? Leanna and Liz were talking about him like he's the life of the party. When is he coming?"

I stopped short. "TOD? Oh, no no no. TOD is not a person. TOD is pure evil." Rob had a raging fire going, and Leanna was spreading out blankets and beach towels around it. There was a cooler of beverages and, sitting on Liz's lap, the dreaded TOD. "Later, guys. Thanks for the lovely evening." I grabbed Adrian's hand. "You are not subjecting him to that. No way."

Adrian seemed amused by the amount of cajoling and convincing the girls launched into. "Tree, it's harmless fun. Come on! It will be a good way to get to know Adrian, and for him to get to know us," Marissa wheedled.

"For example," Leanna said, grabbing the notebook from Liz's lap, "Adrian, read page twenty-three."

Despite my protests, Adrian tilted the battered book toward the light of the fire and followed Leanna's finger across the page. "'*Marissa to Tree—Truth: Did you spit or swallow with Kurt O'Toole? Tree takes Dare, pees in the kitty litter box.*' What is this?"

"It's a game we played in high school. A jacked-up version of Truth or Dare," I said. "All recorded in the book for posterity." I had half a mind to grab it from his hands and toss it into the flames.

"You peed in a cat litter box?"

"Giving a whole new meaning to the nickname you gave her. Mittens was so pissed at you, Tree." Marissa and the others dissolved into hysterics.

"If you don't answer the question, you have to take the dare, whatever it is," Marissa explained.

"Adrian, you don't have to. It's silly." I kicked a bit of sand at my so-called best friends who had promised to behave themselves. "I can't believe you dug TOD out."

"Leanna's idea."

"I don't mind, Kat." He pulled me close. "I can handle it."

"Oh but wait, it gets better." Rob passed Adrian a beer. "I upped the stakes and introduced a strip poker element into it a while back. Otherwise, it gets pretty boring, pretty fast."

"If you answer the Truth question, the asker has to remove an article of clothing," Liz explained. "If you take the Dare, you have to not only do the dare, but also let them remove a piece of *your* clothing."

"I hate you all," I said, shaking my head as Adrian pulled me down next to him and prepared for the first question.

Marissa was to his left. "I'll be gentle. Have you ever murdered anyone? No? See, that was easy. Next!" She took off one bangled bracelet with considerable fanfare and gestured for Leanna to record it in the book.

Liz followed. "What was the first thing that came to your mind when you met Tree?" She blew into her half-empty beer bottle and awaited his answer.

It didn't take him long. "That she was stunning . . . and one day I'd possess her heart."

The group collectively interjected with a long drawn-out "Awwww!"

Liz pulled off her shirt to reveal a tank-top underneath. "Leanna, you're up."

I cringed, waiting for some anti-male diatribe. Leanna could be pretty caustic when her heart was in it. "Do you believe in love at first sight?"

Okay, maybe that was worse.

"Hmmm, no. I don't." He took a long swallow of beer. "I

believe love involves the commitment of many senses, as well as your head and your heart, so I wouldn't just rely on my eyesight," he finished, winking at her. Leanna kicked off a sandal, and the age-old debate ensued as to whether footwear was indeed an article of clothing.

"What is the dumbest thing you ever did while under the influence?" Rob asked.

Adrian stared stonily into the fire, as if secrets and answers were contained in the flames. "I burned my daughter's oatmeal," he finally replied. "Burned . . . her oatmeal." Slowly and quietly, as if he could still hardly believe it.

The chatter around the fire died down. Karen gave a nervous giggle. Liz stifled a burp, and Mitch cleared his throat. Marissa raised her brows, and Leanna rested her chin in her hand, waiting for more. My hand gripped his knee tightly, imploringly. "Such a simple . . . normal task. I tried so hard . . . I was high . . . nodded out. Almost burned the house down, and I lost custody of her. I'd say that was pretty bloody stupid of me."

"Yo man, I had no idea, I'm sorry . . ." Rob started.

"Don't be. It was the catalyst for cleaning up my life, so . . . no worries."

Rob unbuttoned his Hawaiian shirt and apologized once more. This time, for the man-boobs he was about to reveal.

Mitch lightened the mood considerably. "So, Adrian . . . have you ever been with more than one woman in bed at the same time?"

"Mitchell!"

"Relax, Kar . . . it's Truth or Dare!"

"Yes, Mitch, I have," Adrian answered simply.

"Really? How many?"

"Hey, only one question during your turn, mister," Marissa said. Mitch grinned and dropped his shorts to reveal his boxers. Karen's embarrassment was quickly turning to disgust. "Your turn, Karen."

Karen turned to Adrian, shyness in her voice. "If you could choose anyone, living or dead, to meet and have lunch with, who would you choose and why?"

Marissa added, "And it can't be a cop-out answer like Ghandi, Marilyn Monroe, or Hitler, okay?"

Adrian smiled thoughtfully. "Dare."

"Seriously? You can talk about doing drugs and banging multiple chicks and you can't answer that?" Leanna teased. "Karen, think of a good dare for him, and Adrian—you have to let Karen take a piece of your clothing off of you."

Karen was doubly mortified now, but giggled when Adrian held up one foot. She pulled off his sneaker. "I dare you to . . . run down to the lake and scream the chorus to *Maxwell MacGillikitty* at the top of your lungs." Our laughter was drowned out as he belted out Karen's request. A faraway canine howled back in reply.

"And that ends your turn. Tree, you got off easy, you didn't have to ask your man any questions," Marissa said.

"Maybe he planned it that way," I joked, giving him a kiss. "So sorry," I murmured into his mouth. "That was idiotic."

"I've been through worse," he whispered back, pulling me onto his lap. People were losing interest in the game, once the fresh meat was done.

"I think I'd better get Jasper to bed." Karen wiped sand off her capri pants and offered a hand to help her husband up from the sand. Mitch, beer bottle to his lips, waved his free hand and said, "I'm going to stay for a while. You can take the car. It's close enough for me to walk home." Karen gave him a long look. "Or stumble home," he added, and Rob gave a laugh.

"I'll walk you up, Kar." Marissa made sure to kick some sand in Rob and Mitch's direction as she hoisted herself up.

"So . . ." It was Rob's turn to grill Liz. "Who do you achieve the bigger O with? Men or women?" Liz had taken the bisexual route for a while, common knowledge to most of us. Mitch spilled half of his Sierra Nevada in the sand in his effort to scurry closer for her answer.

"Don't give these pervs the satisfaction, Liz." Leanna alternated pouring Jack and Coke into the plastic cup expertly balanced between her denim-clad knees.

"This is turning ugly," I said with a giggle. "We're going for a walk."

Adrian grabbed another beer from the cooler. "Kat?"

Leanna held up her Jack and Coke to me as an alternative. "Take this, I don't want to look at it or smell it." I took it off her hands, and she promptly plopped backward on the sand. "Holy crow, the beach is spinning."

Adrian took my hand, and we walked to the water's edge. There was no wind and barely a ripple as we looked out across the lake. "Where are we in relation to your house?"

Turning my back on the lake to get my bearings, I pointed left. "There're our pines." He nuzzled my neck but didn't say anything more. "They're not usually this . . . immature. Or wasted."

"They're funny. I like them." There was a shriek from behind us. Liz, Mitch, and Rob were all stripped to their undies and racing down to the water. Marissa had brought the dogs back with her, and they were streaking across the beach in pursuit.

"I can't believe Karen got you on that question."

Adrian touched the sand behind us to make sure it was dry and pulled me down next to him. "I know this is going to sound strange . . . but my answer is Peter." It took me a moment to digest his confession. "I would've liked to have met him . . . to hear about you and what you were like back then."

I was blown away. His statement overwhelmed me with its genuine desire and painful impossibility. Words escaped from my lips. "I love you."

Suddenly, I heard every sound of the night around us.

Spring peepers like little bells in the grass, the fire popping as it died out behind us, the panting of the dogs as they ran another lap, and the inebriated splashes down the beach. I heard everything but a response from Adrian, who was silently nursing his beer. I forced myself to down Leanna's strongly prepared drink in a smarting act of self-chastisement. What the hell was I thinking? Opening myself up like a fucking Hallmark card?

"Here, have another." Leanna had gained a second wind and a fresh happy drink. She generously poured half her glass into mine before stumbling down toward Marissa, who was trying to coax the trio of water babies back to dry land. I watched as my two girlfriends hugged, and I longed for the safety and familiarity of that huddle. I hadn't felt this raw, this exposed, since moving back. I allowed more Jack to wash over me like a tsunami.

The evening ended choppily, drunkenly observed in blinks like a slide show. All the children sleeping in a heap like kittens upstairs. Liz passed out in the guest room, Leanna collapsed on the couch. Marissa grilling Adrian before handing my keys over to him. "No, I'm not drunk, and yes, I will drive on what you Colonials call the '*right*' side of the road." My eyes coming in and out of focus as I concentrated on the blackness through the car window, muttering lefts and rights to my chauffeur. "Love Street?" he said as I indicated our last turn. "I never noticed you lived on Love Street!"

"Yes, Love Street. Where I have lingered far too long," I mumbled wearily. Jim Morrison and the Doors had penned the song before it had become my address.

"Isn't that where all the creatures meet?" He put my arm up around his shoulders to help me out of the Smurf.

"Ha . . . Pete said the exact same thing the first time he visited."

Adrian sang softly in minor key as he opened my garden

gate and we stumbled toward the house. "Are we at all alike? Pete and I?"

His question made my head spin. Allowing myself to think so much about Pete brought on an uncontrollable queasiness. I felt the saliva pool into my mouth and I knew what was coming next. The motion-detector lights, on cue, showed me exactly where to puke: neatly over my mother's hydrangeas.

The purge sobered me somewhat. Adrian helped me inside and led me to the bathroom. He handed me my toothbrush, paste already applied, and I gratefully brushed. Next he steered me into my room, pulled my dress over my head, and put me in a T-shirt, singing all the while about wisdom and knowing what to do.

He fell next to me on the futon and curled his body against mine. "I have never been loved . . ." His words poured over me, warming every part, as I lazily kissed up the inky paws on his forearm and wrapped it around my shoulder. I heard his voice catch. ". . . like I have been loved by you," he continued, his voice scratchy yet gentle, like a cat's tongue, deliberate and patient, slicking over the same spot. "And I have never loved like I love you. You've got to know this. My silly drunk girl."

27

WRENCH IN THE WORKS

AN ABBREVIATED ring ricocheted off the walls, raising me from my futon like a horror flick zombie. I was alone, and the room was silent. Phone? Alarm? Door? I rolled up and onto my feet to explore. Water. Brush teeth. More water. My head felt like a martini olive being squeezed of its juice. More water.

"Good morning, sunshine." Adrian was at the kitchen table with a cup of tea. The vivid tattoos on his chest clashed with the faded flowers on the wallpaper.

I fell into the chair across from him. "I feel like Keith Richards looks."

He smiled. "You don't scare me." He pushed his mug toward me.

"Not a big fan of tea. Is that against the law in Britain?"

"No. I can still bring you home to Mum."

"Yee-haw."

"Here, try. Milk and honey in there, what's to hate? Good hangover cure." I gave it a tentative sip, nodded, and had some more. "I thought for sure yesterday *I'd* be the drunk one, not you," he chided.

"Was that the phone?"

"Yeah. I didn't want it to wake you."

"Marissa?"

"No, a Veronica? She said she'd call back."

"Oh." My mother-in-law. "Shit."

"What?"

"Nothing." Figures. "I'm upset with myself."

"Why?"

I played with a few crumbs on the table in front of me, crushing them with my pinky nail. "The first night you share my bed . . . and I puke and pass out."

"It happens."

"I didn't get to wake up next to you."

"That'll happen, too. Another morning. I got to watch you sleep. That was nice."

I pulverized a few more crumbs and thought about my words on the beach. I hadn't expected them to come to the surface when and how they did. And I hadn't imagined the mention of Pete would trigger them. It was hard to think about Adrian and Pete and love all together without feeling guilt and grief as well. But Pete and Adrian *were* alike in that I loved them both. And they both, somehow, had fallen in love with me.

I longed for the words to tumble out, as uncontrollable and as cathartic as my purge last night. I wanted to tell him about who I was before Pete, and what I had been like when I met him. How we had connected, how we had blended our lives together seamlessly. Like a glass vessel, slowly turning, without end. And, inevitably, how I shattered without him, left with nothing but glass shards no one would dare touch. How Abbey, my family, and my friends gathered around me, trying to sooth my sharp edges, bleeding and hurt as well. How time then wrapped around me, working to wear down the points until I was left with sides as soft and supple as tumbled sea glass. Once translucent, now opaque. Changed.

I watched as Adrian's eyes flicked across my face, resting on my mute lips before turning skyward. Had he been trying to channel my thoughts, crack them like a fortune cookie or a code even I couldn't decipher? Without words, I moved to curl myself onto his lap, intertwining and locking limbs into a hug. He had hollows and angles that now fit my worn curves and valleys.

"I'm sorry I upset you last night," he whispered.

I squeezed him tighter, watching his white skin against my black T-shirt form some sort of cosmic yin-yang. "No . . ."

"Yes, I did. You mistook my silence on the beach and proceeded to get hammered before I could gather my thoughts and properly explain. You deserve more than a knee-jerk reaction, better than an automatic response of 'I love you, too.'" He pulled back to look at me. "You are the best thing to happen to me, bar none. You, Abbey . . . all of this. You both walked into my life and . . . I never knew what I wanted until you did."

ADRIAN'S OPEN LIPS, pressed to the nape of my neck as the water from our shower rolled off his body and over mine, turned out to be the best hangover cure. Still, as we bounded out the door into the brilliant morning, coffee was sorely needed.

"Starbucks and then you'll get me to the 10:15?" Adrian knew how I liked my coffee, and he knew all the train schedules by heart.

"I wish you didn't have to leave so early." He had agreed to do two more library programs in neighboring towns last weekend, where he had charmed the children and had given away the rest of his Natalie CDs. A dad in the audience owned a toy store in South Street Seaport that hosted children's concerts on weekends in the summer, and so Adrian found himself with yet another gig.

"I'd love nothing better than a lazy day lie-in with you," he murmured, opening the door of the Smurf for me. "But the sippy-cup crowd calls."

There were more devotees in the coffee shop worshipping their steaming mugs than down the street at Sunday church, but the line went fast. Rob was known for brewing the weakest coffee on the planet, so I grabbed cups for Liz and Leanna as well. We were balancing several Americanos out the door to the adjacent lot when Grant materialized from behind a BMW with Connecticut plates. He made no attempt to grab the door to help us, choosing instead to flick a disdainful glance at our damp hair, our tired smiles, and make his own simple assumptions.

"Ah, Katrina. Walking on sunshine this morning, I see." He turned to Adrian. "Back in school we used to call her group of girls Katrina and the Waves, you know . . . like that one-hit-wonder band. They would walk through the cafeteria like they were on the back of a frickin' parade float." He mockingly smiled and waved. "Very popular. Never consorting with the longhairs or the burnouts. Pristine, know what I mean?" He licked his bottom lip and jutted out his chin, expecting a reaction.

I seethed at his rudeness and audacity. Adrian took a different tack.

"We never properly met." He juggled a coffee into the crook of his tattooed arm to free up a hand. "I'm Adrian."

Grant balked, looking confused at Adrian's smile, but slowly extended his hand as well. A dirt-dusted grease smear was plainly apparent.

"Grant, there you are. I thought we were meeting inside." The handshake didn't happen, for a woman had practically burst between them.

"Sorry I was running late, babe." Grant deftly swiped the

offending hand across the backside of his jeans as he reached
with his other to usher his date back into the coffee shop. The
woman turned to look over her shoulder questioningly at
Adrian and me, and I was reminded of a woman in my yoga
class.

"Are you by any chance related to Jenny Bogancourt?"

Despite Grant's press against her backside, the woman hesitated. "Jenny's my sister." She smiled at me. "You know her?"

"We take yoga together. I'm Kat. Tree. Katrina. Hi."

"I'm Becca . . . I came down from Connecticut to visit her
and do some antiquing, and look what I found instead!" She
turned toward Grant expectantly. He was taking on that just-
eaten-a-bug expression.

"Ah yes, he's a gem," I said with gusto. "I hope you have
Triple-A."

We left her looking quizzically after us, Grant murderously.
Adrian shook his head as we passed the car with the
Connecticut plates, its alignment slightly lopsided. "Barmy
tossbag. Someone's going to pan his head in one of these days."

"How are *you* feeling this morning, Miss Drunkypants?"
Marissa tossed me a paper plate so I could help myself to the
brunch spread.

"Coffee?" Rob held up the pot, half-full of light tan liquid.

"Brought my own, thanks. A bit tired . . ."

"From all the morning sex? Shower sex?" She flicked my
wet ponytail. "Starbucks bathroom sex?"

"Wouldn't you like to know?"

"You mad at me about the Truth or Dare? He was a good
sport. The drug stuff, though . . . shit. Did you know about
that?"

"A bit, yeah." I busied myself with pulling apart some
monkey bread.

"They say what doesn't kill you makes you stronger," she commented. "He's still here." I nodded, wishing he were right next to me now. "Does he see his daughter much?"

"Not really. She lives in England. I guess she's getting married soon."

"Get out! If she starts having kids, you'll be . . . like, a step-grandma!"

"Worse than that . . . she'll be a step-mother-in-law." Rob shuddered.

"That's a lot of cart before the horses, you two. We've only been dating a month! Chill. Speaking of mothers-in-law, however . . . mine apparently called this morning. How am I going to explain why a guy answered my phone at nine o'clock on a Sunday morning?"

"Just tell her the truth. It's not like you picked him up in a bar the night before or something slutty like that. She can't expect you to live like a nun."

Liz emerged on the deck, freshly showered. "Oh thank little baby Jesus." She made a beeline for the Starbucks cup. "I can't drink that brown water you brew, Rob. No offense."

"None taken . . . Big Red."

"Oh, shut up." She pulled a bagel from the basket. "What'd I miss?"

"Slutty nun talk. How's your hangover?" I asked her.

"Mine? You got pretty wrecked last night." She buttered her bagel expertly with one hand while adding sugar to her cup with the other. "Leanna left?"

"Yeah, she got Dylan up and out before I was awake." Marissa stretched. "Wonder if Karen changed the locks on the door. Mitch didn't leave here till after midnight." She smeared a half a bagel with cream cheese. "Something about him rubs me wrong."

"BRINA! ABBEY! MAXWELL'S ON!"

"Joseph Vincent Falzone! No screaming through the screen

door!" She dragged her fingernails through her hair. "We've got people recovering here." The girls streaked past, a tornado of curls and giggles.

"I don't mind him," Liz said to no one in particular. "He's kind of funny, once he loosens up."

A MELLOW GIRLS' day was sorely needed. "Rock and roll power nap," Abbey said happily, curling between Liz and me as we half snoozed, half watched a movie back at the house. It was rare for Liz to have a three-day weekend, and wonderful to have the company.

After polishing off a pizza and three games of Yahtzee Jr., Abbey insisted both Liz and I tuck her in that evening. "Look at my photographs, Aunt Lizzie." Abbey pointed from her bed to the three snapshots she had taken of Adrian performing at one of the libraries last week.

"She takes after her uncle Luke with the photography," I said proudly. "Most of the shots I got were blurry."

"Nice, Abbeycadabra. This one's my favorite." Liz tapped the one of Adrian duck-walking Chuck Berry–style with his guitar.

"Oh," Liz said after Abbey finally fell asleep. "Where's that care package Mariss packed? We didn't even break into this at the party." She brought out a creamy wheel of cheese. "Rouzaire Brie from Zabar's, yum. Can't let this go to waste."

I rummaged through the pantry. "All I've got are . . . goldfish crackers. And grape juice."

"That's fine. We could do with some grapes that aren't fermented." I handed her a cutting board and knife. "Did you know a wheel of Brie is still alive until you cut into it?"

I laughed. "No, I didn't. Is it going to scream?"

We smeared the soft ripe cheese onto the little fish, chatting until we had no chat left in us. "Time to wake up and go to sleep," Liz said with a yawn.

"You sure you don't mind sleeping in Kev's rock 'n' roll shrine?"

"No, on the contrary." Liz gave a languid stretch, then smiled. "Up there, he feels close. I miss him."

LIZ WASN'T DUMB, but she wasn't always the most observant person, either. She rarely recognized neighbors on the street or classmates who came into the bagel shop, and she wasn't embarrassed to admit she simply couldn't place people out of context. So I was mildly surprised to find her holding up a tattered rock magazine from Kev's room and comparing it to the photographs on Abbey's bulletin board the next morning.

"I *knew* there was something familiar about him!" she hissed. "Tree, you sneaky little bee-ach! How the hell . . ." She paused as Abbey came trotting down the hall to use the potty. I put a finger to my lips and motioned her out to the living room.

"Were you even going to *tell* us? And Kev—holy cow, what did he say when you told him?"

"I didn't. And I'm not. Adrian is a fairly private person, understandably. If he wants people to know, I will follow his lead." I had to admit, it was a bit of a relief to be able to talk about it with at least one person.

"Wow, how did he make the leap from Digger to Tigger? You know, from '*roast the babies and use their blood as gravy*' to '*bouncy, trouncy, flouncy,* pouncy, fun, *fun, fun*, fun, fun'?" she marveled, leaning back on the couch in amazement.

"Come on, the lyrics aren't *that* bad!"

"Yuh-huh! Have you listened to that stuff?"

"Some. Not much since Kev used to crank it up to eleven."

"Well, he played a lot of their music for me. A lot. And told me tons of stories. And then he would quiz me!" She ran upstairs and fetched *Necromancer*, which I knew was their heaviest album. "Listen and learn." She put it on the turntable, and we both burst with laughter at the extreme lyrics.

Death is just a
carnival for maggots
who eat your soul
like a midnight snack.

We banged our heads around like a couple of teenagers until we caught a glimpse in the mirror and saw two ridiculous-looking thirty-somethings and a little girl standing behind them with her hands on her ears.

"Sorry, sweetie. Mom and Aunt Lizzie are just being silly." I gave her a kiss on the head and motioned to Liz to pull the plug on it. "Go wash your hands and I'll make you some lunch."

"Wow, I bet he has slept with hundreds of groupies," Liz said once we hit the kitchen.

"Thanks for that image." I began pulling the fixings for PB&J out of the fridge.

"So he simply walked away from it all?"

"No, he barely escaped with his life intact." I left Liz pondering that one as I served Abbey her lunch and got her dressed.

"You can't tell anyone," I whispered as Abbey ran to get in the Smurf; we were taking Liz to catch her train.

"I know, I know. I'm . . . wow. I'm floored."

"Don't look now . . . here comes your new best friend," I murmured. Liz let a giggle escape as Mitch slid up to the edge of my drive in his little hybrid.

"Hey, heading home? I'm going into town to catch up on some work in the office if you want a ride."

Liz turned sheepishly to me. "Beats the train . . . and it's easier than you having to lug Abbey out."

"Get her there in one piece," I instructed Mitch.

"Yeah, I'm precious cargo," Liz quipped, subtly allowing her back to arch, as well as one rogue eyebrow.

"Clean driving record," Mitch vowed, biting a smile into his bottom lip. "You're in good hands."

As Liz reached to hug me, I had to reiterate. "Not a word, Red."

28

WARRIOR STANCE

TUESDAY MORNING YOGA was a welcome way of returning to the week's rituals. Karen and I were working through our warrior poses in the corner when she quietly confided that Mitch hadn't come home the night before. "He was still working on his project at eight p.m. and, poor thing, he slept on the couch in his office." Karen locked her hips and raised her arms strongly. "He figured the traffic home would be bad with the holiday, and he'd just have to go right back this morning, anyway." We glided from warrior one to warrior two position. "Jasper missed his daddy . . . he's not used to waking up without him."

I leaned back into peaceful warrior, not sure of what to say. The image of Liz eagerly jumping into Mitch's passenger seat dared me to consider the resulting consequences, finishing with an unwelcomed vision of Mitch's good hands on Liz's precious cargo. I saw no happy endings there.

Karen looked so unsuspecting and calm, standing in mountain.

~

"YOU LED HIM INTO TEMPTATION!"

"The man hadn't had carbs in a year, can you blame him?"

"I'm not talking about your bagel challenge, Liz. Karen said he didn't come home last night."

"I guess that makes two of us who have secrets." Liz was three counties away, but that was clearly an all-up-in-my-grill comment. I imagined her eyes as a nightmare pool of pure black, all pupils and no iris.

"Yes, but Adrian's secret isn't harming anyone." I clenched the phone hard.

"Are you so sure about that?"

"Liz! Three days ago you were ready to clone him."

"I didn't want to say anything before, but when Kevin dabbled with speed in junior high, and had to get his stomach pumped? He'd wanted to gain 'inspiration' like Digger claimed he got from various illegal substances. Is that the role model you want around for Abbey? You've known him for, what? Two months?"

"*You* don't know him at all." I was done discussing it. Adrian had had to bury enough friends; he considered himself one of the lucky ones. Heroin had ruined enough people in his life to make him know he could never flirt with it again.

"Whatever. You've got your rock star to play 'confess the sins' with," she snarled, "so don't go judging me."

It was impossible to slam a cell phone down like the phones of old, but her defiant click to break the connection stung with the same insult. My own phone barely had time to recover before lighting back up and buzzing with a new call: Adrian.

"Hey."

"Erm . . . hello to you, too." Adrian's husky murmur and the tinny din of Manhattan rush hour tunneled through the line. "Everything all right, luv?"

"Just tickety-boo." Abbey wasn't the only one picking up

Adrianisms. "Liz and I got into a bit of a scrap . . . a bone-throwing match from the skeletons in our respective closets."

"Ah. Care to throw me a bone?"

His quip made me wince. I still hadn't given Adrian so much as a peek into the closet of my past. He was quick to take a shot at any opening lately; the weight of Pete's loss had morphed into the proverbial elephant in the room, too big to be ignored for much longer.

"This had more to do with, um, you. Liz knows."

Adrian was silent on the line, but I could hear him singing loud and clear from the other room. Abbey had started watching yet another episode of *Maxwell*, and the intro song was blaring.

"I didn't tell her, she . . ." *Maxwell MacGillikitty . . . feline private eye!* ". . . figured it out herself. Hold on." I cupped the mouthpiece and hollered, "Abbey, turn it down!"

"What?" The bleat of a siren echoed Adrian through the phone. "Sorry. Trying to cross West End Avenue. How did she—?"

"She put two and two together yesterday morning. I guess we can blame my brother's influence on her. I told you they were inseparable in high school."

"No one else is to blame but me," he said shortly. "I don't want to cause a rift between you and your friends."

"Oh, Adrian. No." Abbey had finally abandoned the TV in search of dinner. I mimed hand washing, shooing her to the bathroom. "There was more . . . I can't really talk about it now, in front of Abbey. Another time, okay?"

"All right." I heard the tinkling of bells and a sudden sweeping silence.

"One thing, though . . . Are you there?"

"Aye, luv. Indoors now."

"I've been meaning to tell you: There's a pancake breakfast at Abbey's school coming up that she's really looking forward to . . . for Father's Day. Just be prepared, she might ask you." I braced myself and strained for a verbal reply. A steady buzzing vibrated through the phone. I pressed on. "I don't want you to feel obligated or put on the spot . . . really, I'm not going to suggest it to her. Let's see what she comes up with on her own. Are you still there?"

"I am . . . marveling . . ." The buzz filled the punctuated spaces. "Just thinking about *all* the money strewn about for *years* on Natalie in pursuit of her happiness, and here is a little girl ecstatic at the mere thought of sharing pancakes with me. Is it as simple as that?"

"It's as simple as that." An uninvited catch in my throat caused me to gulp hard.

"It would be my—*bloody fuckin' hell, man!*—pleasure and an honor, Kat." A crescendo of murderous bees rose up to drown him out.

"Adrian, where *are* you?"

"Tattoo parlor." I could hear his grin through the line. "It's a work in progress."

29

FATHER OF THE YEAR

"Mommy! There's a *taxi* at our house!"

"Yes, I know. You need to get dressed, like now. It's almost time for school."

"Did that taxi bring Adrian all the way from Mad Hatter?"

"Manhattan." I scooted her into her room. "Yes." The 6:40 a.m. train had been the only other option to get him here in time for the pancake breakfast, since we still hadn't extended our playdates to overnights. But that was about to change; Adrian had asked me to break curfew with him in the city that night.

Marissa practically ran over to pack Abbey's bag when I asked her to babysit, so elated we were finally breaking the seal. "Don't let him eat shellfish," she had warned, "or get you drunk and pukey again. I need you to come back with good morning-after stories."

What I really needed was to get through my own story— more aptly, my after-mourning story. Returning to the city, reciting it safely within my lover's embrace without having to say good-bye at night's end seemed finally . . . fine. I could do this.

"Clothes, Ab. Now." I hurried to get the door.

Electric blue Gerbera daisies clutched against a suit of the darkest slate gray greeted me.

"So dapper!"

"It's not every day I get pancakes for breakfast." He kissed me in the doorway, long and lingering. "These are for Abbey, and this . . ." He plucked out a sunny yellow bloom that I hadn't noticed stashed within the bouquet and tucked it into the tangle of my morning curls, behind my right ear. ". . . this makes those green eyes glow."

"I'll put these in water," I said, caressing my hands over his. I was still amazed by the zing his fingers never failed to produce when they came into contact with mine. I loved the feel of his flat fingertips with their calluses and grooves, especially his index finger and its permanent indent from the E string of his guitar. "Coffee?"

"Absolutely." He tossed his suit jacket onto a kitchen chair and grabbed a mug from the cupboard. I wasn't brand-obsessed, but an impressed chuckle slid out at the sight of the Armani label as the jacket slipped lazily over the ladder-back.

"Oh my God, I've never seen you in a tie before," I marveled.

"You ain't seen nothing yet!" he breathed into my ear, sending heat to my brain and down my spine until my thighs actually quivered.

I tried to remember how to breathe, but my intake was sharp, the resulting sigh ragged and full of longing. "I want to see that new tat," I murmured, "and I *will* find it." I had yet to see him unclothed since his visit to the tattoo chair; in fact, this was the longest we had gone without any feasting eyes or other body parts on each other's flesh.

"No doubt I'll enjoy your trying." He grinned.

"Adrian!"

"What's new, pussycat?" he called, pouring himself a cup.

Abbey came waltzing into the kitchen, sporting a half-and-half combo of last year's Halloween costume and this year's never-worn ballet recital outfit. After just five lessons, she had put the kibosh on ballet by pointing at the neighboring karate dojo and pronouncing her sport of choice. I now had to endure the weekly displeasure of Grant cheering his son on as the kid roundhouse-kicked his way through his classmates.

Morning patience was for some reason elusive, my criticism a bow that scraped over the tight strings of my nerves, causing even Adrian to cringe.

"Absolutely not," I said of her kitty cat ears, a ruffled black leotard with a pink-and-black polka-dotted tutu and a long cat tail attached with elastic. "Don't be ridiculous. Go—"

Abbey stamped her foot in response.

Adrian, sensing I was about to lose my mind, calmly addressed her. "It's very stylish, Abbey, but I don't think you should wear that to school."

"Why." *Stomp.* "Not?"

Leaning against the counter, Adrian took a sip from his mug before continuing. "Well, polka dots and cat tails are for fancy dress. Purple and stripey are better for school."

"Oh. Okay!" she quickly agreed, scampering out.

I mouthed a thank-you to him, and he laughed. Abbey was back moments later in her favorite purple leggings with a purple and blue–striped tunic, modeling and pirouetting. Her little plastic pocketbook with its signature happy girly skull dangled from her wrist. "Perfect." I complimented her choice, before turning to Adrian. "Seriously. Thank you."

"Look, I know it can't be easy for you. I was raised by a single parent, remember?"

"How did your dad handle you ... and your brother?"

"Dunno, really. Well, he drank quite a bit. He'd go out for his 'nightly constitutional' down at the Dog and Parrot, maybe meet a lady ... We had some temporary mum types." Setting down his coffee, he raised himself a few inches and affected a thicker accent. "Oi kids," he imitated, propping an unlit cigarette under his top lip and giving me a squinty eye, "say hullo to Doris. She's 'ere to do a bit of the washing up."

"Yikes." I plucked the Marlboro from his mouth and carefully tucked it back into the pack in his shirt pocket. "Waking up to a mother du jour had to be weird."

"It's a bird, it's a plane, it's . . . *SUPerABBEY!*" Someone was clearly overexcited about the prospect of rubbery pancakes and a morning of song. I wondered if I should warn Adrian to limit her maple syrup intake or suffer the consequences. She was careening around the kitchen, arms akimbo and mouth puttering like an engine. "Oh, pretty!" She had spotted the flowers in their vase on the counter. "Can I keep them in my room? Please, Mom?"

She went to reach for them with both hands, and before I could do or say anything, her tiny elbow made contact with the coffee mug Adrian had been drinking from. It went skittering, and I helplessly watched it plummet, then smash with a heartbreaking pop and gush; bone china and morning lifeblood scattered and smattered. "Goddammit, Abbey!" I yelled. Adrian jumped to grab paper towels. "Step back . . . go!" Abbey backed out of the kitchen, lips quivering and eyes brimming. I dropped to my knees as Adrian attempted to staunch the flow and gather the pieces carefully in the palm of his hand. *Oh, no . . .* The whimper never made it out of my vocal chords, the words were trapped painfully in the breath from my chest.

"Christ, Kat, it's not her fault. I set it too close to the edge." He swiftly rose and deposited the entire mess into the trash. "Calm down, luv. It was just a mug."

It was.

Just a stupid blue plate special diner mug from Fishs Eddy. But I had watched Pete drink from it every morning since we met. He couldn't drink coffee from a dark mug. He had fessed up to his quirk with a sheepish laugh; it made him nervous when he couldn't see how much coffee was left in the cup. Couldn't see the bottom. Couldn't see the end coming.

"I know," I whispered.

As he rested his lips on my temple, I heard the jangle of keys coming off the hook behind me. "Shall I?"

I nodded. "See you back around ten thirty? And then we'll go pick her up after school at noon."

Abbey was out on the screened porch, wrestling her feet into her sneakers. I knelt to tie her left, kissing her right knee. "I love you, Abbster. And I'm sorry. I didn't mean to yell."

"I didn't break Daddy's mug on purpose."

The tread of Adrian's shoes on the hardwood ceased.

"I know." My words echoed the response I had given Adrian just moments ago. I slowly rose, feeling his eyes upon me.

He cleared his throat. "Abbey . . . Road? Shall we hit it?"

"Pancakes!" she cheered.

He shook out his shaggy hair, as if to shake away any troublesome thoughts, before ushering her out the door. "See you, Kat."

30

MR. FAHRENHEIT

I WATCHED as Adrian snapped all the correct car seat buckles, smiled wanly at their inaudible banter. Even after the car doors closed and the Mini coasted up the street, I lingered on the porch. What was waiting for me inside? Shards of Pete in the dustbin, the silent husk of the empty house. I was exhausted, and it was only eight fifteen. A tiny funnel cloud of depression was forming, one like I hadn't felt since first moving back to Lauder Lake. Had the futon still lived on the porch, I would have collapsed onto it and slept until Adrian's return.

My gaze dropped to Abbey's boom box. The porch had become her private DJ booth where she spun tunes and danced. Some afternoons it resembled an adolescent version of an after-hours rave club; hands flailing with juice boxes held high, kids dancing the dust up from the floorboards and singing at the tops of their lungs. Other days, it was her ballet studio, where she practiced slow, complicated, and possibly self-invented dance moves, her tiny tongue pushing from the corner of her lips, mirroring her father. Somewhere in the house, harbored deep inside one of the many boxes, was a baby picture of Pete, his earliest documentation of this particular habit. I had observed it many times over the years, while he worked under deadline on various stories and even on our wedding day as he attempted to push that platinum band over my nervous knuckle.

Last night, I had witnessed a pre-bedtime air guitar porch performance, unbeknownst to Abbey. She had plenty of material to draw from: at least a half dozen of Adrian's children's performances and countless other times he had played guitar to her audience of one. Still, I was flabbergasted to see her little mouth twist up and over to one side, exactly like Adrian. It was a tug-of-war of nature versus nurture; fascinating to watch, but one I wanted to remain a tie game. An even draw. A dead heat.

I cranked the player, not caring what CD was in rotation. Anything that could cut through the silence and motivate me to move. I spent the next hour robotically moving every last box into the attic. Sweat and dust formed a protective film that enveloped me, prevented me from thinking about the life and the death within the boxes. Box after box piled up. I stood back to survey the result: a wall built of my life, pre-Adrian, next to a wall of Adrian's life, pre-me. I wished for a way to seal off the attic, for both our sakes. So we could move forward with our present and our future, leaving the excruciating excavation of our pasts for the archaeologists to uncover.

Standing in my now-uncluttered living room, the clocks warned me of the approaching hour. Hastily, I jumped into the shower. There were still my bags and Abbey's to pack for our respective overnights, and Adrian was due back any moment.

Queen was playing on repeat out on the porch when I emerged. I dueted with Freddie Mercury and finished straightening up, swiping at the checkerboard patterns of dust the boxes had left on the hardwood. I watched for the telltale blue-and-white streak to swing into the drive with increasing frequency. Where was Adrian?

Ten thirty had come and gone, as had eleven. His cell rang

until voice mail came on. Could the car have broken down? Did he crash? Had something happened at the building? A fire, a bombing . . . I contemplated calling over to the school, but decided to lay my psychosis on Marissa instead.

"Hey, is Rob back from the Father's Day thing?"

"Yeah, he had to get back to the high school to proctor a test. But we spoke briefly and he said it was beyond cute."

I craned my head toward the street again, seeing nothing but the green hedges and empty asphalt. "Did he . . . did he say Adrian was there?"

"He said Adrian ate as many pancakes, if not more, than he did. You sound freaked, Tree. What happened?"

"He's not back. It's eleven thirty and he isn't home."

"Think he got lost?"

"No, he's been back and forth with me tons of times. Besides, he'd call. Mariss . . . tell me I have nothing to worry about."

"Tree, I'm sure he's fine." I could hear the controlled pitch of her voice, quite different from her usual unrestrained Yonkers tongue. "I'll get both girls if you can't make pick-up. Maybe he stopped to buy you flowers or something."

"He brought flowers this morning. And I went all thirty-two flavors of crazy on him and Abbey earlier." I relayed the story of Pete's mug, pacing the length of the porch.

"I don't blame you for being upset . . . but did you explain why?" she wanted to know.

"No, I told myself tonight would be the night when I tell him everything, but—" I heard the pop of gravel and a door slamming. "He's here." I breathed.

"Go, go . . . see you later."

31

POP GOES THE WEASEL

"Hey." I pushed the screen door open for him. He had stripped himself of his suit jacket again, and his shirtsleeves were shoved up. The dichromatic uniform of white and gray let his eyes steal the show; their hue in the sunlight had an almost lapis lazuli–like quality. Under his tousled blond-gray locks, his cheeks were blotched with red, and it occurred to me how utterly English he looked. "How was breakfast?"

"Breakfast was good." He saluted me with a large construction paper card. I recognized Abbey's scrawl on the front, and one of her better renditions of Maxwell was grinning on what appeared to be a paper necktie. It flapped open to reveal an acrostic poem of his name:

Awesome
Dude
Rocks
I like him!
A dad
Nice

"She made me this, too. A pencil holder." He held up a soup

can decorated with colorful magazine decoupage. "For the desk in my cubicle at work." He smirked, shaking it.

"Adrian, you're bleeding." Three knuckles on his right hand had rivers of red in their creases. "What the hell happened? Where have you been?"

"Nowhere. Just . . . driving." His tone was agitated, and I watched as his eyes dropped a shade of deeper blue, their gold pyrites flecking as he squinted back out into the sunlight. "That pathetic prick . . ." *Oh, God. Grant.* "He isn't worthy of talking about you." He wouldn't look at me.

"Did you *hit* him?" I pictured Adrian decking Grant as the other parents and teachers looked on in horror. I could hear the squeals of the children and the miniature chairs raking across the floor as my boyfriend, Abbey's escort, pounded her classmate's dad.

"Yeah, I hit him! So clever with his little barbs, the cunt. I should've pummeled his bleedin' boat race the first time I laid eyes on him. Shut him up proper." The grimace on his face was circa 1985, shock rocker–worthy and full of malice. I had never seen him so incensed. "Mark my words, his son will be the spitting image," he growled. "Give him a couple of years."

I grabbed his hand. It felt swollen, and blood was smeared down his pinky as well. "Jesus, Adrian. Did the kids see?"

He shook his head. "It was afterward, outside. Behind the building." He winced under my touch and pulled away. Something in me snapped.

"You can't just go around punching people who look at you wrong or say stupid shit to you! This isn't some heroic paparazzi scuffle! What if he had called the cops? Another arrest on your record could get you deported!" I heard a raking, screechy voice and had a hard time reconciling the fact it was mine. "And then you go *driving* all around, and you don't even call . . ." One of the many grandfather clocks in the living room chimed. School dismissed in ten minutes, and I really needed about twelve to get there on time. I grabbed the car keys from the porch ledge where he had banged them down along with Abbey's gifts. "I worried myself sick."

"I was so bloody angry, Kat. I couldn't come back right away!"

I pushed past him. "It was thoughtless and irresponsible! You *know* that—" I stopped myself. But no, he didn't know. I never told him the sickening reality of what "couldn't come back" meant in my world. Pain and shame coursed through me as I stood in the driveway, chest heaving and heavy.

Adrian's palm banged the screen door open, and the rest of him came tripping down the steps after me. "Go on, Kat . . . unfit! And inappropriate. Lacking the moral fiber necessary to supervise a child! Shall I provide you with more colorful adjectives the family court solicitor assigned to me when I lost my parental rights? Thanks, Kat." He strode past me into the road, palms up and outstretched. "Thanks for the vote of confidence."

"Adr—"

"Just go get Abbey."

Turning over the ignition flooded the car with hammering drums and the distorted guitar strut of Adrian's playlist from his drive back. Drowning Pool. I didn't flinch or turn it down as I peeled out of the drive to the whisper-turned-growl of the chorus of "*Let the Bodies Hit the Floor.*" I saw Adrian's back receding in the rearview mirror. He was headed toward the lake.

I breathed deeply along with the music. I could absolutely understand the anger building up and the power of letting that anger loose. *Something's got to give.* Adrian's suit jacket was riding shotgun like a smoky specter, peppered with his scent. I rolled down both windows and gave Lauder Lake a taste of metal for possibly the second time in one hour.

There was no sign of Grant as I pulled into the drive. No

blood sprayed on the asphalt out back, only some colorful kid graffiti and the remnants of a hopscotch game. I imagined Adrian staring down silently at the chalky numbers before decking Grant on the count of five.

I was the last parent for pick-up, but everyone was all smiles when they greeted me. Miss Carly gushed at how wonderful it was to have Adrian join in the day's celebration. She didn't seem to know of the altercation that happened an hour before on school property.

"So kiddo, tell me about your day," I prompted, killing the car radio.

Abbey proceeded to go into great detail about the breakfast: the circumference of the pancakes, the thickness of the syrup, the height and width of various father figures. On and on. I tried to stay focused on all of her details, throwing in a *wow* or *cool* here and there. Her enthusiasm heartened me, but my mind was still somewhere between the coffee and the blood spills. "And Adrian let me try his coffee, even though he said I would probably like yours better because it's sweeter." Her pocketbook swung between her two hands. "Sweeter like you-u!" she trilled.

That got me to laugh. "Did Adrian say that?"

"Yes. Adrian said a lot of nice things. But Jake was mean today."

Ah, so here it was. "What did Jake say?"

Abbey fiddled with the clasp on her purse. "He said, 'Why is *he* here, he's not your dad!' So I told him Adrian *is a* dad . . . he just lives far away from his real daughter, so I'm pretending to be his daughter today so he won't feel like a daddy with no kids."

"Well, that's a nice thing for you to say."

Abbey began pulling items out of her purse and placing them neatly across her lap. I glanced in the rearview mirror as she brought out a Pez dispenser of a kitty cat and a sparkly

green guitar pick Adrian had given her. Next came a pair of
glow-in-the-dark vampire fangs waiting for her mouth to grow
into. She carefully stuffed them between her lips and did a
chomp test; no, still too big. She placed them on her lap as
well.

"Then Jake said, 'My dad says *your* dad is six feet under.'"

I jerked my head up, but she wasn't watching me. She had
pulled a photograph of Pete out of her bag. It had wrinkles
from overhandling, but was still a great shot of him. We had
gone to a marathon party at a friend's apartment that over-
looked First Avenue. Pete was in need of a haircut and shave,
but looked positively radiant in the picture, wolfy teeth and all.

"And what did you tell him?"

"I told him my dad is in the stars and had two feet, not six!
Then I said, 'Your dad must be crazy.'" The way she drawled out
her last word made me long to leap over the seat and hug her.

"Good answer, Abb. You know . . . Dad was smiling right at
you in that picture."

She was holding the photo with both hands, quite close to
her face. I leaned my chest on the steering wheel as we coasted
down our street, trying to hold my heart together in one piece.
"Yep," I managed. "Everyone at the party was looking out the
window watching the marathon runners race up the street, but
you began cooing . . . you weren't even two months old, riding
in the pouch carrier on my chest. And he turned and smiled at
you and I snapped the picture."

"Hi," Abbey said, as if she were cooing at a baby herself.
"Hi, Dad." She neatly tucked the photo into her pocketbook,
replaced her other treasures, and smiled.

"How about we get you lunch and then finish packing for
Aunt Miso's tonight?" Adrian was nowhere in sight. I wondered
if he was still at the lake. Or perhaps he had ventured up to his
metal memory lane only to find I had littered it with the tourist
trappings from my own walk of life.

"Pancakes were my breakfast *and* lunch!" Abbey moaned, rubbing her tummy. "I want to stay out here and dance."

"Suit yourself."

I found a calmer Adrian, sitting on the back steps with what looked and smelled like a double Jack on the rocks. His knuckles were cleaned up, but a Marlboro was burning down to the filter between them. He hadn't been smoking much as of late, and never in front of Abbey. "She all right?" he inquired, stubbing the butt out against the thin sole of his dress shoe.

I squeezed onto the stoop next to him. "Yeah," I answered softly. "She had a lot of fun with you." We bumped shoulders and sat quietly for a few moments. Birds relayed their afternoon chatter through the treetops. I could hear the faint rattle and hum of Abbey's music and subsequent dance steps. "I didn't mean to make you feel . . ." I paused as he took a slug of whiskey. "I'm sorry," I whispered.

"You and Abbey mean the world to me. But you deserve better—"

"Stop, don't—"

"No, let me say this. You make me want to be a better man. I need to remember that before going off half-cocked next time. To think of you and Abbey. If I'm going to throw stones, I need to pay mind to the ripples in the pool."

"Listen, Grant's the type of guy who loves to get under people's skin. He hasn't matured since—"

"Since you slept with him?" Adrian said around a mouthful of ice cubes.

"Is that what he was going on about? At a preschool breakfast? See, that just goes to show you he's obviously living in some sort of warped past."

"Aren't we all?" he asked, sharp and sudden.

"All what?"

"Dealing . . . or not dealing . . . with our past? Kat. You've got to talk about Pete."

Stunned, I couldn't pull my thoughts together fast enough to respond. "If not to me, then at least to Abbey."

"We talk," I mumbled lamely. "I won't ever deprive Abbey of him."

The phone began to ring, but neither of us made a move. Adrian's cheeks were still flushed, from drink or sun or perhaps heated from the confrontation. This was far from how I had expected the day to go. I certainly didn't think I would go ballistic over spilled coffee, and I'm sure Adrian didn't wake up that morning determined to punch someone. Or fight with me.

"You know, I wish someone would write a bloody book about *you*. I can't crack you, Kat. Hard as I try, I can't crack you."

"Mom . . . Aunt Miso's on the phone." Abbey was pressing her nose flat against the metal screen. "Adrian, want to see me climb the tree?"

I hitched my hand under the door from where I was sitting and pulled it toward me. Abbey came hopping down the steps, handing me the phone.

"Initiating Operation Dupioni Silk."

It took me a moment to realize what or whom Marissa was referring to. "Leanna?"

"Major meltdown. At the mall."

"Crap." Meltdowns in your midthirties should not take place at the Lauder Lake Mall. Especially not for Leanna, whose favorite escape was thrifty shopping.

"My mom's here. Bring Abbey."

Abbey was wedged in the crotch of the crabapple tree; Adrian was leaning an arm against the trunk and surveying her progress. I noticed he hadn't loosened the grip on the antique Hawkes whiskey glass in his hand. It was a rare cut-glass tumbler from the six-piece set that normally never left its place of honor in my mother's china cabinet. Had she been here, she'd no doubt trail behind his every move with a pillow, poised to catch it lest his grasp slip.

"There's a crisis," I said quietly. "With Leanna. I'm sorry . . ."

"Go." We were still in the midst of our own crisis, but I could tell his tone was genuine. "It's okay. Go to her."

"Thank you. Abb, come on down. We need to go to Aunt Miso's now. Grab your bag." I touched his shoulder. "You'll stay?"

He shook his head. "I'm feeling a bit . . . penned in. The house today . . . feels like it's coming down on me." His eyes flicked toward the garage. "I'm gonna ride." He handed me his drink.

"You can't ride home!" I pictured Adrian in Armani, weaving through traffic off the GW Bridge. Abbey pulled a move like a lemur and landed in his outstretched arms. His reflexes were quick, but still I worried what would become of him.

"Silly girl." He deposited Abbey neatly on the ground, and she was off running in the direction of the house. "I'll ride to the station, take the train back."

"Please be careful."

"Please be my date tonight? You'll still come down, right? There's something I want to show you."

"As soon as I can," I vowed. "I will be there. I've got some show-and-tell for you myself." Only the sweet whiskey aftertaste lingered on his lips as he rested them quickly on mine before retreating to the garage.

32

MALL RATS

"WHERE DO you think she could be?"

Marissa studied the mall directory in front of us with the interest and zeal of a philologist decoding Sanskrit. "She said she was between Macy's and the Hallmark store . . . Come on, this way." It had been years since Marissa had worked at the mall, but she navigated the various aisles and escalators with a keen homing sense.

"Do you know what prompted the meltdown?"

Marissa shook her head. "I do know she was hella ticked off the other day about something Ed did or didn't do. I thought she was going to send a gaggle of holy crows to descend upon him."

"Murder."

"Oh come on, Tree. That's a little much."

"No, I mean it's a murder of crows. Gaggle is reserved for geese."

"How did I get a friend as freaky as you?"

"Just lucky, I guess." I spied Leanna, sitting catatonic on a bench. We made a beeline toward her, dodging giggling teen girls as they swung their shopping bags and tiny Abercrombie-clad butts in exaggerated mall-walk fashion.

"I went into the card store," Leanna sniffed, "to pick out a Father's Day card. There were romantic ones, and funny ones, and heartfelt ones . . . Things with Ed are not romantic or funny. My heart . . . feels dead."

Sensing the need for reinforcements, we steered her right toward the tiny café tucked between Victoria's Secret and Pretzel Heaven. Halfway through large iced double capps, the floodgate opened. Leanna was oddly calm as she reiterated how, after reading card after card, she realized how utterly inappropriate and hopeless her and Ed's relationship was.

"Come on, Le . . . life isn't supposed to be summed up in a three-dollar card," I reminded her.

"Karen's, maybe," Marissa joked, her cheekbones sucked slim to drain the dregs of her drink. "Can you imagine what mine would say? *To the love of my life, who needs to lose twenty pounds—I'm going to give you amazing head tonight and then we'll watch* The Late Show. *Happy freakin' Father's Day!*"

Leanna managed a smile. "You could have your very own line of Kiss My Lily-white Ass cards."

"Start designing . . . we'll make millions. Build a compound, hire some fine pool boys. Who'll need husbands?"

"I can't believe I was ever sold on the idea of marriage in the first place." Leanna dipped her lips down onto her straw. I flicked my gaze over her head and met Marissa's, who raised one carefully plucked brow. "I think I was afraid of being alone."

"But you're not alone . . . you've got all of us, and we're not going anywhere." I balled up my straw wrapper and flicked it at her.

"Except for Tree, who's going to Manhattan tonight, all night."

Leanna's mouth made a mini lipsticked O. "That's right,

what the hell are you doing here? I'm keeping you from all the hot Central-Park-view sex, Tree!"

"And morning after tea-and-crumpets-with-the-rich-guy sex," Marissa added.

"Forget greeting cards. You guys need to collaborate and write erotica," I joked. "There's plenty of time to get into town. I wanted to make sure you're okay."

Leanna sighed. "I think . . . I'm going to be all right. But it's time to insist he comes to joint therapy . . . and I'm going to ask around about some legal counsel, too."

"Good girl." Marissa nodded. "Face your fears."

"I can't even face the Rubbermaid storage under my bed."

"One box at a time. Right, Tree?"

I thought of the marathon move that morning. I hadn't faced anything; I merely hauled it out of sight. Adrian was right. What was I so afraid of? Pete was just dreams and bones, like in that folk song about the garden on *Songs for Natalie*. But if I built him up with words, would he chase Adrian away? Or was I scared the ghost would abandon me if I verbalized it?

"Take charge, Le. Like you always used to," I heard myself say.

"And speaking of charging . . ." Marissa scraped her chair back. "I think we need to swipe the ol' credit card a few times before we blow this joint. Tree, we're not going to let you wear Pete's old boxers for sexy time with Adrian."

"Hell no. Let's go next door and find her some crotchless panties!" Leanna was back and in her zone, surveying the stores on either side of us. "Then I want a pretzel dog."

"Gotta love the mall!" I laughed.

33

COMEBACK KID

FUELED by espresso and armed with several lacy undergarments whose price tags had been carefully removed by Marissa's teeth, I rocketed down the West Side Highway. *Meet me in the Land of Eternal Youth,* read Adrian's most recent text message. *I'll be there, drinking Guinness.*

Cars were hydroplaning past me in the rain, and there wasn't much time to decipher his clues on my own. I dialed Marissa and got her on speaker. "Hey, are you near your computer? Can you Google 'land of eternal youth' and 'Irish'?" I certainly hoped the place he was referencing was in the borough of Manhattan and not Kilkenny.

"Is this another one of your nerdy cryptic things? It translates to . . . not sure if I am pronouncing this right . . ." Marissa stumbled over the words with her Yonkers tongue.

"Tír na nÓg, excellent! Thanks, Mariss." Many a lunch hour had been spent at the restaurant bearing that name on the corner of 33rd and Eighth. It was painfully close to Penn and my old office. Pushing those thoughts aside, I merged boldly east toward Adrian.

Artificial sun and dry skies awaited under an awning of

black and orange as I allowed myself to be swallowed up by the wide bright mouth of the parking garage nearest Penn station. I stashed my overnight bag in the trunk before relinquishing my keys to the parking attendant. "Wait, hold on." I grabbed Adrian's jacket at the last minute and slipped it on before ascending up the slick ramp to surface level.

The rain had let up somewhat; random fat drops plunked down rudely in strategic spots. It was easily ten degrees cooler than earlier in the afternoon. I crisscrossed the Armani arms across my chest for warmth as I jaywalked swiftly across the avenue. This section of the city was hell this time of day on a Friday; the weary workday commuters and early-bird weekend revelers were not quite where they wanted to be, forming a slow-moving purgatory across the sidewalks and pissing me off.

"Kat!"

Adrian pulled me from the crowded path and kissed me under the bar's golden sign. A cement column and a large ornamental potted tree blocked us on either side from being jostled back into the fray. His hands found mine, lost under excess inches of his jacket sleeves.

"I started to think you wouldn't . . ." A wayward raindrop broke against the top of our lips as they met again. "I'm sorry, Kat. Earlier . . ."

I shook my head, leaning my temple on his cheek. "No. Don't you apologize," I whispered. It was easy to close out everything, with my eyes pressed shut and his arms around me. But when I opened them, I was staring straight across at the last doorway I ever saw Pete walk through. My ghosts were gaining on me.

"You're shaking."

"I'm all right." Through the bar window, I saw a strange mixture of rough-looking longhairs, suited professionals, and Hell's Kitchen locals. "Are we going in?"

"No time. Unless you're famished, we could grab something

somewhere quick." He gestured vaguely toward the other corners.

It took most of my faculties to keep my eyes off both the doorway into Penn Station and the lacerations on Adrian's knuckles. I shook my head, antsy and ready to roll wherever it was we were going.

The rain and sidewalk crowds had disappeared as we hurried up the block. "So am I dressed right for where we're going?" I was still in the silky kimono wrap top and jeans I had thrown on after my cleaning binge and shower.

With a smile, Adrian flicked his eyes over me. "It'll do. Trade jackets with me, though. You'll probably be more comfortable in my leather. There . . . biker meets bohemia. You never fail to look beautiful, Kat."

An irritated hipster with a swoop of stupid-looking hair bumped shoulders hard with Adrian. "Jeez, walk much?" We had disrupted the flow of foot traffic, apparently.

"Easy there, mister cockedy man." Adrian's murmur was more amused than offended. What a relief, and a far cry from the day's earlier events. He let the rude guy push past us, yet we continued to shadow him up the street.

As we approached the pale-bricked front of the Hammerstein Ballroom, the hipster and Adrian made similar abrupt right-angle turns under the UFO-bright lights outside. "Guest list?" Adrian asked the bouncer at the door, who motioned toward a will-call window. Hipster got stopped in his tracks yet again at the end of a long line behind swags of velvet rope.

I had missed the name on the marquee, such was my preoccupation with street etiquette. "Who's playing?" I whispered excitedly in Adrian's ear as he showed his ID and was handed a plain white envelope. From the crowd, it was hard to tell. Although it appeared many of the long-haired clientele had moved up the block from the bar.

"Dead Can Dream. They're kind of new prog metal meets post-hardcore."

"Translation?"

"I think you'll like them."

I wasn't the only one wearing a leather jacket in June. As we were sucked deeper into the cattle-crowd, I understood Adrian's earlier comment about feeling more comfortable in it; it provided a tough barrier and a camouflage of similar skin to protect me. Adrian, meanwhile, appeared perfectly at ease in his Armani and denim. "Just a small piece of my world," he shouted over the din. Screeching guitars and tribal thumping competed with the roar of three thousand throats. Evidently, the band of the hour had taken the stage. "Another stop on the Digger Graves five-quid tour."

We squeezed down a narrow aisle toward the bright lights of the stage and the sea of writhing bodies on the floor. "We're not going into *that*, are we?"

"Gen pop? Wouldn't think of it." He led us up a tiny staircase and showed his tickets to security at the top. We were ushered into a decent size opera box, the lowest one stage right. I could see three similar boxes across the venue from us, jutting from each curved balcony level. All were packed with people, but ours stayed relatively empty. Those who were in the box with us wore satin VIP sticky passes of green and black. Adrian pulled ours from the ticket envelope. He nonchalantly stuck one on his denim-clad thigh and applied mine to my top, above my right breast. "Hello, Miss VIP."

The band was impressive. I had a hard time deciding where to look as the lasers, lights, and backdrops pulled my eyes from each band member and back again. The singer was a stump of a guy with a long black ponytail and a powerhouse voice that ripped through the rafters of the building. He was flanked by one guitarist and a bass player, but the sound was large, heavily melodic, and constant. Our vantage point provided a great view of the drummer, who was mesmerizing to watch. I could see the grim set of his mouth, lips pressing closed in concentration, as his muscular arms, colorfully sleeved in tattoos from his shoulders to his elbows, snapped out from his body.

"That's my friend Jim." Adrian nodded in proud approval with each beat, but he kept his arms crossed for most of the show. I watched him survey the audience every now and again, his eyes flicking cool and calculating over the crowd.

The house lights came up as the band exited for a short set break. The low buzz of the crowd and Gabriel-era Genesis from the PA took its place. Adrian found my belt loops under the leather and silk and hooked his fingers through them, pulling me close. "Whaddaya think?"

I was thinking I wanted to model my lingerie for him, but stuck to the topic at hand. "Killer. Like Porcupine Tree meets Coheed and Cambria."

He seemed to enjoy that reference. "Let's go say hi to Jim." He took my hand, and we scurried down the stairs and through a side door that led backstage. Every security guard inspected our passes with a silent nod. We found ourselves making our way up a steep stairwell, then down a cramped hallway full of chatter and pot smoke. The tiny greenroom was impossible to access. I plastered myself to Adrian's side as he checked his phone. "He's in the dressing room. One more flight up."

Another round of stairs put us in a much quieter, although still diminutive, space. Luckily, there were far fewer people in the room. In fact, it held just the four band members who had occupied the stage moments ago. The singer smiled shyly as he passed, towel tucked around his shoulders, on his way down to his friends. The guitarist was wolfing down a limp turkey sandwich from a deli plate on the counter while talking on his cell. Jim was in deep conversation with the bass player, but as he caught Adrian's reflection in the mirror that spanned one long wall, he spun and grinned. "My brother of steel. What is up, my friend?"

They greeted each other with a solid hug, one so long that the bass player and I smiled at each other and began laughing. Introductions were made all around, and Jim played a tired but happy host, offering us catering and beer. Out from behind the drums, he was over six feet tall, with chiseled good looks and a neat dark goatee similar to Adrian's. I put him around my age. They chatted about the tour, and Adrian asked after Jim's family. It occurred to me he was the first person I'd met in person from Adrian's past life. "How long have you known each other?" I asked.

Jim turned to Adrian. "You didn't tell her?"

Adrian laughed. "You tell the story better than I."

Jim ran his hand over the damp bandanna knotted to his head, smoothing the wavy brown hair that escaped through the back. "It was the *Metastasis* World Tour, I was fifteen. Kat, if I tell you Corpse was my favorite band, I'd be downplaying it. Huge fan! So they're playing an amphitheater in my small hometown—"

Adrian rubbed at his graying goatee. "Was that the Merriweather?"

"Yes. Don't interrupt! So they're playing my hometown. Columbia, Maryland. Not only is this my first Corroded Corpse concert, it's my first rock show *ever*. The band was on fire. I was right up front, caught Riff's pick, the whole nine yards. And after the show, my buddy and I decided to wait behind the stage to try to meet them."

"You and about forty birds . . . Guess who got backstage?" Adrian joked.

"My friend got tired of waiting, and his mom was driving us, so he totally bailed. I didn't care. I waited for, like, two hours, and finally it paid off. I met every guy in the band but you,

Digger; you were the last to come out. I thought I had missed you."

"Me and Cass," Adrian recalled. "He had a hired car and we were headed back to the hotel."

"The hotel that I knew was right near my house," Jim added. "So after you gave me your autograph, I summoned up the nerve to ask you for a lift home. And you said—"

Adrian laughed. "Fuck off. Or was it bugger off?"

"Adrian!" I gasped, giggling.

He raised his brow at me. "What? He was a cheeky little git."

"So that was that; they drove away," Jim continued. "Out of luck. Five minutes later, I was looking around to find a pay phone to call home when their car pulls back around." He paused and smiled at Adrian. They were like an old married couple, fondly finishing each other's stories.

"And I said, 'Get in the bloody car'—I couldn't just leave him there!"

"And then my mom made you the best damn she-crab soup you had ever had—"

"The *only* she-crab soup I had ever had . . . the best damn thing I had tasted Stateside."

"And so twenty years later"—Jim spread out his arms —"here we are. Do you kids need a ride home tonight?"

"Seriously . . . you've stayed in touch all this time?"

"Yeah . . . pretty much. Every northeast Corpse gig after that. Then I started DCD in '93, and I guess we've seen each other, what? Maybe a dozen times since? Not enough, man. You look good." Jim turned to me. "Kat, seriously. It must be you, because normally he looks half in the bag." Adrian squeezed my hand, and I squeezed back, smiling. "Dig, so you wanna?"

"Depends. Which one?"

"'Syndrome.'"

"When?"

"Second segue."

I glanced from one to the other, trying to get a handle on this line of conversation. Along with unique facial hair, musicians apparently shared their own tonal language.

"Nah."

"Come on."

"All right. No intro."

"Deal. Outro?"

"Fine."

The tour manager was rounding the band up like a large pissed off mother hen, trying to herd them back onstage. Jim gave me a bear hug, hissing into my ear, "Keep him around, okay?" With a slap handshake to Adrian: "Staying for the aftershow?"

"Don't press your luck."

The band thundered down the stairs, and a few moments later, we heard the crowd raise a massive cheer and the room thump with muffled acoustics from below.

"Quickie in the dressing room?" Adrian suggested, stripping off his jacket.

"What, are you—"

"Kidding, Kat. Kidding! I'm sitting in with the band in a moment." He chuckled.

"That's what you guys were going on about? I had no clue. Seriously?"

"Yeah. It's actually a Corpse song they're covering. They play it better than we ever did, in fact." He handed me his jacket. The tour manager popped his head over the stair railing.

"Sean wants to know if playing his Roadstar is okay for you."

"Absolutely, mate."

I followed them down the stairs, which was an entirely different experience now that the band was back onstage. The manager used a Maglite to direct me to a safe spot backstage as a guitar tech rigged Adrian up. Whatever song they had been playing segued right into "Syndrome Dreamer," whose opening bars now sounded vaguely familiar to me. In fact, I was pretty sure I had pinpointed Adrian's mobile ringtone. I recalled Kevin commenting years back that the rarely played song displayed a "cerebral side" of Corroded Corpse. At the time, I had considered that description as the mother of all oxymorons, but now, as I concentrated on the lyrics while watching its creator shred a complex composition so melodic it brought tears to my eyes, I was glad to be proved wrong.

Pieces of darkness
haunt the unusual
painting the world
of the syndrome dreamer.
Fate is the key
chance, the answer
unlock the door
to the unknown.

From my perch tucked between the monitor board and half the road crew, I could see down into the pit. As Adrian had once described, only the first several rows of the crowd were illuminated and visible, but I detected an incredible wave of response coming from the entire house as I watched arms swaying in unison and heard the appreciative whistles and screams. I wondered where in the crowd Irritated Hipster Guy had ended up. Had he realized his brush with greatness? The opera box we had vacated held several more bodies now, nodding and staring with rapt attention.

Star-tipped whispers
refrigerated doubts
a man of many colors
answers number zero.

Although the band had respectfully shifted to allow him to come front and center, Adrian chose to hang back. My eyes delighted in taking him in from head to toe. The lights wove crazy patterns over his shaggy hair and bounced blindingly off the tiny silver trails of the pickups as he moved. His stance was one of accomplished nonchalance as he leaned slightly back, his gaze shifting only from the frets to the other musicians as his fingers nimbly up-stroked and pulled off from impossibly high frets to create the most spine-tingling arpeggios.

Untame the obvious
despondent fear of shadows
recalling the morose
at the hands of the syndrome dreamer.

Jim grinned as his arms swung like a demented octopus, making contact with every skin and cymbal as the song's crescendo thundered to the rafters.

"Mr. Digger Graves, ladies and gentleman!"

Adrian didn't stick around to witness the response of the singer's pronouncement; I watched as the neck of the guitar swung back with his sudden movement and he pivoted on the heel of his motorcycle boot. He was shrugging off the guitar strap and handing the axe back to the guitar tech with a nod as the band played the last dwindling notes of his song. The crowd's cacophony tunneled behind us down the cement ramp and out a back exit door near the loading dock. We were practically to Eighth Avenue before he released his grip around my waist and spoke.

"You don't see that every night, now do you?"

"Adrian," I began as he pulled me close to fumble into the pockets of his leather to find his cigarettes, "that was incredible! Do you realize what—"

"What being outed onstage after fifteen years of silence means? Pretty sure it means fuck-all." He exhaled smoke toward the summer sky, then fixed his gaze pointedly on me.

"I was going to say what that meant to your friend Jim, to

play with one of his heroes. And what it meant to me, to finally see you *really* play . . . a song you created," I blurted.

He stomped on the barely smoked cigarette and proceeded over the zebra-crossing without a sideways or a backward glance. I stood defiant, allowing my words to plow after him rather than my feet.

"We believe in you. But if you can't even give yourself that courtesy, then yes—it means fuck-all!"

A taxi's horn provided an exclamation point, punctuating my outburst. It whizzed narrowly by Adrian as he strode back across the avenue. The rise of his chest and his sigh was a complete surrender. I pulled him off the sewer grate and into my arms, and his lips fell on mine with a hard crush.

"You've got all this. . . this love—no, it's louder than love. It's passion and beauty built up inside you that deserves to burst out," I whispered against his mouth as we came up for air.

"Where's your car?"

"That's all you've got to say?"

"For now . . . yes."

34

BLOSSOMING

WAKING up in Manhattan was both comforting and surreal. Opening my eyes to find Adrian lying next to me on the bed in peaceful slumber was almost dreamlike, especially after the intensity of the evening's events.

We had scrambled up to his apartment and had barely made it through the door fully clothed, not bothering to flick a light switch. I was still quivering with the memory: my silky lingerie lay forgotten in my bag as he stripped me down bare and spread me across the Persian rug. His tongue urged me toward a screaming finish, but I denied myself, instead pulling him roughly toward me, yanking off the rest of his clothes. Adrian deftly flipped me over and I bent invitingly, yielding to him by the expanse of his living room windows. His hands cupped my breasts, protecting them from the cold glaze of the glass as he slid into me from behind, a foot propped on the low sill for leverage. We both came rapidly, suspended above the rustling treetops in the deep violet sky, Adrian's breath over my shoulder fogging the scenery and my mind. It had been easy to fall back against him, mewing and crawling into his naked lap, kissing every inch I could find in the dark.

Now the dawn sifted in through a gap in the curtain, motes of dust sparkling in a lone spotlight leading to the newest tattoo on my lover's body. So there it was. On his side with his arm thrown over his head in slumber, Adrian provided me a luxurious full view of a beautiful flowering desert cactus that ran from his hipbone to his armpit. The stem was various shades of green and rose up to mid-rib, with spiny clusters—some curving, some straight, projecting out in every direction; some black fading into gray, others yellow into white. Smaller ribs of the plant undulated from the body, and it was then I noticed a slim smooth snake, brown and gray, coiling carefully between the spikes on its mission upward. Its reward was apparent: A lush funnel-shaped bloom fanned up toward his armpit, the colors flaming orange bleeding into dark red. The lower buds harbored a few remaining spikes near its base before changing to smooth and waxy petals. The detail inside was incredible, complete with a thick nectar chamber and dozens of thready pink stamens at the center.

Adrian had once likened me to a desert flower, soon after my Memorial Day purge and clam-up. "You bristle to keep people at bay," he had commented. "But your blooms keep them coming back." I hadn't taken offense; I knew the quality had mutated in me during those dry and barren years after Pete. Perhaps Adrian saw himself as the snake, an unlikely suitor stereotypically unequipped to bring solace but determined to do so. Who was more likely to injure the other? I didn't want to currently contemplate it, not on our first real morning together.

Like a film in reverse mode, I slipped naked out of bed and into one of my new negligees. Marissa and Leanna had tried to sway me away from my choice, saying it was too bordello red with too much black lace, but I had insisted. The bathroom mirror agreed with my choice; I smiled at the way the bottom hem graced my legs, how tiny my waist looked as the red silk ruched up tastefully over my chest, and how the black lace straps flattered as they widened over my ivory shoulders. I brushed my teeth and completed my loop back into bed.

"Oh my . . . my, my, my," Adrian murmured; he was just stretching and blinking as I eased back down next to him. "Let me drink you in . . . wow."

I straddled his sheet-swathed midsection and let him admire the view. "I match your flower," I whispered, leaning to kiss the complex corolla of the fresh tattoo.

"You *are* my flower," he whispered back, fingers moving along the lacey hem as if to memorize where it met my flesh. "My *Echinocereus triglochidiatus*. Yes, big word . . . I know. Trying to impress you."

I pressed my chest to his bare one, allowing my hands to run over his smooth, strong shoulders. "Oh yeah? Tell me more."

"The desert flower takes five to ten years after sowing to bloom." He ran his fingers around the lacy straps and down the neckline. "Then the flower only opens for a few days at a time."

"Sounds like beauty worth waiting for," I breathed, kissing his cheek and sliding toward his ear. "Like you and me." I felt him squirm under me. I knew the combination of my whisper and just the slightest pressure of my lips and tongue was delicious torture to that particular erogenous zone.

"Kat," he groaned. "Come 'ere, love." He pulled my face gently to his. "I was an utter prat last night. You must think me some fool drama queen. I'm sorry."

"Shhh, no." My lips found his neck, and the silky barrier between us aided me as I shimmied slowly lower, my mouth never breaking contact with his skin. When I licked the spot where the *misericorde* ended and his scars began, I heard a sharp intake of breath, felt his frame stiffen. For once he didn't attempt to stop me as I dipped my head farther. I felt his fingers through my hair, lifting it off my face from where it was blocking his view. He wanted to watch me. I flicked my eyes up for a moment and saw his flutter in conflicted rapture.

Somewhere deep within the house, his landline phone began to ring. I didn't slow my pace or break my rhythm, and he uttered a strangled groan of approval. I felt his toes curl under the sheets. "Kat, baby . . . you're amazing . . . please, not yet . . ." I acquiesced, rising only to lower myself upon him. Silk and lace pooled across his tight tattooed torso. "We're not using anything . . . are we okay?"

"It's a safe time." My words were lost to his mouth as he leaned up to press it tightly to mine. Our slow movements kept him so close and deep, all we could do was stare at each other in wonder. The landline began to ring again. "Maybe you should—" He thrust my breath wordlessly out of me, and I began to shake as my climax rained down from deep within.

I could tell Adrian was ready; he had been holding off and waiting for me. His cell phone began to peal on the nightstand as I felt him buck under me, rear up as I rode him harder toward the edge, and then I felt his release.

"Robyn!"

35

BATTLE CALL

MY EAR WAS PRESSED against his neck, but I clearly heard him utter his ex-wife's name. My mouth froze midkiss against his shoulder, and I felt him steadily shrink within me.

It took me a moment to realize he was acknowledging her call and not, as I had ridiculously assumed, calling out her name in the throes of passion. I awkwardly attempted to disengage myself from him and not eavesdrop as the verbal sparring began.

"No, I wasn't screening my calls . . . because last I checked, New York is five fecking hours behind London. You do the math," he snapped. "All right, you have my attention now, so what—*What?* When?" Whatever Robyn was relaying, Adrian's face took it in and boomeranged it back out with a hurt grimace. "Can you not play the blame game, just tell me what the doctors . . . Can they stop it without surgery? Do they know . . . Robyn . . . Okay. Well, what is the success rate of that? When will they start?" He was up and rummaging through his bureau, raking a pair of boxers up his slim frame with one hand. "I'm not going to wait here while . . . Honestly, I could give a fuck what *Leopold* recommends . . . Yes, well, *I* prefer to call him that, thank you . . . I don't know, I'll ring you when it's sorted."

I stared at the compass rose that spanned my lover's back, watched as his shoulders shook slightly. "Adrian . . ."

"It's Natalie." He paced toward his laptop, wrenching it open and firing it up. "She had an accident. Horseback riding. Robyn waits half a bloody day to tell me, and then has the nerve to tell me *not* to come? That it's my fault for buying her a horse in the first place?" His laugh came out as a bitter bark. "I may be five hours behind, but who's the one living in the past?" He paced back to the dresser drawers and began plucking items out. "That notion is so ridiculous, I'd laugh . . . if it wasn't so damn dire. The swelling is putting pressure on her brain. They've medically induced a coma, pending surgery."

I scrambled off the bed. "You pack. I'll find a flight." My hands shook across the keyboard, and I willed my mind to stay on task. "Here's one, nonstop from Newark. It leaves at 6:25 p.m. and gets into Heathrow at 6:40 a.m."

"Nothing earlier? Gatwick?" He leaned over my shoulder.

"No, nothing nonstop. We've missed the morning flights."

"Book it." He tossed a credit card onto the desk and fled from the room.

I stood bent over the laptop, mouse arrow hovering near the "ticket quantity" dropdown box. The result of our unprotected union trickled slowly down my thigh. "One . . . ?"

"Yes, one way." He was back, leather shaving case in hand. "Robyn and Leopold will no doubt loathe my indefinite existence, but I don't give a flying monkey's."

"Abbey and I have passports. If you need . . . We could . . ."

"Not necessary." He began to fatten up his rucksack with shirts and sock rolls. "It will be enough of a mad scene without having to explain you."

I knew Natalie was the focus, but his words stung. I

continued booking his flight, biting my lip in feigned concentration.

"Come on, love. You know I don't talk to them much, they're so wrapped up in themselves." He sidled up to me, kissing my shoulder as I clicked through the confirmation process. "I need to get some cash, dollars and pounds. And I've got nothing here to speak of in the way of food. My bank is on Fifth; we can stop there and then go to the Naked Bagel. Ah wait, but Liz . . ."

"She's never there on weekends."

"Still on the outs?"

"Yeah. I miss her. And her damn bagels."

Adrian's master bathroom shower put the facilities I had regrettably passed up at the Plaza Hotel to shame. Not only did he have a luxury showerhead about as big as a Seattle rain cloud, but there were several other sprayers at various angles and pressures as well that worked to invigorate and calm. I wished we could've stayed in there until we drained the borough dry, but Adrian's boarding time was creeping closer.

On our way through the lobby, we passed by the dentist whose office was on the ground floor of the building. His face was a familiar one, and pleasantries were often exchanged when we passed in the hall. But today he was eying Adrian with wary respect. "That was you, wasn't it? At the Hammerstein last night?" He didn't wait for acknowledgment before stammering excitedly, "I had no clue . . . you! And you *live* here?" He shook his head. "How cool is that? Wow!"

Adrian gave a smile and a nod as he took my arm and didn't break his stride on his way out the door.

"Metalhead dentist . . . Maybe he has a musician discount?" I laughed as Adrian gave my comment a dismissive yet modest roll of the eyes.

We swept into the cold confines of the bank right before its noon closing time. "Oh, for fuck's sake," Adrian muttered, his hand shaking as he penned his withdrawal request. "Do you hear that?" The piped-in Muzak filtering down was unmistakably a light instrumental version of "Simone." "Goddamn Wren..."

"Try to ignore it," I said, pulling him through the velvet ropes to the waiting teller. The Muzak droned on ridiculously, Adrian's blistering guitar solo replaced by the pan flute.

"Yes, can't you see I'm laughing . . . all the way to the bank? Ho ho ho," Adrian remarked sardonically, pocketing the many pounds sterling, dollar bills, and traveler's cheques.

"Call me when you arrive? No matter what time?" I had escorted Adrian as far as security would let me.

"And I will call you every day after that. Promise. Kiss Abbey for me?" I nodded my head close to his, allowing the peppery comfort of him to sink into my skin. "Sorry I'm going to miss your parents' visit."

Tears were brimming, but I laughed. "No you're not." I had forewarned him the moment my parents had announced their plans to stop en route to Kevin's annual Independence Day cook-off.

"Okay, admittedly I was terrified." He pressed his lips into a tiny smile. "But still."

"But still." I squeezed his fingers in mine. "Love you . . . God, I love you. Hoping for the best for Natalie."

"That means . . . that means the world to me. Thank you. I want her to meet you. And Abbey . . . my world."

I felt his kiss long after it broke; I needed to.

There's something heartbreakingly intimate about watching your lover carefully remove his shoes and offer them up to strangers for inspection, along with his cache of toiletries. His eyes caught mine right before he crossed the last security checkpoint; his lips formed clear, legible words of love, and then he moved swiftly through to the other side.

36

PARENTAL CONTROLS

ADRIAN'S CALLS weren't daily, as promised. He was having trouble with his phone and putting in long hours at the hospital, but his news regarding Natalie was heartening. The doctors had placed shunts and were expecting a full recovery, pending physical therapy. One silver lining, he relayed via e-mail, was the postponement of her wedding.

My parents arrived in their usual fashion, fussing over Abbey and hijacking my bedroom for a week. Secretly, I didn't mind moving into the boogeymen room. I slept under Digger's watchful eye, his secrets safe with me. On occasion, I would scan the various metal forums and news sites online for reactions to his brief Hammerstein appearance. It had already become the stuff of legend among the die-hard fans and had piqued the curiosity of the newer, younger Corroded Corpse fans who had missed seeing the band play live in their heyday. Rumors raced through the threads, and speculation as to an eventual reunion racked up the post counts and started many a heated discussion. New York fans had the bragging rights, and several claimed to have seen their elusive hero on the streets of the East Village or drinking in local haunts. Blurry photos, captured with phone cameras during the brief window of opportunity Adrian's cameo had allowed, began popping up one by one on blogs and social networking sites. Unseen by the public for nearly two decades, he had become the metal world's Bigfoot, their Loch Ness monster. And here was proof. He still existed.

I reasoned it was conveniently best for him to be out of the country now, of all times, although there was no way to convince my mother of the same. She took it as a personal affront upon arrival, and subsequently made daily barbs, bringing into question his actual existence.

"Abbey darling," I overheard her ask, "tell me what you like about mommy's new friend Adrian."

"I like that he lives in the park."

"He lives in a *park*?" Great. Now she'd have him pegged for a homeless man. Or a woodland sprite.

"Not *a* park, Grandma. *The* park. Central Park! He lives above it." She paused to pull Adrian's quip from the stores of her young mind. "Twenty-six hundred square feet of the Manhattan sky. But not quite in the stars. That's where Daddy is."

Grandma was very interested now, but remained cautiously skeptical.

"I can't believe we're missing him by mere days," she moaned. "Phil, should we change our flights? We *can* change our flights."

"Mom, no . . . there's no sense. He'll be jetlagged, and you need to get to Kev's for the big showdown."

My parents took great pride in watching their son's restaurant go head-to-head against several of Portland's finest every July Fourth. Although to this day, my dad just shakes his head at the commercial success my brother has eked out for himself with BITE ME. "I don't get it," my dad would say of the restaurant, which specializes exclusively in hors d'oeuvre–sized portions. Thimble-size flights of soups, dollhouse hamburgers. He was once served a miniature replica of fish and chips. "It was a flake of fish on top of a French fry. Jesus Christ, for five dollars?"

"Do you at least have a picture of him to show me?"

I rolled my eyes, thinking ironically of the entire top floor of her house and its decades-old shrine devoted to him.

"I've got one!" Abbey galloped a loop from kitchen to bedroom and back, clutching a picture Miss Carly had snapped at the pancake brunch.

"Handsome," my mother allowed. "He's quite gray, isn't he?"

"And purple. And red and black and blue and green!" Abbey crowed. She was fascinated with Adrian's indelible ink and loved to add to his landscape with her own washable marker doodles; he patiently allowed her to use the available bare spots on his arms like a live-action coloring book.

I stared at the photo. Debonair in his suit, with his hands on Abbey's shoulders and his cheek pressed close to hers, Adrian grinned as if he knew the picture would eventually fall into my hands. Abbey's eyes sparkled up at me, tiny pearls of teeth displayed in a sweet smile. Nothing about the photo indicated the mug-breaking incident that had preceded it, nor the single-round sparring match that was next to come. Just another beautiful blip of time, caught frozen on film.

THE ATTIC ROOM was like a sauna, but it was the one place guaranteed to give me privacy. A week in my parents' company had me crawling the walls, but the knowledge they were departing within the next twenty-four hours kept me sane. As the over-sixty and under-thirty crowd were taking afternoon siestas downstairs before dinner, I relished the opportunity to laze around, daydreaming of their departure and Adrian's eventual return.

A portable fan spread relief across my bare skin as I lay on the bed in just my bra and panties. Its oscillating current breathed life into the flat photos of Adrian and his bandmates, and I watched, entranced, as some billowed and others rattled against their sticky restraints. A small, poorly taped poster fluttered down and plastered itself to my stomach, having lost its battle against the wrath of the fan. Peeling it off, I saw it was my lover, captured in grainy black-and-white. Shirtless. Sweating. I held the cool damp scrap to my chest and felt the tears, hot and humbling, roll down my cheeks and back behind my ears. I missed him so goddamned much.

I reached for the phone and dialed, if only to make some connection. His recorded voice was at least preferable to silence.

"Mobile of the in*de*fatigable Digger Graves!"

"Uh . . . um . . ." I scrambled to sit up at the sound of a real live human voice. Female voice. British. "Is he . . . um, there?" I could hear raucous pub din, laughter, and the scraps of jukebox melodies.

"Sure, 'ang on. He's up buying the next round."

I waited, suddenly feeling exposed. As if this disembodied Englishwoman could see me in my underwear, right through the phone.

"Shite phone is working, then?" I faintly heard, then a more audible, "Hello?"

"I guess it only works when girls answer it." I swallowed hard.

"Kat! Gawblimy, it's good to hear your voice. Blasted phone's been useless. Especially in hospital."

"The hospital sounds strangely like a bar."

A static-filled laugh met my ear. "Left there 'round an hour ago. Ran into Sam's sister Tess and 'er lot passing through Earls Court."

"Snogging-behind-the-garage Tess?" I had heard stories of

how Sam had freely offered up his sister for Adrian's first kiss. "That's who answered the phone?"

"Very same. I wouldn't snog Tess now, mind you. 'Er bloke's as immense as said garage!" His accent seemed thicker, competing over the clinking of ale bottles. "And 'ow's my Abbey?"

"Your Abbey is fine," I stated. "Your *Kat*, on the other hand, is losing her mind."

"Oh, that's right . . . your parents!" he rasped. "I plum forgot their visit."

I snapped the fan off. Its breeze, once a relief, was now stinging. The conversation also stung, as did the notion of another woman answering his phone on his behalf. I shouldn't have called.

"It doesn't matter. I'm gonna go, okay?"

"Ach, Kat. No. Don't." His voice lowered. "Please, I miss you, luv."

"Then come home," I found myself saying. I winced. It sounded weak and whiny. "I have to go. Love you." I hung up. Weaker than weak. Under the rafters of rock stars, I felt puny and petty. Not even strong enough to sustain the shortest absence.

37

SPARKLE AND FADE

PETE'S BIRTHDAY, without fail, arrived in a jarring fashion, as the neighborhood kids set off squealing bottle rockets and M80s down at the lake. Abbey had never had the opportunity to help her dad blow out his birthday candles, but each year at 9:55 a.m. on July Fourth, we lit a sparkler to honor his arrival into the world. It was crackling and exciting, and sometimes a bit out of control—not unlike life. And like Pete, it was ours to hold for much too brief a time. Abbey carefully conducted a silent "Happy Birthday" chorus, smiling as this year's sparks flew in different directions before sizzling to a stop.

Pete's brother and I had a tradition as well. Starting with the Carousel Prints that first year, Luke and I made sure to visit and gift items of Pete's to each other, as if husband and brother would live on if we swapped tokens like the Rubik's Cube from his childhood bedroom or, like this year, his coveted MTV shirt. The unspoken rule was to pick a destination in the city to take Abbey, a place Pete and I hadn't been able to show her together, and make a day of it.

And it remained an unspoken rule when Adrian surprised me with a phone call the evening before.

"How about a date at Coney Island tomorrow? I hear they're serving hot dogs."

"Adrian—oh my God! Are you home?" He wasn't due in for two more days.

"Yeah, chanced an earlier flight." He sounded exhausted. "Natalie was released from hospital yesterday, so Robyn and Leopold whisked her off to my . . . to *their* country house in Essex to convalesce. I saw no point in hanging about London." He paused. "Time to come home and detox."

I tried not to think about the various pubs and girls of his past he needed to detoxify from. Girls who knew him as Digger . . . and described him as "indefatigable."

"I need to see you. Pack up Abbey and come into town."

"She's already in bed," I said lamely.

"Wake her up, she won't care." His flippant tone was foreign to me, and not exactly welcome.

"She'll be cranky, and *I'll* care. I'm not some groupie who can drop everything and follow the tour bus, Adrian." The words stomped out of my mouth before I could halt them, and I could sense they had trampled over all of Adrian's most sensitive places.

"And I," he said slowly, "am going to pretend not to be highly offended by that comment. Christ, Kat. I thought you'd be happy I came back early."

"I'm glad you're home," I backpedaled. "It's . . . I . . . We really need to have a talk, Adrian."

"I agree. As opposed to whatever it is we are having now," he finished flatly.

I sighed, feeling a pileup of words as they hit the brick wall of my heart. He needed to know, and he deserved to know.

"So meet me," he pressed. "I've got somewhere fantastic I want to take you two tomorrow. I promise it's not Coney Island."

"We can't during the day. I'm sorry." I paced the floor, hating his silence, hating my inability to just spill the beans.

"You can't change your plans? I haven't seen you for two bloody long weeks."

I paced the length of the hallway and paused, gazing at the Carousel Prints. "I'm sorry," I repeated softly. Pete smiled out at me. "I can't break these plans."

Luke was meeting Abbey and me at the Cloisters for a tour of the museum and a picnic on the grounds.

"We can meet you later," I offered. We had had an open invitation to Luke and Kimon's for the evening, but I knew it would be okay to beg off. "Dinner and fireworks . . . and we'll take it from there?" The guys would be more than willing to take Abbey overnight if I asked them, giving me time alone with Adrian.

"Your call, Kat. I'm knackered," he said wearily.

I wanted to climb through the phone and curl into his lap. I wanted to rewind the clock and start the conversation over. I wanted to change the date on the calendar and put us in a more neutral spot. I wanted to get through tomorrow with my sanity intact.

I needed him to understand.

"I'll text you tomorrow," I managed, "and we'll make a plan."

38

MYTHICAL BEASTS

ABBEY and I carpooled with Leanna and her family, who were making their annual July Fourth trek of misery to Jones Beach. The museum was on the way, and Leanna was grateful for the buffer in the car. She and Ed seemed more civil toward each other, I observed, since starting joint therapy. Their only disagreement in the car involved whether to take the Throgs Neck or the Whitestone bridges after dropping us off. Leanna spent most of the ride craning her neck over the front seat to talk to me, with Dylan's blipping video game and Abbey's singsong observations providing lively background noise. I chatted distractedly, my thumb and my brain rolling through the texted conversation Adrian and I had had earlier.

> **K:** How about dinner @ Ollie's—can you meet us at 5?
> **A:** I might be drunk by 5.
> **K:** Where's your patience and fortitude now?
> **A:** They've turned to stone and crumbled to dust. Just like your resolve.
> **K:** ???
> **A:** I'm tired of waiting Kat.

K: Please. I promise. Tonight.

A: Not soon enough. I'll be where the myth surrenders to the maiden. 4 p.m. Venture out of your comfort zone and meet me there. Abbey too . . . this place has her name written all over it.

K: I can't handle a riddle today!!!

K: Please . . . let's just start at Ollie's. Or @ your apt. But I can't before 5. I'll explain later.

K: xoxo

His texts had stopped an hour ago, but I continued the conversation one-sided, first in text and then in my head. What did he mean, *where the myth surrenders*? What comfort zone? A place with Abbey's name . . . none of it was ringing a bell. And I told him I couldn't meet earlier. My brain and my nerves felt pushed to the limits. Of all days . . .

Ed was hunched unhappily behind the wheel of the family Volvo rather than his precious truck, and barely grunted as we said our thanks and hopped out at Fort Washington Avenue and 190th. "Call me and let me know where you end up." Leanna waved out her open window. "We'll figure out a time to meet back up tomorrow."

"Will do. Try to have fun."

"You too." *Take me with you?* she mouthed. I laughed in response, and she threw a defeated laugh back. I touched her outstretched hand as Ed slowly nudged the Volvo back into the flow of traffic.

"Unkie Luke!" Abbey was off and running to our appointed meeting spot, the main pedestrian entrance of the Cloisters. My brother-in-law caught her in his well-built arms, hurtling her up into the air and swinging her a full three-sixty before hugging her to him.

It hurt to look at Luke. I still saw Pete in him, yet I knew he and Pete looked less and less alike with each passing day. I thought of that old tale of the mountain climber who had died in an avalanche and the son who had followed years later in his father's footsteps, climbing the same summit only to find his father staring out at him from a block of ice, frozen at an age younger than the son himself. I wondered who Luke saw when he looked in the mirror.

He propped Abbey on one hip and reached to envelop me with his free arm.

"Hey, girlfriend. Happy Pete's Birthday."

"Happy Pete's Birthday to you, too," I whispered against his cheek as I kissed him hello. "Is this where the tour starts?"

Luke grinned. As a professional photographer, he had shot countless weddings in the park surrounding the museum. "You bet! Welcome to Margaret Corbin Circle."

"Who's she?" Abbey wanted to know.

"A really brave lady. When the British attacked, she took control of her fallen husband's cannon."

Abbey's little mouth formed an impressive little ring.

"Now . . . on to your lawn, Miss Abbey." He took her hand and we headed along the promenade.

"For real?"

"Yep, for reals. There's even a sign to prove it. Abby with no E, though."

Luke pointed out various flowers in the Heather Garden as we passed. I looked on with a smile as he snapped photos of Abbey sniffing the fragrant little purple bells, her tiny fingers fondling them as if to ring them.

"Mommy, look! A bride! Unkie Luke, take her picture!"

A wedding party was moving toward a part of the park where trees formed a natural canopy. Two photographers and a videographer trailed in their wake, documenting madly.

"Looks like she's got it covered, Abb. That's Linden Terrace. Amazing spot for a wedding." I detected a blush creep across his cheeks, similar to the one that never failed to betray Pete when he tried to keep a secret. I bumped my hip against him, hoping to break his resolve, but he stayed on course.

"Here we are. Abby's Lawn." A wide green expanse met us, boasting majestic views of the Palisades across the river. Luke handed me his camera bag in order to unhook his backpack.

"Lunch from Cowgirl Hall of Fame."

Abbey squealed. She loved the kitschy restaurant around the corner from her uncle's apartment, with its campy wagon-wheel décor. "Frito pie?" she asked hopefully.

"And mac and cheese." He spread a blanket and began unpacking the unlikely picnic lunch. "Stealth margaritas, too." He handed me a sports bottle.

"Yum, happy drink!" I guzzled a gulp. Cowgirl served theirs up in glass mason jars, but this way tasted even better.

"Go on. Open it."

After lunch, Abbey stalked squirrels while Luke and I lingered on the last of the margaritas. The MTV shirt I had presented to him moments ago was already on display.

"Excellent!" he had complimented, pulling off his own T-shirt and giving the park a gander at his gloriously smooth shoulders. The shirt was tight on his pecs; his long-term partner, Kimon, was built like a Greek god, and Luke certainly got his money's worth out of his own gym membership keeping up with his lover's buffness.

I turned over the white letter-size envelope he had handed me. It was wrinkled and felt old. On the front, in their mother's slanted small script, was written the words *Peter's teeth.*

"Teeth? Was your mother a witch doctor?"

Luke laughed. "She gave it to me last time I visited. Let's open it."

I carefully slid my finger under the aged gummed flap, and

it gave way. "There's . . . there's nothing here." My fingers
explored the empty cavity.

"Holy . . . do you think they disintegrated?" Luke wondered,
leaning his chin on my shoulder as he peered into the
envelope.

"Hey, wait . . . I feel something!" My pinky hit something
sharp inside the envelope, and I carefully dug it out with my
fingernail. Sure enough, one tiny baby tooth of Pete's. I held it
between my thumb and index finger and was about to call
Abbey over to show her when it made a tiny pop and literally
crumbled to dust and disappeared.

Luke and I stared. I didn't know whether to laugh or to cry.

My hand slowly dropped open, and I let whatever was left
get taken by the wind. He squeezed my shoulder, then ambled
over to get Abbey. I pocketed the envelope and busied myself
with the packing up. It was time to move on.

Luke hoisted Abbey onto his shoulders and we began to
make our way toward the vaulted passageways of the museum.
While many New Yorkers and tourists alike were migrating
toward Lady Liberty and sticking to the shores outdoors, I was
so glad our trio stayed north to the hushed confines of the
Cloisters. Only a handful of visitors dotted the landscape
around the medieval-looking structure, and an occasional
cyclist whizzed by on the larger outer paths.

Abbey rested her chin on the top of her uncle's hair, which
he had always kept groomed shorter than Pete's, with a bit
more product. I walked in reverse ahead of them so I could
snap a picture of them with Luke's camera.

"You and Abbey are coming to my exhibit, right? It's the last
weekend in August."

"Of course! We wouldn't miss it for anything."

"I've got your buddy Liz catering it."

"Really." I gave a wry smile. "Did she tell you we aren't
speaking?"

"What? Get out! What happened?"

"Long story . . . and little ears." I motioned toward Abbey. "Another time."

"Well, this is a good enough time for me to share something with you guys . . ." Luke looked about to burst. "It's going to be a combination art opening–engagement party. Kimon and I are getting married."

"Oh my God!" It had been what I expected and wanted to hear. "That's so awesome!" I stepped sideways to throw my arms around him. Abbey used the opportunity as a group hug and reached down to pull me close. Luke's one arm went around me and the other reached up behind Abbey's back to steady her. "I am so happy for you, Luke."

"Have the wedding here!" Abbey begged.

Luke laughed. "We don't want to wait. New York is taking too long to get its act together. It will be up on the Cape, most likely. Next summer."

An elderly couple smiled at us along the stone walled path. "I must say," the woman remarked, "your daughter is a spitting image of the two of you."

"Thanks," Luke said with a laugh as they passed, and I elbowed him in the ribs. "Same DNA, I guess. If you ever get the urge to give Abbey a sibling, I would willingly make that minimal contribution, Tree. In a cup, of course."

"Duly noted."

We entered the museum, Abbey still a monkey on Luke's strong back. "How old are you now?" he teased, extracting her. "Ten?"

"Unkie Luke." She laughed. "You know I'm only four. And a half."

"Okay. Here are four postcards. See the pictures on the front? Each of those four items is in this castle. Let's go find them."

"Brilliant!" I praised as Abbey trotted importantly ahead of us, past ancient and imposing stone portals. "That will keep her busy for a while."

Abbey found the roundel with the scene of the attack on the Castle of Love from her first postcard. Next came the only known complete deck of illuminated fifteenth-century playing cards. "Mommy, is that a jester?" Abbey asked, pointing at the knave card.

"Wow, yeah, I think so."

"Adrian would like him."

The third item was a pretty stained glass window, and finally, the fourth card revealed the Unicorn Tapestries. "Oh," breathed Abbey as we entered the room. "I love him."

The tapestries told the story of the unicorn being found, chased, attacked, killed, and then miraculously coming to life again. "Poor unicorn," Abbey moaned at the sight of the unicorn surrounded.

"Look at this piece," Luke pointed out. The fifth tapestry was just fragments. "See the look on the woman's face? She's taming him." I thought she looked shrewd and bewitching. The poor creature stared lovingly at her. "They call this one *The Mystic Capture of the Unicorn*."

For some reason, this tattered piece saddened me the most. It had been a tough two weeks without Adrian, and now a very emotional day with my brother-in-law. The tears I brushed away did not go unnoticed by him.

"You okay?"

I nodded. "Can we get back outside for a while? It's so dark in here. And cold."

39

OPEN THE HEART

LUKE LED us right out of the tapestry room into an enclosed square garden. The warmth of its pink marbled columns and fragrant plants instantly cheered me. Abbey made a beeline for the center fountain.

"What a day, eh?" Luke took my hand.

"Yeah." I sniffed. "I wanted to tell you . . . I haven't been too sure how to share it, but I—I've met someone."

"Oh, Tree. I think that's great." Luke squeezed me hard, and Abbey came running back down the path, bumping into our legs. "Really." He pulled back and looked into my eyes. "You are entitled to every happiness. I look forward to meeting him."

"Thank you," I whispered, standing on tiptoes to kiss his cheek.

"My brother was a lucky man," Luke said softly, "and he knew it, Tree."

There's a position in yoga that opens your heart: your face toward the sky, shoulders down, while your hands are clasped behind you and pulling down. I had my head tilted up toward Luke, and Abbey was running in circles around us, tugging my hands back in her solo game of chase. As Luke said those

words, I truly felt it was a heart-opening moment. I had loved
Pete, and he had loved me. There was enough love in me for
Adrian, Abbey, Luke, and all the wonderful people in my life
without feeling like I was shortchanging anyone—or anyone's
memory.

We smiled at each other.

"Unkie Luke, what's a cloister?" Abbey wanted to know.

"See all these walkways and covered paths surrounding us?
Those are cloisters. You usually find them in a church or an
abbey."

"But *I'm* an Abbey!" She laughed. "I'm gonna go visit the
unicorn again."

"Look at her march," Luke observed with a smile. "Right at
home in this place."

This place has her name written all over it.

Oh my God. The Cloisters. Abby's Field. Fort Tryon. When
Adrian had mentioned it once as his favorite park, I had told
him I never ventured above 125th Street.

Venture out of your comfort zone.

"Luke, what time is it?"

"Just after four. Why?"

I scrambled after Abbey, back into the tapestry room. She
was standing in front of the tattered fragment, her little face
studying the lovesick face of the doomed beast.

Where the myth surrenders to the maiden.

40

CLOSE THE DOORS

"OH MY GOD. We have to go."

"Tree, are you all right?" Luke watched, concerned, as I swiveled my head toward every possible exit.

"I'll call you later, okay? Come on, Abbey!" She threw her arms around Luke in a quick hug and grabbed my hand.

We raced out, retracing our steps. Abby's Field was green and wild, alive with children running. No trace of Adrian. Had he been here? Had he been inside, waiting in vain with the unicorn?

As we approached the exit of the park, my heart took a sickening dive. Two police cruisers ringed the large paved circle normally meant for pedestrians. Long barricades had been placed for what appeared to be crowd control reasons, although people were drifting away from the area and an officer was dismantling the blue wooden sawhorses.

"What happened?" I asked a woman standing to my right. She wore a large baby carrier backpack and was chugging from a water bottle.

"I'm not sure," she responded. "I think maybe that guy got mugged." She gestured toward an agitated man standing with another cop. The baby on her back gummed a cracker and stared at Abbey.

A nearby pretzel vendor leaned over his cart. "No, he got his camera smashed." He pointed to two teenagers on the other side of Fort Washington Avenue. "Those kids were with another guy—"

"It was some celebrity; the boys asked for his autograph," chimed in an older woman. "Then *that* man"—she nodded toward the upset man with the cop—"ran up and began hollering and snapping pictures. I was waiting for my son to pay the cab fare and was practically knocked down!"

"Celebrity?" The pretzel vendor shrugged. "Didn't know him from nobody. Polite guy, though. Bought a soda from me earlier."

The woman's son shook his head disgustedly. "No respect for privacy. To hound someone like that! Trying to make money on some gossip site, I'm sure. I would've broken his camera, too, if he had blocked *my* path."

I glanced toward the parked police cars, half expecting to see Adrian in the back of one of them. "So where'd the guy . . . the celebrity go?"

"Jumped right into the cab we'd vacated."

The baby laughed; Abbey was making funny faces at it.

"Only in New York!" I heard the pretzel vendor say as Abbey and I jaywalked toward the teens.

One was smoking a cigarette, and both were loud and hyper. The other people waiting at the bus stop with them were edging away in irritation. Their uniform of shaggy hair, jeans, and black band T-shirts was enough to confirm my suspicions. But the familiar-looking signature, freshly inked on one of the teens' messenger bags, left no question in my mind. "Dude," the kid with the messenger bag was saying to his friend, "your mom is going to totally freak."

"Who gives a shit?" The other teen moved to take a puff

from his cigarette, and I spied a similar autograph Sharpied onto his bare forearm. "Totally tattooing it!" He gave the air a couple of victory punches. "Digger Graves, muthafucka!"

"Note to self," messenger bag kid said with a laugh. "Ask him for his autograph, but never for a picture. Did you see how postal he went on that dude?"

I scooted Abbey into a cab. "Sixty-eighth and Broadway, please."

The cab careened out of Washington Heights. With one hand in Abbey's and the other on my phone, I shakily dialed and got his voice mail. "Hey . . . it's me. I got the riddle . . . too late. Um . . . are you okay? Heading to Ollie's now." I slowly pushed the phone into my pocket, frowning to myself. I could only imagine how this latest scuffle had ruffled him—it must've been like the vampire paparazzi in the all-night diner with Simone all over again.

"Are we meeting Adrian?" Abbey asked.

"I hope so."

As we exited the cab and crossed over toward the restaurant, Abbey began waving at someone. It was Dirty Stroller Man from our pilgrimage to the hot dog stand. I gently admonished her, but all she said was, "He waved first. I was just being polite."

We stood outside Ollie's and waited. I pulled out my phone and quickly texted.

We're @ Ollie's. Where R U?

Abbey smushed her nose against the glass, watching waiters as they carried plate after plate of steaming noodles past. My eyes drifted from corner to corner, waiting to catch sight of that familiar gait.

More and more diners pushed past us into the noodle shop. Abbey was beginning to fidget. 5:20. "Okay, Abb. Maybe we should try his place." I checked my phone. Nothing. *We're on our way to you*, I wrote.

The hostess was smiling through the window at us. She held up a fortune cookie and pointed at Abbey, nodding her head. Abbey quickly ran in and retrieved it.

I hailed a cab, and we sailed across 64th, Abbey buckled safely into the middle seat. I squinted and read her fortune aloud as we bumped along. "*One joy scatters a hundred griefs.*' That means you can have a lot of sad things happen in your life, but having one happy thing happen can make you feel much better about all of them," I explained.

The cookie was right. I thought back to my epiphany in the gardens, surrounded by Luke and Abbey. Bolstered by Luke's good news and his positive reception of mine, I knew I could finally share with Adrian everything I hadn't had the courage to before. He had laid all of his skeletons out for me, ugly and bare, and we had gotten through it. Now it was my turn. Not Truth or Dare. Only truth. My resolve was stone solid. No crumbling this time.

My cell phone beeped, and my heart jumped upon sight of the tiny fat envelope icon at the top of the screen. A text.

Too many ghosts, Kat. I can't com(pete).

Can't come.

Can't compete.

Pete.

You don't have to compete. I'm putting the ghosts to rest. My fingers couldn't push the keys fast enough to keep up with the racing of my mind and heart. *One joy scatters a hundred griefs.* I don't know why I texted him the fortune. I had planned on sharing it in person. When I shared everything else.

"Good afternoon, Ms. Lewis. Hi, Abbey. Is he expecting you?" Hector, the doorman on duty, picked up his phone as we trooped into the lobby.

"Kind of. I think." My laugh was shaky. "We got our lines crossed."

Hector turned his back slightly, and after a moment, slowly hung up the phone. "I'm sorry, Ms. Lewis . . ."

"Did he pick up? We were supposed to meet him." Hector was shaking his head apologetically. "Can't we just go up and—"

"I am sorry. I can't let anyone up on the floors who doesn't have a key." He avoided my eyes. I felt as unwelcome, as intrusive as the curious fan, the pesky paparazzi. I was being shut out.

"Mommy, when can we see Adrian?" Abbey asked.

"Thank you, Hector," I managed, and pulled Abbey outside.

"I want to go in!" Abbey protested.

"Hold on a second, Abbey."

Another text was waiting.

My grief lies onward, and my joy behind.

What the hell . . .

I must've muttered under my breath, because Abbey began pulling on my hands, trying to look at my phone. I shooed her away like a fly, and Adrian's Shakespeare ring on my finger caught the late afternoon sun sifting through Central Park.

Shakespeare.

I quoted a fortune cookie.

He quoted fucking Shakespeare.

WE KNOW WHAT WE ARE, his ring mocked.

You are caution, I am chaos. Like the Zoas, split by experience, his next text read.

Why was he doing this? I couldn't imagine his reason.

Stop. I love you. My fingers ached as much as my heart. Couldn't he sense my passion?

Good-bye, Kat.

"I'm hungry. I want Ollie's," Abbey said, pouting.

"Okay," I heard my voice tell her. "We're leaving."

It was the magic hour when taxis went off duty—the changing of the cabbie guard. We began to walk as yellow cab after yellow cab passed us, lights off. I periodically carried Abbey, starting out strong but ending with a shaking finish a few blocks later. The pack holding our overnight items felt like an anvil on my spine.

Ollie's was absolutely mobbed when we arrived back. Bodies were jammed into the tiny vestibule, and faces looked hungry and hostile.

"Come this way, sweetie." At this point, we were heading south, but walking blindly. I didn't know what to do next.

"Mommy, I am so *so* hungry!"

"We'll get something in a minute. There's a good Chinese place on the next corner."

As we approached the maroon awning of what I thought was Happy China, where Pete and I used to share dishes when we were in college, my heart sank. It had turned into a trendy Pacific Rim fusion place, far too complicated for Abbey's palate. Behind the window, diners ate and drank happily, confident with their places in the world. I was beginning to feel like one of the relics from the museum. The Manhattan I once knew like my backyard was a foreign land. Familiar corners transformed to unrecognizable, no cabs to be found. A bus rumbled slowly past, but I didn't dare stick Abbey and myself on it. I didn't trust my sense of aboveground public transportation enough.

Finally, we found an available cab. I was done with the city. "How much to drive to Westchester?"

The cabbie turned. "Lady. Are you serious?"

"You must go up to Stewart Airport, right?"

"Not today. Traffic will be nuts getting back into town. Everyone's coming in for fireworks. I can't lose all my fare tonight waiting on the bridge. I can take you to Grand Central."

"Fine." Panic was rising in my throat, but I didn't want to let on to Abbey. She seemed content sitting and riding in the air-conditioning and had temporarily forgotten about food. Until, of course, we arrived at Grand Central and she began begging me for McDonald's.

I was so freaked out by the prospect of taking the train that I progressed on autopilot, grabbing Abbey a Happy Meal and racing through the main terminal in search of the right ticket window.

"Mommy, look! Daddy!" I had been pulling on her little arm like a dead weight, trying to read the departure board and get to the ticket window in time to catch the next train.

"What?"

"The stars! Look! They're so pretty!"

In all the hustle-bustle, I hadn't realized this was the first time my child was looking upon the ceiling of Grand Central Terminal, filled with its marvelous constellations. She gaped like a tourist, and it practically broke my heart. While trying to insulate our shattered little unit from further pain, I had unwittingly denied Abbey another of her birthrights. Every child in New York should have the luxury of staring and dreaming up to the heavens, whether it was the true blue skies above Central Park or the mottled plaster stratosphere of the landmark station. Adrian was right. I owed Abbey . . . so much more.

"Sweetie, we just don't have time today." I pulled her onward.

Outbound Metro-North trains were on a holiday schedule, few and far between. By the time we got seated and moving, the sky was beginning to grow dark, I was drained, and Abbey was still crying hunger.

"You wanted this Happy Meal, so eat it," I snapped, flinging down the tray table in front of her and laying out the lukewarm food on napkins that grew instant grease spots. She was still kvetching as we burst out of the dark tunnel and aboveground. I leaned my forehead against the window and stared out at the endless tracks ahead.

Everything was metal and stone. No spot of grass . . . as if no living thing could possibly exist anywhere near these tracks. Life was transported back and forth across the tracks daily, but nothing that lingered behind could stay alive for long.

Abbey ate one piece of chicken and pushed it away. A rage came over me. I slammed the cardboard container back in front of her and demanded she eat more or she would go to bed hungry.

"I hate you," Abbey wailed. "And I hate Mad Hatter. I'm moving to Large Vegas. Away from you."

I was horrified—what kind of mother had I become? Yelling in public, forcing crap food down my daughter's throat? "I'm sorry, baby . . . I'm so sorry. Mommy is sad right now . . . I didn't mean to . . ." Abbey let me kiss her head and hug her, but she stayed quiet, except for her sniffling and the occasional sipping from her juice box.

Every creak and rock of the train car had me white-knuckled, squeezing the armrests. *Home, I just want to get us home.*

As we neared our station, we saw the first cascade of fireworks light the sky, somewhere up above the Hudson. Deep inside me, I felt like I had explosives popping in every direction, fearful I wouldn't be able to keep them under control.

Marissa's minivan was waiting silently for us in the lot. I had texted her from the train. "No questions, please," I said wearily, and that was all I needed to say. I snuck a peek at her as we drove in silence. She was wearing blue denim capris, a red T-shirt, and a red, white, and blue headband in her hair. I had no doubt pulled her from fireworks with her family, but I was too exhausted to apologize or thank her. My hug good-bye would have to do. Inside, I gave Abbey a proper dinner and broke my number-one Mom rule: I tucked her into my bed.

"Where's Adrian?" she wanted to know.

I looped her hair behind her ear and kissed her forehead gently. "I don't know, Abb. But I'm trying to . . . figure that out." She looked so worried and forlorn. It nearly crushed my already devastated heart. I put on my best game face and softly sang one of her favorite renditions from Adrian's mix CD. *"Who lives in a pineapple under the sea?"*

"Abbey Lewis," she whispered, her eyelids finally beginning to waver.

I stared at my phone long into the night before finally working up my courage to call him. *Don't do this to me,* my brain chastised him. *To Abbey. She can't lose someone again.* "Leave me a message," his voice dared on both his home and mobile voice mail. It occurred to me he never made the expected promise of "and I'll call you back."

41

PEACE TREATY

THREE DAYS WENT BY. Nothing. His trail was gone again.

He was as inaccessible to me as every other rock star was, hovering above my head.

I tortured myself by calling again, wanting answers. Gaining no peace. The messages with his voice had been replaced by the generic phone company voice mail. I didn't know what was worse: hearing his voice or that disembodied computer telling me to leave my message. All I knew was I couldn't keep putting myself through this. No more calls.

Once again, the comfort of my friends was my salvation. I opened the door to a knock one Wednesday to find Marissa standing there, two steaming cups of coffee in her hands. "If Moses won't come to the mountain," she announced, "the mountain comes to Moses."

To my surprise, Liz was lingering on the step behind her. "I am asking both of you to remember the Teal Dupioni Silk Accord of 1993," Marissa continued. "We agreed at Leanna's wedding to never leave a woman down."

"I'm so sorry." Liz hugged me hard.

"Me too." We supported each other into the house.

"I never slept with him, Tree. Honest. We kissed and stuff, but in the end . . . neither of us had the guts to go there." She breathed deeply. "I don't know what possessed me. I just got so goddamn sick of thinking all the good ones are taken, and . . . well, I wondered if I could lure someone else's good one away. It was a shitty thing to do."

"Oh, Lizzie. There are still good ones out there. Hiding somewhere."

"You just have to wait for some of them to outgrow their inner Peter Pan," Marissa advised.

Liz snorted. "And move back from Oregon."

I smiled; she was the closest thing I had to a sister, and she did bring out the best in my brother. I could see a happy ending there. "I missed you, Red."

"Aw, I missed you, too, bitch."

Marissa clinked her paper cup to both of ours. "A toast to the real good guys out there, taken and untaken."

"And to the Teal Dupioni Silk Accord," I proposed. "Where is Le, anyway?"

"Her therapist *prescribed*," Marissa explained, while Liz air-quoted, "a *date*. She and Ed are *lunching*."

"Good to hear."

"Tree . . . I struggled with whether I should tell you this." Liz set her coffee down. "Adrian's been to the Naked Bagel. A few times, since . . ."

I nodded. As much as it hurt me to the core, I was relieved to know he was still out there, walking the same earth as me. "How did he seem?" I asked quietly.

"Well . . . miserable. Until he noticed me staring at him, and then he looked pissed off *and* miserable." Liz's eyes flashed with a sympathetic glow. They still held Adrian's secret, I knew. The past he had so boldly and unapologetically shared with me. If only I had given him an inch . . . I thought back to the day of the pancake breakfast and Adrian's agitated words to me. How he wished someone would write a book about me. And how I needed to talk about Pete. We had spent so much time slaying Adrian's demons, it never occurred to me that mine could be even bigger, kept under wraps.

42

13 DE AGOSTO

AUGUST ROLLED IN, oppressive and long. Abbey was enjoying summer camp during the weekdays, but we were always at a loss with ourselves come the weekend. My sweet girl no longer asked to watch *Maxwell MacGillikitty*. And she no longer asked about Adrian. I must've worked through my stages of grief from sadness to anger. Because any time I thought of him, I wanted to burn the second floor of my house down, eliminating all evidence of my loss.

"Come to the city, doll." Liz was insistent. Luke and Kimon were taking Abbey to Cape May for the weekend to give me some "me" time, and I didn't have the heart to tell them I wasn't very good company to myself. I was grateful for Liz and her plan to find a cozy Irish bar for us to relax in and have a few drinks.

We ended up at a dance club in Washington Heights after meeting some Argentinean soccer players with really nice legs at the Irish bar. Clubbing was the last thing I was in the mood for, and I knew it was a mistake the moment we walked in to the pulsating lights and pumping house music. Liz tried to sway me, pointing out one cute guy after another. I didn't want to hit on anyone or be hit upon. I was rude to any member of the male tribe who came near and gave fake names to anyone who asked. "Your friend Ingeborg needs to lighten up," one guy informed Liz as I laughed from behind my drink.

"Tree, come on. Let's have some fun. Dance with me." Liz pulled on my hand, shaking her rump and trying to sway me out onto the dance floor.

"Let's dance with that guy." I pointed to a dark-haired guy wearing a Corroded Corpse T-shirt.

"Oh, come on. He's barely legal. And I am sure he is wearing that shirt to be ironic. Oh, Los Fabulosos Cadillacs! I love this band!" She started swinging her arms to the Latin rock beat and, not surprisingly, she had a *fabuloso* dance partner in no time.

"Miz Katrina! You come dancing here?" It was Ana. Adrian's cleaning girl had traded in her sweats and flip-flops for a cute dress and crazy-high heels. The only thing I recognized on her was the little cross of gold at her neck. She explained she was here celebrating her brother's birthday, and proceeded to point out every friend and relative, including the birthday boy himself, Santino, Liz's current dance partner. Whistles and drums and trumpets were blaring, and people were partying like it was Carnival in Rio.

"How is he?" She was my only lifeline to Adrian, and I needed to know.

"Senhor Graves, he has been in a bad mood. I worry for him . . . He drinking a lot." Her thick arched brow furrowed. "For a time he only come out of the bedroom when I do the cleaning of it, but now, he not even let me in the room to clean it. He stay in there now, most time." Her hands fluttered anxiously as she continued in the best English she could. "Yesterday I see a man let himself out the big door as I come in, man with tattoos all over . . . Oh, he even had his head tattooed, looking like he want to swallow me whole and he carrying plastic baggie full of needles and I am *scared* for Senhor Graves. I knock on door of bedroom, he not answer. I hear the loud music he plays, he turn it on and off, so I know he alive in there. But he isn't wanting to talk to anyone. Is so sad, Miz Katrina. I am scared for him. You can't talk to him?"

"Ana, I tried. He won't speak to me."

The young girl shook her head and said something in her native tongue. She crossed herself. "I know sound silly. But I put broom behind the front door, keep away bad visits. Old trick in my country, *superstição*—how you say that?"

"Superstition?"

"Yes. I try not to think of him alone today. *13 de Agosto.*" Her full lips quivered with the words. I realized what she meant—it was Friday the Thirteenth. "This month, August. *Agosto,* like *desgosto.* Your word is, I think, *sorrow,* no? Unluckiest."

We hugged each other because there was nothing else left to do or say. I saw Ana's brother and Liz looking at us quizzically from the dance floor and motioning for us to join them. I wasn't quite sure how or if we should explain how we knew each other.

"'El Matador'!" Ana brightened. "Is my favorite song. Come!"

She introduced her brother to me over the loud music, and he grinned, arms around Liz's waist as he swayed her to the trumpets and the "hey, hey" chorus. I danced, eyes closed, allowing myself to get lost in the unfamiliar tongue and beats. Keeping me from thinking about *desgosto.* Sorrow. I saw myself down at the shore of the lake. I heard him sing.

Lures me to her like a matador . . .

"Oh Tree, I know you don't want to be here. I don't, either. This sucks." Liz and I tumbled out of the club as the next song cued. "Come on, let's go. Anywhere, your choice. We can go home; I've got a whole box of Beard Papa at my place. Or we can go to Junior's. Anywhere you want."

"I don't want cream puffs, I don't want cheesecake. I just want Adrian."

"Tree, don't do this to yourself . . . please, don't. Look. What he did was cruel and cowardly." We had a stare-down on 125th Street. "Nothing you did—or didn't do—deserved such treatment. Let him hide in his fancy penthouse, or behind whatever facade his stupid stage name has built back up. It's time to move on."

I had no reserves with which to protest. She was right.

I WANTED to sleep without end, yet I was scared to close my eyes. Each morning I awoke feeling beaten up, as if I had been trying to wrestle myself out of a straitjacket. Or perhaps into one. My arms felt dislocated, like I had been hugging myself hard through the night to keep myself grounded to the bed.

My dreams were horrible. They even had sound tracks.

The latest one started out innocent enough. Abbey and I were in the car, singing along to the radio. Abbey was the Pips to my Gladys Knight as I sang about a man going back to find what was left of the world he left behind. My dreaming self smiled up into the rearview mirror. Abbey and Adrian were sitting in back, holding hands.

Suddenly, Pete was riding shotgun, dressed in his Washington interview suit that never made it out of the garment bag that day. He was smiling at me and tapping his fingers on the window and singing along with our chorus about leaving on midnight trains.

My dream shifted. Adrian was now next to me in the front of the Mini, dressed as if he'd stepped right off the walls of my brother's bedroom. I sang a warning about superstars who didn't get far as he lay prone against the seat like he had after his allergic reaction. Instead of an EpiPen, a syringe was dangling out of his arm.

Pete and Abbey were back again, sitting side by side in the backseat. Abbey her current age, Pete looking like the day I met him. She was holding his available hand. The other, along with the arm it was normally attached to, was gone. I screamed the silent scream of dreams, trying to wake myself up.

I woke in a pool of sweat, knowing what I had to do. If I couldn't have him in my world, I needed to go find him in his.

43

COME TO BLOWS

WITH ABBEY, Brina, and Joey off at summer camp every day, Marissa and I were free to shop. Today we were conquering the grocery store. Karen had joined us, too, with Jasper riding safely ensconced in a nest of organic cotton that protected him from yucky supermarket cart germs.

If carts were places, Marissa's would be Las Vegas. Or as Abbey would say, Large Vegas. Everything was supersize and over-the-top, in shiny boxes and shimmering plastic. Decadent and not very healthy. Karen's cart was a Buddhist temple; sparse and containing only what was necessary to survive. Organic, macrobiotic, and natural, in minimal packaging. And my cart was Switzerland. I stayed neutral as they peered into each other's carts with disdain.

I turned on my own down the magazine aisle and found myself staring at the rock magazines. A headline and byline caught my eye: *HEAVY METAL MASTERS—WHERE ARE THEY NOW? By Alexander Floyd.* In the corner was a small inset picture of Digger and Riff, circa 1983. That tinny refrain from my dream played in my head again. Could I try to live in his world since he refused to be in mine?

I picked up the magazine and flipped to the feature. It was titled *IS IT TIME TO PUT OUR BELOVED CORPSE TO REST?* and featured a bevy of photographs from their humble beginnings to the most recent—a blurry capture of Adrian onstage at the Hammerstein and a candid photograph of Rick's profile taken at LAX. He looked nothing like his pictures of old, with a shaved head, a beard, and a T-shirt that sported Go GANG GREEN across his midsection. The article opened with the rumors of Digger's return to the stage. My eyes skimmed to the last sentence eloquently penned by Mr. Alexander Floyd. "Until I see a death certificate for one of them, I will remain ever-hopeful the Lennon-McCartney of the metal world will resurface."

"Find anything good?"

Marissa was bearing down on me from the opposite end of the aisle. Her cart was positively brimming.

"Just a magazine for Kev. He told me to be on the lookout for it." I tossed it into my cart on top of Abbey's yogurt. "Where's Karen?"

"I lost her as I passed the Nature's Marketplace section." She shivered.

"One woman's hell is another woman's sanctuary," I joked.

"Ah, the Lauder Lake Ladies of Leisure!" Grant had turned up the aisle behind me. If his cart was a place, it would be back-woods Pennsyltucky: beer, beef jerky, and scratchy toilet paper. "What's shaking, ladies?"

He peered into my cart. "What, no spotted dick? No beans on toast? I heard your Cuppa Tea made tracks. And I don't mean the ones on his arms, covered by all those tattoos."

I couldn't think, couldn't move. Certainly couldn't speak. If I hadn't been holding on to the cart, I think I would have slid underneath it.

Marissa's voice broke through my meltdown, crisp and clear. "Grant, you'd better get your ass out of here before I use

your face for a cleanup on aisle four!" She looked like she
wanted to pull an Evel Knievel right over me and the top of my
cart in order to run him over with hers.

He pasted a look of faux innocence and indignation on his
face as he backed his cart up and out of our aisle, but I could
see he was holding back a smile.

"My God. Does the whole town know the widow got
dumped?"

Marissa made a face. "Please. Grant's no longer got a football team to hoist him on their shoulders or cheerleaders
waiting to give him victory blow jobs. He's a legend in his own
mind here in Lauder Lake."

"Great. I get to see the legend again at karate class in an
hour."

"Do you want me to take Abbey there today?"

I shook my head. "It's my battle, I can take him."

~

"WHAT IS OUR GOAL?"

"BLACK BELT EXCELLENCE, SENSEI."

"What is our quest?"

"TO BE OUR BEST."

Abbey could now recite the martial arts student creed as
automatically and precisely as she could a *Maxwell
MacGillikitty* episode. As the kids, barefoot and in uniform,
broke line to begin warm-ups, I saw Jake Overhill come scram-
bling onto the dojo floor. The smell of Drakkar cologne told me
his father wasn't far behind.

Right behind my chair, as a matter of fact.

Thanks to alphabetical seating arrangements since fifth
grade, I had fallen in love with the back of Grant's neck,
watching it go from scrawny and giraffelike to toned and

tanned. Now, as he began to breathe down the back of mine, I felt my skin crawl.

"Underwood." He cooed my maiden name like a filthy pigeon. "No hard feelings, right?"

"Right." I crossed my arms and kept my gaze straight ahead. "I have no feelings for you at all, Grant. Hard or otherwise."

"Come on now, Tree. Just 'cause he pulled a runner doesn't mean you have to take it out on me." He chortled. "You're better off anyway."

I concentrated on Abbey, who was swiftly swiping the air in unison with the other students, first left, then right. Tiger claws. How I wished I could tiger claw Poster Boy's face.

"Lauder Lake is no place for a washed-up junkie has-been trying to reinvent himself," he continued loftily.

"Is *that* what you said to him at the school?" Grant received a lash by my hair as I swung to finally face him. "And why he hit you?"

"Did he *really* think he could come to that pancake breakfast and pass for Mr. Normal? I don't care *how* much he spends on wine or suits. Once a loser—"

"You don't know—"

"I know plenty. Surprised?" He practically spit. "*He* was. Till I told him he wasn't the *only* guy you've had up in your attic bedroom. Maybe you'll think twice next time before you let the riffraff in." His cruel laugh was laced with the scent of beef jerky.

I felt sick.

"He's like that stupid cat he sings about," Grant continued. "He lands on his feet and moves on. Let's see." He ticked off his examples on his fingers. "He left *one* life up there in your brother's room, then he walked out on the life he faked in *your* bedroom . . . I'm sure he's on to the next dumb groupie's bedroom by now."

Could I hit him? I wanted him down for the count. *Let the bodies hit the floor.*

A murmured gasp rippled from the seating area. But it wasn't our drama the other adults were focused on. Abbey had delivered a spinning crescent kick, freakishly powerful for her age and belt level. Knocked on his ass and scowling, Jake looked unhurt except perhaps for his pride.

"Tree, you totally missed it! Abbey nailed that kick!" Brian Jensen, a friend of Kevin's whose kids were purple belts in the class, crowed from the back row of seats. "Wow!"

"Shut up, Jensen! She's supposed to nail the pad, not my kid."

"Chill, Overhill. *Your* kid needs to learn about personal space."

"Gentlemen . . ." Hanshi Steve, the owner of the school, pointed in warning toward the door. Before he turned back to the class, I saw his eyebrow arch in impressed amusement, and he gave me a wink.

44

INFORMATION DISSEMINATION

GRANT'S BOMB sat ticking in my chest as I sat in my living room, surrounded by the ticking of time.

Washed-up junkie. Has-been. Not the only one.

Bad enough Adrian had had to endure Grant's barbs and misleading sexual rumor-mongering that day; he had had to come home to my neuroses. For every time he opened himself to me, I had rattled my cages shut. No wonder he let our relationship give up the ghost . . . because I hadn't trusted it enough to let my ghosts go.

I stared at the magazine and at the picture of Rick. I remembered my promise to Adrian, how I would try to find his childhood friend. It was time to step into his world.

Rick Rottenberg, aka Riff Rotten, consider yourself researched.

I worked fervently through the evening, one hand scrolling through LexisNexis while the other scrawled as many leads as I could find on a legal pad. It turned out Rick's paper trail was far easier to find and follow than Adrian's had been. Then again, Adrian had given me a lot of fuel to find Rick.

"Go Gang Green" was a slogan for the Oregon Ducks. Why

would an aging rock star wear a college team's T-shirt . . . unless his kid went to school there?

- Son Paul = Natalie's age (twenty)
- No Rick, Richard, Paul, or Simone Rottenberg in the Oregon directories. (It would have been ironic had my brother's idol been living mere miles from him.)
- Maybe they're listed under Simone's maiden name?
- 1982 *New York Times* wedding announcements: Simone Banquet
- Nothing under the name Banquet. Divorced?

I turned back to the magazine to see if I could spot a wedding band on Rick and reread the last line: *Until I see a death certificate for one of them* . . .

- Simone: Twenty in 1982, DOB 1962. Adrian said she was American. Check Social Security Death Index.

Oh, poor Simone.

It had to be her. Died in 1994. Last known address: Hanalei, Kauai, HI 96714

- No Rottenbergs listed in Hawaii directories. No Banquets.

I had hit a dead end. Back to the Oregon Trail.

- U of O student directory: Paul Banquet, junior. Major: Nanoscience.

Could it be? Only one way to find out. I shot an e-mail off to him.

"Mommy, I found these."

Abbey was clutching her Father's Day crafts in her fists. Someone had been snooping in my room. Adrian didn't take them that day. He also never cashed the check from the library, according to the inquisitive phone message Gwen had left earlier that day.

"I know, sweetie. He forgot them when he rode his bike to the station." I fingered the paper tie that proclaimed her acrostic poem for him.

"Doesn't he want them?"

"I think deep down . . . he does."

"Can we mail them?" Her look was so genuine and so hopeful that nodding was all I could do to keep from crying.

> Date: Thursday, August 19, 2004 2:05 p.m.
> From: pabanquet@uoregon.edu
> Re: Friend of Digger Graves
> To: bibliomama@gmail.com
>
> My dad is the Rick Rottenberg you are looking for. I
>   speak with him daily, and depending on his
>   mood, he may be receptive to talking to you. I
>   will pass along your number.
> PB

The call did come, but not exactly as I had expected. I picked up the phone during dinner with Abbey and got an earful of Cockney curses. "How *dare* you harass my son and track him down at school? If I had a dollar for every reporter who tried to worm their way in—"

I quickly moved to another room. "I'm not a reporter . . . just a really good researcher. I'm a friend of Adr . . . Doug Graves. Digger."

"Dandy. I am sure Billy No-Mates needs all the friends he can get. Please refrain from—"

"Wait . . . *að blanda blóði saman*. The blood oath. I know about that. And the *misericorde*. Please don't hang up."

There was a silence. I held my breath and prayed. "You are quite the wealth of information, aren't you?"

"Just a librarian with a really good memory. He said your last words to him were '*See you in hell, me old China*.'"

"Now *that* I don't remember. But I've been told I have a flair for the dramatic." I heard a clinking of what sounded like ice into a glass. I pictured him pouring himself a fistful of fingers' worth of scotch over those rocks in preparation for the rest of our conversation. "So, Katrina. Care to catch me up on the last sixteen years?"

"You can call me Kat. And in all honesty . . . Adrian—he goes by Adrian now—he came into my life four months ago." Saying it out loud made it seem so insignificant, and therefore even less possible. Could it really only have been four months? Did it really happen at all? Some nights I have dreams that span longer periods of time. "Corny as it sounds, I feel like we've lived a lifetime together." I ignored Rick's snort and plowed on, thinking of what Adrian might want him to know. "He's been clean for over a decade. He's still making music, some great music. More for himself and for those around him than for mass public consumption . . ." I chose my words carefully. "He's found some peace with his past, and love . . ." I swallowed hard. "I know he's still hurting, though. He feels a lot was left unsaid with you . . . with Simone. He shared a lot with me . . . but I know there are some things he wants to tell you, and you alone. I told him a while back I would try my best to find you."

"A for effort, luv," came his gruff reply.

"God, I know this must seem out of left field. A complete stranger out of the blue telling you things about you that you yourself haven't thought of in years—"

"Who says I haven't thought of them? Who says I don't

spend each day of my life wondering what I could have done differently? If Simone were still . . . You know about Simone, I'm assuming? Stomach cancer. Ticked her off your tidy little research list, I reckon?" His voice was caustic, causing me to cringe.

"Yes . . . I . . . He doesn't know. I can say I . . . I know how you . . . I lost my husband four years ago. I still flounder, lost at sea daily."

Rick backed down a bit, his voice resuming its normal octave. "It doesn't get any better after ten years, I'm sorry to say." We both paused to reflect on this. "Have you ever been here?"

"Where's here?"

"Hawaii, Miss Marple." He chuckled. "Here on the island of Kauai, there's a beach called Polihale. It's the westernmost point in the United States, actually. Miles and miles of beach, mostly deserted; there's no swimming or surfing there, as the currents are just fierce. Simone and I were on holiday, right after that blasted last tour finished. I stood on that beach for, I don't know, hours it seemed. It's got these incredible sand dunes, like a hundred feet high, and in the distance you can see the beginning of the cliffs of the Na Pali."

"It sounds incredible."

"It's the kind of place that makes one realize how insignificant one really is in the grand scheme of things. Pulled my ego down a few pegs and got my priorities in line straightaway. We relocated here with the children shortly after; family became my number-one priority, and it still is to this day. After Simone died, I went off of my head. The locals talked about the powerful Polihale heiau just north of the beach, a sacred site. It is believed to be one of the points from which the souls of the dead depart the island into the setting sun. It sounded so beautiful, so peaceful. I wanted to go and die there, to travel with her. The kids were the only things holding me back."

"My daughter, too, she was the only thing that kept me

sane." I curled my legs up under me and switched ears. Abbey was eating ravioli and singing a song to herself in the kitchen.

"How old?"

"She's turning five soon. Adores Adrian. He's so good with her." It took an effort to stay in the present tense.

"Really. I remember his Natalie at five. Damn shame. I hope he's managed to salvage that wreck of a relationship."

"He's been trying." Silence buzzed through the line.

"So if I call him . . . it's not going to spell instant reunion of the band. Just so we're clear."

"I think you're of the same mind on that front."

THE PHONE CUT through my dreams the next night. Twelve thirty a.m. *Please. Just let it be him.* I picked up the phone and tried my best to mask my startled and sleepy salutation as one that exuded casual and confident. "Hi?"

"Where did you say you and Digger met again?" It was Rick.

I rolled onto my side. "I don't think I did say. At the library."

"The library, seriously?" He laughed.

"It was a case of mistaken identity, I suppose." I yawned.

"The phone numbers you gave me, luv. They're both out of service."

My heart sank into the futon mattress, where I could feel it struggling to beat. "Shit." I couldn't help it. I was so tired. The tears came too easily. "Damn him."

"Ah, luv." Something was being poured into a glass. "How did it end? Did you piss him off, fuck him off, scare him off?"

"The hell if I know. He never let me in on the punch line."

"I'm so sorry you're sad, luv." And he sounded as if he truly was.

"I was sad. Now I'm more angry than anything. How could

he just remove himself like that? Why was it so easy to walk away?"

"Because it's easy to live with your eyes closed . . ."

"And to misunderstand what you see," I automatically replied before I knew what I was doing. I saw Adrian in my mind's eye, leaping over the Imagine mosaic and into my heart.

"The problem with Digger is that everything was always so black-and-white with him. He was never able to accept the gray matter. Either the hero or the victim . . . he couldn't seem to find a way to exist in between. He's always been like that, since I've known him. Hero to victim in three seconds flat."

I pondered that for a moment. If I had been beyond fighting for, did that mean I was the enemy?

"Got a pen, luv?" I scrambled through my bedside table drawer to find one, and took down the digits he dictated. "If you talk to him . . . you can pass him this number. You take care, now."

45

HANDLE WITH CARE

Dear Adrian,

I once told you how proving something didn't exist was infinitely harder than proving something did exist. Well, you haven't replied to any of my e-mails or my calls, so I guess my theory has been blown out of the water—you have proved there are things that really don't exist. I thought we had stumbled upon something, the two of us. And that we were beginning to explore it together. But as the days go by and the silence in this house becomes unbearable, I am convinced there must've never been anything there. And I can't continue to exhaust my resources trying to prove it otherwise.

Here is something that is real: your friend Rick. He'd like you to call him. And Abbey wanted you to have these.

There's been enough grief. I wish you only joy.

Kat

I CLOSED the letter with Rick's phone number, slipped it into Abbey's handmade card, and placed it in a small box with the pencil holder she had made. With a heavy heart, I worked Adrian's ring over my knuckle and dropped it into the container. *WE*

KNOW WHAT WE ARE, it twinkled its reminder at me once more as I reached for the packing tape.

"Anything fragile, perishable, or potentially hazardous?" the postal worker asked as she reached to take the box that now contained my hopes, dreams, and fears about the future.

All I could do was shake my head and let it go.

A MAN SAID TO THE UNIVERSE

A man said to the universe:
"Sir, I exist!"
"However," replied the universe,
"The fact has not created in me
A sense of obligation."

— STEPHEN CRANE

BETTER MAN

"SOHO. RHYMES WITH *HO-HO*."

"And don't forget *yo-yo*."

Abbey and I were playing games as we walked toward Luke's photography gallery. We hadn't strolled together on a city block since July Fourth. It was on my mind, but I hoped it wasn't on hers.

"Wooster. Rhymes with . . . *rooster!*" she crowed triumphantly, pointing at the street sign.

"Now that's a silly but good one."

"Silly . . . rhymes with *Philly!*"

Abbey was excited to see Unkie Luke and the rest of my in-laws, but she was especially excited to travel with Pete's parents to their house in Philadelphia after the opening. They were both high school teachers and they enjoyed spending the last week of their vacation each year with their only granddaughter.

"Here's Spring . . . rhymes with?" I prompted.

"Spring! *Ring* and *sing* . . ."

The scent hit us both, seemingly at the same time. Peppery, with a hint of bergamot. Maybe basil.

"Spring Street smells like Adrian," Abbey said matter-of-factly.

My head had jerked up, pivoting around to every quadrant in search of him. "Oh, look." I pointed to Molton Brown, a shop well known for their luxurious grooming products. "That must be where Adrian buys his cologne."

It's amazing how a simple scent can heighten all the senses. One whiff and I was lost. My eyes wanted to search for him; I longed to hear his voice. And the thought of his touch ignited me. A thousand memories and moods flooded my mind.

The large double *L* sign ahead was like a beacon. I ushered Abbey into the cool confines of Luke's gallery. All year long he had exhibits and installations of photographers from around the globe, but it was the first time he had the entire place filled with his own work.

We were immediately enveloped by Veronica and Ben, my in-laws. Several other relatives and friends of the Lewis family were on hand as well. Kimon and Luke both looked suave and artsy in crisp white buttoned shirts and linen khakis. They each took Abbey by a hand and led her toward a display of color shots from the trip to the Cloisters and large black-and-whites from their Cape May weekend.

Liz had arrived through the back door, a covered tray of food in her hands. "Tree? A hand, please?" I helped her slide the mammoth tray onto a long table and followed her down the long hallway to the service door. "I brought an assistant," she announced, stepping aside and allowing me to peer out the square of mesh wired glass.

Adrian was slouching and smoking against the open back end of her catering van, cigarette barely leaving his lips as he puffed anxiously. I jumped away from the window before he could spot me. "How in the hell . . . ?"

She shook her bob of red hair, a small smirk on her lips. "He was waiting at the shop when I arrived this morning. What a sight."

"Was he ... high?"

"Drunk. Tenacious. Tearful." She began a one-woman dialogue alternating between a British accent worse than Marissa's and her own fly girl–speak. "He got up in my face with 'I know you didn't approve of me, but,' and I was like, 'Get out of town,' and then he was all, 'Just tell me wot I need to do to get 'er back. I don't give a flying monkey's wot she did.' And I go 'What *she did*? You're delusional if you think she did anything but love you, warts and all!' And he was like, 'Come again?' So then I got Doom Boy some coffee, sobered him up, and told him he was coming with me." She smiled proudly.

"Does he know it's me ... that I'm here?"

"He's about to."

Before I could protest, Liz pushed open the door and marched toward him. He barely reacted as she went through the motions of scolding him for smoking near the food. I watched the scene play out like a comical silent movie as she plucked the cigarette from his fingers, smoked the rest of it, and directed him to grab another tray of food to bring in. He did as he was told. And found himself face-to-face with me.

"You can bring it right in to the table here." I tried to keep my voice even.

I turned quickly, not wanting to linger on his shocked expression for fear it might morph into something even more unfamiliar to me. The corridor felt as endless as a cathedral aisle. I could feel his eyes on me as my heels clicked manically, but I didn't dare turn to look or speak any more. He deposited the tray as he was instructed. I watched his hands, normally so dexterous and assured, shake slightly. The Shakespeare ring was back on his left pinky finger.

"You're drunk again," I said softly.

"And you're still beautiful."

I felt my heart surge with love, even as it was breaking apart.

I had dreamed of him before I met him and had fallen for him the moment he had stumbled into the library that April day. "Tree, is everything okay? Do you know this guy?" Luke had left Abbey admiring the photographs with Kimon and warily approached us. Behind him, the quizzical faces of my extended family looked on.

"Oh, she knows me. But do I know *her*? And do you?" He gulped a half laugh. "Ah, Kat. And Schrödinger's cat." He poked a stunned Luke in the chest. "Are you in a superposition of states? Are you alive or dead? Do *you* even know?"

"Quantum physicist?" I heard my father-in-law ask Liz.

"No. Rock star," came Liz's stage-whispered reply.

The entire room was staring at the scene now, the art forgotten. Kimon and Abbey rounded the corner, and stopped in their tracks. I tried to keep my voice calm and controlled. "Everyone, excuse me. Give us a minute. Please." To Abbey, I said, "Stay here, baby. I'll be right back." She said nothing, just gaped at Adrian as I pulled him into Luke's office.

Staying calm was not working; I was so relieved to see him, I wanted to cry, to yell, to push him and hold him all at once. "Tell me what made you feel you had to rip apart my life and my daughter's life all over again? After all we had lost! What possessed you?"

He immediately began pacing the small room, hand running through his hair. "I did what I thought was best, but it killed me to walk away from you."

"Best? *Best?* Putting Abbey and myself on a train home that day was the *worst* thing I've had to go through since . . . since . . ." Tears strangled my words.

"Since what, Kat? I don't *fucking* know because you wouldn't ever tell me!" He punched his heaving chest in emphasis.

"Since Pete died! He got on a goddamn train and left me!" I thought of the bullet holes engraved across his heart, hidden from view. I felt each word rip through both of us, riddling us with the sorrow, the knowledge . . . the burden and the relief. "And then . . . and then you left me," I choked out quietly, my hands finding my face.

"I had to. After seeing you that day. With him." I jerked my hands away to stare at him. Biting his lip, he continued. "England, my family . . . the bloody fans and press coming out of the woodwork, they all mucked about with my head, and I missed you so terribly. I wanted to whisk you away somewhere beautiful and peaceful. I wanted to show Abbey the Cloisters. Even without crenellations, it's the most castlelike, amazing place in the city. And there are these unicorn tapestries there, they tell a story of a creature in captivity. The poor beast has magical powers, does great things, and *everyone* wants a piece of him. They hunt him down. Trick him and attack him. Destroy him! Does that sound like anyone you know?" His voice gained a hard edge. "In the end, he is miraculously reborn. I wanted to show you that. But you refused to meet me and you wouldn't tell me why. But there you were," he spat. "With him. And the three of you looked so goddamned happy."

"I can explain—"

"*Now* you can explain? I *never* forced you to talk about Pete. I used to see the bleedin' picture every day I entered your damn house; I tried to make peace with the fact I was competing with a ghost. I tried to be there for you, but you refused to be pried open. Time, you said to give you time. And I did, because I thought you loved me like I loved you and we would have all the time ahead of us. Then I leave for three weeks and you bring a bloody carbon copy of him into the picture?"

Picture.

I calmly, quietly walked behind the desk and picked up a frame. Putting it in his hands, I then turned to walk to the window, my back to him.

It was my wedding picture. I could see it in my mind's eye. Smiling with Pete, surrounded by my parents and Kevin, Pete's mom, dad, and Luke. The photo was almost a decade old. Luke was scrawnier back then, perhaps with a bit more hair, but other than that, he looked the same . . . and so much like Pete.

"His brother. Luke. The three of us spend every July Fourth together. Pete's birthday. This party . . . it's Luke's engagement party. His partner, his parents, Abbey . . . they're all in the next room. But I'm going to stay in here with you until you hear what I have to say."

I turned. Adrian seemed rendered speechless. He put the picture down. Picked it up again, put it back down.

"I opened my heart to you . . . but not my heartbreak. I was afraid, so I kept it private. To deal with on my own. Because I do love you . . . but I am always going to have moments when I miss him. And when I miss him, I am not the same person you know. So, yes, I am probably as flawed as you feel everyone else in your life is. That's life! I never wanted to be your saint!"

I was crying now, and he was, too, as we locked in a tangle of arms and long-overdue kisses.

"You." His voice shook. "You are the best thing that ever could have happened to me. When I thought I had lost you, I realized everything else I had been mourning for, that I thought I had lost—a good relationship with Natalie, my career—it had all been synthetic. Those things are still there in front of me, and I can do something about them if I try hard enough." I felt his lips on my temple, and the warmth of his well-worn ring as it found my finger once again. "You and Abbey were the real thing, what mattered most. I know what we are. And you've shown me, Kat. It really is harder to prove something doesn't exist."

My arms encircled him, pulling him closer. "I saw you," I softly stated, "in those tapestries. Digger *and* Adrian. Abbey and I fell in love with that amazing creature. We were so sad for him, we wanted to protect him. But in the end, we knew he'd be okay." I smiled and ran my hands up his arms.

"Captured, but okay." He smiled back. It was then I noticed two fresh tattoos.

"Ah, yes. During my period of self-imposed house arrest. Too afraid I'd be a danger to myself if I went out. Luckily, my tattoo artist makes house calls."

I traced the cat. She had green eyes and was sitting serenely on his left bicep, wearing a key of gold around her neck. Trailing behind her was a smaller striped cat, one with wings. Her tiny paws splayed jauntily, midflight. In her mouth she carried a tiny heart. In true macabre Digger fashion, it wasn't a cartoon heart, but a small-scale replica of a real one, valves and all.

"You've got the key to my heart," he said. "And then Abbey stole the whole blasted thing."

Ana's man with the "bag of needles" had done an amazing job.

I sighed and smiled with relief. Adrian leaned back to look me in the eye. "I'm going to LA in two weeks. I called Rick. We talked for hours. He's flying in from Hawaii, and we're going to see if we can get back some of that old magic. All thanks to you."

"That's great!" I was truly happy to hear that, although butterflies of terror beat their wings at my heart. It was like looking into the bottom of a black mug and not being able to see what was coming next. *That's life,* my mind echoed.

"I don't want you to leave my side till I go. Come stay with me in the city. Bring Abbey, too." He smiled at the sound of her name.

"Abbey spends this week with my in-laws. It helps me—all of us—get through September first."

Adrian gripped my hands, exactly like he had that first day we met. I remembered his words that first time: *Bloody hell, Kat.* He had been ready to jump into the trenches that day, without even hearing my war story. He was a fighter, and he was a victor. He had conquered a lot of demons in his lifetime, alone and with me by his side. It was time I gave him—and myself—the same chance and courtesy. I fixed my eyes on his. No looking away, no looking back.

"Pete was my world. No matter where we were, when I was with him, I was *home*. Everything synched; everything made sense. Together we created this life, this great, great life. And just when I thought it couldn't possibly be more perfect, we *created life*. Abbey. I couldn't imagine her before her existence, how perfectly complete she would make us. How I could look at her and love Pete more than I already did. But one year. That's all we had, the three of us. That hectic newborn first year, and there was no time to even tell him all of this. Because I was tired and I thought I'd have all the years in our lives to tell him."

I watched as Adrian swallowed hard. His thumb spun the ring on my finger by nervous habit as he continued to hold my hands.

"It was a train wreck. Caused by a heat buckle in the tracks: a sun kink. A lot of people . . . were okay. But I knew . . . I knew he wasn't going to be one of them. Like your blood oath story, like Ingeborg knew about Hjalmar the minute she saw his ring." He gathered me into his arms, like he had that hungover morning in my kitchen after Marissa's party. I recalled the thoughts I had held back from sharing then. Of the glass vessel, slowly turning, without end. "My world shattered, Adrian. Everything that made sense imploded." I thought of my friends and family, Abbey. Everyone gathered around me, trying to sooth and smooth my jagged edges. "My mind, my body . . . everything was in shards, felt sharp. Dangerous. I didn't dare touch anybody or let myself be touched."

"My desert flower," he whispered, and I nodded. His fingers were on the hollows of my cheeks, touching my lips as I spoke. I leaned into his caress and closed my eyes as the tears began.

"Time took care of the wound. Smoothed some of the edges."

"Just enough," he breathed into my hair, arms encircling my waist. I gripped him tight. "Look how we fit."

I gulped a laugh, felt his lips find my temple. "Exactly. But you were like a sun kink, too. Blinding and bright, hot. Threw me right off course, but it was right where I needed and wanted to be." I remembered that day at the Plaza, Adrian grabbing my hand. Being ready for, not scared of, the adventure. "It really was like jumping into the fountain."

ABBEY WAS the first to see us emerge; she ran to hug him. I looked on as he talked softly into her hair; she looked at him and hugged him again. "I'm sorry I was the ogre under the bridge. Can I be the jester again?" She nodded against his chest.

Next, he hugged Liz. I loved that she had him beat by a few inches, even when he was wearing his motorcycle boots. "Thanks, Red," I heard him say.

"Just so we're clear, Doom Boy," she said as she squeezed his shoulders, "I'm naming that cranbagel after you, and you won't see a penny of royalties."

"Top notch!" He laughed.

"His pop-ins," Liz said, turning to me, "always result in a gaggle of Corpse fans straggling in after. Good for business."

"I don't quite think the collective noun would be *gaggle*," Adrian said, pondering, rubbing his goatee. "Kat?"

"How about a grommet of metalheads?" I laughed.

I thought it would be harder to introduce him to Luke and my in-laws, but he somehow made it easier. "It is an honor to meet you all." Their smiles and open faces made it easier, too. My dreams of Pete and his assurance of "different kinds of love" rang true.

48

IN TOUCH

"ROCK STARS only crash in little planes, not commercial jets. You needn't have worried," he teased me, calling the moment he landed in LA.

"Hey. You do your job, and I'll do mine," I sassed back. "So what's on your agenda?"

"Meeting Rick in Hollywood. He just dropped the twins off at UCLA. Freshmen in college, I can't believe it. We're grabbing lunch and taking it from there."

"There" turned into renting a place in the Hills and writing together, catching each other back up on the last two decades. Sam, who lived and did session work in Los Angeles, was more than happy to come back on board. They did a few small club shows in LA under the name the Rotten Graves Project. *What would you find in a rotten grave?* he e-mailed me. *A Corroded Corpse, of course!* It was a clever loophole around Wren's copyright, and for the hardcore fans to discover three-quarters of their favorite band playing under a secret moniker . . . a marketing gold mine. Word got out, the music industry was .buzzing again, agents and managers sniffing around. *We can perform all the songs; we own the publishing. Wren can collect his few pennies in royalties if he wants. But we are doing it this time on our own terms.*

We talked on the phone, e-mailed, and messaged every day. Abbey got into the action, too, offering up her latest Matt the Bat lyrics.

> **K:** So I had to find out from my fanboy BROTHER that RGP, aka CC, is playing a one-off show at MSG on Halloween? He is freaking. He said he's flying here for the show and pissed that he missed the secret gigs in LA. Don't worry, I didn't let the kitty out of the bag.
> **A:** Sorry, luv—it was only confirmed today!
> **K:** Just kidding. It's the Information Age. The fans get the info before the artists do.
> **A:** Curse that Internet!
> **K:** Yeah, what happened to Patience?
> **A:** And Fortitude. Speaking of which . . . we are holed up here, practicing till then. Jim is flying in—remember him from Dead Can Dream? He's taking Adam's place.
> **K:** That's amazing!
> **A:** I have to run. Tell your brother not to bother buying tickets when they go on sale tomorrow. Looking forward to meeting him.

That week, a FedEx package arrived. Its note read: *The jewel of my collection. I usually take them, but never have I given one.* Inside was a key. His key. I recognized it immediately, dangling from his Chelsea FC keychain. *I'm coming home on the 25th but will be squirreled away in rehearsals and doing interviews and such. And I know you'll be busy with Kev once he arrives. So I will see you and Abbey the night of the show. Love you, my Kat.*

My brother arrived on the twenty-ninth, walking through the security gate wearing a vintage Corpse T and a smile so big, he could barely contain it. With his short bleached blond spikes and earrings, he looked more rocker than hot-shot chef. Liz had traveled to the airport with me after promising to sign over the Naked Bagel to me if she so much as breathed a word about Adrian.

"Hey, Dooley," he greeted her with a bear hug.

"Hey, Underwood." Her eyes shined clear and brighter than any of the green pressed glass in my mother's china cabinet as the hug broke and she stepped away on unsteady legs.

As we hit the outskirts of Lauder Lake in my Smurf, my brother began to snicker and point. "Lame-ass loser ex-boyfriend at ten o'clock!"

Sure enough, there was Grant. Bent over his pussy wagon on the opposite side of the road. Karma couldn't have dreamed up a more fitting scenario. He was struggling with the lug nuts of his flat tire as the first promising drops of a soaker of a rainstorm began to fall. We slowed to a crawl, and I beeped my horn, causing him to jump a foot. "Aw, nuts too tight?" Kev leaned over me and called in mock sympathy. I flipped Grant a righteous, defiant, and totally deserving middle finger out the open window as we sped off. "They don't call you Tree*bird* for nothing, sis!" Kev laughed.

Kev reclaimed the boogeymen room. I had, with the help of friends and family, reduced the boxes up there to a manageable number. One box at a time. When Abbey was old enough, she would probably appreciate many of the items contained in them.

With Kev came good meals. Abbey found his chopping hypnotizing. After a fabulous dinner and Abbey ensconced in bed, we stayed up talking into the night. I felt closer to my brother, or rather, more tolerant of him. I was dying to tell him everything, but was also having fun by not.

"So tell me how this works again," he wanted to know for the tenth time. "Are you sure we've got tickets?"

"I've got a friend who knows some people in the music business, and he is giving us tickets." I handed over the last pot for him to dry.

"I hope they're good seats," he grumbled.

"Liz is coming, too," I baited, waiting to gauge his reaction.

"That's cool." He began to slowly dry the pot, and I could tell the cogs in his noggin were turning. "Very cool." A small smile played on his lips. "Now, your friend. He's not going to stand there with his arms crossed the entire show, too cool for his own good, is he?"

I tried to hide my amusement. "No . . . I think the music will . . . move him."

"Thank God, I hate guys like that. Fucking New York City hipster music snobs."

49

BIG NIGHT

WE ROCKETED DOWN the Taconic State Parkway, an amped-up Kev riding shotgun and Abbey in the backseat, all sugared up from her earlier Halloween take. No one did much talking during the trip, all lost in our own thoughts of what the evening would bring.

We snaked through traffic down Twelfth Avenue. "You can drop me at Eighth and Forty-deuce." Kev was going to meet up with fellow fans for dinner at Virgil's BBQ.

"How are you going to know one another if you've never met?" Corroded Corpse's extended hiatus had kept fans apart, but the Internet message boards had not. He was meeting with fans he'd been chatting with on a daily basis for years. In fact, he probably spoke to them more often than with all his family combined.

"Believe me, we'll know. This is like the Corpse family reunion. Everyone will be in black. Drinking heavily and singing at the top of their lungs."

I laughed. "Don't forget, eight thirty. Meet me under the big clock on the corner of Eighth and 34th."

He gave Abbey a knuckle bump before jumping out of the Smurf, and we were free to cruise uptown.

There was no waiting in the lobby, no doorman having to announce us; Abbey and I went right up with our key and entered the quiet apartment. *Ten minutes behind you,* Adrian's last text read. Roses were waiting there for me on the kitchen island. A note lay next to them. *Abbey, your present is in the library.* We both tiptoed in, like kids on Christmas morning. In the farthest corner lay a cage, and a tiny striped tabby kitten was curled cozily in a fleece bed. Abbey squealed, but the kitten slept on.

"So cute! Oh!"

"Shh, let's let her sleep. We'll go get dressed."

I took Abbey upstairs to the room formerly reserved for Natalie's visits. There on the bed was another item waiting for Abbey: a plush Maxwell doll with a card. "Abbey, it's from Adrian's daughter. She says thank you for the get-well card, and she heard you really loved Maxwell MacGillikitty."

"She sent him from English?" Abbey was astounded.

"From England, yes. How nice, right?"

I began to unpack our bags. In honor of the red-and-black outfit Digger was known for onstage, Abbey chose a red miniskirt, black and red–striped tights, little black boots, and a black T that said *FUTURE HEADBANGER* in red on it. Uncle Kev had gotten the shirt for her a few years ago, but he had no clue about kids' sizes. Finally she had grown into it and had the perfect occasion to wear it. She topped the whole ensemble off with her black cat ears and tail. "For fancy dress, remember?" she said, twirling.

Hmm, now what does the girlfriend of a rock star wear?

By the time I figured that out, Adrian was home. California and the company of old friends had been kind to my lover. His skin had a healthy glow, and his eyes looked as if they had absorbed a bit of the Pacific Ocean into their blue during his travels. They practically danced as he shook his shaggy hair, considerably longer and lighter, from them. He hugged us long and hard. "So, Abbey Road. What are we calling the cat?"

"Chelsea!"

"Good girl," he said, laughing.

He barely had time to grab a shower before a call came, announcing a limo was waiting for us down front. Abbey's first sitter, Ilana, was now in graduate school at NYU and studying child psych. We had been in touch throughout the years, and she had been my first choice when considering a caregiver for the evening. We swung by to pick her up before heading to the Garden. She and Abbey became quickly reacquainted, playing with every gizmo and button in the back of the stretch limo.

Adrian rested a hand on my knee and smiled. He didn't look nervous at all, considering he was about to step onstage in front of twenty thousand people.

I hadn't been in a limo since the funeral. As it passed by the very door into Penn where Pete and I had last stood, it was like watching a movie—time as another dimension. A young metal-head couple happened to be kissing under the doorway this time. I smiled, touched the window, and said a silent good-bye.

Everything began moving at high speed. Doors flew open and uniformed men escorted our entire party to the side entrance door of the arena. A couple of the fans in line noticed the commotion, causing a flurry of excitement and outbursts from the crowd gathered outside. "DIGGER! I love you, Digger!"

Backstage at Madison Square Garden. Heaven for most music and sports fans alike. I was in awe. And happy we had Adrian to lead us through the maze of security guards and road cases. All the cement-bricked walls backstage looked the same. Luckily, several doors had paper signs hanging from them, indicating catering, hospitality, and the production office. We sent a hungry Abbey with Ilana in the direction of food. The catering area looked strangely like a nice restaurant, complete with linen cloths on the tables and candles for ambiance. It was funny to see the burly stage crew and other tattooed hairy types breaking bread politely in there.

Adrian led me past more curtains and cement walls until we came to a door labeled *Riff—Practice Room*. He rapped his knuckles on the door as he turned the handle. The first thing I saw was the headstock of a guitar, with its big silver keys. A chill ran up my excited spine. "Ay up Dig," came a murmur before its owner turned. As he did, his eyes caught mine and brightened. "Ah, Kat . . . it is you, eh?" He quickly shrugged off the strap of his guitar and freed up his hands. Placing them on my shoulders, he pulled me close and announced, "Thank you. From the bottom of my doomed black heart." I couldn't help it. My goosebumps gave way to tears. We hugged. "You have brought my brother back."

He turned to Adrian, who was standing back with an amused smile. "And you pulled this bird at the library, you say?"

"While drunk," I added. "In front of a roomful of children."

"Nice, mate."

"Oh, and look, Kat." Adrian pulled something from his pocket.

> *We observe*
> *the ideals*
> *of how things should*
> *be*
> *the vastness*
> *of burrowing realities*
> *abridges our gaze*
> *dilating into*
> *a dry cut*
> *a cold sun*

a fragrant decay
the porcelain purity
uncelebrated

I knew instantly what it was. Coffee stains dotted the napkin's border like muddy teardrops. "Simone kept it?"

"That whole time. My goddess," Rick breathed. "She always believed in you, Dig. In us. I used to hate that you knew her so well . . . enough to write what I just couldn't see." Rick rubbed his hand over his shaved head. "But now I'm touched you did, and you cared enough to."

"She helped me learn to know myself, too." Adrian leaned in, one hand on his friend's shoulder and the other grasping mine.

Jim popped his head into the room to say hello. He was the kid in the candy store personified, which quickly lightened the mood again. The smile on his face as he bantered with his idols, now bandmates, was infectious. Sam, a tad heavyset and a head taller than his companions, arrived boisterous and British, just as Adrian had described him. His pocked cheeks became ruddier with each sip from his pint of bitter. Or as he called it, "bih-ah", his tongue barely registering the *T*s and *R*. His accent was thicker than both Adrian's and Rick's, but I believe I made out the words "Fancy checking out the New York City Ballet wif me after?" in one of his sentences as he and Jim moved onward down the hall.

"Don't be impressed by his cultural prowess, Kat. He visits the local 'ballet' in every town he's played in," Rick explained.

"And by 'ballet,' he means 'strip club,'" Adrian finished with a laugh.

It was time for me to go meet Kev and my friends. Adrian called a runner over. "She needs access." The runner handed him an all-access laminated pass, which Adrian slipped over my head. "Hide that when you are out front," he advised with a kiss. "Only show it to security. Here are tickets and a pass for your brother."

I went out to wait for Kev, who was late, not surprisingly. That was nothing new. I had also told Liz, Marissa, and Rob to meet me by the clock. Liz, of course, was in on the antics. My only regret was not being able to convince Leanna and Karen to come, but a concert on both a school night and Halloween was a tough sell.

Marissa greeted me with a cheek kiss. "I thought we were going to a club to see Adrian do his little guitar thingy."

"This," I said, sweeping my hands up toward the lit marquee flashing *ROTTEN GRAVES PROJECT*, "is his little guitar thingy."

Marissa screamed. Rob merely said, "Hot damn!" It wasn't exactly his normal genre, but I could tell he was impressed.

Kev came bouncing up, hugged Liz, and shook me by the shoulders. "Got the tickets, huh huh huh, lemme see!" He grabbed them from my hands and stared in disbelief. Adrian had made sure to pull some of the best seats in the house. Kev whooped and swung me around. "Hey, what's this?" He pulled the laminate that had poked him in the chest out from under my shirt.

I grinned. "You. Come with me." I slapped the sticky VIP pass on his jacket. "We'll see the rest of you at the seats." Kev stood there catatonic as I doled out the tickets and grabbed his hand.

"Holy crap, I am shaking. Where are we going? Is there a greenroom? Do you think any of the band will be there? How do you know your way around?"

I wound my way down the corridors, ushered by guard after guard once they caught sight of my pass. We cut through the small curtained section for hospitality, containing friends and the few lucky fans with guest passes. They were all chattering excitedly and sipping comp drinks as they no doubt wondered, like Kev, if they would glimpse a member of the band that night.

A tall, scraggly blonde with a beard strode out of the production office on his way to the front of house. "That's Miles," Kev whispered, "Corpse's sound guy. Holy shit, I just saw Miles! He's like a celebrity in his own right, he's been with the band since—"

Suddenly, he stopped dead in his tracks. We had walked beyond a long black curtain into the hallway where the dressing rooms were—the inner sanctum. Small groups of people had gathered to talk outside one of the rooms. Standing next to the wall, chatting to some industry types, was Adrian.

He had since changed into his stage clothes, consisting of black leather pants, black boots that raised him at least four inches, and a red and black leather vest. He was shirtless underneath and was holding Abbey in his arms as he chatted with a guy who was nodding and holding on to Adrian's every word. Abbey was content to just snuggle and run her small fingers around the Celtic cross tattoo on his bicep.

"Omigoddigger. Andhe'sgotyourdaughter." Kev seemed ready to faint.

Rick came sauntering out of his dressing room, blocking our path. "Oh, hey, Kat. Have you seen Sam about?"

"I saw him a while back in catering. Rick, this is my brother, Kevin. He is a huge fan."

He shook a stunned Kevin's hand. "Hey man, thanks for coming out."

"Riff, I . . . you . . . your music . . . so many of your songs have been the soundtrack of my life for the past twenty years!"

Rick gave a modest chuckle. "Scary!" he murmured. "But great to hear, mate. Glad you have enjoyed listening to it as much as we enjoyed making it. See you after the show, awright? Cheers." He patted Kev's shoulder and was gone.

"I . . . duh . . ."

"Uncle Kev!" Abbey had spotted us. She jumped down from Adrian's arms and came running. "It's like a party, Uncle Kev! And there's going to be music."

Adrian was watching, smiling. Abbey grabbed her uncle's hands, swinging them, but he was still in a stupor. Adrian winked at me, excused himself from the people around him, and sauntered over. "Hello, Kevin." He stuck out a hand.

"Hello, Digger." Kev couldn't stop staring at their hands as they shook.

"No, that's Adrian, silly Uncle Kev. Mommy's friend. Not like her best friend, because Aunt Miso is her best friend, but he's a extraspecial friend, and he's my friend, too. And *I* got to help him put on makeup!" Our laughter was ice-breaking, and Kev recovered from his shock.

"When . . . How . . . Sis, you have a lot of explaining to do!" he sputtered. "I am so psyched you guys are doing this project. Have you written any new music? Think you will record a new studio album? Are you in contact with Adam?"

"He takes after my mom," I explained. "Lots of questions."

"Shut it, Tree!" Kev turned back to Adrian. "Any plans to tour the West Coast?"

Adrian laughed and rubbed his goatee. "Well, we wanted to get our feet wet first with this gig. New York has always been our strongest market, tons of metal fans. Honestly, we went in thinking we would play a smaller room, but the offer came in from the Garden and then it sold out in a couple of hours, so yeah, I guess the need is there. We're working on routing now for next spring. As for Adam, he was happy to hear from us. But he's got other things going on in his life and wasn't interested in being a part of the band at this time. Jim, the new drummer, kicks serious . . ." He glanced at Abbey and finished, ". . . double bass drums. Oh, and yes, I've been writing some new music. Kat has heard some."

Kev looked at me as if I were some rare exotic animal all of a sudden. "It's good stuff," I assured him.

"Rick and I also worked on some new material out in LA; you'll hear a few new songs tonight. He's staying on for a month, and we'll go into the studio next week to lay down some tracks. How long are you in town for?"

"Just a few more days." Kev, although considerably calmer, still looked amazed to be in the conversation.

"Cool, you should come down and listen," Adrian said.

"That would be SO awesome!"

Ilana popped her head out from catering. "Sorry, Ms. Lewis, I was talking to Paul and we lost track of time. I'll take her."

A more modern version of 1980s Rick appeared next to her. He had the Rottenberg hair, although with considerably less volume. But his eyes, I could tell, were directly from his mother. Cavernous blue. Adrian introduced us. "I couldn't miss this reunion," Paul explained to me with a shy smile.

"The last time I remember you at a show," Adrian recalled fondly, "you were upsetting the catering tables by playing hide-and-seek underneath!"

The tour manager, a big Scottish guy named Martin, came flying through. "Okay, band goes on in five minutes. I need everyone to clear this area; we need a couple of minutes. Only the band in the dressing room. Family can watch from the side of the stage."

Adrian reached over to Abbey, now in Ilana's arms. "Good night, you! I won't see you before the show's over." He kissed her forehead; she was already looking sleepy.

"Break a leg, Adrian Graves," she murmured.

"Go get 'em," I whispered as he leaned down to kiss me. Grabbing the sides of his vest, I pulled him close once more. "I love you."

He grinned, kissing me again. "Easy, tiger."

The four of us followed some other guests to watch from

side-stage. Kev hugged me as we rushed to find a place before the stage lights dimmed. Spotlights began to spin, the dry ice hazers creating a dramatic fog around the drum set as Jim began to thump. We couldn't see but could hear the audience instantly begin to clap along, roaring. The drums beat faster and more frantically, and without warning, Rick and Adrian came galloping out from the side, with Sam strutting behind. Multiple spotlights struck each of them, and the crowd volume reached deafening proportions. Thank heavens for amplifiers. They jumped right into "Spoils of War," with Riff growling the lyrics and Digger howling the chorus as the entire sea of people out front pumped their arms and chanted in unison, "Spoils! Of! War!" Kev was doing it from the side, but toned it down after he got a few looks. Most of the people side-stage were acting cool and collected, nodding their heads and acting semi-unimpressed. Even Paul wasn't paying all that much attention, talking to other people back there. Well. They may have seen countless shows from a few feet away, but it was our first. I tapped Kev on the shoulder and yelled in his ear, "They rock!" He nodded wisely and gave me the devil horns sign.

Abbey had in her earplugs and was bopping along in Ilana's arms. After the first song, they prepared to leave. I gave Abbey a ton of good-night kisses. "I will see you in the morning, baby-doll. Be a good girl."

"THANK YOU, NEW YORK!" Riff yelled. "How the hell are ya?" The crowd shouted back as an unintelligible body, the house lights illuminating every raised fist. "It's great to be back, feels like no time has gone by. Are you ready to ROCK AND ROLL? Are you ready to SCREAM AND SHOUT?" Digger took a moment during this call and response to flick his eyes side-stage to locate us. He nodded with a smile as Riff bellowed, "Are you ready to PLUNDER AND PILAGE, YEAAAAAHHHHH!"

Digger started hammering on his guitar and head-banging as the next song started up.

"Holy crap, they haven't *ever* played this song live! This is *history* in the *making!*" Kev yelled in my ear, frantically grabbing his phone and texting someone, no doubt one of his Internet metal buddies.

"How 'bout we check them out from the front?" I hollered, and he agreed. We tramped down a small set of stairs and a ramp, heavily guarded by security. They ushered us into the long narrow space between the barrier and the stage. Photographers scuttled past us like crabs, trying to capture their big money shots.

The heat and the energy coming off the fans in the pit were insane. Kids were holding up banners and waving T-shirts with Corpse Guy on them, and fists and fingers triumphantly displaying devil horns were pumping in the air. Some people were pogoing and attempting to crowd surf.

I turned my attention up to my man onstage. I was right below him, and he had big smiles waiting for me. In fact, his looks in my direction were so frequent, they began to draw the attention of others.

"Hey, you're fucking with his momentum," Kev shouted in my ear.

"Jealous much?" I loved that we could have sibling rivalry in front of twenty thousand people.

"Seriously, is he making you wet with those looks?"

"KEV!"

"Well, I know *I'd* get a little wet if I were a girl and he was smiling at me like that."

"Okay, maybe people are starting to look," I confessed.

"Fuck 'em. Let them look."

Kev slung his arm over my shoulder, and we did some quality head-banging before heading to our seats across the arena. Along the way, we ran into John Duff, the music critic from the *Observer*. He had worked with Pete, and I hadn't seen him since the funeral. He and I smiled in mutual recognition and surprise, but the concert made it impossible to talk as we passed by each other.

To get to our seats, we actually had to go back along the side of the stage, down a corridor, and then back out into the halls of the arena. We hiked quickly up a stairwell, not wanting to miss a thing. As we got to the landing, I suddenly felt Kev's hands grab my shoulders. "Wait a minute. Have you slept with him, Tree?" His voice echoed through the stairwell, still sounding muffled compared to the wattage reverberating throughout the Garden.

I found myself resorting back to preteen indignation. "Chuh —I can't believe you! Tsk. God!" What a question to come from a brother.

"Seriously, Tree. Tell me you've communed with the blade."

"Is that what the kids are calling it these days?"

"I mean, the knife tattooed on his chest—have you seen it up close?" he hollered.

"The misericorde, you mean?"

"Oh my God, you know what's written there, don't you? *Nobody* knows. Only Riff and Digger; no one else has ever gotten close enough. Well, maybe Simone. But seriously, no photographer has ever captured it; no journalist has ever been given an answer. And no fan has *ever* gotten close enough to decipher it."

We flashed our tickets at the usher, who stepped aside to let us pass. As we walked up the dark ramp to the seats, I leaned close to my brother. "Get to know him, okay? He puts his pants on one leg at a time, just like the rest of us."

Now it was Kev's turn to *chuh* and *tsk* me.

Rob and Liz were up out of their seats doing some serious head-banging. Marissa had a booty-shake going to each drum beat, keeping her fist in the air. They all hugged me as we squeezed across them to the open seats. "He is so awesome up there, I can't believe it!" Marissa screamed, shaking her head.

"You freakin' knew, Dooley! Didn't you, ya dirtbag?" Kev accused, grabbing Liz around the shoulders and miming a noogie with his knuckles to the top of her head.

"She swore me to secrecy! I didn't put two and two together until I was in your old room and took a good look at one of your old rock posters."

"Hey, whoa, has *he* seen my room?" He turned to me. "Did he think I was totally dorky? Hey, could he *sign* all those posters?"

"Shut up and watch the show, Kev!"

Riff was prowling from stage left to stage right, beckoning the crowd to yell some more if they had any yell left in them. "Thank you . . . thank you all. Awright, awright, we're going to slow down for a moment and play a new song for your listening pleasure. It's called 'Cat with the Emerald Eyes.' Hit it, Dig."

Adrian began picking out a familiar-sounding melody. My entire body sizzled with a delicious zap of nervousness as I realized it was the song he had played for me at his apartment that first time I was there. Now the song had words, words he breathed clear and crisp into the mike.

You said
Easy tiger . . .
Not so fast,
First I have to make peace with my past.
So I twined my fingers through your hair
And waved my smudge sticks to clear the air . . .

The guitar and bass began to gallop, drums keeping the beat, and the song took on that heavy groove I remembered loving so much in his room, watching him play, so alive.

The demons descended and swooped 'round my head
Tricksters who switched the live for the dead
The smoke cleared and I feared you were lost in their lies
Hadn't known the truth shone in your emerald eyes.

I put my fingers to my lips in a point, smiling and listening. I could feel my friends' eyes on me, but I couldn't take my gaze off the man onstage.

Who's to say
What exists
What is lost
What is this
I have found
In your eyes
In your kiss. . .
In your kiss
Fragile stinging
A narrow miss
And you're bringing
Me back to life with those
Emerald eyes.

He burst into a scathing guitar solo, borne out of what I could only imagine was the anguish he had felt while we were apart those months. It sounded as tightly wound as I myself had felt those lonely, endless days and nights. But slowly it began to unravel, to loosen, to soften and come to a quieter place. His eyes were closed as he performed the last verse a cappella to the spellbound crowd.

Easy Tiger . . .
Make it last
Arms wide, incantation, the spell's been cast
No smoke and mirrors, no saints here,
only saviors, survivors, no fear
catch a glimpse of the future
Emerald eyes hold it clear . . .

I was a biased party, but I thought it sounded amazing. Judging from the looks of wonderment around me, however, strangers and my friends alike seemed to agree. Perhaps Adrian was in the running again for another shot at a Christmas number-one single. I knew, though, it probably didn't even matter to him. I had a feeling he would have played that song to an audience of one and been just as happy and proud of it. And I would've been happy and proud to listen, too.

I heard a sharp whistle from below. Martin had come out from backstage and was trying to get my attention. I fought the flow of the exiting crowd to reach him. "Aftershow passes for your whole crew, courtesy of Digger Graves," he announced.

Everyone peeled and planted their sticky passes on, excited and chattering. I laughed as I caught a glimpse of Marissa rearranging her boobs as we made our way backstage. A small party had gathered in back, hanging on to cups of beer and standing around. The anticipation and thrill pre-show had morphed into a relaxed and accomplished vibe post-show. Sweaty band members mingled with everyone. Martin attempted to talk up Liz, but my brother had glued himself to her side. I had planned on giving Kev my Smurf and house keys later, but had the feeling Liz wasn't going to let him leave the borough tonight.

Rob went off to smoke a doob and bond with the sound guy, leaving Marissa and me on our own. We watched as the band got ushered away to take pictures for *Rolling Stone*.

"Girl, you are full of surprises." She bumped my shoulder.

"I told you I wasn't afraid of the unknown . . ."

"And get a load of that." She nudged me and nodded toward Liz and Kev, who were locked in a pretty tight squeeze. "Between her chemical red and his bleach blond, what color hair do you think your niece or nephew will have?"

"Still a lot of cart before the horses, Mariss. But if you care to make a bet . . ."

We giggled against each other.

"Excuse me, Kat?" A tall gentleman, dressed crisply and casually, exuded a business air as he came at me with an extended hand. "Oliver Owens, High Ace Artists."

"Oh, hey." I recognized the name of Corroded Corpse's US booking agent instantly.

"I hear I've got some competition." He laughed at my surprised look. "Ending the King of Doom's sixteen-year hiatus by booking him to play a children's library program has become somewhat of an industry legend," he explained, but then took a more professional tone. "Seriously, I think there is amazing cross-marketing potential with the demographics. I'll call you when I get back to the LA office and we can brainstorm a way to bring his best to two generations of music fans."

"Do you think Adrian will want to play for the kids after all this?" Marissa asked me as we watched Oliver move on through the crowd.

"I think the King of Doom likes being the jester sometimes."

"So, you staying in town tonight?"

"Yeah . . . the first night that the three of us are under one roof. Kind of a big deal." I smiled, watching as Adrian made his way toward us.

50

ALL IN

THE LIMO SILENTLY SLIPPED UPTOWN. Adrian was still in those leather pants and boots, stretching out his legs and pulling me close to kiss him. We were both thirsty, but all we found in the back of the limo was San Pellegrino. Laughing, Adrian got the limo driver to pull over at an all-night grocery to get us some plain old bottled water.

We found Ilana curled on the couch with a book from Adrian's library. I had a feeling we'd be seeing more of her that week, as Rick's son Paul appeared pretty sweet on her. "My brother wants to come and cook dinner for the band this week. You should come," I told her.

"Tell him *no* shellfish, though!" Adrian laughed. "Now *there's* a fact the fans don't know yet." He walked Ilana down to the waiting limo after we said our good-byes and thanks.

At last, Adrian pulled off his boots and we quietly wound up the spiral staircase, holding hands. Abbey was sleeping soundly in Natalie's old room, with Chelsea the cat a furry comma-shape next to her.

I lit the familiar peppery candle as Adrian showered away any evidence of his grueling physical performance and joined me in bed. Legs mingled and skin was softly touched as we talked into the night.

It was three a.m., then five. We'd been dozing and kissing, and he kept singing in my ear, and I kept squeezing him to make sure I wasn't dreaming, I so wanted this to be real. And it was.

At around 6:20, I heard the shuffle and drop of two little feet to the floor and the machine-gun pitter-patter of Abbey rounding the corner and coming down the hall.

"Are you ready for this?"

The slightest smile played upon his lips, curling up higher on one side. He had a memory on his mind; I could see it shimmer in his eyes like a sharp cut sapphire.

"Count me in."

ACKNOWLEDGMENTS

I recently read a quote about how the brain cannot be in a state of appreciation and a state of fear at the same time. I whole-heartedly agree, because when I think about the gratitude I have for the following people, I feel fearless on my journey down this writing path. Thank you for believing in me, reading my words, and entrusting me with your time.

Amanda Usen, who pushed me to finish this book and who keeps pushing me toward positivity in all facets of my life. I will never forget your mitzvahs, my friend!

Ever grateful to my agent, Nalini Akolekar of Spencerhill, and to everyone at Berkley who helped bring the first edition of this book to an audience of fabulous, gracious and voracious booklovers.

Now, I dedicate this current edition to all of you, too many to name but I will try:

To the amazing Goodreads gang – Irene, Mo, Michelle, TeriLyn (thanks for buddy reading LTL in your Canaries group!), Elizabeth H, Lana DG Romance, Jx and Deanna (the PinkLadies), Maida, Baba in Switzerland (I still swoon over your graphics), Kelly, AJ in Australia, Amanda in Malaysia, Michelle (Helen Geek), Dee M., Caren, Iryna, Alleskelle, Brandi, Jennifer K, Wendy'sThoughts, Katy Loves Romance, Alex is the Romance Fox, and all the other fabulous and creative GR readers who continue to delight me with their fan art and reviews – thank you x 1000 for your support!

Heartfelt thanks to all the amazing bloggers who have included my books in their pages, roundups and reviews: Maryse @ Maryse's Book Blog, Cheri @ Kindle Crack Book Reviews, Aestas Book Blog, Hikari @ Folded Pages Distillery, KT Book Reviews, Open Book Society, Mary @ Bookhounds, Sharon Slick @ Guilty Pleasures, Sophia Rose @ Delighted Reader, Lana @ Dirty Girl Romance, and to Irene (again!) and Nina @ The Literary Gossip for their wonderful blog tour work. A special horns-up to rock star writer Susan Helene Gottfried @ her Rock of Pages and West of Mars blogs, too.

To my writer friends within WFWA, RWA, WNYRW – from writer retreats to conference confabs to online brainstorming – I'm proud to be in such good company. Eternal gratitude to Amanda Usen, Alison Stone, Stephanie Haefner and Natasha Moore for their wisdom and wisecracking, and to Pat O'Dea Rosen and Kristin Contino for their fabulous friendship and critiquing over the years. To Molly O'Keefe, Barbara Claypole White and Laura Drake – I give big Wayne's World "We're Not Worthy!" bows to your blurbing!

Much love always to Steph for letting me turn her poetry into Adrian's lyrics. And to Alysa, Michelle, Naomi, Liz and Natalie for their forever friendships.

Last but not least, thank you to my Rosokoff, Gallo and Topper families for their love and support – and to my daughter Millie, who inspires me every day.

And in loving memory of those I've lost along the way: Helen Rosokoff, Pete Phillips, Lisa Witt, and John Gallo – you are never far from my heart or my thoughts.

ABOUT THE AUTHOR

Jessica Topper has been in love with the beauty of the written word ever since she memorized Maurice Sendak's *Chicken Soup with Rice* at the age of three.

After earning a B.A. in English Literature and her Master's Degree in Library Science, Jessica went on to work as a librarian in New York City before trading in the books for book-keeping. For seventeen years, she worked in the production office of an international touring rock band.

Jessica broke the rock romance mold with her 2013 debut novel LOUDER THAN LOVE. Her follow-up romantic comedy, DICTATORSHIP OF THE DRESS, was named one of Publishers Weekly's Best Books of 2015.

She lives in Western New York with her family - including two cats that love to walk across her keyboard.

Visit her online at jessicatopper.com

facebook.com/JessicaTopperAuthor

twitter.com/jesstopper

instagram.com/jessicatopper

goodreads.com/jessicatopper

CPSIA information can be obtained
at www.ICGtesting.com
Printed in the USA
LVHW041651231120
672481LV00006B/1418

9 781953 863003